Y0-BDF-977

JASMINE CRESSWELL

is a multitalented author of over forty novels. Her efforts have gained her numerous awards, including the RWA's Golden Rose Award and the Colorado Author's League Award for best original paperback novel. Born in Wales and educated in England, Jasmine met her husband while working at the British Embassy in Rio de Janeiro. She has lived in Australia, Canada and six cities in the United States. Jasmine and her husband now make their home in Sarasota, Florida.

KRISTIN GABRIEL

is a transplanted city girl who now lives on a farm in central Nebraska with her husband, three children, a springer spaniel and assorted cats. She received a B.S. in agriculture from the University of Nebraska before pursuing her dream of writing. Two-time winner of the prestigious RITA® Award for Best Traditional Romance of the Year, Kristin is the author of nine books for Harlequin. Her first novel, *Bullets Over Boise*, was even turned into a made-for-television movie called *Recipe for Revenge*. Kristin enjoys hearing from her readers and can be reached through her Web site at www.KristinGabriel.com, or at Kristin Gabriel, P.O. Box 5162, Grand Island, NE 68802-5162.

JASMINE CRESSWELL

KRISTIN GABRIEL

THE TROUBLE WITH LOVE

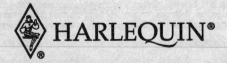

HARLEQUIN®

TORONTO • NEW YORK • LONDON
AMSTERDAM • PARIS • SYDNEY • HAMBURG
STOCKHOLM • ATHENS • TOKYO • MILAN • MADRID
PRAGUE • WARSAW • BUDAPEST • AUCKLAND

ISBN 0-373-83545-0

THE TROUBLE WITH LOVE

Copyright © 2003 by Harlequin Books S.A.

The publisher acknowledges the copyright holders of the individual works as follows:

THE PERFECT BRIDE
Copyright © 1996 by Jasmine Cresswell

MONDAY MAN
Copyright © 1998 by Kristin Eckhardt

CONTENTS

THE PERFECT BRIDE

Jasmine Cresswell

CHAPTER ONE

SAM ALWAYS CHOSE five-thirty Friday afternoon to throw a tantrum. The staff at Services Unlimited had grown accustomed to having their weekends kicked off by Sam hyperventilating over some crisis or other. This time, unfortunately, Sam had decided to stage his weekly scene over one of Caitlin's projects.

He stormed into her office, looking as threatening as a man can look when he's chubby, five foot four and blessed with no more than a dozen silvery hairs carefully arranged over his bald pink scalp.

He shook a fistful of papers under Caitlin's nose. "This reference from the Countess of Yardleigh stinks. How come you're still recommending this Tittleswit guy for the job? Why didn't you recommend Jackson? Jackson is already in Washington, and he's got a slew of solid American references."

Caitlin drew a deep breath and managed a reassuring smile. She loved her job, her colleagues and her life in general. Most days, she even loved her boss, Sam Bergen. This afternoon, however, she admitted to feeling frazzled. It had already been a long tough week. "The man's name is Littlethwaite, Sam. Algernon Littlethwaite. Not Tittleswit."

"Yeah, and his references stink."

"Sam, I called the Countess of Yardleigh and spoke to her in person for twenty minutes. She thinks Algernon Littlethwaite is an excellent butler, but she's very restrained and uppercrust British. Her definition of lavish praise is to say that Algernon 'fulfilled his duties to the best of his ability.' Don't worry, Sam, we've found the perfect butler for the Japanese ambassador."

Sam had no intention of being mollified. Late on Fridays, he seemed to enjoy worrying. "What about Littlethwaite's work permits? God knows what kind of runaround they'll give you at Immigration if his paperwork isn't in order."

Caitlin reminded herself that she was paid an excellent salary and that the job market in Washington, DC, was tight. "As you can see if you've read the file, Sam, Mr. Littlethwaite faxed us copies of his visas and documentation three weeks ago. He has absolutely everything he could possibly need to work legally in this country, and I'm sure he'll arrive from London tomorrow afternoon right on schedule."

A tap on the door of her office was followed by the immediate entry of Dot, her secretary. "Sorry to interrupt, Sam, but Caitlin has to sign these letters right away if we want them to catch tonight's mail. As it is, I'll have to take them to the late pickup box."

Caitlin flashed her secretary a grateful smile. "Sorry, Sam, but I really must read these through before I sign them."

Sam left Caitlin's office, gloomily predicting that Mr. Littlethwaite would turn out to be a con man and that Services Unlimited would be dragged into bankruptcy as Sam valiantly tried to fend off lawsuits from the disgruntled Japanese ambassador.

Dot shook her head. "What is it about Friday nights?" she asked. "From Monday morning until quitting time on Friday, Sam Bergen is an intelligent, considerate, efficient employer. The clock strikes five on Friday and suddenly he grows fangs and turns into a monster."

"I think he misses his wife. Friday nights used to be special for them. It was the only time he absolutely refused to allow business to intrude. Now he has nothing to look forward to except an empty house and a lonely weekend."

"Poor man, but Shirley's been dead for two years now. He should get out and about more. Find himself a nice woman to liven up his lonely weekends."

Caitlin finished signing letters and handed the bulging folder back to her secretary. "Dot, I left home so that I wouldn't be surrounded by people who think getting married is the cure for all the world's problems. Don't you start, please."

Dot held up her hands in protest. "Caitlin, honey, I never said one single word about Sam needing a wife. I said he needed a nice woman he could date, that's all. I'm no fan of matrimony."

"Sure. That's why you've been married three times."

"Right, and divorced twice and widowed once. It's taken me twenty years, but I finally got smart. From now on, the men in my life are gonna be strictly short-term and strictly by appointment. Marriage is a one-way street, with all the advantages going in the man's direction."

"You're too cynical," Caitlin said, although in her heart of hearts she didn't really disagree with her secretary.

"Wait until you're married—then we'll have this conversation again."

"We'll have to wait a long time. I'm not planning to get married for the next hundred years or so."

"Huh, you're too pretty to stay that smart. Chestnut hair, green eyes, curves in all the right places. Honey, you're a surefire bride-in-waiting if ever I saw one." Dot grabbed her jacket and purse, tucked the package of mail under her arm and waved from the doorway. "See you on Monday, boss. Have a good weekend. And if you're seeing that gorgeous hunk Alec Woodward tonight, give him a kiss from me."

"Gorgeous hunk? *Alec?*"

Dot shot her a curious glance. "In case you haven't noticed, honey, he's endowed with one heck of a body hidden under those conservative lawyer's suits of his. Not to mention that he has a pair of wicked blue eyes, expressly designed to make any normal woman sit up and beg for attention. If you're determined to stay single, I recommend you keep away from Alec Woodward."

Caitlin chuckled in genuine amusement. "I'm not in the least danger, Dot, I promise you. Alec and I don't think of each other that way."

"You're not blind, girl. How can you avoid thinking of him that way?"

"Easily, because he's my friend. Alec moved in next door when I was eight. That means I've known him for twenty years, and in all that time, I can honestly say I've never noticed his wicked blue eyes. So I don't suppose they're going to start driving me insane with longing any time soon, do you?"

"Keep it that way, hon, and you'll live a happy life. Lovers and husbands are two a penny. Good friends are a heck of a lot harder to find. Especially of the male variety." She shrugged, gazing at Caitlin thoughtfully. "Of course, if a woman ever did manage to find a lover who was also a friend, then I guess she'd have a match made in heaven."

Caitlin grimaced. "Don't hold your breath."

"Honey, I've lived long enough to know that anything can happen in this world. Sometimes even the good things. Have a nice weekend." Whistling under her breath, Dot ran for the elevator.

Relieved of the secretary's cheerful presence, the office suddenly seemed so quiet as to be oppressive. Thank heaven it was Friday, Caitlin thought, as she tidied away the papers for her newest client. It was good to know that her hard work had paid off and that she personally had filled three important positions during the past week. In addition to Mr. Littlethwaite, she'd found a housekeeper for the chairman of the World Bank and a sous-chef for the White House, but she'd worked too many fourteen-hour days recently, and she desperately needed a break.

Perhaps she'd call Alec and see if he could join her for a drink after work. Or, better yet, they could spend the entire evening together. They could have a pizza at Mama Maria's, the Italian restaurant they'd discovered a few months ago, and then catch the late show at one of the nearby movie theaters.

Talking to Dot had reminded her it must be more than two weeks since she'd seen Alec. Now that she stopped to think about him, Caitlin realized she'd missed Alec a lot. In fact, she was surprised how much she hoped he hadn't already made a hot date with one of the luscious female law students who swarmed around his office.

She stopped filing papers and reached for the phone, but before she could dial the number for Alec's office, her other line buzzed. She almost didn't answer the call, then discipline won out over personal feelings. She switched lines and responded politely.

"Hello, this is Caitlin Howard."

"Oh, Lin, can you believe it? I'm pregnant! The doctor confirmed it this afternoon. He says I'm seven weeks pregnant and everything's fine. Jeff and I are so happy we're practically swinging from the chandeliers. Or we would be, if we had any chandeliers."

Her sister's excitement fizzed and bubbled over the miles of fiber-optic cable. Caitlin experienced the oddest little lurch in the pit of her stomach. It was a second or two before she managed to reply, and her sister's voice came again, more tentatively.

"Hey, Lin, are you still there?"

Caitlin shook off a wave of sudden, inexplicable exhaustion. "Yes, I'm here. Merry, that's wonderful news. Congratulations! I'm so pleased for you and Jeff. I know how much you both wanted to start a family. It's going to be a first grandchild for Jeff's parents, isn't it?"

"Yes, they're almost as thrilled as we are. After two years and no success, we were beginning to wonder if I'd ever get pregnant!" Merry giggled. "And it sure wasn't for want of trying, believe me. Jeff and I really worked at this project! Gosh, this is the most exciting day of our lives. We're driving into Youngstown this weekend to look at cribs and to buy curtains for the nursery. Megan and George are coming, too, but they're leaving the boys with Mom and Dad—you know how carsick they get."

"I sure do," Caitlin said with feeling, remembering a disastrous outing at Christmas when she had been responsible for entertaining her two young nephews, Zach and Matt, the sons of her other sister, Megan. She'd learned the hard way that toddlers of two and three can't consume hot dogs followed by ice cream followed by popcorn and then drive home in the back of a station wagon without disastrous consequences.

Merry laughed sympathetically. "You're so smart, Lin, but I swear you don't have an ounce of common sense. I don't know how you manage to run that agency of yours when you only need to *look* at a vacuum cleaner to have it break down."

Caitlin had long ago given up trying to convince her family that providing trained domestic help for the ambassadors, senators and other dignitaries of the nation's capital did not require her to run out and personally dust furniture. "So when is this special baby due exactly? Sometime next spring?" she asked. "I'll have to be sure to save some vacation time for visiting with my new niece or nephew."

"May fifteenth, can you believe it? Wouldn't it be wonderful if our baby arrived right on your birthday?"

"The best present I could have," Caitlin said. "And I plan to lobby hard to be chosen as one of the godparents."

"You're already chosen. Jeff and I couldn't think of anyone we love more, even though we don't understand you." Merry's cheerful voice became somewhat wistful. "Megan and I were talking about how the baby's due on your birthday and all. Do you realize you're going to be twenty-nine next May, which is only one year away from being thirty? Gosh, Lin, aren't you worried?"

"What about?" Caitlin asked, although she knew very well what her sister was trying to say. "Last time I checked with the dentist, she assured me my teeth aren't going to fall out any time soon. And the doctor seems to think I can hold off on ordering my wheelchair for at least another five years, maybe even ten.''

Merry refused to be diverted. "You know that isn't what I mean. It's not your health we're worried about—it's the fact that you're still single. With all those glamorous men in Washington, Megan and I can't understand why you haven't managed to get yourself settled yet. Haven't you met any exciting men recently?''

Merry sounded almost pleading, and Caitlin resisted the impulse to snap at her youngest sister. She forced a laugh. "Sure, I met this marvelous English butler, who wears starched wing collars and is called Algernon Littlethwaite. I didn't believe there were people outside TV sitcoms who had names like that, did you?''

"Caitlin, don't joke. I meant have you met any *eligible* men. Men you've gone out with on a date. Men you might want to marry.''

Caitlin sighed. She knew from long experience of dealing with Merry—not to mention the rest of her family—that it would prove quicker and easier to tell her what she wanted to hear. Nobody in Caitlin's family was prepared to believe the simple truth: that Caitlin had no particular desire to get married, that she liked her life and her career just the way they were.

"I had dinner with a congressman from Kentucky a couple of weeks ago,'' she said. "He's very good-looking and very sincere about wanting to improve government funding for rural education. You know how strongly I feel about that, so we had a lot in common.''

Merry, who had a low opinion of politicians, seemed unimpressed by the congressman from Kentucky. ''Anyone else?'' she asked.

''Last weekend I went sailing with one of the assistant curators at the Smithsonian. He was very nice. He's a graduate of Georgetown University, five years before me, so we had lots to talk about.''

''What's his name?

''David.''

''Did you really like him?'' Merry couldn't conceal her eagerness, or the faint undertone of anxiety. ''I mean are you going to see him again soon?''

''I hope so,'' Caitlin said lightly. ''But I wouldn't start making any wedding plans for another decade or two.''

''Gosh, Lin, you're so hard to please. Who are you waiting for, for heaven's sake? Prince Charming? Superman?''

''I'm not that picky. Any millionaire who looks like Mel Gibson and has the soul of a poet could capture my heart in a minute.''

''You always joke about it, Lin, but it's not a joking matter. What's going to happen ten years from now when you're president of Services Unlimited but all alone in your fancy Washington apartment, and the only person who calls on Saturday night is a client complaining that the chef you sent around to the embassy doesn't know how to cook frogs' legs, or toads' knees or whatever gross thing they're eating in Washington that month.''

It had been a long day on top of a *very* long week. Caitlin tried hard not to feel angry with her sister. Merry never meant to pry, or to intrude, or to push her own values onto Caitlin. The trouble was, Merry and Megan were throwbacks to the fifties who couldn't believe that any woman was truly happy until she was married. Caitlin's enthusiasm for working hard at a demanding job in a huge city like Washington, DC, struck her sisters as both inexplicable and sad. They had been on a nonstop, five-year campaign to get Caitlin married and comfortably ''settled down,'' preferably in their hometown of Hapsburg, Ohio.

''You know, Lin,'' Merry went on, ''if you were honest with yourself, you'd admit that a woman's never really fulfilled until she has a home and a husband of her own.''

Caitlin's self-control snapped. She was on the verge of saying something she probably would have regretted for years when a familiar friendly face appeared in the doorway.

She sprang from her chair, dropping the phone onto her desk. ''Alec, oh, thank heaven you're here!''

Alec's casual smile hardened, just for an instant, into an expression Caitlin found unreadable. Which was odd, because she usually knew exactly what Alec was thinking. Over the years, they'd grown to understand each other so well that sometimes they were like an old married couple, communicating in jumbled half sentences and vague gestures.

"Alec?" she said uncertainly.

The split second of tension vanished, and his smile resumed its usual teasing form. "I should stay away more often. It's great to receive such a welcome."

"It must be telepathy," she said. "I was going to call. Boy, am I happy to see you." She retrieved the phone and apologized to her sister. "Sorry, Merry, someone just arrived unexpectedly in my office and I dropped the phone. Clumsy of me. What were we talking about?"

"As if you didn't know." Now it was Merry's turn to sigh. "I suppose this unexpected visitor is another of your important clients, and now you'll waste the weekend locked up in your apartment writing a presentation for him."

It was late and Caitlin was tired. She couldn't think of any other excuse for the imp of mischief that seized her. "Heavens, no, this isn't a client," she said. "It's a hot date." She gave Alec a conspiratorial wink, while Merry spluttered into the phone.

"Oh, great! What's he like?"

"Well, let's see, how should I describe him?" Caitlin pretended to consider her sister's question. "He's thirty-five, he's intelligent and very successful in his career. He also has a great body and wicked blue eyes that would make any woman sit up and beg to be noticed."

"I can't believe what I'm hearing. Caitlin, is this

really you talking? And is he still there? Can he hear what you're saying?''

"Yes, he's listening to every word. I think he's stunned by what I just said about his sexy blue eyes. But heck, this is the nineties. Why shouldn't I let him know I think he's attractive?''

Alec leaned against the doorjamb, his much-discussed eyes dancing with laughter, but his expression somewhat quizzical. "Twenty years, and I never knew you cared,'' he murmured. "Tell me more about my great body.''

She grinned, covering the mouthpiece of the phone. "Don't you wish.'' She uncovered the phone. "Merry, I hate to cut you off, but my date is waiting, and he's such a dynamic man he hates to hang around doing nothing. I'll talk to you later, okay? Tell Jeff congratulations on becoming an expectant father, and good luck with the crib hunt.''

"You know what, Lin, you sound really strange. All sort of discombobulated. Oh, boy, I can't wait to tell Megan. I think maybe you've met the right man at last.''

She should have denied it at once, but Caitlin wasn't in the mood to fight a losing battle. She glanced at Alec, inviting him to share the joke. "You're right, Merry. He's far and away the most attractive man I've ever dated. In fact, I don't think I'll ever find another man to compare with him.'' She said goodbye quickly and hung up the phone, feeling a smidgen of guilt for having deceived her sister.

Alec pushed himself away from the doorjamb and crossed the room to give her a brotherly hug. "What was that all about? I assume it was Merry on the phone."

"It was. And she was so desperate for me to have a date tonight, I transformed you into my hot new prospect for a romantic evening."

"Well, you can't lie to your sister, so I'd better *be* your date for the night. Would you like to go out for a pizza?"

She smiled, not at all surprised that their thoughts were running in harmony. "Great idea. Mama Maria's?"

"Definitely. The house special. Double cheese, no onions, no anchovies."

"Cappuccino coffee with dessert?"

"Mmm…sounds good. You've booked yourself one sizzling date, lady. Let me tell you, I can't wait to hear some more about my great body and wicked blue eyes."

"Wish I could oblige, but there's nothing to add." She grabbed her purse and, with the ease of long friendship, hooked her arm through Alec's. "Those aren't actually my own opinions. I borrowed them from Dot."

"Your secretary? Hah! I always knew she was a woman of outstanding perception."

Caitlin laughed. "She's a fantastic typist, too. A hundred words a minute." She yawned, resting against the wall as they waited for the elevator.

"Whew!" she said. "You arrived just in the nick of time. Merry was doing her usual job of putting me through the wringer."

"Is that why she called? To give you a hard time about your single state?"

"No, she has good news. The best, in fact. She's pregnant! The doctor says she's in good health, and the baby will arrive in May."

Alec stood aside to let Caitlin into the elevator. "That's terrific. Jeff must be ecstatic. He's such a great teacher, and he loves kids. He'll make a perfect father."

"Yes, I'm thrilled to bits, except for one thing. Now that my family can stop fretting about Merry's failure to conceive, they've got nothing to worry about except me. Poor old spinster Caitlin, toiling away at her job in Washington because she can't find a man to look after her."

He grinned. "Well, love, you have to face facts. In less than two years you'll be turning thirty, and your chances of snaring a man are fading fast. Heck, if I held you up to the light, bet I'd already see the gray hair and wrinkles."

"A few more weeks like the one I've just had and you won't need to hold me up to the light."

They stepped into the downstairs lobby. "Bad week?" Alec inquired with genuine sympathy.

"No, a great week, but too busy." She beamed, unable to conceal her accomplishment and pride in it any longer. "I managed to find a housekeeper for the chairman of the World Bank. And he's accepted our bid on janitorial services for his entire office complex.''

"Way to go, Caity!" Alec's hug was full of warmth and shared pleasure. "I know how hard you worked to get that cleaning account."

She tried to look modest and failed completely. "Sam's made me a junior partner and given me a five-thousand-dollar raise."

"Hey, this calls for a *real* celebration. Champagne, fancy French restaurant, dancing under the stars…"

She groaned. "Don't tempt me, Alec, I'm too tired. Mama Maria's is about all I can handle tonight. I need the noise and the clattering plates to keep me awake. Too much quiet French refinement and I'll nod off into my stuffed partridge."

"Okay. We'll save the French and fancy for next weekend."

Caitlin's heart gave a curious little lurch of excitement. The prospect of getting dressed up and enjoying a real night out on the town with Alec had an appeal she couldn't quite identify.

"I'd like that," she said, and then lapsed into a silence that wasn't as easy as silences between them usually were.

Alec spoke crisply. "Eight o'clock, next Saturday. It's a date. I'll pick you up at your apartment."

They stepped out onto M Street. The sidewalk was thronged with pedestrians and the road was bumper to bumper cars, trucks and delivery vans. Georgetown was patronized by yuppies, diplomats, doctors, college students and a lot of tourists, so its narrow, cobbled streets tended to be impassable at most hours of the day or night.

Caitlin assessed the bustling scene with a practiced eye. "No point in waiting for a cab," she said.

Alec agreed. "The restaurant's only ten blocks, and it's a good night for walking. Not too hot, not too cold. No humidity, no wind and a glorious sunset." He drew a satisfied breath. "I love fall."

Caitlin turned her face to catch the pleasant evening breeze. "September and October are terrific. The only problem is that five months of grungy winter come next." She zigzagged expertly between a band of street musicians and a gaggle of college students cheering a young man who had managed to balance six empty beer cans on the top of his head. She laughed, shaking off her tiredness, and seized Alec's hand.

"I'm so glad you stopped by tonight. I've missed you. What've you been doing these past couple of weeks?"

"Hiring another paralegal, trying to understand a new computer program that was supposed to cut my research time in half and is currently driving the entire office crazy. And defending Dwayne Jones on a murder charge without much success."

She looked up quickly, knowing that this was a case that had troubled him. "The verdict's in?"

"No, the trial isn't over yet, but the prosecution

has the jury convinced Dwayne is guilty—I can tell by their faces.''

''I haven't seen anything about Dwayne's case in the papers.''

''Why would you?'' Alec said with a trace of bitterness. ''What's one more murder in a city that has a dozen or so each month? Drug-related shootings in the inner city happen so often they aren't news anymore. Dwayne's story isn't interesting to anyone except his mother and his sisters, and they're convinced he's going to get convicted despite the fact that he didn't kill anyone.''

''Do you agree with them? Do you really believe he's innocent?''

''Nobody growing up in Anacostia is *innocent*. The kids in that project are born streetwise, or they don't survive. But Dwayne's bright and he's stayed in school, and if he can just beat this rap, he'll graduate with honors in May. Lord knows, that's a miracle all in itself. Dwayne's probably shoplifted, he may even have snatched a purse or two. But he didn't murder anyone that night, I'm sure of it. The poor kid had the bad luck to be in the wrong spot at the wrong time, and now he's facing life imprisonment for a crime he didn't commit.''

''I thought you'd found witnesses to say he hadn't done the shooting.''

''I had,'' Alec agreed grimly. ''Now my witnesses have gone underground.''

''Disappeared, you mean?''

"Yes, either they're afraid of offending one of the local gang leaders, or else they're simply afraid of messing with the police and the law courts. In the neighborhood Dwayne comes from, they don't view cops and lawyers and judges the way we do. I'm not a friendly civic protector—I'm the enemy. But unless I can persuade those two witnesses to trust me and resurface, Dwayne Jones doesn't have much hope."

"Do you have private detectives out looking for the witnesses?"

"You bet. Three of them, all old-timers. They're the best. If anyone can find those witnesses, they will."

Caitlin was still holding Alec's hand. She gave it a comforting squeeze, not needing to say or do anything more to let him know she understood that this sort of case ate at his professional conscience like acid. She knew that Alec had taken on Dwayne's case as a favor to the public defender's office, which meant that he would receive no pay for his work, and that the expenses connected with the case would all come straight out of Alec's pocket. If Dwayne Jones had any chance at all to get his life together, Alec Woodward was that chance. At moments like this, Caitlin felt proud to have him as a friend.

They turned onto Wisconsin Avenue. "Mama Maria's!" she exclaimed, sighting the restaurant. "Mmm, I can smell the oregano already, and the melted mozzarella."

"Keep your fingers crossed there isn't a line. I'm

starving. I skipped lunch and my stomach is not happy with the situation.''

They were in luck; the restaurant was crowded but not yet full. Maria Rossi, a second-generation American with the flashing black eyes of her Italian ancestors but a svelte figure straight out of *Cosmopolitan* magazine, personally directed them to a secluded table in a quiet corner of the dining room.

''You look like you need some time alone,'' she said, handing them the oversize menus. ''Me, I always know when lovers are in turmoil. My mother was Sicilian, and she emigrated to America because the neighbors accused her of witchcraft. She had second sight, and me, I inherited her gift. Or at least some of it. I always know when a couple's love life is in crisis. You two are deciding whether to get married, right?''

''Er...not exactly—''

''Sure you are. You want some Chianti like always, yes?'' With a cheerful smile, Maria wound her way back to the reception desk, not waiting for their answers.

Caitlin chuckled. ''Last time I heard that story, Maria's mother had to flee from the Nazis before they could imprison her for being such a brave resistance fighter against Mussolini's fascists.''

Alec leaned back against the comfortable leather banquette. ''Maybe her mother was a brave resistance fighter *and* a witch. That would be a pretty useful combination, I should think.''

"Well, Maria didn't inherit her mother's gift if she thinks we're lovers, but at least she gave us the best seats in the house." Caitin crunched contentedly on a bread stick. "Gosh, it's great to relax. Remember to look like a tormented lover when Maria comes back with the wine. We don't want her to be disillusioned."

"Like this?" Alec asked.

She looked up from the menu, and for a bewildering second thought she saw such love and frustrated longing in Alec's gaze that she actually shivered. "Hey, Alec, cut it out," she said awkwardly. "You're too darn convincing."

He laughed, his eyes once again gleaming with good humor and nothing more. "Lawyers have to be three parts actor, didn't you know that?"

Maria returned with a small, straw-covered bottle of Chianti and two glasses. "Enjoy," she said, removing the cork with a single expert tug and leaving Alec to pour the wine himself.

A college student in a minuscule miniskirt brought them warm bread, bowls of green salad and wrote down their order for pizza. "It'll take twenty minutes," she explained. "The kitchen prepares each pizza to order."

"No problem. We're not in a hurry." Alec smiled and the waitress smiled back. She leaned over to top up his wineglass, making sure he received the best possible view of her generous cleavage.

Caitlin watched the waitress weave her way

through the crowded tables. "You made a conquest," she said, amused. "Those hip wiggles are all for you."

"Jealous?" Alec inquired, smiling lazily.

"She's not your type."

"Isn't she? What is my type?"

Caitlin started to answer, then realized she had nothing to say. She stared at Alec in blank astonishment, holding a forgotten forkful of salad in midair.

Alec gently guided the fork back to her plate. "What is it?" he asked. "Caitlin, what did I say that was so shocking?"

She blinked, then laughed a bit stiltedly. "Your question surprised me, that's all."

"After twenty years, I'm glad I can still surprise you."

"Well, you did. The fact is I've no idea what sort of woman appeals to you. For all I know, a perky college student might be your ideal date."

"She was—fifteen years ago when I was a perky college student myself."

She smiled. "Alec you were never perky. Pseudo-sophisticated, maybe, but perky, never."

"You're nearly seven years younger than me. When I left for college you'd barely turned ten. Maybe you didn't see me as I really was."

"I *know* I didn't see you as you really were. Alec, surely you realized what a terrible crush I had on you. I thought you were God's gift to women. For years I had this recurring nightmare that you'd marry someone else before I had a chance to grow up and marry you myself.''

"I seem to remember your telling me something of the sort when you were about sixteen."

Feeling a jolt of nostalgia, Caitlin took a long, slow sip of wine. "You were halfway through law school and your parents told me you were unofficially engaged. To a nurse called Jeannie Drexel, remember?"

"How could I forget? We got as far as setting the wedding date before Jeannie got smart and pointed out to me that unless we were in bed we had nothing to say to each other. I've always been grateful to her for being so perceptive."

"I was furious with you," Caitlin said. In her mind's eye, she could see the skinny, graceless young girl she'd been, red pigtails flying behind her in the wind as she cycled to the stream where Alec had gone fishing. "I told you you were making a big mistake."

"And you were quite right."

Caitlin smiled wryly. She had gained a lot of wisdom and common sense since those days, but somewhere deep in her heart she felt a little ache for all the passion and emotion she'd lost along the way. Growing up, she reflected, wasn't entirely a change for the better.

"You were very kind to me," she said. "Not many young men would have been able to let down an overwrought teenager so gently."

"You wanted me as your link to the big exciting world outside Hapsburg, Ohio, not as a husband,"

Alec said. "So being gentle wasn't difficult. All I had to do was remind you about going to college, and how you could have an interesting job, and your very own apartment, and the car of your choice." He grinned ruefully. "In fact, it's humiliating to look back and remember how easily I persuaded you that a career would be much more satisfying than marriage to me."

"The sixteen-year-old heart is notoriously fickle," Caitlin said. "You should never have mentioned the car. It was the prospect of owning my own BMW that did it."

The pizza arrived and the waitress took the opportunity to give Alec another wholesale review of her charms. Alec seemed too hungry to notice. He proceeded to silence his rumbling stomach with a couple of hefty slices of pizza, then poured them both a final glass of wine.

"That was delicious. The food gets better each time we come," he said. "What do you think?"

"Better and better," Caitlin agreed. "You eat the rest of the pizza, though. Otherwise I'll have to spend the entire weekend at the health club working off excess calories."

Alec helped himself to another slice. "I'm glad you were free tonight," he said after a few moments of contented munching. "I've been wanting to talk to you about something important for weeks, and I've just never managed to find the right opportunity."

"Something personal?"

"Very personal." He seemed absorbed in the task of wiping his fingers on the huge paper napkin. He looked up suddenly. "I've decided to get married."

Caitlin felt a sharp constriction in her lungs, as if someone had placed a heavy weight on her rib cage and then ordered her to carry on breathing normally. Alec was going to get married. Why was she so shocked? Perhaps because she had always assumed that Alec would remain single, like her. She swallowed hard, trying to make herself feel enthusiastic. Alec was her friend. If he had fallen in love—found a woman to marry—she ought to feel happy for him.

"Congratulations," she said, injecting as much zing into her voice as she possibly could. "I'm so pleased for you, Alec. Who is...who is the lucky woman?"

Alec smiled cheerfully. "I've no idea. Not yet."

Caitlin stared at him blankly. "What on earth do you mean? How can you decide to get married without knowing who you want for your wife?"

"Easily," he said, "with your help. You're my best friend, you've known me for years, plus you're a woman with years of professional experience interviewing job applicants. I'm counting on you to find the right woman for me."

Caitlin was so shocked she couldn't do anything except stare at Alec in speechless amazement. She had known this man and his family for twenty years. For the past couple of years she'd have sworn she understood his thoughts and feelings almost as well as she understood her own. Listening to him, Caitlin wondered if she had ever understood him at all. The thought was so bizarre it made her feel as though the universe was tilting.

"I can't find a wife for you," she said finally. "Good grief, Alec, the very idea is absurd. We're heading into the twenty-first century, for heaven's sake. Arranged marriages have gone the way of the dinosaurs."

"Maybe it's time to reintroduce the concept," he suggested. "You know, like everyone thought plastic and polyester were the miracle products of the future. Then we realized that maybe cotton and wood had a lot to recommend them, after all."

She reached for her wineglass and took a hefty swallow of Chianti. Her teeth chattered against the glass, and she spared a moment to wonder why Alec's decision to look for a wife should have such a strange *physical* impact on her. She realized she felt obscurely angry, as if he had betrayed an element of their friendship by even suggesting he wanted to get married.

"I don't understand why you feel this sudden need for a wife," she said, trying to smile. "Personally I'd recommend hiring a good housekeeper. They're much easier to get rid of if they don't work out."

He leaned forward and looked at her, his eyes dark and shadowed in the flickering candlelight. "Caitlin, I'm soon going to be thirty-five. I've spent fifteen years running and pushing and striving to climb the career ladder. I don't regret those years—I'm proud of them, proud of the work I've done as a lawyer. But I've reached the stage in my life when I need something more than professional success. Getting promoted from junior partner to senior partner in my law firm isn't going to cure this ache in my gut. That's an ache caused by loneliness.''

''So increase your social life,'' she said, refusing to acknowledge a flash of fellow feeling. ''Get together with one of those nubile young law associates who are dying to date you.''

''I'm tired of playing the dating game, and I'm tired of dating the people I meet professionally. The law is a fascinating occupation, but there's more to life than tort reform and indemnity clauses.''

''Then take up a hobby,'' she snapped. ''How about skiing? I remember last winter we both said we'd like to learn to ski, but we never did anything about it. Maybe this winter—''

Alec sounded impatient. ''Caitlin, get real. Sports and hobbies can be a fun part of married life, but they can't be a substitute. I guess I've finally grown up. I've realized over the last couple of years that having a great collection of wine, a fabulous stereo system and a Persian rug to complement the leather couches in my living room doesn't turn my apartment into a home. And that's what I want, Caitlin—a home I can share with a congenial companion. I want a wife. A loving wife, a woman who'd like to help me build a home, and be the mother of my children—''

''You can hold it right there.'' Caitlin knew her

smile was brittle, but she couldn't help it. Alec's words were pricking her skin like needles, and the more he said, the more painful it became. "You've just hit on the major problem with your neat little scenario. Finding the right wife isn't an easy job, you know—otherwise half the marriages in this country wouldn't end up in divorce court. Why do you think our agency does such a thriving business in placing nannies and housekeepers? Most of the time we're placing our recruits in a family split by divorce."

"True, there are a lot of failures, but we both know marriage doesn't have to end in the divorce court. Look at your family. Look at mine. Our parents have been contentedly married for years. Your sisters and mine couldn't be happier with their husbands."

"They're satisfied by their standards," Caitlin said. "But the women in both our families have sacrificed their entire lives to their marriages. Is that what you want from your wife? A woman whose interests are so narrow she's prepared to stay home all day experimenting with new recipes and taking your babies for walks in the park? For heaven's sake, Alec, what will you talk about to this wonderfully domesticated wife of yours five years down the road?"

"Everyday things," he said. "Maybe whether the baby got a new tooth, or whether we should treat ourselves to a vacation in Hawaii. Maybe we'll discuss ways she could combine her career with motherhood."

"How about ways that *you* could cut back on your

career so that *you* could stay home and baby-sit while
your wife worked full-time?''

''That, too,'' Alec said quietly. ''I'd certainly be
willing to consider taking time off from my career if
that's what my wife needed in order to feel fulfilled
and happy in our marriage.''

He was really serious about getting married, Caitlin
thought, feeling a stir of panic deep inside. She didn't
want Alec to find this wonderful wife, she realized,
because there was no way their unique friendship
would survive after he was married.

She felt a sense of loss so acute it was physically
painful, but she ignored the ache and forced herself
to smile. The necessity for deception was painful in
itself. In the past, she'd never had any reason to conceal her true feelings from Alec. Drat and damnation,
she thought. Why did he have to change things when
we were so happy?

She stretched her smile a notch wider and raised
her wine glass in a toast. ''Well, old friend, I can see
you're determined to become a married man, so
here's wishing you good luck in finding the perfect
wife.''

He raised his own glass in reply. ''Thanks. How
soon can you start your search? As you can imagine,
now that I've finally decided to take the plunge, I'm
anxious to start interviewing candidates.''

''Alec, I can't find you a wife! There are a few
things in this life that people have to do strictly for
themselves, and finding a mate is one of them. Be-

sides, I'm the worst person you could possibly ask. You know how I feel about marriage. I've never made any secret of the fact that I think it's a trap for women.''

"But nobody's asking *you* to get married, Caity. We're talking about me. You're a professional personnel recruiter. Just because you don't personally know how to be a butler or a nanny doesn't mean you can't find excellent butlers and nannies for your clients.''

"It may have escaped your notice," she said dryly, ''but there's a difference between the duties performed by a butler and those that would be required of a wife. Our company has listings for literally hundreds of domestic helpers. We don't have any files headed 'Potential Wives.'''

"Improvise. I'm willing to pay all expenses and a five-thousand-dollar fee.''

The waitress arrived to clear their plates and take orders for dessert. Caitlin had lost her appetite, but she ordered a cup of cappuccino for appearance sake. Alec ordered fresh fruit, then ruined the health effects by asking for ice cream on the top. His appetite, Caitlin thought resentfully, didn't appear to be suffering in the slightest from his sudden crazy desire to get shackled for life to some sweet young thing who would bake him cookies, bring him his slippers—and warm his bed. So far, their conversation had remained amazingly decorous, all things considered. Alec hadn't said a word about how he and his mythically perfect wife were going to conduct their affairs in the bedroom, but if rumor could be believed, Alec was going to want someone whose skills in bed were as superlative as her skills in the kitchen.

"You're blushing," Alec said softly. "What are you thinking about?"

"It's the wine," she lied. "You know I can't drink more than a glass without getting all hot and bothered."

Alec leaned across the table and clasped her hand. "Help me, Caitlin. I really do want to find a wife as quickly as possible, and with the caseload I'm carrying right now, I don't have the chance to meet many suitable women."

"If you're too busy to find a wife, I'd say you're too busy to sustain a worthwhile marriage."

Alec turned away, his shoulders rigid with tension. When he turned back, his expression was determined, his voice grim. "You know, Caitlin, some of the most important decisions we make are the hardest ones to explain. You may not understand my reasons, but the fact is, I've decided to get married. I'd like your help in finding a wife, but if you don't feel up to the job, then I guess I'll go to some other employment agency and offer the assignment to them."

She had absolutely no idea what bug had gotten into Alec, Caitlin thought testily, but she certainly wasn't going to have him take his silly assignment to some other company. "Services Unlimited is the best employment agency in town," she said. "If you're determined to go through with this crazy scheme, then I'm sure our company will be able to find you the perfect bride.''

Alec beamed. ''I'm sure you're right,'' he said. ''In fact, I'm counting on it.''

CHAPTER TWO

DOT MARCHED into Caitlin's office and slapped a file folder on the desk. "I know this must be a joke," she said. "But it's Monday, and I'm half asleep. Would you please explain the punch line so we can both have a good laugh?"

Caitlin picked up the folder and read the label, although she knew quite well what it said. She'd written the tag herself a couple of hours earlier. "Client: Alec Woodward, Attorney-at-law. Position available: Wife, full-time, live-in."

Caitlin flipped open the file and glanced at the papers nestled inside. "Everything seems to be in order," she said, pretending not to notice that her secretary hovered on the verge of apoplexy. "Yep, it's all here—detailed job description, photo of client, profile of the ideal applicant, salary and benefits for the prospective wife, and details of our agency fee. Alec has agreed to pay us five thousand dollars by November first, provided I've presented at least four suitable candidates before then. If he actually marries one of our candidates, then we get a five-thousand-dollar bonus. All our usual expenses will be reimbursed by him of course."

Dot leaned down and peered closely at her boss. "You don't look crazy," she said. "You don't even look as if you have a fever. So that means this has to be some kind of a bad joke. In the first place, we're a personnel company, not a hearts-and-flowers dating agency. And in the second place, Alec Woodward doesn't need to hire anybody to find him a wife. He's got a body to die for, great teeth, thick hair and bedroom eyes. Plus he's intelligent, successful in his career and has enough money to keep the wolf from several doors. Heck, from what I've seen, he's even quite a nice guy—or at least no more of a rat than most of the men in this world. Now, explain to me why a guy with those qualifications would need to hire a domestic-services company to find him a wife."

"He's too busy to find one himself?" Caitlin suggested.

Dot's eyes popped in astonishment. "Too busy to find his own wife, but not too busy to take on the responsibilities of married life? That's a new one. Even my ex-husbands wouldn't have come up with an explanation that dumb."

Caitlin closed the file with a brisk snap. She'd had an entire weekend to rethink her Friday night conversation with Alec, and she could no longer understand why she'd been so reluctant to accept the assignment. A job search was a job search as far as she was concerned, and she prided herself on her outstanding professional ability to match client and applicant. Right now, she couldn't think of a single reason that finding a wife for Alec should be any more difficult than finding an English butler for the Japanese ambassador. On the whole, Alec's requirements for his future wife seemed a great deal more flexible than the ambassador's requirements for his butler. Caitlin returned the folder to her secretary with a cheerful smile.

"It's too late to back out now, Dot. I've accepted the assignment, and Sam's quite pleased I did. He says that with the fast pace of life today, maybe there's a renewed need for a topnotch matrimonial agency in a big, impersonal city like Washington. He wants us to consider this search for Alec's wife as a test case for our company, and if the search proves successful, he's going to evaluate merging with a major dating agency and upgrading their services to the same high standards we apply to all our other personnel services."

"Sounds to me like you and Sam stood out too long in the rain we had Saturday afternoon. You both lost your marbles in the storm." Dot tucked the offending folder under her arm. "This isn't gonna work out the way you planned, Caitlin, believe me. But of course I don't expect you or Sam to listen. I'm just the typist around here."

Caitlin grinned. "Right. I've noticed how shy and hesitant you are about expressing your opinions. Sam and I are both so intimidating."

Dot didn't deign to give a reply. With a withering

look, she retreated to her own office. Two minutes
later, she stuck her head back around the door.
"Don't forget you have a three-o'clock appointment
with Michelle Morreau. She's the fancy chef who
would like a live-in position with one of our Washington bigwigs."

"I have her résumé here. On paper, she sounds like
a great find."

"Yeah, but the way this day is going, she'll probably turn out to have warts on her nose and fungus
growing on her chin."

Dot's gloomy predictions couldn't have been more
wrong. In the flesh, Michelle Morreau proved every
bit as marketable as her résumé suggested. A petite,
vivacious woman in her late twenties, with sparkling
eyes and a cap of shining, dark brown hair, she had
trained in Paris and Switzerland before returning to
the States a few weeks earlier. She arrived for her
interview carrying a tray of homemade goodies so
delicious even Dot was forced to admit that the applicant's skills as a pastry chef were beyond dispute.

Michelle explained that she wanted to buy a home
in the Washington area and had decided that a live-
in job would help her to save enough money to ac-
cumulate the down payment on a small town house
before her thirtieth birthday.

Caitlin felt an immediate kinship with this woman,
whose age and ambitions were not dissimilar to her
own. "I have several excellent nonresident positions
I could recommend to you," she said. "Unfortunately

I have only one live-in position on the books at the moment. It's for a member of the cabinet who's looking for a cook.''

Michelle perked up. "That sounds interesting."

"Unfortunately there's a catch. He has three young teenagers, and he wants the cook to supervise the children when he and his wife go out of town. I suspect that your cooking skills would be underutilized, but he's offering excellent pay, and their house in Chevy Chase is lovely. In view of the possible child-care duties, would you still be interested in going for an interview?"

"Yes, I think so," Michelle said after considering for a few seconds. "A cabinet member must throw a lot of big parties, which would give me the chance to show off my fancy cooking. And I come from a huge family, so I'm used to being around kids. Occasional baby-sitting would be no problem." She smiled and gave a very Gallic shrug. "My grandmother can't understand why I'm not surrounded by my own babies. She always thought I would marry young and have a clutch of children at my knees long before now."

Caitlin returned her smile. "Your family sounds like mine. My sisters have rounded up every bachelor within a fifty-mile radius of our hometown in an effort to provide me with a husband. I'm trotted out like a brood mare every time I go home on a visit."

"I'm sure they mean well." Michelle fell silent for a moment, and some of the sparkle in her expression died. "I was married once. It was the love match of the century as far as I was concerned, except that my husband asked for a divorce on our second wedding anniversary.'' She broke off abruptly. ''I'm sorry. None of this has anything to do with the member of the cabinet and his need for a cook.''

But it might have a lot to do with Alec's quest for a wife, Caitlin thought with sudden excitement. Here was a young attractive woman who liked children and didn't seem in the least opposed to the idea of marriage, despite the unhappy experience with her first husband. Caitlin felt the tingle of anticipation that always came when she was on the verge of tackling a challenging assignment. She leaned forward, elbows resting on her desk.

''Ms. Morreau, I hope you won't be offended by what I'm going to ask. It's a personal question, and you have absolutely no need to answer if you prefer not to. Whatever you reply will have no bearing on my recommendation to the cabinet member. Rest assured I'll be happy to arrange for that interview no matter what answer you give to my question.''

Michelle looked intrigued. ''This sounds interesting. Go ahead and ask.''

''All right, here goes. Would you consider marrying again in the near future?''

''If I met the right man, I might,'' Michelle said. ''But I sure don't have any prospects at the moment. If I take a job through your agency, Ms. Howard, you needn't worry that I'll quit any time soon.''

''That wasn't why I asked the question.'' Caitlin

realized she was drumming her fingers on the top of her desk in a nervous rhythm. She stopped at once, clasping her hands loosely in front of her. There was no reason for her to be jumpy, no reason at all. Finding Alec a wife was a straightforward business assignment, and that was exactly how she was going to approach it. Caitlin decided not to beat around the bush any longer. She plunged ahead, leaving no time for second thoughts.

"Ms. Morreau, I have a somewhat unusual position on our books at the moment, and I wonder if you might be interested in hearing about it."

"I certainly would. I often prefer unusual assignments."

Caitlin drew a deep breath. "A well-established professional man in this city is looking for a wife," she said. "Our company has agreed to select possible candidates for him to interview. Would you care to meet our client?"

Michelle recoiled visibly. "And apply for a job as someone's *wife?* Good heavens, no! This isn't a dating service, is it? I'd never have come here if I'd known it was a dating service."

"We're not a dating service, or at least not yet. I wish you'd reconsider your answer, Ms. Morreau. The man in question is an old friend of mine, and I've taken on the assignment partly as a favor to him, and partly as a test case for our company. We are the nation's premier domestic-placement company, and we believe there's scope for us to bring our expertise to bear in an area that hasn't received much attention from trained professionals. Sam Bergen, our president, feels that the modern world is doing such a terrible job of pairing up potential spouses that maybe the time has come to rediscover some of the older methods.''

"I think the modern world has moved past the point of needing arranged marriages."

"Perhaps. Frankly, you'd be participating in an experiment if you agreed to meet with this client of ours."

Michelle shook her head. "In my wildest dreams, I can't imagine that some stranger from your files would make a suitable husband for me. Besides, how do I know that he isn't a weirdo? He's almost bound to be a creep. A man who needs an employment agency to find a wife for him doesn't sound like very promising husband material."

"I've known this man and his family since grade school, and I can assure you there are no skeletons in his closet, no hereditary health problems and no reason you wouldn't find him a very attractive date." Caitlin smiled encouragingly. "My secretary insists that he's a prime hunk, and he also happens to be a very successful criminal lawyer."

"Then what's his problem? Is he ninety years old or something?"

"Thirty-five. A veritable spring chicken. Think about it, Michelle. From your point of view, what do you have to lose? Agreeing to meet my client doesn't commit you to marriage. It doesn't even commit you to a second meeting. And you just might decide that you like each other enough to pursue the relationship.''

Michelle ran her fingers through her neat cap of hair. "I can't believe I'm even listening to this. It's crazy. It's insane.'' She half rose from her chair, then sat down again with a tiny, self-mocking laugh. "Okay, I'll admit you've caught my attention. I *am* crazy, crazy enough to be curious, at least. Have you got a picture of this man?''

"Right here,'' Caitlin said, pleased at her forethought in insisting Alec provide a photo. They'd gone back to his apartment on Friday evening and spent nearly three hours composing Alec's biographical statement, striving to make it as appealing as possible to prospective wives. Then they'd outlined the practical and financial arrangements that Alec wanted to include in a legally notarized prenuptial agreement. He might be reckless enough to consider finding his wife through an employment agency, but it seemed he still retained enough lawyerly caution to want a rock-solid prenuptial contract.

Michelle took the file. As she inspected Alec's photo, Caitlin could see her expression change from skepticism to dawning wonder. Finally she looked up and met Caitlin's gaze.

"This picture's been fixed, right? I mean, the man doesn't look this fabulous in real life. Good Lord, why would he be scrounging for dates? The man is sex appeal personified. And those eyes—those eyes of his are lethal. That color comes from contact lenses for sure.''

''He doesn't wear contacts.'' Amused at Michelle's enthusiasm, Caitlin leaned over and looked again at the familiar picture. It was a publicity shot taken when Alec was elected to the partnership at the prestigious law firm of Smythe, Howell, Bernstein and Gemelli.

Alec looked amazingly handsome, Caitlin admitted. His eyes—his much admired blue eyes—seemed to laugh up at her, teasing, friendly and yet oddly provocative, promising a woman all sorts of exciting adventures if she once surrendered to their owner's magnetic charm. Caitlin had seen the photo a dozen times. Strange she'd never noticed Alec's incredible sexiness until Dot and Michelle both pointed it out.

She tucked the picture back in the file. ''This picture isn't touched up at all,'' she said. ''Alec looks just like that.'' Her voice sounded oddly husky, so she cleared her throat and continued briskly. ''Would you like to read his personal bio? It's on that sheet of green paper.''

Michelle read no more than a couple of paragraphs before her head jerked up. ''I know who this man is,'' she said, sounding breathless. ''He's Alec Woodward, the defense attorney.''

''Right.'' Caitlin's sense of humor had returned, and she found Michelle's awed reaction diverting. ''You say that as if you recognize his name.''

"*Singles* magazine voted him Washington's Most Eligible Bachelor. There was a big spread on him in last month's issue. He's the lawyer who defended Cindy Carstairs on a charge of murdering her husband on an abandoned movie set."

"And won. What can I say? Services Unlimited prides itself on listing only the best clients," Caitlin joked, although inwardly she admitted to feeling impressed. Being declared Most Eligible Bachelor in a city known for its attractive, powerful and wealthy men was no small achievement. It was typical of Alec, of course, that he had never mentioned it. Caitlin and his family had only discovered he was class valedictorian at Harvard when he stood up to make his valedictory speech.

"'Five foot eleven, 180 pounds, state of Ohio junior tennis champion,'" Michelle read aloud, her voice rapt. "That's an interesting coincidence—I was captain of my high-school tennis team." She pulled out the yellow sheet that listed Alec's requirements for marital bliss.

"He wants at least one child, possibly two if his wife is agreeable, and we can reconcile the needs of the children with the demands of our careers. He'd like to stay in Washington for the next few years, but he's willing to consider living in other major cities if his wife prefers that. He doesn't like living in the country, although eventually he'd like to buy a cottage for weekend retreats." Michelle sighed happily. "Alec, baby, you sound like my perfect man."

Springing to her feet, Michelle closed the file and returned it to Caitlin's desk. "Ms. Howard, do me a favor and arrange a meeting for me with Alec Woodward as soon as you can. I'm sure he'll turn out to have some horrible major drawback, but from his file, he seems the perfect mate. The man looks sexier than a movie star, and writes with more sensitivity than a poet. Unless the full moon turns him into a werewolf, why did the women of Washington, DC, leave him on the loose for so long?"

Caitlin laughed. "Don't worry, I personally guarantee that he has no fangs. He's single because he's been too busy to think about getting married until recently. Besides, not every woman in the world wants to get married, you know, even to a man like Alec Woodward. Maybe he had an unhappy love affair, or loves the wrong woman."

Now why in the world had she said that? Caitlin wondered. She knew quite well that Alec wasn't suffering from an unsuccessful love affair. He'd had a few serious relationships in the past ten years, but they'd all been broken off by mutual consent relatively painlessly. She knew him well enough to be certain of that—didn't she?

"I guess it's possible he's nursing a broken heart," Michelle said, although her tone suggested she couldn't imagine Alec Woodward being rejected by any sane woman. "Anyway, if he's been wounded in the battle between the sexes, so much the better. I've been a victim, too, so we can comfort each other."

Caitlin bit back the retort that Alec didn't need comforting and that—if he did—she was perfectly capable of providing all the solace he needed. She knew her reaction was irrational, but perhaps it wasn't surprising that she felt this spurt of jealousy at the prospect of Michelle or some other woman taking the number-one spot in Alec's life.

The trouble was, deep down inside, she hadn't yet accustomed herself to the idea that he wanted to marry. She'd always assumed he viewed marriage much as she did: as a trap that locked men and women together in a lifelong bond that snuffed out excitement, creativity and personal growth. Of course, even in today's supposedly liberated society, women sacrificed far more than men in most marriages. Alec's independence wasn't going to be compromised just because he took a wife. Even so, there was no denying that in her heart of hearts, Caitlin felt a knife thrust of betrayal. Alec was her best friend, darn it! She'd been counting on him to be there for her— always.

She pretended to rummage through her papers for a moment while she regained control of her emotions. It wasn't more than a few seconds before she managed to pin on a bright, professional smile.

"So, Michelle, when can I arrange a first meeting for you and my client?" *Yes, that was better. Think of him as "my client," not as "my dear friend Alec."*

Michelle smiled back, a cheerful, uncomplicated smile. "The sooner the better! As you know, I'm not working at the moment, so my hours are very flexible. Any time Mr. Woodward is available, I'm willing to meet him.''

''What's your favorite restaurant?''

''Maison Blanche, you know the one? Right by the White House.''

''Great choice,'' Caitlin commented, relieved to find her professional instincts once again completely in charge. ''That's a favorite with Alec, too. I'll call him this afternoon and try to set up a lunch or dinner date within the next week. In the meantime, would you like me to contact the cabinet member and arrange an interview for the position as his cook?''

''I think you'd better do that,'' Michelle said, her voice wry. ''I need to line up something a bit more mundane than a date with Alec Woodward if I'm going to keep my head out of the clouds.''

Escorting Michelle out to the reception area and the bank of elevators, Caitlin dismissed her earlier moment of doubt. ''I'll be in touch some time this week,'' she promised, thinking that the wife-search was really going far better than she'd expected.

''I'll be waiting.'' Michelle blushed at her own eagerness, then smiled with just a hint of sauciness. ''Goodbye, Ms. Howard. This has surely been an interesting afternoon!''

Alec would really enjoy Michelle's company, Caitlin decided, returning swiftly to her office. What's more, she was just the sort of cute, cheerful young woman that Alec's mother would like to have as a daughter-in-law. Yes, all in all, this had been a very successful interview. Caitlin had every reason to be pleased with her first candidate for the role of Mrs. Alec Woodward.

"Did I hear right?" Dot demanded. "Are you recommending that woman as a prospective wife for Alec Woodward?"

"Yes. Any objections?"

"None you'd be willing to listen to."

Caitlin grinned. "You're just a man-hater. She's sweet and I'm sure Alec will love her."

"For a smart woman, boss, you are sometimes amazingly dumb." Dot sighed gustily. "But then, I guess I can't talk. Smart women are always dumb where men are concerned. We're made that way so men don't have to walk around feeling permanently inferior."

Caitlin sat down at her desk, ignoring Dot's disapproving glower. In a world where time was replacing money as the commodity in shortest supply, why shouldn't busy, successful people hire professionals to find ideal spouses for them? If she could provide Alec with a suitable wife, Sam Bergen would appoint her vice president in charge of the new "matrimonial services" division. And if she made a success of that new division, maybe her dream of a full partnership would come true years earlier than she'd hoped.

Caitlin smiled ruefully, well aware that she was building tall castles on shallow foundations. Before she could dream of partnerships, she'd first have to get Alec successfully married off. She reached for the phone and dialed his office.

His secretary answered with the expected news that he was still in court. "He'll stop by to collect his messages as soon as he leaves the courtroom," she added.

"Tell him I'd like to come around and see him tonight, Betty, maybe after dinner, if that's okay. I have some exciting news for him."

Betty was middle-aged, super-efficient and devoted to Alec's well-being. For reasons Caitlin had never been able to fathom, Betty seemed to dislike her intensely. On this occasion, as always, she sounded as if talking to Caitlin was slightly less pleasurable than sucking on a lemon.

"Thank you for calling, Ms. Howard. I'll see that Mr. Woodward gets your message. However, he's very tired, and this Dwayne Jones case is causing him a lot of extra work."

"I won't keep him up late," Caitlin promised, wondering how Betty managed to make her feel so guilty when, in reality, she had nothing to reproach herself for. "The news I have is going to please Alec a lot, I promise."

"I'll pass on your message," Betty said dourly, and Caitlin could almost see the disapproving flare of the secretary's nostrils. *Oh well,* she thought, hanging up the phone. *I guess I can't expect everyone in the world to like me.* But tonight when she saw Alec, she'd ask him just what she had done to offend the woman.

CHAPTER THREE

CAITLIN COULD SMELL the coffee brewing as soon as Alec opened the door to his penthouse apartment. "Mmm, you're a wonderful man," she said, brushing her cheek against his in an absentminded greeting. "How did you know I skipped coffee and dessert?"

He grinned. "Because you always skip coffee and dessert whenever you come to visit me."

She yawned and stretched luxuriously on his expensive leather sofa, adjusting the throw pillows behind her back for maximum comfort. "You shouldn't keep imported Belgian chocolates in your fridge, and then I wouldn't be such a miserable scrounger."

"But how could I be sure you'd keep coming to visit me without my fancy chocolates?"

She laughed. "Darn, my secret's out! I love you only for your Belgian truffles."

Alec feigned heartbreak as he disappeared into his small but state-of-the-art kitchen. "Betty says you have important news for me," he called out over the rattle of coffee cups.

"The best. I've found you a wife. Or I should say a potential wife." She chuckled. "I'm not insisting that you propose to my first candidate, although she is terrific.''

The cups stopped rattling. Silence descended for a second or two, and then Alec reappeared in the doorway, holding two mugs of coffee in one hand and a gold-foil box of chocolates in the other. He set both coffee and chocolates on the low table in front of the sofa before sitting down next to Caitlin.

"You don't look very pleased by my news," she said. "I thought you'd be amazed and impressed by my efficiency. Not even twenty-four hours on the job, and already I've lined up a prime candidate."

"I *am* impressed. I'm overwhelmed." Alec appeared afflicted by sudden restlessness. He got up from the sofa and walked over to the stereo, flipping through his collection of CDs with none of his usual dexterity. "I guess I'd expected to discuss my basic requirements some more before you went ahead and set up the first interview."

"Alec, we spent most of Friday night discussing your ideal wife. I feel I have a really good handle on what you're looking for. Trust me, Michelle is going to be perfect. I brought you a copy of her résumé." Caitlin handed it over, then turned her attention to choosing a chocolate. "Michelle's a cordon bleu chef," she pointed out. "Trained in Paris. Twenty-nine years old, loves children, likes to play tennis, and she's really cute."

Alec looked up from the résumé. "Blond? Brunette?"

"Dark brunette, with a pixie smile that'll melt your heart."

"She certainly sounds intriguing. When can I meet her?"

"As soon as you have some spare time. She'd like to join you for a meal at the Maison Blanche restaurant."

"The one right by the White House?"

"Yes. Naturally, she wants the first meeting to be somewhere public."

"Of course, I never expected anything else. Maybe you could set up a dinner for Friday night? I should be free by then. The Dwayne Jones trial goes to the jury tomorrow, and I don't imagine it will take them more than a few hours to reach a verdict."

Caitlin looked up anxiously. "Did you find your witnesses?"

"One of them. He's an ex-druggie in a rehab program, so the jury may or may not believe him, but at least he took the stand and swore that he and Dwayne were in a café eating dinner, not in the liquor store where the shooting took place. The DA kept hammering him, but he told the same story as Dwayne— they only ran away because they didn't want to be caught up in the fighting, not because they'd fired the shots."

"That should be enough for reasonable doubt, shouldn't it?"

"I hope so." Alec finally found a CD to please him. He put the disc into the player, and the strains of a Debussy prelude drifted with soft, full-toned clarity into the living room. Caitlin listened in unaccustomed silence until the final chord had died away, her former exuberance pierced by a shaft of melancholy.

Alec hadn't rejoined her on the sofa. He sat in a chair to one side of the empty fireplace, his expression remote, almost austere, as he sipped his coffee. "What's bothering you, Caity?" he asked quietly.

Embarrassed by her thoughts, she felt herself blush, but she answered truthfully, because honesty was at the core of her relationship with Alec. "This sounds selfish," she admitted, "but I was feeling jealous of your future wife. I enjoy your company so much, Alec. There'll be a real gap in my life once you're married."

If she had expected him to reassure her, to tell her that nothing would change, she was disappointed. "Yes," he agreed. "Things will be quite different when I'm married." Politely he added, "But of course we can still be friends."

"Not friends like we are now," Caitlin said. "Your wife wouldn't be too pleased if she had to put up with my dropping in for coffee and sympathy whenever I'd had a rough day at the office."

"I guess that would be a bit much," Alec agreed. "I'll miss all the wonderful times we've had, Caity, but I've reached the stage in my life where I realize that having a successful career and a wide circle of acquaintances will never be enough to stop me from feeling lonely. I'm finally ready to make a full-scale commitment to a woman, despite what I'll have to give up." He smiled wryly. "Of course, I feel like I'm about to jump off a high cliff without a parachute, but I'm willing to make the leap. I'm tired of hot dates that lead nowhere. I'm tired of tiptoeing around my deepest emotions for fear of blundering into someone else's space. I need a woman who's willing to relate to me with total honesty. I'm tired of secrets, Caity. After a while, they poison any relationship."

He couldn't possibly realize how much his words hurt. Caitlin's body jerked ramrod straight in protest. "But you and I already have that sort of intimacy, Alec! Good grief, we tell each other *everything*. I can't imagine a more honest relationship than ours!"

"You're deceiving yourself," he said, his voice laced with weariness. "For people who've known each other as long as we have, Caity, the amazing thing is how much we *don't* reveal, how many secrets we struggle to keep hidden from each other."

If Alec had grabbed a stick and physically beaten her, Caitlin couldn't have felt more shocked. "Maybe you feel that way," she said, her voice shaking. "But I have absolutely no secrets from you, Alec. Not one."

"You can't mean that. I can think of dozens. Most of them important."

"Name one!"

He looked at her consideringly for a long, tense moment. "All right," he said at last. "Are you a virgin, Caitlin?"

Her mouth opened, but no words came. After several edgy seconds she found her voice again. ''That's not a secret, it's just irrelevant. My sex life is something intensely personal, something that there's no reason for the two of us to discuss.''

''But it's rather a fundamental thing for a man not to know about a woman he sees so often, wouldn't you agree?''

She shook her head. ''Our relationship is based on longterm friendship not...not physical attraction. We're friends, not potential lovers.''

''Even friends talk about sex occasionally, Caity, but we never do. It's a taboo subject between us. Why?''

She stirred restlessly against the cushions. ''Maybe because everyone else talks about it all the time and, frankly, I think the whole subject is somewhat boring.''

''Sex is overrated—is that what you're saying?''

''Some people seem to think it's important,'' she said carefully.

''But not you?''

She shrugged. ''Surveys show that, by the time they've been married for two years, couples rarely make love more than three times a week. But each week they spend, on average, a hundred hours together. Let's say the lovemaking takes up three hours of their time. That leaves ninety-seven hours each week when they need to find something else they have in common. With statistics like that, how important can sex be?''

"Statistics show that one-third of the children in southeast DC suffered from malnutrition last year. That's an alarming fact, but does it help you to understand how a mother feels when it's dinnertime and she has no food to offer her kids? Statistics aren't weighted for emotional content, Caity, which is just one of the reasons they so often lie. Your statistics don't show the relative importance of those three hours of lovemaking in comparison to the ninety-seven hours spent sleeping or doing the laundry.''

"I don't need statistics to know the importance of sex is overrated. I'll bet the couple who shares a passionate interest in baseball stays married longer than the couple who shares a passionate interest in sex!''

"How about sharing a passionate interest in baseball *and* sex?'' Alec suggested mildly.

Caitlin was too full of nervous tension to sit still any longer. She jumped up and began pacing the room. "I'm beginning to think you're right about one thing—I don't understand you, Alec. These past few days, you've sprung a lot of surprises on me.''

"In that case, we're equal,'' Alec said. "You finally realize you don't understand me, and I admit I haven't understood you since the day you got engaged to David Wallace. That was four years ago last May, in case you've forgotten.''

Caitlin's heart began to pound with unreasonable speed. She paused by a pot of chrysanthemums in full bloom and tugged at a withered leaf. "I never made any secret of the fact that my engagement to David Wallace was a terrible mistake."

"Why was it a mistake? He seemed like a nice guy."

"I got engaged to David to please my family, not because I'd fallen in love with him. My sisters wanted him for a brother-in-law, and my parents thought he'd make the perfect son. The only problem was, I didn't really want him for a husband. Even so, I agreed to marry him, and when I broke off the engagement, I hurt him quite a lot, and I feel very guilty about the way I behaved." She swung around accusingly. "You know all this, Alec. You were the man who lent me his shoulder to cry on when I was trying to break off the engagement, remember?"

"Vividly," he said. "And I've been waiting for the past three years for you to admit the truth of why you really ended your engagement to David."

Caitlin stopped shredding the chrysanthemum leaf and stared at Alec in bewilderment. She rubbed her forehead, trying to ease the start of a nagging headache. "I'm sorry," she said. "I've no idea what you're talking about."

"On the day David got married to Kirstin Steinbeck you left their wedding reception and came to see me. You spent the entire night in my apartment. We sat up in this very room and talked for ten hours straight. And you know the most amazing thing of all? Somehow we managed to spend all that time together without once mentioning your engagement to David. So let's not kid ourselves about how honest and open and confiding our relationship is.''

"You never asked me about my feelings for him! You've never mentioned his name from that day to this!''

Alec smiled tiredly. "The night of David's wedding, you wanted comfort from me, Caity. Comfort and companionship, not soul-searching inquiry and reckless honesty. And you still want the same things. I know the rules of our relationship. I knew I wasn't allowed to ask about David. We're not allowed to probe each other's deepest emotions. That's how we keep our friendship in balance.''

"How can you say that? We don't have rules,'' she declared vehemently. "For heaven's sake, Alec, you're picking on isolated incidents and inflating them out of all proportion.''

"If you really believe that, then I guess we have different opinions about what's important. It's eighteen months since David married. Eighteen months, according to you, during which we've been best friends without a single secret between us. And yet I still don't know why you were so upset by his marriage. *You* broke off the engagement, after all. *He* didn't dump you. Did you expect him to remain single and grieving forever?''

"Of course not.'' Caitlin felt stifled, as if the intensity of her feelings had somehow drained all the oxygen from Alec's apartment. She walked over to the window, keeping her back turned toward him. After a long silence, she heard herself say, "I've never told anyone this. In fact, I've scarcely even admitted the truth to myself. It wasn't the reality of *David* getting married that upset me—it was something more subtle. Seeing him and Kirstin together and so much in love forced me to accept that I was never going to get married myself. And that realization hurt a lot more than I'd expected. I've always claimed that I want a career and an independent life-style, but deep inside me, I guess I had this secret belief that there was a man somewhere out there in the big world who was going to sweep me off my feet and make domesticity seem like heaven."

"And David wasn't the man."

"Much more than that. Watching David get married, I realized that for me there wasn't *ever* going to be a Mr. Right."

Alec had crossed the room to stand behind her. Gently he put his hands on her shoulders and turned her around, tilting her chin up so that she was forced to look at him. His eyes were dark and intent but, she was relieved to see, contained no trace of pity. "Why not?"

"Because I'm not capable of falling in love," she admitted, trying her best not to sound self-pitying and knowing she failed. "David was just the last in a long string of men I liked, but never managed to love. He was the nicest, kindest person you could ever hope to meet. I wanted to love him, and I simply couldn't.

The earth didn't move when he looked at me. Heck, half the time I didn't notice whether he was looking at me or not. When he kissed me…'' She broke off, not sure whether to laugh or cry.

"When he kissed you…" Alec prompted.

Caitlin confessed the humiliating truth. "I realized after we'd been engaged for a couple of months that I used the time when David kissed me to plan my work schedule for the next day. I'd close my eyes and visualize the agenda for my upcoming meetings while David was pouring his heart and soul into a caress. As soon as I realized what was happening, I knew our engagement had to end."

Alec laughed, and she shook her head ruefully. "Honestly, Alec, it's not funny. I've thought about this for a long time, and I've decided I must have some sort of defective gene or a missing hormone or something. I'm envious when I see other couples genuinely in love, but I can't begin to imagine what they feel."

"For a woman with defective genes, Caity, you'll be delighted to hear that you look entirely normal. In fact, you look great."

"Thanks for the vote of confidence. But the truth is, Alec, I'm twenty-eight years old, and I've never come close to feeling all those crazy things everyone else seems to feel a dozen times before their twentieth birthday. By the time they were in the fifth grade, my sisters were already romantic veterans. Contrast them with me. I was so clueless I never understood I was supposed to fall madly in love with Tommy Winkler because he kept pulling my pigtails!''

"Caity, love, you aren't defective—you were clearly surrounded by clods. Now, a suave Cassanova like me never went in for crude tactics like pulling pigtails. Lord no! I found that tripping girls in the playground worked *much* better.''

Caitlin laughed. "If you'd tried tripping me up, I'd have bopped you over the head with my schoolbag. Which probably proves I've been a lost cause since third grade.''

"Mmm. Or it might prove you had amazingly well developed common sense.''

She sighed. "Common sense isn't necessarily a blessing, Alec. From what I've seen, common sense is the last thing you need if you're planning to fall in love.''

"You fell in love at least once,'' Alec reminded her. "Remember our dramatic confrontation on the banks of the trout pond when you declared passionate and undying devotion to me?''

"My one and only experience of a genuine teenage crush,'' Caitlin agreed. "But you're forgetting something important.''

"What's that?''

"It took you less than half an hour to talk me out of my supposedly lifelong devotion. When Megan was sixteen, she cried herself to sleep for a whole month because Greg Bardok decided to take someone else to the senior prom. And she didn't even like Greg all that much!''

"Your sisters are lucky people. They realized early on what they wanted out of life to make them happy. Some of us take a lot longer to learn who we are and what we're going to do with our lives.''

"True. And I guess I learned at David's wedding that I was never going to fall in love deeply enough to make a good marriage.''

"Come on, Caity, you're too young to be making such sweeping statements.''

She shook her head. "Falling in love isn't anywhere close on my horizon.''

"Don't tempt fate. The poets all seem to agree that's one of the strange things about love—it so often takes you by surprise, creeping up when you least expect it. And then, wham! Before you know what's hit you, you're suffering an acute attack of love sickness.''

Her laugh held just a touch of wistfulness. "I don't know how I did it, Alec, but somehow, somewhere, I got immunized against that particular disease.''

He looked down at her, his gaze sober. "Okay, maybe you're never going to fall wildly, insanely, passionately in love with someone, but that doesn't mean you can never find a man who would make you an acceptable husband and a good father for your children.''

She could feel herself blush fire-engine red. "All right, I admit it. I'm a romantic at heart and I can't imagine promising to share my life with a man unless I've fallen head over heels in love with him. Women make so many sacrifices when they marry that it seems to me you need to be fathoms deep in love before the arrangement is worth it.''

"Then you must disapprove of my decision to find a wife through your agency. Realistically, we both know I'm not likely to fall in love with any of your candidates.''

"Marriage means different things to different people,'' she said. "You're a man. Perhaps falling in love isn't so important to you. After all, your life is likely to change far less than your wife's.''

His gaze darkened. "Love is very important to me,'' he said softly. "But I guess to a certain extent I'm like you. I've just about given up on the impossible dream.''

She'd been so intent on their conversation she hadn't noticed how close they'd moved to each other. To her surprise, Caitlin realized their bodies were almost touching. Alec's arms were clasped lightly around her waist and the pressure of his hands at the small of her back suddenly made her feel hot and restless deep inside. From a long way away, she heard herself ask, "Have *you* ever been in love, Alec?''

"A long time ago.''

He didn't say anything more, and she prompted him. "With that nurse, Jeannie Drexel?''

"No. Like I told you, Jeannie and I shared nothing more than an acute attack of lust.'' Alec stared into the distance, obviously conjuring up memories that still had the power to hurt. "There was someone else.... It must be more than four years ago that I fell in love with her."

"Things didn't work out for you?"

"No."

The monosyllable sounded unbearably bleak, and Caitlin's throat had become so dry it hurt to draw breath. She swallowed hard. "I think, maybe, right around that time...your mother hinted to me that you were hoping to get married. But she never mentioned anyone's name.... And then I got engaged to David, and I didn't see much of you for a while...."

"My family never really knew the whole story, just that I was deeply in love and the woman had decided to marry another man."

"Alec, I'm so sorry. You sound as if it still hurts."

He looked down at her, visibly dragging himself back into the present. "Yeah, well, I've learned to live with the situation, I guess. Sometimes we can't have the one thing we want most."

Caitlin was so accustomed to thinking of Alec as striding through life, successful, confident and unscathed by trauma, that it was hard for her to readjust her mental images. Looking up at him, and seeing the shadows that still lingered in his eyes at the memory of his unsuccessful love affair, she felt an unexpected rush of protective sympathy. She reached up and stroked his cheek in a hesitant gesture of consolation. To her surprise, Alec caught her hand and held it tight within his own. Then, even more astonishing, he turned her hand over and dropped a kiss in the center of her palm.

"Trust me, Caity, twenty-eight isn't too late to fall in love," he said softly. "Maybe you should let a few of your barricades down and see what happens."

She and Alec were still standing uncomfortably close. Her skin prickled where Alec's fingers held her, and deep in the pit of her stomach she felt the flicker of a hot, hungry flame. The sensations were odd, unfamiliar—and she didn't like them one bit. She leaned against the window frame, creating an inch or two of welcome space between herself and Alec.

He was usually sensitive to her moods, but tonight he didn't seem to notice her warning signals. Instead of dropping his hold and moving away, he leaned forward, his head bending slowly toward hers.

"Sometimes common sense can be taken too far," he murmured.

"Wh-what do you mean?"

His lips hovered no more than a hairbreadth from hers. "I mean this," he said, and brought his mouth down on hers, hard and commanding.

Caitlin closed her eyes. She wasn't planning her work schedule; she wasn't thinking about anything. Except, maybe, that Alec didn't kiss in the least like David. Or the congressman from Kentucky. Or the curator from the Smithsonian.

Alec tightened his hold around her waist. The flame deep inside her flickered once more, then roared out of control.

Caitlin surrendered herself to the conflagration.

CHAPTER FOUR

DOT GLANCED at her watch. "It's nearly five-thirty," she said. "And it's Friday the thirteenth. What's happened to Sam? How come he's missing such a golden opportunity for predicting disaster?"

"He's already left the office," Caitlin said. "He went to meet his daughter at the airport. Remember, she's arriving home from Europe today."

"No wonder the place is so peaceful. Well, if Sam's already left, I'd better go home right away, before you decide to throw a tantrum in his place."

Caitlin winced. "Have I been that bad to work with this week?"

"Oh, not too terrible, all things considered. Probably no worse than a lion with raging toothache."

"Good Lord, Dot, didn't they teach you anything in secretarial college? You aren't supposed to be honest with your boss—you're supposed to soothe my irritated nerves. I need sympathy—this has been a tough week."

"True, and from what I've seen, Michelle Morreau's frequent phone calls have been right at the top of your problem list. If you don't want her to marry your hunky lawyer friend, how come you fixed up their date tonight?''

Caitlin blinked. ''Michelle's dinner date with Alec isn't causing my bad mood, of course it isn't. Why should it?''

''You tell me.''

''Good grief, I'm thrilled about their meeting! It's a positive first step in an interesting business project—''

The door to the office flew open with a crash and Sam, white hair spiking into a halo around his bald pate, burst into the room, ''My car has a flat tire and I can't get a cab to take me to the airport! Jodie's going to arrive and I'm going to miss her!''

Caitlin checked her watch. Five-thirty on the button. She and Dot exchanged half-amused glances. ''Don't worry, Sam, I'm sure Jodie's much too sensible to do anything foolish.'' Caitlin spoke soothingly as she reached for the phone. ''What airline is she flying with? We'll leave a message to say you're on your way and that she should wait in the baggage-claim area. Then I'll call for a limo. You've used Bob Cox's service before, and you're a good customer. I'm sure he can get someone around here within twenty minutes, even on a Friday evening.''

Sam's shoulders hunched forward in dejection. ''The airlines never pass on messages,'' he said gloomily. ''Jodie will have left before I get anywhere near Dulles airport. You know what traffic's like at this time on a Friday.''

His air of subdued defeat was so unusual that Caitlin felt a spurt of concern. She walked around to the front of her desk and looked down at her diminutive boss. "Sam, what's really the problem here? Your daughter is a competent grown woman, who just graduated from college with high honors. She isn't about to vanish in a puff of smoke if you're a couple of minutes late to meet her plane."

"Jodie isn't a grown woman, she's a girl!" Sam roared with some of his old fire. "What's more, she's a girl without a grain of sense in her head."

"Uh-oh," Dot said. "Now I get it. You've been up to your old tricks, Sam, don't try to deny it. You've been fighting with Jodie, haven't you? Good Lord, you shouldn't be allowed anywhere near a long-distance phone when your children are out of town."

Sam's round pink cheeks flushed bright red. "Jodie and I had a bit of an argument," he admitted.

"How big is a bit?" Dot demanded sternly.

Sam scowled. "I guess if I don't arrive at the airport right on time, Jodie will think I'm not coming to meet her. And I don't know where she'll go next." He crossed his arms, managing to look pleading and defiant all at once. "Jodie hung up on me when I tried to talk some sense into her last week. I don't know what's getting into kids these days. She's twenty-two years old, wears three earrings in one ear, and thinks she knows more than a man who's fifty-eight—"

"Tell me the sob story while we're driving," Dot interjected briskly. "I'll give you a ride out there."

"You will?" Sam's chubby face creased into a smile of pathetic gratitude. "Thanks, Dot. Thanks a million. I'll never forget this. I really owe you one."

"Just remember that when you're handing out the Christmas bonuses," Dot said dourly. "And next time your daughter goes overseas, don't call her unless you can manage to be pleasant."

"She's not going abroad again!" Sam yelled. "If she thinks I'm going to have her studying tsetse flies in Africa or any other damn fool thing, then she's mistaken. Environmental biologist, indeed! Why can't she be a teacher like her sister, or stay at home like her mother did? She doesn't need the money. She should concentrate on meeting a nice young man so she can get married and settle down in Washington, near her family."

"So you can yell at her in person, instead of just over the phone?" Dot asked sweetly. "Come on, Sam, quit talking and let's get rolling. And you'd better promise me right now that you're not going to start arguing with Jodie as soon as you meet her, or else I'll withdraw my offer of a ride to the airport. People who get into my car are expected to behave themselves."

Caitlin watched in astonishment as Sam meekly promised to be the soul of discretion and trotted behind Dot out of the office. At moments like these, she wondered if she understood even the most superficial details about the male sex. Who would have thought Dot could control Sam's volatile temper with such apparent ease? Although, come to think of it, Dot was usually the person who calmed his Friday-night jitters.

With Sam's explosion taken care of, there was nothing to stop Caitlin from catching up on the week's paperwork. She returned to her chair and shuffled listlessly through the stack of files needing her attention. Before very long, she was stifling yawns and staring at the dial of her watch. Five-fifty. Time seemed to be moving incredibly slowly. In about two hours from now, Alec would be meeting Michelle Morreau for the first time. She wondered what Michelle would wear. Nothing too elaborate if she was smart enough to follow Caitlin's advice. Alec disliked frilly, fussy clothes on a woman. Perhaps she should give Michelle a call and remind her to choose something casually elegant and understated.

Caitlin reached for her Rolodex in search of Michelle's number, then let her hand fall back onto the desk. She shouldn't repeat her advice, shouldn't work too hard to make this evening a success. When Alec and Michelle met, they would either hit it off or they wouldn't, and Caitlin would be doing neither of them a favor if she tried to push them into a long-term relationship that wasn't exactly right for both of them.

She forced herself to read a few more files, realized she hadn't understood a word in any of them and finally admitted defeat. Her mind wasn't on work. She didn't want to think about finding a nanny for the assistant editor at the *Washington Post*. She didn't want to think about candidates for a housekeeping position at the White House. For some reason, she especially didn't want to think about perky, attractive Michelle Morreau. All she wanted to think about was last Monday night and how it had felt when Alec kissed her.

Terrifying was the word that sprang into Caitlin's mind. When Alec kissed her, she had felt as if she were tumbling downward on the fastest, most frightening stretch of a giant roller coaster. But terror wasn't the only emotion she'd experienced. For a few amazing, wonderful seconds her body had sprung into vibrant life, quivering with the shock of a dozen new and intriguing sensations. It had seemed as if, in Alec's arms, the whole world took on new meaning, and she trembled on the very edge of self-discovery. Then exhilaration turned to panic, and she pushed him away, clamping her lips together in a hard, straight line to stop them from trembling.

Alec hadn't attempted to take her back into his arms or to renew their kiss. Instead, he stood quite still, not touching her, just looking. Just looking— with those bright blue eyes that everyone suddenly seemed determined to point out were lethally sexy. He looked at her, damn him, and didn't say a single word.

"Why did you do that?" she'd demanded finally just to break the silence. Her voice sounded high and squeaky rather than cool and sophisticated, but that couldn't be helped. At least she'd resisted the urge to do something adolescent and melodramatic like slapping his face.

He didn't smile or apologize and his gaze never wavered. "It seemed like something we both wanted—something we've both wanted for a long time."

"Not me," she responded instantly and with absolute conviction. "Alec, we're *friends* and that wasn't a friendly kiss."

"No," he agreed. "It sure wasn't."

He still hadn't sounded as if he was apologizing, and Caitlin hadn't been willing to pursue the conversation any further. She turned her back on him, wrapping her arms tightly around her waist, as if a firm grip on her body could get all her rampaging feelings under control again. She hated the way she was feeling, and she was angry with the man whose kiss had made her feel that way. She breathed deeply, searching for calm.

"I should leave," she'd said, staring blindly at her watch. "It's late."

"But maybe not too late."

"It's nearly midnight."

"Yes," he'd agreed. "So it is."

Superficially their conversation had made little sense, and yet once again she'd chosen not to probe beneath the surface of his words. The past few days had produced too many shocks as far as her relationship with Alec was concerned, and she hadn't had the mental fortitude to deal with any more surprises that night. Her life was going just the way she wanted it to go, with short- and long-term goals neatly in place. Her course had been mapped out ever since she'd graduated from high school, with every stage of her career carefully charted—in a straight line up. A kiss, however odd it made her feel, couldn't be permitted to make an impact on such well-laid plans.

Determined to conquer her strange skittishness, Caitlin had swung around and glared at Alec. "Thanks for the coffee and chocolates," she muttered. "Like I said, it's getting late. I'd better leave."

"Right. Well, come back any time. I enjoy your company." He'd suddenly seemed amused, and that infuriated her. He kept up an easy flow of polite conversation while she stuffed her arms into the sleeves of her jacket and collected her purse. She answered him in gruff monosyllables, longing to escape.

Caitlin had left Alec's apartment still seething. By the time she'd arrived home, she realized her anger was out of all proportion to the events that had taken place. In today's freewheeling society, a kiss—any kiss—ranked about a minus-three on the Richter scale of emotional significance. But that insight didn't seem to change her feelings about the incident. What was even odder, her anger hadn't faded over the past five days. It still lodged, like an ill-digested meal, somewhere in the pit of her stomach. Right now, remembering Alec's kiss, she could feel a familiar arrow of emotion pierce her, and she didn't like the hot, sharp feeling one little bit.

Abandoning the pretense of resuming her work, she locked her papers into a file cabinet before shrugging into her suit jacket and picking up her briefcase. She would stop off at the health club and join one of the aerobics classes. Perhaps vigorous exercise would ease her attack of Friday-night blues. What was happening to her well-ordered life? She was never at loose ends or stressed out by overwork, and yet this was the second Friday in a row she'd felt on edge and…lonely.

The elevator doors slid open just as she walked out into the lobby. Alec, looking tired but cheerful, waved in greeting. "Hi, Caity! You're the very person I came searching for."

"Well, here I am." She didn't say anything more because her breath was suddenly coming in quick, jumpy little gasps and she didn't want him to notice her strange reaction.

Of course he noticed at once. "Your voice is husky," he said. "Are you catching a cold?"

"No, not at all. I'm fine."

"Good." He took her arm and followed her into the elevator. With tremendous difficulty, she refrained from jerking away. The doors glided shut and her heart started to thump hard against her ribs. He was standing so close she could smell the cologne he wore, something exotic she didn't recognize. For a moment she had the craziest urge to bury her face in the crook of his neck and breathe deeply. Fortunately, common sense reasserted itself before she gave in to the ridiculous impulse.

Nevertheless, she felt clammy with relief when the doors opened and they emerged onto the sidewalk. Alec moved away from her as he pushed back his shirt cuff to look at his watch. "You're leaving work early tonight, aren't you?" he said. "It's barely six o'clock."

"I have a date," she replied, which wasn't exactly a lie. She supposed the seven-o'clock aerobics class could be termed a date.

"Going somewhere exciting?"

Last week she would have told him the truth without hesitation. But ever since their dinner at Mama Maria's, Caitlin knew their old intimacy had vanished, disappearing into this uncomfortable tension she had no idea how to handle. So she smiled brightly and evaded a direct answer. "Oh, just the usual Friday-night sort of stuff. How about you, Alec? Did you get a verdict in the Dwayne Jones case?"

"We sure did! The jury found Dwayne not guilty. Isn't that terrific?"

"It's wonderful," she said. "Congratulations on a major victory, Alec."

He beamed, the picture of a relaxed man, balanced on the crest of success. "This has been a pretty good week, all in all. Justice is served in the Dwayne Jones case, and tonight I get to meet the woman who may agree to become my wife. I guess this is a night for celebration."

"I'm delighted you're so happy with life." Caitlin felt ashamed of the acid she heard in her voice. She forced herself to meet Alec's gaze, then wished she hadn't when her stomach looped into a tight knot. "Are you all set for the big meeting with Michelle?" she managed to ask.

He grinned. "Shaved, showered and groomed for success. Didn't you smell my new cologne? The saleswoman assured me it's guaranteed to send women insane with desire for my manly body." He leaned closer. "Is she right?"

Caitlin swallowed hard. "Not in my case, but I'm not the woman you're hoping to attract."

"True, but she promised a one-hundred-percent success rate." He smiled. "Maybe I should demand my money back."

He sounded so cheerful Caitlin's black mood darkened even further. She felt a sudden burst of resentment at his insensitivity. The world's most thick-skinned clod should have been able to see the sparks of tension flying off her body, and Alec had never been either thick-skinned or insensitive, at least until last week. In fact, his instant awareness of her moods had always been something she'd particularly valued.

Tonight, however, Alec seemed impervious to her signals. He put his arm companionably around her waist as they crossed the street and didn't notice when she stiffened. "Let's grab a drink at Hogan's bar," he said. "I want to show you the gift I've bought for Michelle. You can tell me if you think it's suitable."

"I don't really have much time...."

"No? Oh, well, we can skip the drink. Just take a quick peek at my gift and tell me what you think." Alec stopped outside the bar and delved into a foil bag from the city's most expensive jewelry store. He extracted a deep blue gift box and pulled off the lid with a flourish. "What do you think?"

Nestled in a bed of pale blue satin was an exquisite miniature of a crystal princess kissing an ugly, but ecstatic-looking crystal toad.

"Do you like it?" Alec asked, sounding anxious. "Do you think it'll appeal to Michelle?"

"It's lovely," Caitlin admitted. "And I'm sure Michelle will like it a lot."

"That's a relief," Alec said. "First impressions are so important, don't you agree? Once a woman has a certain idea of a man fixed in her head, I've found it's virtually impossible to change it. Take you and me, for example. We've considered ourselves next-door neighbors and childhood friends for so long, I can't imagine what it would take to change our relationship, can you?"

A week ago Caitlin would have protested that nothing could change their relationship, ever. Now she knew better. "Our relationship has already changed," she said. "In fact, I realize now it changed as soon as you told me you were planning to get married."

Alec looked at her. For the first time that evening,

he wasn't smiling. "I didn't think you'd be honest enough to admit that," he said quietly. With an abrupt movement, he shut the lid of the jewelry box and put it back into the bag. "Remember our date tomorrow night, Caity, to celebrate your promotion. Eight o'clock at your apartment. I'll pick you up."

"You're having a busy weekend, aren't you? Twirling around the dance floor tonight with Michelle Morreau and with me tomorrow."

"Do you twirl on the dance floor?" Alec asked. "You know, we've never danced together, not even at your sisters' weddings. I wonder how that happened?"

"Coincidence," Caitlin said with a shrug. "It must have been sheer coincidence."

"Yes, I'm sure it was." Alec squinted into the gathering gloom and spotted a taxi at the nearby intersection. He stepped out to the curb, waved his arm, and twenty seconds later the empty cab screeched to a halt beside him. Laughing, he turned to Caitlin before entering the cab.

"Hey, did you see that? A single snap of the fingers and I got a cab! I must be on a winning streak! Keep your fingers crossed for me, Caity. By the time I meet you tomorrow night, I may be seriously in love!"

He didn't wait to hear her answer, and Caitlin scowled at the rear of the departing cab. "Great," she muttered. "Just great. That's all I need to make my weekend totally perfect—Alec Woodward spending our dinner together telling me how much he loves Michelle Morreau and what a perfect wife she's going to be.''

"MICHELLE HAS a wonderful sense of humor," Alec said. "And that's a really important quality in a wife, don't you think? She kept us both laughing all evening long. Did I mention that before?"

Caitlin unclenched her teeth and tried for a smile. "A couple of times, actually. You also told me she's cute, pretty, intelligent, great at her job and has a fascinating perspective on French politics." She set down her fork, no longer feeling any appetite for the chocolate torte she'd ordered for dessert.

"Sorry if I'm repeating myself, but I want to be sure you know how much Michelle and I enjoyed ourselves last night. You had a lot of reservations about using your professional skills to find me a wife, so it's important for you to know how much I appreciate your efforts. You should urge Sam to go ahead with his plans to establish a matchmaking division at Services Unlimited, Caity. You obviously have a real gift for pairing up compatible people. I knew you'd select just the right person when I asked you to help me find the perfect bride, and you haven't let me down."

"Is it settled then? Have you…have you and Michelle decided to get married? That's…that's great news. Professionally for me, I mean. And for you personally, of course.…"

Caitlin snapped her mouth shut, stopping the inane

babble. Her smile had been fixed rigidly in place ever since Alec had picked her up nearly three hours ago, and her jaw muscles were beginning to feel numb. The rest of her body, by contrast, was alive with feeling. Her nerve endings seemed to explode every time Alec mentioned Michelle's name.

Alec laughed easily. He'd been laughing and smiling all night long, but *his* laughter seemed entirely natural and carefree. "Hey, Michelle and I need to know each other a little better before we make such an important decision, but to be perfectly frank with you, I can hardly wait for our next meeting."

Caitlin reached for her wineglass. "And when is that going to be?"

"Tomorrow. We're going to the zoo."

Caitlin gulped down a swig of wine. "How lovely."

"She wants to see the new baby gorilla." Alec's expression softened and his voice lowered. "Michelle loves babies. She wants to have children right away, and I've realized I want that, too. As soon as possible."

"This is a rather sudden urge for instant fatherhood, isn't it?"

"Not really. The truth is, Caity, I've felt a lot of gaps in my life recently, and my career isn't going to fill any of them. I'm envious of your sister and her husband, waiting for the birth of their first child. Aren't you?"

She avoided his gaze. "In some ways, but unfortunately women have to make enormous sacrifices in order to raise a baby to adulthood.''

''True, but think of the compensations! And nowadays fathers share more of the child-rearing burdens, which means women don't have to give up all their independence and abandon their careers just because they're also mothers.'' He took her hand and stroked it absently, running his thumb over the vein pulsing in her wrist. ''I went to bed last night and lay in the darkness imagining what it feels like to watch your wife's body grow and change while she carries the child you've helped to create. I tried to imagine how it would feel to watch my wife give birth to *our* child, a living being the two of us had made together. Don't you ever wonder how it would feel to hold your very own baby in your arms, Caity?''

He was conjuring up images Caitlin rarely allowed herself to dwell on. Deciding not to marry had been easy for her, and the disastrous experiment with David had merely confirmed her decision. She'd seen what marriage meant for women, and she didn't believe the game was worth the cost. But in the darkest, deepest, most secret corner of her heart, she had never quite accepted the fact that if she didn't marry, she probably ought not to have a child. She didn't want to answer Alec's question, for it was too painful, but she also knew he deserved more from her than a flip, easy evasion.

''I held both my nephews when they were only a few hours old,'' she said at last. ''Newborn babies have a special feel, sort of warm and solid, even though they look so fragile." She stared into her empty wineglass. "I've never felt so envious in my entire life as I did when Megan first put Zach into my arms. At that moment, I would have given almost anything to change places with my sister, to be Zachary's mother instead of his aunt."

"Zach is four," Alec said thoughtfully. "And four years ago you got engaged to David. Is there a connection?"

"Perhaps," she admitted. "But in the end, you know what happened to David and me. I told you last week. Our big mutual-confession night."

He squeezed her hand, eyes smiling. "Yeah, you told me this great sob story. But what I heard was that you and David weren't really suited to each other, and that doesn't prove anything about the long term. Take my word for it, Caity, any day now, the love of your life is going to explode onto the scene, and you'll think to yourself, Wow! This is what true love feels like. Thank heaven I wasn't dumb enough to marry good ol' Dave."

She laughed, her first unforced laugh of the evening. "When that happens, Alec, you'll be the first to know."

"I'll be waiting. In the meantime, shall we dance?"

"Dance?" She looked over toward the corner of the restaurant, where a trio of musicians played romantic tunes from the forties and fifties. Two middle-aged couples, obviously enjoying themselves, were revolving slowly around the small dance floor. She shook her head. After what happened on Monday night, the idea of stepping into Alec's arms again was...unsettling. "I'm sorry, Alec, but I need something livelier. After all, my sisters and I grew up with John Travolta and *Saturday Night Fever*. Unless there are strobe lights and hundred-decibel amplifiers, my feet won't move."

"Then I know the place for us. There's a genuine disco just around the corner from here if you'd like to go and check it out."

She looked up eagerly. "Black velvet walls, terrible drinks, and a laser light show every ten minutes or so?"

He grinned. "You've got it. Sound like your kind of place?"

"Sounds perfect. What are we waiting for?"

ALEC DREW HIS CAR to a halt in the parking lot outside Caitlin's apartment building in Arlington. She stirred sleepily. "Do I have to move?"

"Only if you want to get out of the car."

She yawned and forced herself to sit upright. "I suppose I'd better get some sleep."

"There's not much of the night left."

She glanced at her watch. "Four o'clock! Good grief, no wonder I'm exhausted."

"The night went fast, didn't it?"

"Too fast. My feet are worn down to the ankles,

but that was the most fun I've had in years. How come nobody ever told me what a fantastic dancer you are?''

"My family doesn't know all my secrets," he said lightly. "Come to that, how come nobody ever told me you can do the splits? Not to mention back flips."

She groaned. "And I'll have the aching muscles tomorrow to prove it! Alec, you don't think we were maybe a touch—uninhibited—during that last dance?''

He grinned. "Just because the DJ whistled and the bartender dropped his tray of glasses? Nah—you were great, Caity.''

"I should go in. If I can find my shoes…" She scuffed around on the floor with her toes and Alec leaned across to pick up her sandals. "Are these what you're looking for?''

"Yes, thanks.''

"Here, let me help you put them on. It's too cold to walk across the parking lot barefoot.''

He leaned down and Caitlin found herself staring at the back of his head while he slipped her shoes onto her feet and buckled the straps. His dark hair curled thick and unruly against his neck, and before she could stop herself, her hand stretched out to touch. Her fingers ruffled up through the springy thickness of his hair and Alec grew very still.

As soon as she realized that he'd noticed what she was doing, Caitlin snatched back her errant fingers. Alec straightened and returned to his own side of the car. "Does my hair need cutting?" he asked, his voice oddly strained.

"No, no. It's fine just like it is." *Fool!* she chastised herself silently. *If you'd agreed it was too long, you wouldn't need to find another explanation for why you were stroking his neck.*

"My hair grows fast," Alec said.

She let out her breath in a sigh of profound relief that he wasn't going to make a big deal out of her momentary aberration. "Does it? Well, anyway, thanks for a lovely evening, but I must get to bed. I've agreed to meet a friend for brunch tomorrow, and I'm going to be lousy company unless I get a few hours sleep."

"Anyone I know?"

"I don't believe so. He's an assistant curator at the Smithsonian. He's very nice."

"Ah, nice." Alec fell silent, then got out of the car and came around to open Caitlin's door. "I'll see you upstairs," he said. "I'd better make sure there are no ghoulies and ghosties waiting to attack in the corridors."

They didn't speak again until they stood in the hallway outside her apartment. Alec looked down at her, his face shadowy in the muted light. "Good night, Caity. Sleep well."

She wished she could see his expression so that she could guess what he was thinking. His mouth was very close to hers. If she tilted her chin just the tiniest fraction, he would hardly be able to avoid kissing her.

But of course she wasn't interested in kissing Alec. She'd been angry at him all week precisely because last Monday he'd chosen to kiss her. Why provoke an action that made her angry? She would say goodnight and leave.

Caitlin tilted her chin. Her lips touched Alec's. For a moment suspended in time he did absolutely nothing. Then his arms slowly closed around her and he drew her tight against his chest. He took her mouth in a long, passionate kiss, while his hands held her clamped against the taut, hard length of his body.

Caitlin's head spun dizzily; her veins fizzed with fire. Then her stomach knotted and the familiar fear returned, swamping her with panic. She jerked her head away, but Alec wouldn't let her go. He caught her face in his hands and lowered his head toward her. "You give such wonderful kisses," he murmured against her lips. "Kiss me, Caity. I need you to kiss me."

If she'd been smart, she'd have taken to her heels and run. If she'd been smart, she'd certainly have reminded him that he was escorting Michelle Morreau to the zoo tomorrow. But Caitlin wasn't smart. Like the fool she was, she kissed him back. And this time, she was so far gone into craziness that she wished the kiss could have lasted forever.

Finally, much too late, sanity returned. She drew back, huddling her arms around her waist. "We shouldn't have done that," she whispered. "Alec, we're friends, and friends don't exchange that sort of kiss.''

''You're right,'' he said, his voice abstracted. ''There was nothing friendly about that kiss.''

She looked at Alec and, instead of the familiar boy next door, saw a dark, forceful, sexually riveting stranger. Panic washed over her in a cold, engulfing wave, and she did what she should have done five minutes earlier. She fled.

CHAPTER FIVE

CAITLIN'S DATE with Richard, the curator from the Smithsonian, had not been a success. Either because she was tired, or because she was in an unusually critical mood, she'd found his company boring in the extreme. She wondered why she'd never noticed before that he was incapable of discussing anything without dragging the conversation around to the habits of primitive tribal peoples, living in obscure corners of the globe.

"Yes, that *was* an entertaining movie," Richard had agreed, when she tried to introduce a subject that had nothing at all to do with folk customs of the world. "Some of its underlying suppositions reminded me of the Anawoponga tribe in the South Pacific. Did you know that the Anawoponga believe that murdered souls always come back to haunt their murderers?"

"No, I hadn't heard of the Anawong... Anapong..."

"Anawoponga. They're a fascinating society altogether, a unique cultural relic that Western society needs to cherish. At puberty, the males are initiated into adulthood by the medicine man..." And off he'd rattled on a ten-minute lecture on the circumcision ceremonies of the Anawoponga, to be rapidly followed by a dissertation on the burial rites of the Betuni and the religious education of the Monguyvu, a particularly obscure tribe recently discovered in the heart of the Ecuadoran rain forest.

Caitlin hadn't been required to contribute to any of these lectures, merely to nod appreciatively and listen quietly. She'd found herself wondering with increasing frequency how Alec and Michelle were enjoying themselves at the zoo. She couldn't help thinking they were having a wonderful time. Alec was such good company it was hard to imagine Michelle *not* enjoying herself. Caitlin wished she'd been lucky enough to spend the afternoon watching baby gorillas at the zoo, with Alec to share her laughter at their antics.

The telephone rang, jolting Caitlin out of her reverie and into the reality of the present, which was Monday morning at the office, a stack of phone message slips waiting to be answered and a desk drowning in paper. The phone call was from the Japanese ambassador, calling personally to say how delighted he was with Algernon Littlethwaite, his new butler, and could Services Unlimited please find him an equally splendid English nanny to take care of his grandchildren when they visited next month?

Caitlin promised the ambassador her best efforts. Screening out all errant thoughts, she managed, by dint of nonstop work, to return all her phone calls, contact three prospective nannies and reduce the pile in her "pending" tray to the point that the folders no longer toppled over if she accidentally jostled the desk.

Late in the afternoon, she was trying to decide which urgent project to tackle next when Alec walked into her office unannounced. "Dot wasn't at her desk," he explained. "Could you spare me a couple of minutes?"

"Sure, take a seat." Caitlin's breath was suddenly coming faster, and she could feel the heat flaming in her cheeks. She smiled, hoping Alec wouldn't notice anything out of the ordinary in her manner. "Today's been a good day, so I'm only about a week behind on my paperwork. What's up?"

"Slightly more chaos at the office than usual. Leon Mancuso has asked me to defend him."

"Wow! That's a biggie." Leon Mancuso was a world-famous pianist accused of murdering his mistress while his blind wife slept in a nearby bedroom. The publicity surrounding his arrest had been enormous, and Caitlin could imagine the media interest aroused by the news that Mancuso was changing defense attorneys. "Do you think you can make a decent case?" she asked.

"It isn't going to be easy, but we'll give it our best shot. Anyway, Mr. Mancuso isn't why I came. I'd like to catch you up on my news about Michelle."

Caitlin couldn't read his expression and she discovered that her heart was pumping nineteen to the dozen. Had he come to announce his wedding plans?

The prospect of Alec married to Michelle Morreau produced a tumult of emotions too complex to analyze, but powerful enough to leave her feeling battered. It took a couple of seconds before she could unclench her hands and produce a smile. "I hope everything's going smoothly. How was your trip to the zoo yesterday?"

"We had a lot of fun. The better I know Michelle, the more I like her. She's really a terrific person."

Personally speaking, Caitlin hadn't found her *that* wonderful, but Alec's eyes glowed every time he mentioned the darn woman. Caitlin turned away. Alec seemed to be watching her much too closely, and she wasn't willing to have her feelings probed right at this moment. She jumped up and walked briskly across the room, closing a cabinet drawer that could just as well have remained open. When she was sure she had her voice and smile under control, she faced Alec again.

"Let me guess," she said with false cheer. "You've come to deliver your check."

"My check?"

"For professional services successfully rendered." She swallowed. "I assume you're here to announce that you and Michelle plan to get married."

She had the oddest impression that Alec was disappointed. The impression was so fleeting, however, she couldn't be sure.

"No," he said after a tiny pause. "I'm afraid we're not going to get married. In fact, I've just come from driving Michelle to the airport. At this very moment, she's taking off on the evening flight from Dulles to Paris.''

"To Paris! Why is she going there? Good grief, she only just flew back to the States a couple of weeks ago!"

Alec's familiar grin returned with all its insouciant charm. "I thought you'd be surprised, but her ex-husband is in Paris, you know. Tall, dark, handsome Philippe.''

"Right, and that's precisely why she left. To get away from talk, dark, handsome Philippe and to put her failed marriage behind her.''

"Her feelings are more complicated than that. Have you noticed that human emotions tend to be far more complex than they seem on the surface? Michelle admitted to me yesterday that she's still in love with Philippe. Madly in love, in fact.''

"What? She certainly didn't sound as if she cared two cents for him when I interviewed her last week.''

"Maybe you didn't ask the right questions," Alec said quietly. "Remember, you were assessing her job qualifications, whereas I was trying to understand her as a person. Besides, I've been in a similar situation myself, and so it was easy for me to recognize the signs of a woman still deeply involved with her former husband. I suspected something of how Michelle felt on Friday night, and by the time we'd spent a couple of hours together on Sunday, I was sure of it.''

Good heavens, what a mess, Caitlin thought. Why

in the world hadn't Michelle discovered she was still in love with her ex-husband before she started to date Alec? And yet, even as she posed the question in her mind, Caitlin realized she wasn't entirely surprised by the news. Past experience with friends and acquaintances suggested that this was precisely the sort of weird behavior typical of people in the throes of love and passion. Never having been in love herself, Caitlin was constantly amazed by the emotional tangles lovesick people got themselves into.

In the meantime, while Michelle winged off to Paris, Caitlin was left behind to sort out the mess. She hoped Alec wasn't seriously disappointed by his failure to make a match with Michelle, although she suspected this must be why she'd seen his expression darken into that earlier look of fleeting disappointment. He must be suffering the pain of dashed hopes and wounded feelings. Thank goodness the relationship between the pair of them hadn't really had time to develop into anything truly serious.

"Oh, Lord, I'm sorry," she murmured, returning to her desk. "What a horrible letdown for you, Alec. If I'd suspected any of this, I'd never have arranged your initial meeting. The last thing I intended was to reopen painful memories of your experience with that woman you loved."

"I don't have painful memories, Caity, so don't blame yourself for something that didn't happen. I fell in love with a woman who didn't return my feelings, but I don't regret the experience one bit. Loving someone is always worthwhile.''

His words carried the ring of truth, and Caitlin, with relief, set aside her guilt. Then the full impact of his news burst over her, and she realized with a little shock of delight that Alec wasn't going to get married, after all. A heavy burden lifted from her shoulders, a burden she hadn't been aware of carrying until it disappeared. The stiff smile she'd kept pasted to her lips changed into one of genuine warmth, and she leaned back in her chair, ready to relax.

"I'll be honest with you, Alec. I'm really happy that your relationship with Michelle didn't develop into anything more serious. I'm pleased she's going to give her marriage to Philippe another try, and I'm even more pleased that you aren't going to marry her.''

He chuckled. ''Aha! Now we get to the real truth. Come on, confess, Caity. You were jealous of Michelle because you always planned to marry me yourself. Not right now, of course, but in ten years or so, when your biological clock ticked right down to the last possible moment.''

Caitlin stared at him blankly, then saw his eyes sparkle with laughter. Surely that meant they were back on their old footing. He was teasing her, just the way he always did.

''Hey, you found me out. Now, shall we get serious for a few minutes? After your experience with Michelle, I'm sure you want to call off this crazy deal with our company to find you a wife. Since Services Unlimited never completed our part of the contract, I'm more than willing to return your fees. I suggest we bill you strictly for office overhead and expenses incurred so far. Does that sound fair?''

''More than fair. Except what makes you think I'm ready to call it quits? I want to get married, and your company promised to introduce me to at least four prospective brides. So far I've only met one.''

''You don't plan to continue with this ridiculous search? Alec, you *can't* mean to continue.''

''Why not? My needs remain the same as they were when we first talked about this. I want to marry as soon as possible, and I need help in finding a suitable partner. Just because Michelle and I aren't rushing to take out a marrige license doesn't mean I've given up on the idea of finding a wife with your professional help.''

Caitlin discovered that, for some obscure reason, she was starting to feel angry. ''Fine,'' she snapped. ''When I come across a suitable candidate, I'll let you know. However, custom-designed brides are in scarce supply, and I should warn you that the average age of job applicants interviewed by this company is forty-three. So don't expect a stream of luscious young nubiles to be wafting your way any time soon.''

Alec stood up, appearing totally unruffled by her peevish tone. ''I'm not looking for a luscious young nubile. I want a mature woman, willing to take the risk of committing herself to a serious relationship.''

"I'll keep your requirements in mind."

"Thanks." He smiled blandly. "Remember, I'm paying your company a hefty fee for this service, and finding me a wife is your best bet for promotion if you want to be a vice president by Christmas."

"Prospective wives don't grow under cabbages," she muttered.

He grinned and began moving toward the door. "No, that's babies. Didn't your mother teach you anything?" He gave her a friendly wave, then stopped abruptly in the doorway. "I almost forgot. I need a favor, Caity. I have to take the president of Ergon Industries out to dinner tonight, and he's bringing his wife. Would you be an angel and come with us? I need a warm female body to even up the numbers."

"Hey, what a flattering invitation."

"Okay, I need a warm, beautiful and intelligent female body to even up the numbers. How's that?"

"Too little too late. Anyway, I have a lot of work to catch up on—"

"We're not meeting till eight, and you could come straight to the restaurant if you like. The Pear Tree— it's one of your favorites—and since you have to eat dinner, you may as well eat somewhere nice. Besides, I need your company tonight. I'm feeling depressed and rejected now that Michelle has left me—"

"All right, quit with the sob story—you've talked me into it." Caitlin pulled a bulging file toward her.

"Now go away, Alec, or I'm going to be fired by Christmas, not promoted to VP."

He gave a mock salute. "Yes, ma'am. See you at eight."

Caitlin refused to think about Michelle's defection to Paris or Alec's absurd insistence on interviewing more candidates for the role of wife. She couldn't afford to waste the time. For a solid hour she worked with robotlike efficiency, setting up interviews, checking references and drafting letters. At five-thirty, Dot stuck her head into the office to say goodbye. The building grew quiet and Caitlin's pace of work picked up. This part of the day was often her most productive time, and she had no intention of blowing it by allowing her mind to wander.

She was concentrating so hard she literally jumped in her chair when Dot suddenly burst back into the office, eyes gleaming with the light of battle. "Sam's on his way," she announced. "No time to explain, but I'm warning you, Caitlin, whatever he says, just keep answering no. I'm going to bring that man to his senses if it's the last thing I do."

"I thought you'd left."

"I would have if I'd been smart. Sam asked me to help him with a special project, and one thing led to another. Psst, here he comes."

Sam strolled into the office. Dark suit immaculate, silver hair neatly brushed, he bore little resemblance to the frazzled father who had begged a ride to the airport the previous Friday.

"Caitlin, how's it going?" His smile was so wide she knew Dot was right. Sam was up to something. He favored the no-nonsense approach unless he was planning something outrageous.

"Busy. But I guess that's good."

"Business is brisk at the moment, that's for sure, but you've had too many projects pushed onto your desk recently. I feel guilty about the amount of overtime you're putting in."

"I don't mind."

"I know you don't, but I've no interest in turning my employees into slave laborers, so you'll be pleased to hear that I've hired some extra help. Remember that candidate I asked you to chat with a couple of weeks ago? José Menendez?"

"I liked him a lot, as I told you. He seemed well qualified, and a nice, coolheaded guy to boot. That's always a definite plus when things heat up around here."

"I agree, and his final reference came in today. Everything checked out fine, so I've offered him a job as a recruiter."

"Great! I'm sure his special expertise in hiring Hispanic workers will be very valuable for us."

"Yes, and apparently he's a real whiz at unsnarling visa problems."

Caitlin eyed her boss. "We went over all this after the initial interviews, Sam. You may as well tell me what's really on your mind. This facade of sweet reason isn't getting you anywhere, because Dot's already blown the whistle on you. You didn't come in here to tell me about José Menendez.''

"Hah!" Sam swung around to glare at Dot, who was standing in the doorway, arms crossed. She glared right back. "I might have known you couldn't be trusted to keep a secret," he spluttered.

"How can your crazy plan be a secret from Caitlin?" Dot demanded. "You're expecting her to put it into action.''

"It's not a crazy plan. It's brilliant strategic thinking!" Sam's cheeks puffed out in annoyance, but since it was the start of the week, a safe four days from the loneliness of Friday night, he quickly regained control of his temper.

"I have a new client for your matrimonial-services division," he said to Caitlin, with another wide smile that didn't quite cover his nervousness.

"A man?" Caitlin asked, wondering if Sam planned to suggest himself as a client. He struck her as the sort of man who needed a wife, not to mend his socks or cook his dinner, but to fill the emptiness of his evenings and add color to the drabness of his weekends. "Is this new client a friend of yours?" she prompted tactfully.

"It's not a man," Sam said. "It's a girl—"

"Woman," Dot interrupted. "Jodie is a *woman*, Sam, not a girl, and that's what you keep forgetting.''

"Girl, woman, what's the difference? Anyway, I want Caitlin to fix her up with that lawyer fellow. Send them out on a date and see what comes of it.''

"Jodie has agreed to be taken on as a matrimonial client?" Caitlin asked, stunned. "When did she decide she wanted to get married? I thought she was planning to go to Africa for a year of postgraduate work in environmental biology."

"That's exactly what she's planning," Dot said.

"She's planning nothing of the kind!" Sam roared. He swallowed hard and his expression became pleading. "She doesn't know what she wants," he assured Caitlin. "If she could just find the right man, I know she'd settle down and get married in a shot."

Caitlin didn't even bother to dispute this dubious premise. "Well, Sam, I'm sorry, but I don't see how I can help you. As you know, Alec Woodward is the only client on our books at the moment—"

"And he would be perfect for my little girl!" Sam declared triumphantly.

Caitlin wondered if she had heard right. "Sam, Alec's almost thirty-five years old, a sophisticated man about town. Jodie's barely twenty-two, and still trying to grasp the alien concept that there's a whole world outside the confines of the lab and her test tubes."

"A dozen years' age difference, that's nothing, and Alec would soon teach her what's what. Besides, I read his file over the weekend, and he sounds like just the sort of man I want for a son-in-law. Hardworking, successful, healthy, well-rounded..." He trailed off. "You've known him for years—there's nothing wrong with his health or his background, is there, Caitlin?''

''No, but—''

''It's settled, then. I'll bring Jodie into the office tomorrow and you can fix her up with this fellow.''

''Fine,'' Caitlin said. ''I'll do that. As soon as Jodie comes into my office and gives me all the pertinent details, I'll arrange a date with Alec.''

Sam beamed in satisfaction. ''Tomorrow,'' he said. ''She'll be here first thing.'' He cast Dot a look of unconcealed triumph. ''I'm glad some people in this office have functioning brain cells,'' he declared.

''Right,'' Dot agreed. ''It's a pity you're not one of them.''

Sam bristled, but he didn't deign to reply. As soon as he left the office, Dot walked over to Caitlin's desk. ''You aren't really planning to set Jodie up with Alec Woodward, are you, Caitlin? My Lord, the poor kid doesn't need you hounding her, as well as her father.''

''Of course I'm not planning to set her up with Alec, but there was no point in upsetting Sam.''

''Why not? That's his problem. Since his wife died, everyone humors him, instead of telling him point-blank when he's making a total ass of himself.''

''Maybe you're right. But what are the chances of Jodie's agreeing to come into the office and get her name entered into our books? One in a million?''

Dot didn't look reassured. ''You don't understand. Sam will keep nagging at her until she says yes.''

Caitlin didn't know Sam's daughter well, but she'd met her often enough to suspect that she would beat out any mule in a competition for stubbornness. The more Sam nagged, the more likely Jodie would be to dig in her heels and refuse to budge. But since Dot looked really worried, Caitlin tried to reassure her.

"In my opinion, Jodie and Alec wouldn't enjoy each other's company, so even if Jodie comes to see me, I can simply recommend against a meeting. That would be a professional judgment on my part, and Sam wouldn't question it. Give him his due—once he trusts an employee's professional skills, he never second-guesses business decisions. Jodie isn't going to get pushed into a relationship with Alec Woodward, even if Sam *does* own this company."

"You make it sound so simple."

"That's because it is simple. Trust me on this one, Dot. Jodie will be on her way to Africa right after the holidays, just like she planned."

"And where will Alec Woodward be?"

"Living the bachelor life here in Washington, I guess."

"With those looks and that personality?" Dot picked up her coat. "Sometimes I wonder where supersmart women like you park their brains after office hours."

Caitlin laughed. "What does that cryptic comment mean?"

"Stick around, honey, and maybe you'll find out."

CHAPTER SIX

CHARLIE KERRICK and his wife, Brenda, turned out to be fascinating people, and Caitlin was glad she'd accepted Alec's invitation to join them for dinner. Charlie had inherited a small engineering company from his uncle when he was barely out of college. Now, some thirty years later, he'd successfully turned Ergon Industries into a major manufacturer of tool-and-die equipment, headquartered in Pittsburgh, but with interests and subsidiaries all over the world.

The Pear Tree was a restaurant conducive to relaxed conversation, and over a meal of shrimp Creole followed by lemon soufflé, Charlie explained to Caitlin that he was in Washington to discuss the opening of Ergon offices in several former Communist countries.

"I want to help rebuild the economies of Eastern Europe," he said. "My mother's family immigrated to the States from Poland right before the Second World War, so I feel a real attachment to the place. I even understand a few words of Polish, which helps a bit when I'm over there, talking to the people who might like to work for me one day. But I'm dealing with stockholders' money, so I have to think like a businessman, not like a philanthropist, and the harsh economic reality is that conditions in much of Eastern Europe are still too unsettled for capitalist enterprises to be commercially successful.''

''Somehow, I don't think that's going to stop you from rolling up your sleeves and pounding the pavement until you find a way to make the investment profitable,'' Alec said. ''You get a gleam in your eye every time you say the word 'Poland.'''

His wife laughed. ''So you've noticed that, too? I think we'll be living in Krakow or Warsaw some time within the next six months. Fortunately our youngest child started college last year, so I'm already packing my bags and figuring out how many pieces of paper I'll need from various government departments before I can get myself licensed to practice medicine over there.''

''Alec never mentioned you're a doctor,'' Caitlin said, a little surprised by the news, partly because Brenda looked so much like the typical suburban homebody.

''I'm a dermatologist, with a subspeciality in childhood skin diseases. I met Charlie while I was in medical school and decided he was too good a catch to let go.''

Her husband bowed. ''Thank you, dear.''

''Don't get swollen-headed. I might change my mind any day now.'' She flashed him a smile that showed he had absolutely no need to worry. ''When Charlie persuaded me to get married, I had to change my career plans just a little," she continued. "I'd intended to become an obstetrician, but that's a very demanding speciality, since babies have a perverse habit of deciding to be born at three in the morning, or in the middle of Thanksgiving dinner, or some other totally inconvenient time."

"Our son was born on my brother's wedding day," Charlie remarked. "Four weeks early."

"At least he started the way he planned to go on!" Brenda said. "He's never had a lick of patience from that day to this." They both smiled fondly, exchanging a look Caitlin had seen many times on her sister's face when her sons, Zach and Matt, did something outrageous, such as planting their toy trucks in a flower bed to see if they would grow. Parents, she decided not for the first time, loved their children for the oddest of reasons.

"How did you manage to cope with raising a family and being a full-time doctor?" she asked, genuinely curious.

"I didn't always work full-time," Brenda explained. "I couldn't see much point in producing babies who would be raised by nannies, which is what would have happened if I'd specialized in obstetrics. On the other hand, I'd sweated blood getting through medical school, and it seemed criminal to throw away so much training and education. So I decided to forget about being an obstetrician and became a dermatologist, instead."

"I can see that dermatologists aren't likely to have many emergencies," Caitlin said.

"Almost none, thank heaven. Once I got through my residency, I was able to find a practice willing to hire me part-time, and I didn't begin working forty-hour weeks until the kids were in junior high. Now Charlie is burned out and getting ready to retire, and I tell him I'm just getting into my stride. For the next twenty years, when we come back from Poland, he can stay home and cook supper while I climb the professional ladder."

Caitlin didn't need to ask if Brenda was satisfied with the choices she'd made; both she and Charlie radiated contentment with their lives and with each other. Some women might not approve of the compromise the Kerricks had worked out, but Caitlin thought they'd achieved a fair balance. True, Charlie had forged ahead building his industrial empire while Brenda made all the career changes and sacrificed her personal goals to keep the home front afloat. But would Brenda have been happier if she'd rejected Charlie and stuck to her original dream of becoming an obstetrician? Caitlin was sure of the answer to that question. Brenda's face glowed with affectionate pride when she mentioned her three children, and her eyes softened every time she glanced at her husband. Brenda was obviously a woman who felt truly fulfilled.

Caitlin said as much to Alec as he drove her home. "Brenda and Charlie have been lucky," he agreed.

"But I think most couples are likely to have a harder time juggling their careers and their personal lives than those two did."

"I expected you to hold Brenda over my head as an example of how easy it is nowadays for a woman to combine a career with marriage and motherhood."

He smiled. "Then I'm glad I'm not a hundred percent predictable."

She could have told him that for the past two weeks she'd found him about as predictable as a tiger deciding whether to target a deer or an antelope for his supper, but she decided not to say anything that might spoil the rapport they'd finally managed to reestablish. "Want to come in for a cup of coffee?" she asked. "It's only ten-thirty."

Alec looked wary, and she laughed. "Don't be afraid—it's safe to say yes. Richard, the guy who took me out to brunch yesterday, gave me a present of real coffee beans from a fancy boutique in Georgetown. He brought a tiny bottle of whiskey and some whipping cream, too. We could make Irish coffee."

"Clearly a smart man if he's already discovered that he needs to bring his own coffee supplies when he visits you."

Caitlin grinned, not in the least offended. "Smart, kind and a total bore. Believe me, I envied you and Michelle yesterday, watching baby chimps at the zoo."

He shot her a peculiar sideways glance as he parked the car. "Want to come to the zoo with me next weekend? There's another chimp expected to give birth any hour now. We might get to see a newborn.''

''I'd love that.'' She was surprised at how pleased she felt at the prospect of spending an entire afternoon in Alec's company. Surprised, because there had been so much tension between them ever since he'd announced his plans to marry. But it was getting late, and she felt agreeably sleepy, so she smiled at him, not wanting to destroy her good mood with too much analysis. ''Are you coming in now that you know the coffee's safe to drink?''

''Sure.'' He held the door open so that they could walk into the lobby of her building. ''Although it's depressing to think my chief role in your life is as a human coffee percolator.''

She shook her head with mock severity. ''Not the *chief* role, Alec. There are other things you do that I value more.''

''Name one.''

''There must be something, although making great coffee is a major talent of yours.'' She yawned and pressed the button to summon the elevator. ''It's too late at night for serious conversation. Trust me, Alec, you're the most important man in my life.''

The words slipped out, and she would have called them back if she could. Fortunately Alec chose not to make any comment. Perhaps he didn't realize how revealing her bantering remark was, but Caitlin knew she'd inadvertently spoken the truth. Alec *was* the most important man in her life, and she was going to feel devastated when he married. She felt like a complete dog in the manger where he was concerned. She didn't want another woman to become the focus of his attention and she couldn't bear to contemplate a wife usurping her position as Alec's best friend.

But his marriage still lay in the future, maybe even far in the future. Tonight it seemed that Alec was willing to return to his familiar friendly role, and Caitlin felt her happiness blossom. They joked around with easy camaraderie while he brewed coffee in her tiny neat kitchen. Then she poured generous servings of Irish whiskey into the bottom of two cups and topped the steaming coffee with scoops of sweetened whipped cream. Alec carried the mugs into the living room, searching for coasters while she rummaged around for the package of family photos that had arrived in yesterday's mail from her mother.

Finding the photos, she kicked off her shoes and curled up against the soft, plum-colored cushions of her sofa. Alec tossed his jacket onto a chair and sprawled at the opposite end of the same sofa, chuckling as he admired shots of Zach and Matt creating toddler mayhem in their backyard sandbox.

"I saved the best till last," Caitlin said, holding up a grainy black-and-white snapshot. "Take a look at this."

Alec stared in silence at the blur of gray shadows. "What's it supposed to be?" he asked, twisting the photo to various angles. "It looks like a close-up of static electricity on your parents' TV set."

She laughed. "You thought that, too? Which just shows how ignorant we both are. That, my dear Alec, is a picture of my new niece- or nephew-to-be. Mom insists it's a wonderfully clear ultrasound picture of Merry's new baby."

Alec gave the snapshot another concentrated examination, then grinned. "Yeah, I can see it's a really cute baby. One problem. Is it a boy or a girl?"

"Even Mom and the doctor can't tell that detail yet, but everyone agrees the baby is perfect in every way—right size, perfectly formed spinal cord, arms and legs in place, fingers and toes all present and correct."

"Why did Merry have the ultrasound, or is it routine nowadays?"

"Pretty much routine, I guess. But in her case there were some questions about precisely how pregnant she actually is. And it turns out she's further along than they'd first calculated. The doctor estimates the baby will arrive right at the end of March, not mid-May."

"Are Jeff and Merry pleased about that?"

"Over the moon. They only have to wait five more months to see their baby, instead of nearly seven. As far as I can tell, they're both counting the hours, not just the days."

"I have good news from home, too," Alec said. "My father's found a buyer for his hardware store, so he and my mother are having a marvelous time planning a retirement vacation. They're thinking of taking a cruise to the Bahamas.''

''Alec, that's fantastic!''

''Yes, the deal looks solid, and they got a decent price.''

''I'm so happy for them. I know how worried they've been, what with the economy in the doldrums and small businesses having a hard time getting bank loans.'' Caitlin was so pleased for her old neighbors she acted without thinking. She leaned across the sofa and flung her arms around Alec's neck, hugging him exuberantly.

Too late, she realized she'd made a serious mistake. Because of the way they'd both been sitting, she ended up crowded breast to hip against Alec's side, her thigh thrust intimately against his. Through the thin silk of her blouse she could feel the hard muscle of his chest pressing against her body, and her heart leapt—with anticipation?—as he slowly closed his arms around her waist. He didn't speak, just held her, looking at her searchingly.

For a moment frozen in time, neither of them moved. Then Alec pulled away, jumping up from the sofa and striding toward the kitchen. He paused in the doorway, turning around to give her a cheerful smile. ''I'll make a fresh pot of coffee,'' he said. ''We don't want to find ourselves exchanging any more of those hazardous, nonfriendly kisses, do we?''

"What? Oh, no, of course not. I don't know what's come over us recently."

"It's called sex," he said dryly. "It can happen to anyone, even to friends."

Fortunately he started running water into the coffeepot before Caitlin needed to come up with a reply. She collapsed against the sofa cushions, her body shaking. *This is ridiculous,* she thought. *What's happening to me? He didn't even kiss me, so why am I getting all hot and bothered?*

Because she *wanted* him to kiss her. The unwelcome answer slipped into her mind too quickly to be pushed aside. With some reluctance, Caitlin acknowledged the appalling truth. Irrational it might be, but she did want Alec to kiss her. She wanted to recapture the magic she'd found in his arms. She wanted him to fold her into his embarace and hold her tight against his body. She wanted him to twist his fingers into her hair and hold her head captive while he teased her lips into a heated response. She wanted to lie next to him, clinging to him, skin to skin, body to body. Most of all, she wanted to feel the throb of her own desire reflected in the hot, passionate demand of his touch.

She knew exactly what she wanted, what she needed—and the knowledge sent the fear surging back.

Alec threatened everything she had carefully mapped out for her future, everything that would make her life different from that of her sisters. Her career, her independence, her freedom, would all vanish if she let herself fall in love. And Alec was especially dangerous to her plans because she found him so attractive and liked him so much. If she once allowed herself to make love to him, the experience would be so intense she suspected she would never willingly let him go. She must take care and watch her feelings, or they would race out of control. Then her happiness would be in Alec's hands, her destiny in his keeping.

The prospect of such deep and overwhelming love would be scary enough even if she was sure that Alec returned her feelings. But in fact, she had no reason to suppose he did love her. She'd just turned eight when he moved into the house next door, and he had already been fourteen, a freshman in high school. He was naturally kindhearted and he'd tolerated her tagging along on fishing trips and family vacations, but for years she'd been nothing more to him than the bratty little kid who was best friends with his sister.

Their relationship had changed when she started college. She'd come to Georgetown University, where Alec was just finishing his law degree, and somehow the age difference hadn't seemed nearly so important when she was eighteen and he was almost twenty-five. They'd gradually become friends, and that friendship had deepened over the years, becoming more important to both of them, until they'd ended up as each other's best friend.

And that's what they still were. Just friends. Even

now, when he'd decided to search for a wife, Alec hadn't considered asking Caitlin if she was interested in taking on the job. Of course, she would have rejected him outright, but it would have been nice to be *asked*.... In fact, now that she thought about it, Alec's attitude toward her was positively insulting. How could he choose to date perfect strangers in preference to Caitlin, a woman he'd known and liked for practically a lifetime?

True, his thoughts and feelings recently had been less than totally clear to her. And they had shared those utterly amazing kisses. But Alec probably hadn't found those kisses as earth-shattering as she had. On the contrary, tonight when they'd hovered on the brink of another passionate embrace, he'd simply walked away and announced he'd like more coffee!

"That's a ferocious frown," Alec said, strolling back into the living room, a coffee cup in each hand. "I'll drink fast and get out of here before you throw me out on my ear."

"If you want to leave, just say so," Caitlin snapped. "There's no need to use my frowns as an excuse."

He set the cups on the table and looked at her without a trace of his usual teasing humor. "Caitlin, if you're angry with me, will you tell me why?"

She shook her head. "I'm not angry at you, Alec."

"Then what's the problem? You sure look angry."

"Not angry. I think...I'm confused."

"What about?"

She looked up at him, at the man who was exerting this uncomfortable, sexual tug on her senses, at the man who was also her closest friend. "I don't know," she admitted wryly. "I'm so confused, I don't even know what I'm confused about."

"Maybe things will seem easier to understand in the morning."

"I sure hope so."

He touched her lightly on the arm, and her muscles tensed in immediate, frustrating reaction. He didn't say anything, just moved a little farther away. "I'll give you a call sometime next week," he said. "Thanks for helping me entertain the Kerricks."

"Thank you for inviting me. They're a delightful couple." She flushed. "I'm sorry, Alec. I sound so stilted. I don't know why."

"Forget it. Neither of us seems to be at our best tonight." He ran his hand through his hair in a gesture that spoke of sudden, intense weariness. "Good night, Caity. I'll see myself out. Don't forget to lock the door after me."

The silence after he left was appalling. Caitlin carried their empty coffee cups out to the kitchen and tried to wash them. She broke both saucers before she decided it would be smart to leave the tidying up until later, when her fingers might prove a bit more cooperative. She was almost grateful when the ring of the telephone interrupted the chaotic whirligig of her thoughts.

She picked up the phone. "Hello."

"Caitlin, this is Jodie Bergen."

It took a second or two for the name to register, a split second more to register that this was a very late hour for Sam's youngest daughter to be calling. "Jodie, how are you? Nothing's wrong, I hope?"

"I'm at the hospital." Jodie was normally a vivacious young woman, with a bubbly, breathless way of speaking. Tonight her voice sounded dull and heavy, drained of energy and life.

"Has there been an accident? Are you hurt? Injured?"

"Not me. Daddy. He got sick right after dinner. The doctors think he's had a mild heart attack. They're checking him out now."

"Jodie, I'm so sorry. I'll come right over. Which hospital are you at?"

"Georgetown University, but you don't have to come, Caitlin. That isn't why I called."

"No, I'll come. I want to see Sam. Besides, you shouldn't have to wait alone—"

"Thanks, I appreciate the offer, but my brother-in-law is on the staff here, and my sister and brother are both here with me. Dad's going to be fine, but he's not allowed visitors right now. We're trying to keep his anxiety level down so that he can get some rest, but the doctors say he's worrying about his schedule tomorrow at the office and he won't relax. Apparently he has the entire day filled with interviews and appointments. To be honest, I called chiefly so I can tell my father you've taken charge at work and everything is under control.''

"Everything will be under control," Caitlin promised. "I'll call his secretary—"

"That's just it. Sylvia left town on Friday to go to her twenty-fifth high-school reunion. Remember? She's out of the office for the next week."

"How could I have forgotten! She's spent six months tormenting us with her diet while she prepared for the occasion. But even with Sylvia gone, there's still nothing for Sam to worry about." Caitlin devoutly hoped she wasn't lying. "I'll call Dot, *my* secretary, and make sure she comes in early. Between the two of us, we'll soon have everything taken care of."

"Thank you. I appreciate your help."

"I wish there was something more I could do." Caitlin paused for a moment, wondering how she could find out the seriousness of Sam's condition without upsetting his daughter. She framed her question carefully. "How long is Sam likely to be in the hospital, do you know?"

"They won't say. It seems this is the second heart attack he's had. He didn't tell anyone in the family about the first one." Jodie's voice sounded even flatter than before, and Caitlin realized that the poor girl was struggling to avoid breaking down completely. The lack of color in her voice was caused by too much emotion, not an absence of it.

"Sam will be fine, Jodie," she said, wishing she

felt as confident as she sounded. "Gosh, your dad is as tough as army-boot leather, and it's going to take more than a little heart trouble to keep him down. He'll be yelling at the doctors and reorganizing the nurses' workstation before you can say Jack Robinson."

"His family's very important to him," Jodie said, not really responding to Caitlin's comments. "Since my mother died...I don't know..." Her voice trailed away into uncertainty. "Someone else is waiting to use the phone, so I should hang up, but I'm planning to come into the office tomorrow, if that's all right with you, Caitlin."

"Of course! I'll prepare a summary sheet for your father, Maybe that will reassure him we've taken care of all the urgent work waiting on his desk. Tell him tonight, and perhaps it will help to ease his mind."

"I'll tell him right away. Would three o'clock be a convenient time for us to meet?" Jodie asked. "I think I'll need about a half-hour, if you can spare it."

"Three o'clock will be fine." Caitlin mentally juggled her already hectic schedule. "And give Sam my love," she added. "Tell him I'll be in to see him as soon as they allow visitors."

"I'll do that. See you tomorrow afternoon." Jodie sounded marginally more cheerful, as if her load of worry had been lightened just by sharing it.

"Call anytime if you think of some way I can help," Caitlin said.

"Thanks, but I hope I won't have to. You've already helped a lot."

Caitlin wasn't sure *how* she'd helped, but she was glad Jodie seemed more upbeat. Hanging up the phone, she glanced at her watch and saw it was barely eleven-thirty. At ten-thirty, she'd been inviting Alec to come in for a cup of coffee. Good Lord, she felt as if she'd survived about a year's worth of emotional drama during the past hour.

Still, the extra pressure looming at work wasn't all bad. Worrying about Sam, calling Dot, getting ready for bed, setting her alarm for an extra-early start in the morning, she was almost able to put Alec out of her mind.

Almost.

CHAPTER SEVEN

THE NEXT DAY, Caitlin plumbed new depths in the meaning of the word "busy." She and Dot both arrived at the office promptly at seven, but by lunchtime, despite nonstop work and a lot of help from their colleagues, they were barely managing to stay afloat. Talking into the phone at the same time as she tried to read and sign a contract prepared by a relatively new employee, Caitlin began to feel overwhelmed by the sheer volume of work. Her heart sank when a short, swarthy, handsome man came into her office, smiling as if he expected to be welcomed.

She ended her phone conversation, trying not to sound too abrupt, and scrawled her signature on the contract, which she devoutly hoped was as standard as it looked. Then she walked around her desk to greet the newcomer.

"José," she said, extending her hand and managing a weak smile. "José Menendez. How, um, nice. Were we expecting you today?"

"Sam asked me to stop by and fill out a few routine papers—tax forms, health insurance, that kind of stuff. The receptionist told me Sam was in the hospital, so I decided to let you know I was available. I figured you might be able to use some help, even though I'm not officially slated to start until next week.''

"We sure do need help," Caitlin said. "But to be honest, I don't have time to show you where to get started.''

"No problem. I'll just pitch in where I'm needed— someplace where I can't make too many mistakes. At least I could answer the phone and take messages.''

Caitlin didn't see how José could screw up too much just answering phones, and he had seemed an extremely capable young man at their interview. She smiled at him in gratitude. "If you're willing to pick up the slack for a few hours, it would be terrific. I knew you were going to be a great colleague, José. I just didn't know how great.''

He smiled back. "Wait until I've been here a couple of weeks, then you'll be truly stunned.''

José proved a godsend. The number of phone calls switched through to her office tapered off almost at once, and Caitlin found she could make time to draw up a coherent roster, assigning Sam's commitments to other staff members, saving only the really complex meetings for herself. She worked solidly for a couple of hours, barely glancing up from her papers until José returned to her office carrying a plate of chocolate-chip cookies, together with a cup of lemon tea for her and a mug of aromatic black coffee for Dot.

"Wendy tells me this is what you both like to drink

at this hour of the afternoon," he said, carefully moving files and setting the tray on Caitlin's credenza.

Dot sipped her coffee and rolled her eyes in ecstasy. "Heavens, it's perfect! José, where have you been all my life? Until you brought this, I hadn't realized I was about to faint for lack of nourishment."

"José, this is wonderful," Caitlin agreed, sipping her tea and feeling the knot in the pit of her stomach start to dissolve. She'd been dangerously strung out and should have realized she needed a break. "Have you taken any phone calls I ought to know about?"

"Three inquiries from job applicants. I arranged to interview them next week when we're more caught up on things. Half a dozen inquiries about Sam's health, which I answered with the latest bulletin from the hospital and the assurance he'd be back in the office soon. A furious call from a chef we placed with a senator last month. He claims he's quitting because the senator only wants to eat hamburgers. Plus we had inquiries from a couple of potential new customers for our janitorial services. I've taken all the details and I'll give you the files tonight. As far as I can tell, I haven't seriously messed up so far."

"It sounds like you've done a fantastic job," Caitlin said, finishing her cookie. "What did you tell the furious chef?"

"That we'd try to find him another position where his creative genius would be appreciated. He's coming in tomorrow. Since he's been through our company's system before, I figured he would be a relatively easy client to take care of.''

Dot gave a bark of cynical laughter. ''Chefs are never easy,'' she said. ''Trust me, they make mad scientists and crazy artists look like normal people.''

José smiled, but didn't appear too worried. ''I'll give him my grandmother's secret recipe for quesadillas. That ought to get him onside. Which reminds me, speaking of chefs, there's a fax for you, Caitlin, from somebody called Michelle Morreau in Paris. She apologizes for not keeping her appointment in Chevy Chase with the member of cabinet, but she was busy getting married.''

''*What*?'' Dot shot out of her chair, cookie crumbs flying in all directions. ''Alec Woodward married Michelle Morreau? In Paris, France? I don't believe it!''

Caitlin wondered why Dot sounded so totally astonished. ''Calm down,'' she said. ''Michelle didn't marry Alec. She remarried Philippe, her ex-husband.''

Dot collapsed back into her chair. ''Remarried? Huh, what a fool! At least I never got that stupid. Poor Michelle. If Philippe didn't appreciate her the first time around, why would he get smart the second time?''

''Some of us do learn from our mistakes,'' José suggested.

''Not men,'' Dot said. ''They just get more stubborn. Look at Sam. He's known for six months—'' She stopped abruptly. Looking as close to flustered as

Caitlin had ever seen her, she returned her coffee mug to the tray. "Well, I guess it's back to the salt mines for all of us. I swear the pile on my in-tray gets higher the harder I work."

"And I'd better check the phone messages at the switchboard," José said. "I'll get rid of this," he added, picking up the tray and leaving the room.

"How did we ever survive without him?" Caitlin remarked, after he'd passed out of earshot. "Can you imagine? An executive who's willing to make tea and coffee—what a treasure!"

"Yeah, and his body ain't bad, either. Short, but plenty of muscle and no flab. In my book, that beats lean and lanky every time."

Caitlin laughed. "Dot, you're incorrigible. Good grief, he's twenty years younger than you!"

"So? Last I heard, window-shopping was still legal in this country." Dot went to her desk and returned with two folders. "This is the summary of today's activities you wanted typed up for Sam, and those are the letters you ought to read before you sign."

"Thanks. And I'll need the cabinet member's folder when you have a minute. With Michelle dropping out of the running, we need to find another good candidate for that position right away."

"I'll get on it now. Maybe José's disgruntled chef would be willing to do a bit of baby-sitting on the side. By the way, it's past three already. Didn't you tell me Jodie Bergen was planning to stop by about now?"

Caitlin glanced at her watch in sudden worry. "Yes, she did say that. I hope nothing unexpected happened to Sam."

"We called the hospital an hour ago. He was fine then."

As if on cue, Jodie appeared at the entrance to Caitlin's office. She looked tired, but extremely attractive, with her thick brown curls spilling out of their clip and onto her shoulders, and her slender, athletic figure shown off to advantage in a casual emerald green sweater and faded jeans.

"I met some new guy, José something. He said I should come through." She gestured to her outfit. "I'm sorry about the casual clothes. I was running late…came straight from the hospital…."

"You look fine," Caitlin said reassuringly. "We're glad you could make it."

"How's Sam?" Dot asked, sounding surprisingly curt, and Jodie seemed almost to flinch before she answered.

"He's very tired. He keeps dozing off, which isn't like him, as you know. But none of the tests so far have revealed anything really serious. The doctors say he just needs to rest and stop worrying so much about everything."

"May we visit him this evening?" Caitlin asked.

"Yes, anytime before nine, two visitors at a time."

"That's good news," Dot said gruffly. "Okay, I'm out of here while you two talk. I'll look up that cabinet member's file you wanted, boss."

"Why don't you sit down and relax for a moment?" Caitlin suggested to Jodie as soon as Dot left the office. "I recommend the blue chair—it's more comfortable than it looks."

Jodie obediently sat, although she perched on the edge of the chair, the picture of tension, her hands clasping and unclasping in her lap. Caitlin tried to put the young woman at ease by chatting about Sam's good test results and his uneventful recovery, but the mere mention of her father's health seemed to make Jodie even more nervous. If it hadn't been for the fact that Caitlin had conferred at length with Bruce, Sam's son-in-law and himself a surgeon, she would have begun to worry that Jodie knew something about her father's health she wasn't revealing. Having spoken to Bruce, however, Caitlin knew her boss's prognosis was about as good as it gets for a man who has suffered two minor heart attacks and still scowls at the mention of the word "exercise."

In the end, she gave up her attempts at reassurance and switched to business. Perhaps Jodie, as the only child still living at home, felt a special burden of responsibility for the handling of Sam's business affairs.

"We've already prepared a summary sheet of today's transactions for your father if he wants to review it," she said. "Basically we've tried to reassure him that everything here at the office is under control, and that none of his clients has been neglected. He doesn't need to read any of this material if he feels tired, but maybe he'll rest easier if he can keep his finger on the pulse of things.'' She handed over the file. ''I've kept copies, so don't worry about losing papers. I'll bring my file when I visit Sam this evening. Please take your time reading through the material, and if you have any questions, I'll do my best to answer them.''

Jodie took the folder but didn't look at it. ''Actually, Caitlin, to tell you the truth, I didn't come here to talk about business. I'm not qualified to make any useful contribution, so I wouldn't dream of second-guessing your decisions. Dad trusts you completely.''

''Then why did you come?''

Jodie pushed nervously at a cluster of curls tumbling across her cheek. She looked young, vulnerable and extraordinarily pretty as she plucked up the courage to speak. For a moment, seeing the lingering traces of childhood in Jodie's troubled gaze, Caitlin could almost sympathize with Sam's desire to keep this daughter, the baby of his family, home in Washington, DC, where he could protect her.

''Take all the time you need,'' Caitlin said. ''And remember I've had a lot of experience in listening to people discuss their personal situations. That's one of the requirements of my job. So if you have a problem you think I could help solve, all you need to do is ask.''

''You can help me for sure,'' Jodie said, then lapsed again into strained silence. With a final, impatient flick of her curls, she straightened in the chair, shoulders squaring with grim determination. She drew a deep breath. "Here goes. I would like you to arrange a date for me with Alec Woodward. I understand he's using Services Unlimited to find him a wife, and I'd like to be considered for the position."

Caitlin felt an instant of stunned disbelief, followed almost at once by understanding—and sympathy. "Jodie," she said gently. "You don't have to do this."

"I know I don't have to do it. I *want* to meet Alec Woodward. It's the least I can do for Dad...."

"Because your father has been so worried about you recently? Because he wants you to get married and stay here in Washimgton?"

Jodie kept her gaze fixed on her hands. "Yes."

"Guilt is a lousy reason for deciding to do almost anything, especially something as important as getting married."

"My dad is a generous, wonderful man. I owe him."

"Yes, you do. You owe him love and affection and respect, but not control over how you live your life."

"I've got to do *something* to make up for all the arguments we've had recently."

Caitlin leaned forward. "Listen, Jodie, your father didn't have a heart attack because you want to go off to Africa next January. He got sick because his cardiovascular system wasn't functioning properly, and maybe because he didn't take proper care of his body. You're a biologist, so you should know I'm telling you the plain and simple truth.'' She smiled slightly. ''Men don't have heart attacks because their daughters argue with them, otherwise the world wouldn't be able to build enough hospitals to accommodate all the harrassed, middle-aged fathers.''

Jodie didn't crack even a tiny smile. ''Dad was showing me Alec's photo and I yelled at him, told him to stop behaving like a crazy old man. Then his face twisted into this horrible grimace of pain and he fainted.'' She looked up, cheeks paling at the memory. ''The ambulance took twelve minutes to get to our house and I was giving Dad CPR all that time. Those minutes while I waited for the paramedics to arrive were the worst twelve minutes of my whole life. I'd yelled at him—screamed at him, truthfully— and he fainted. It was cause and direct effect.''

Caitlin got up and walked across the room to put her arm around Jodie's rigid shoulders. ''Jodie, stop punishing yourself. Your father would probably have had his heart attack at the precise same instant even if you'd been discussing bridesmaids and flower arrangements for your wedding day.''

She shook her head. ''He wants me to get married. He's obsessed with the idea that I need to settle down.''

''Then your father must learn to cope with his own misguided obsession,'' Caitlin said briskly. ''You sure don't have to mess up your plans for your own life just to accommodate his harebrained vision of your future.''

"I'm twenty-two. My mother already had her first son when she was twenty-two."

"Times have changed," Caitlin said. "And even if they hadn't, there's only one valid reason to get married, and that's because you *want* to get married. Apart from anything else, have you considered this great scheme of Sam's from Alec Woodward's point of view? Can you imagine how Alec would feel, going out on a date with a woman who's offering herself up as some sort of sacrificial lamb? Come on, Jodie, get real. You're acting like the heroine in a bad Victorian melodrama, not like a sensible woman heading into the twenty-first century."

Jodie finally gave a tiny smile, her first one of the afternoon. "A bad Victorian melodrama?" she murmured.

Caitlin grinned. "Very bad. So bad, in fact, that if you like, I'll forget you ever mentioned this nonsense about marrying Alec, and we can get right back to boring stuff like reviewing the work file I gave you earlier."

"No, as I said before, there's no reason for me to review business information you want to pass on to Dad. My specialty is the life cycle of the tsetse fly, not opportunities for profit in the employment industry."

Jodie got up and paced nervously around the room. "Caitlin, I know everything you've said about my plan to date Alec Woodward is true. At least I know *logically* that you're right. But that doesn't seem to help the way I feel. Wait until you see Dad tonight before you lecture me any more. He looks so tired, so gray and weary, as if keeping up with daily life suddenly seems more bother than it's worth.'' Jodie scrubbed her knuckles at the corners of her eyes and sniffed. ''Damn, why don't I ever have a tissue when I need one?''

''Here.'' Caitlin handed her a box from the credenza. ''Jodie, you're a brilliant student, a beautiful woman and a loving daughter. You don't owe your father another darn thing.''

''I don't owe him, maybe, but I could choose to give him something, couldn't I?''

''Not something as crazy as a promise to marry Alec Woodward—or any other man you don't love.''

''No, not marriage, maybe. But how about a date? I could tell Dad I've arranged to go out on a date with Alec Woodward, and that might cheer him up enough to make him take an interest in getting healthy again. How about that, Caitlin?'' Jodie's cheeks grew pink with sudden enthusiasm. ''Heck, who am I kidding? It's no sacrifice to go out on a date with Alec Woodward. The guy's a total hunk.''

''You sound as if you've met him,'' Caitlin said.

''Oh, no, just saw him on TV. That's what started Dad off last night, you know. They did a segment on the local TV news about Leon Mancuso and his new lawyer. Alec Woodward not only looked good enough to eat, he came up with all these witty replies when the interviewer asked him the usual dumb questions. Dad saw I was impressed, so he pulled out this folder of information about Alec. Then, of course, he couldn't understand why I didn't leap at the chance of going out on a date with the guy. Dad belongs to the generation that believes if a woman admires or likes a man, she must want to marry him.''

From the point of view of Sam's health, the idea of his daughter dating Alec wasn't totally without merit, Caitlin realized. Her stomach gave a quick, uncomfortable lurch at the thought. All her advice to Jodie so far had been solid, sincere, reasoned and from the heart. Suddenly, at the prospect of arranging a date for Jodie and Alec, she found her basic instincts at war with each other. As a professional representative of Services Unlimited she could, of course, refuse point-blank to set up the meeting. However, Sam owned the company, and after several years of working closely with him, Caitlin understood him well, and she agreed with Jodie's basic premise. In family matters, Sam was a stubborn man, with his mind set on a certain life-style for his daughter. It was likely to speed his recovery, and certainly his will to get better, if he knew Jodie was dating a man as eligible and attractive as Alec Woodward. Which was all fine and dandy—except that Caitlin was extremely unwilling to set up a meeting for the two of them.

''Alec Woodward has come to this company with a request to utilize our professional services,'' she said at last. ''He wants to meet women who are potential marriage partners, and I don't think it would be fair or even ethical to send him out on a date with you, knowing that marriage is out of the question.''

Caitlin was voicing a valid objection, but she squirmed a little in her chair, knowing she wasn't being entirely honest. Buried somewhere inside her was the fear that Jodie and Alec might find each other so congenial they would forge ahead and actually get married. And the prospect of Jodie and Alec marrying sent shivers of anxiety rippling up and down Caitlin's spine. Only because they were so unsuited, she reassured herself, not for any other, more personal reasons.

Jodie leaned forward pleadingly. ''Caitlin, call him and arrange just one date for me. I promise to be honest with him as soon as we meet. I'll tell him I don't want to get married and that I agreed to the date because of Dad's state of health. We can take it from there.''

''I will call Alec, but I have to tell him the truth upfront,'' Caitlin said after a tiny pause. ''I'm not going to describe you as a serious candidate for wedding bells, because you're not.''

''What will you say, then? That I want a date with him, but I'm not sure about getting married?''

''I'm going to tell him about your father's heart attack and your belief that Sam will recover more quickly if he knows you're dating Alec. That's the best deal I can offer you, Jodie. Take it or leave it.''

Jodie stood up. ''I'll take it. And thanks, Caitlin, for being so understanding about all this. Dad always says you're one of the few people he knows who is both clear-sighted and kindhearted. I see now why he feels that way.''

The compliment was beautiful, and Caitlin wished she merited it. Right at this moment, she couldn't imagine anyone less deserving of either part of the compliment. The truth was that she didn't understand a single thing about her feelings toward Alec Woodward, and she knew for sure that her heart didn't feel nearly as much kindness toward Jodie as it should. Her cheeks grew hot, and she stood up, hoping she didn't look as embarrassed and guilty as she felt.

''Sam assumes other people share all his own good qualities,'' she said. ''Don't count on that date with Alec Woodward, Jodie.''

''I won't,'' Jodie said, but her sparkling eyes gave the lie to her words.

Caitlin sighed, feeling a hundred years old. ''I'll try to get back in touch with you sometime tomorrow and let you know one way or the other.''

''I really appreciate all your help.''

''It's nothing, don't mention it.'' Caitlin smiled, feeling totally hypocritical. Alec, thank heaven, rarely took personal phone calls during the day, which meant she had another hour before she needed to screw up her courage and face the prospect of speaking to him for the first time since their uncomfortable parting the night before. And when they did speak, she'd have to be brisk and businesslike, convincing him how sweet and intelligent and attractive Jodie was, and how it would really be worth his while to meet her. The prospect filled her with gloom.

Two weeks ago Caitlin had thought there wasn't a subject in the world she would find difficult discussing with Alec. Over the past few days, she'd begun to wonder if the exact opposite wasn't true. Was there a single subject she and Alec could discuss without her stomach going into a nosedive and her heart starting to gallop at twice its normal speed?

Life, she decided, smothering a sigh, was sometimes very confusing.

SHE PHONED ALEC'S OFFICE at six, just before leaving to visit Sam at the hospital. Betty achieved the impossible and sounded more unfriendly than usual. Her dour response reminded Caitlin that she'd never gotten around to asking Alec why his secretary disliked her so much.

"Alec is with a client, Ms. Howard, and he has meetings scheduled until seven this evening." After four years, she showed no sign of breaking down and calling Caitlin by her first name. "The Mancuso case is exceptionally demanding."

As always, Caitlin found herself stumbling over her apologies. As always, she wondered just how Betty managed to make her feel so guilty. "I'll try him at home this evening," she said. "It's rather important, so could you tell him to expect a call around nine-thirty or ten?"

"If I must," Betty said.

It was the first time the woman had ever been flat-out rude, and Caitlin decided there would never be a better occasion to ask for an explanation of her hostility. "You know, Betty, I don't believe you're an impolite person, or an incompetent secretary, which means that you do know how to answer the phone courteously if you want to. So would you please tell me what in the world I've done to make you dislike me so much?"

There was a moment of silence during which Caitlin was sure Betty hovered on the brink of answering the question honestly. Then the moment passed, and Caitlin knew, even before the secretary spoke, that she wasn't going to tell the truth.

"I'm very sorry, Ms. Howard, I didn't intend to sound so abrupt. It's been a long day, but that's no excuse for my lack of courtesy. I was rude, and I apologize again. Please be assured that I'll pass on your message to Alec as soon as he's available. I've no doubt he'll be waiting for your call at nine-thirty this evening."

"The perfect secretary recovers her poise," Caitlin murmured. "If you ever want to change jobs, Betty, come and see me. I'm sure I could find a great position for you. On the other hand, if you ever decide to answer my previous question truthfully, give me a call. I'd really like to know the answer." She hung up, hurt by the exchange even though she'd rarely met Betty and had no real reason to care if the woman had taken a dislike to her.

Her visit with Sam in the hospital did little to dispel her growing depression. Despite Jodie's warnings, she hadn't been prepared to see her feisty boss looking so ill.

"I'm not feeling as bad as I look," Sam told her with a hint of his old humor. "Here's some free advice, kiddo. Get smart and stay out of hospitals. The way they prod and poke you in this place is enough to make even a strong man feel ready to call the undertaker."

Caitlin laughed, but the trouble was, Sam didn't look strong. Surrounded by machines, his body invaded by tubes and an IV drip, he looked downright frail. No wonder Jodie had been willing to take drastic action like dating Alec Woodward in order to boost his spirits.

She tried to interest him in cheerful anecdotes of the day's progress at the office, but she knew he wasn't really listening. Only when Dot arrived, carrying a bottle of expensive single-malt Scotch, did he perk up a little.

"This'll be waiting for you when you get out of here," she said, waving the bottle enticingly under his nose. "Jodie can drive you over to my place and I'll cook you a low-fat dinner that'll taste so good you'll think cholesterol is the chief ingredient."

"I'll drive myself!" he spluttered.

"Not if you want to eat my good food, you won't," Dot said calmly. "And for sure not if you want to have a wee dram of this whiskey."

Sam fussed and protested slightly, but after that, Caitlin was relieved to see a little color return to his cheeks and his manner no longer quite so apathetic.

Still, it hadn't been pleasant to find her ebullient boss looking so under the weather, and she found herself thoroughly depressed by the time she left the hospital. Exhaustion didn't improve her mood, either, she decided, dragging into her apartment and wondering if she had the energy to fix a bowl of soup. She wasn't hungry, but she probably needed some sustenance. Now that she thought about it, apart from an orange when she got up, and the cookie José had brought her in the middle of the afternoon, she hadn't eaten all day.

In the end, she brewed a pot of tea and toasted a slice of whole-wheat bread because that was less trouble than opening a can of soup. She still had to call Alec, and her stomach jumped nervously at the prospect of speaking to him. In two short weeks, her relationship with Alec had changed from relaxed, easygoing friendship to the point where she needed to screw up courage to pick up the phone and dial his number. *How in the world did we come to this?* Caitlin thought in bewilderment.

Procrastination was getting her nowhere. Drawing a couple of deep breaths, she picked up the phone, and punched Alec's number with nervous fingers.

He answered after the first ring, but his voice sounded tired and distracted. "Hello."

"It's Caitlin."

The pause before he responded was infinitesimal, but she heard it. "Yes, Betty told me you might call."

His voice remained flat, hovering somewhere between bored and weary. She spoke quickly, fighting an absurd impulse to burst into tears. "Sam's in the hospital. He had a minor heart attack and they're keeping him in for tests."

"I'm sorry to hear that. Sam has always seemed like a really good guy. You must be pretty busy at work."

"Very busy."

"Please give Sam my best wishes when you next talk to him."

This was awful, Caitlin thought despairingly. They sounded like two acquaintances making polite conversation because neither one of them could think of an excuse to hang up. She cleared her throat. "Betty told me how busy *you* are, so I won't keep you, Alec. In fact, this is really a business call. About your search for a wife."

Another pause, this one much longer. "Yes?" he said at last.

"Sam's daughter would like to meet you, although she doesn't want to get married right away. Her name's Jodie, and she's very young, only twenty-two—"

"I'm up to my eyeballs in depositions and pretrial motions in the Mancuso case. I don't have time to—" He broke off abruptly, then started again. "If Jodie has no interest in getting married, why does she want to meet me, for heaven's sake?''

''Her father wants to see her married and settled down,'' Caitlin said bluntly. ''She's willing to humor him since he's in the hospital. Alec, I understand completely if you don't want to meet her.''

Caitlin assumed this would be the end of the conversation. To her astonishment, she sensed Alec's interest level suddenly perk up. ''You're sure she's not interested in getting married?'' he asked.

''As far as I know, she's bound and determined to take off for Africa right after the New Year. She's convinced no man on earth can compete with her interest in the life cycle of the tsetse fly. If you ask her about sleeping sickness, larval worms, or other similar fascinating topics, she can talk nonstop for hours.''

''We sound like ideal companions right now,'' Alec said, his voice containing a hint of its usual laughter. ''I can drone on about briefs and depositions, while Jodie jabbers on about insects. In the meantime, Sam will be happy to know his daughter's dating a solid citizen.''

''You mean you're willing to meet her?''

''Sure, why not? We can go to the movies together or something equally harmless. She needs a couple of hours away from the hospital, and I need a break from the Mancuso case.''

''Well, if you're sure, I'll give her a call tomorrow.''

''Why don't you give me her phone number and

I'll call her myself? Since this is kind of an informal arrangement, and I already know her father, we could relax the etiquette a little, don't you agree? This way, Jodie and I can arrange a convenient meeting spot without you having to act as go-between. Busy as you are, you could save yourself some time.''

Caitlin knew Jodie would have no objections to being called directly, and Sam would be delighted to hear that things were moving so swiftly. She gave Alec the Bergens' home number, wondering why her stomach had stopped swooping and diving, only to congeal into a cold, hard knot of anxiety. Alec's behavior seemed totally out of character. He wanted a wife, so why was he willing to invite determined-not-to-marry Jodie out to the movies?

She decided to make one more attempt to clarify the situation. ''You do understand that Jodie isn't willing to marry anyone right now? She wants this date with you strictly to please her father.''

''I understand completely. But we'll see how things work out. You never know, she may change her mind, and I'd certainly like to help Sam over the hump.''

''Well, if you're sure...''

''I'm sure,'' Alec said. ''Got to go, Caity. I have a pile of paper to wade through before bedtime.''

''I need an early night, too. Good night, Alec.''

''Talk to you soon.'' He disconnected with a brisk click.

Caitlin hung up the phone and paced angrily around her apartment, stripping off her neat business clothes and tossing them over whatever piece of furniture happened to be handy. "This is crazy," she informed her TV set. "This is totally crazy."

The TV set made no comment, and Caitlin marched purposefully into her bedroom. Rummaging around in the dresser drawer for a clean nightgown, she straightened and found herself staring at a photograph of herself and Alec, taken the previous year at the Ohio State Fair. They were eating neon-pink cotton candy and were posed in front of a ferocious-looking prize bull. Alec's sexy blue eyes twinkled with laughter, and his mouth—his infuriatingly kissable mouth—seemed to invite her to come closer. The same photo had stood in the same place every day for the past fifteen months. Tonight she could hardly bear to look at it.

With a groan of frustration, Caitlin turned the photo toward the wall. Then, to her everlasting astonishment, she burst into tears.

CHAPTER EIGHT

THE REMAINDER OF THE WEEK was so busy that Caitlin's life was reduced to a survival routine of work, eat, sleep, repeat. Miraculously, late on Friday afternoon the pace seemed to slacken. Staring at her in-tray with blurry eyes, she realized that the stack of pending files had shrunk to near-normal proportions, and that there wasn't a single folder on her desk bearing an orange sticker marked Urgent.

Dot came into the office with a collection of letters requiring Caitlin's signature. "If you don't have anything too important, boss, I'm planning to leave right now and go visit Sam."

"Sure." Caitlin scrawled her signature on successive pages. "It's great that he's finally back home and perking up a bit. You have the latest office update to take to him?"

"Yes, José prepared it and he's done a terrific job. I'll tell Sam you plan to stop by tomorrow morning and catch him up on the details, right?"

"Right." Caitlin leaned back in her chair, stretching muscles that ached from too many hours hunched over her desk. "Lord, I can't remember when I last looked forward like this to the weekend. I'll be glad when Sam is fighting fit again.''

''He's improving rapidly since he came home. And Jodie is certainly making him happy right now.''

Caitlin yawned. ''What's Jodie up to?''

Dot gave a wide smile. ''Dating Alec Woodward, of course. Surely you know all about it? You set up the initial contact and they've been together every night this week. Sam's thrilled to pieces.''

Caitlin realized her mouth was hanging open. She snapped it shut. ''Dating? Jodie and Alec Woodward?''

Dot's smile stretched even wider. ''I have to hand it to you, boss. You saw the matchmaking possibilities where those two were concerned, and the pair of them sure have hit it off.''

''Wait a minute.'' Caitlin clutched the edge of the desk, feeling a sudden spurt of dizziness. Work this week had been so hectic she'd never followed up on the tentative arrangements Alec had made for meeting Jodie. ''Dot, what are you talking about? Jodie isn't serious about Alec. She agreed to date him once, to please her father. She wanted to give Sam's recuperation a little boost, but she has no intention of getting involved in a real relationship with Alec Woodward.''

Dot laughed. ''Jodie may have told you she didn't intend anything serious, but that was before she met Alec in person. Honest to goodness, Caitlin, you should see the two of them together—the air positively sizzles when they hold hands! I've never seen such a couple of lovebirds in my life.''

''But Jodie isn't interested in falling in love!'' Caitlin protested. ''She's going back to Africa. She's a scientist, obsessed with creepy-crawlies! Besides, she's only twenty-two and Alec is almost thirty-five, a very sophisticated, cosmopolitan thirty-five....''

''I guess love doesn't pay much heed to the calendar,'' Dot said with a sentimental sigh.

Caitlin shook her head. ''Dot, listen to yourself! Since when did you get all sappy about love and romance? What's happened to the woman who three weeks ago warned me to stay smart and single.''

''This is different,'' Dot said vaguely. ''Some couples are just so right for each other even a cynic has to be touched.''

''Jodie and Alec aren't suited to each other!'' Caitlin said, wondering if overwork had affected her brain or everyone else's.

''Why do you sound so put out? You ought to be pleased that Alec's found a woman he likes. It's not as if you wanted to marry him yourself, is it? Anyway, I've gotta run, Caitlin. Sam isn't ready to be left alone just yet, and I know Jodie wants to go out tonight. Alec's taking her to the new play at the Lincoln Center.'' She waved cheerily. ''Bye! See you Monday. I'll mail these letters on the way to Sam's house.''

As soon as Dot left, Caitlin cleared her desk with feverish haste, stuffed a few leftover papers into her briefcase, thrust her arms into her jacket and ran for the elevator. She hailed a cab and arrived at Alec's downtown office building almost before she realized where she was heading.

The prospect of confronting the gorgon-like Betty before being admitted to Alec's office gave Caitlin no more than a few seconds' pause. Sweeping past the astonished receptionist, she stormed down the richly carpeted, oak-paneled corridor. Betty's desk sat in a screened nook directly outside Alec's office.

The secretary's pleasant smile faded to a frown as soon as she recognized Caitlin. Her greeting was chilly enough to freeze steam. "Good afternoon, Ms. Howard."

For once, Caitlin spared no time wondering why Betty looked and sounded so disapproving. "Is Alec in?" she demanded.

"He's in, but he's very busy—"

"With a client? With a partner?"

"No, not that, but he's on the ph—"

"I need to speak with him." Without waiting for permission, Caitlin knocked on Alec's door. "It's me," she said. "I have to talk to you." She pushed open the door.

Alec was on the phone. He looked up as Caitlin burst into the room, but he didn't offer his usual welcoming smile. Instead, he swiveled around on his chair, presenting her with a partial view of his profile and an excellent view of his hunched shoulders.

He laughed softly into the phone. "It's Caitlin,"

she heard him say. "No, I wasn't expecting her." He paused for a moment. "Right, I agree completely." His voice took on a husky tone. "Darling, this entire week has been incredible."

Darling? Caitlin's eyes were in danger of popping out of her head. She realized belatedly that this was a private phone call and that she shouldn't be listening. She walked over to the far corner of the office and tried to appear fascinated by the leather spines on a collection of law books.

Alec's conversation became more muffled, but she couldn't help hearing the throaty chuckle that marked its ending. "Bye, darling. I can hardly wait to see you." He made a kissing noise into the receiver.

Caitlin couldn't contain herself any longer. She swung around just as Alec faced forward again. He returned the phone to the cradle, giving her a smile that was cool and a touch impersonal.

"Hi, how are you? I wasn't expecting to see you today."

"Who were you talking to?" she blurted, then blushed scarlet. "I'm sorry, it's none of my business, of course. Forget I asked that."

"Don't be embarrassed." He sounded kind, almost paternal. "I was talking to Jodie. We were making the final arrangements for our date tonight. We're going to the Lincoln Center Playhouse."

"Yes, so Dot told me. It seems everyone knew how well you and Jodie hit it off except me."

"You were busy. I didn't like to bother you with

personal calls. Dot mentioned that you were up to your neck in paperwork.''

"You've been talking to Dot? She never mentioned it.''

"Dot and I have gotten to know each other quite well since Sam got sick. She and Betty seem to have become bosom buddies.''

"Dot and Betty?'' Caitlin exclaimed. ''They like each other?''

"Why do you sound so surprised? They have a lot in common. Same age. Same profession. Both super-efficient. I understand they met for cocktails one evening and had a great time complaining about their respective bosses.'' Alec smiled blandly. ''They seem to think we're doing a very bad job of managing our personal lives.''

"They disapprove of your dating Jodie,'' Caitlin said quickly.

Alec's smile deepened. ''On the contrary, they both think she's exactly the person I should be dating right now.''

Caitlin found herself clutching her briefcase so hard her knuckles had turned white. She set the briefcase down and tried to achieve a casual smile. ''I'm surprised you're having so much fun. I didn't expect you and Jodie to hit it off. There's, um…there's kind of a big age gap between the two of you.''

"Twelve, thirteen years is nothing these days. Jodie and I find we have the most amazing number of things in common. Attitudes to life, reactions to people, family values. All sorts of things.''

Caitlin smothered a disbelieving snort. ''Since when did you develop a fascination for the life cycle of the tsetse fly?''

''Gee, Jodie hasn't talked all that much about insects.'' Alec's mouth curved into a tender, reminiscent smile. ''I guess we found more interesting ways to spend our time.'' He reached for a legal brief, then stopped in mid-motion, as if he'd just remembered Caitlin was in his office and he needed to mind his manners. ''I'm sure you came here for a reason, Caity. A busy career person like you doesn't take time off in the middle of the afternoon just to shoot the breeze. Is there something I can help you with?''

So many things, she thought. *Dear God, so many things.*

Too late, she realized why Dot's news about Jodie had so upset her and why she had rushed to Alec's office: she had been fiercely, savagely jealous.

Things that had been opaque suddenly became crystal clear. Her flight across town had been the instinctive, reflexive action of a wild creature running from danger to the security of its lair.

Except that Alec was simultaneously both the safe lair, and the danger from which she was running.

How in the world had it taken her so long to recognize a truth so basic to her well-being, so fundamental to her life? For years now she had been fighting the knowledge that she loved Alec, that she desired him physically with a hunger that was fast becoming an incurable ache—and that she wanted to spend the rest of her days as his wife.

Putting the truth into words, even though she didn't speak them out loud, made her dizzy. Disoriented, she glanced vaguely around the office, wondering what she should do next in a world that had lost all its familiar bearings.

Alec got up quickly. For the first time that afternoon, he really seemed to see her, and he put his arm around her waist, guiding her to a chair. "What is it, Caity? You went white as a ghost." He spoke into the intercom. "Betty, could you please bring me some hot tea or coffee? And maybe a cracker or two? Whatever's available in the lunchroom."

His voice hardened when he turned back to speak to Caitlin. "You should take better care of yourself. Making yourself ill with overwork isn't going to be much help to Sam or anyone else."

"I'm not planning to work this weekend," Caitlin said. "For the next two days I'm on vacation."

"Good." He didn't suggest getting together with her over the weekend. He didn't mention their tentative plans for a visit to the zoo.

Betty came in with a pot of tea and a plate of small cookies. Looking at Caitlin, her frowns disappeared and her face softened into an expression of kindly sympathy. "My dear, you don't look well," she said. "Would a couple of aspirin help? It's all I've got to offer, I'm afraid."

Caitlin wished—fervently—that aspirin could cure what ailed her. Unfortunately lovesickness required more potent medicine. She forced herself to sit up straight and accept the cup of tea with a bright smile. She was darned if she'd betray weakness in front of the gorgon. "Thanks, Betty, but once I've had a leisurely dinner and a good night's sleep I'll be a new woman. This has been a busy week, that's all."

"Shall I call a cab for you?" Betty asked. "There might be a wait at this time on a Friday evening."

Alec spoke at once. "Don't bother with cabs, Betty, I'll take Caity home."

"You're forgetting your other appointment," Betty said, and her voice took on an odd sort of warning note. "You know you can't leave the office, Alec. Not now. Not with Ms. Howard."

"But, surely, in the circumstances…"

"I don't think it would be at all wise," Betty said firmly.

Alec walked over to the window and looked out into the gathering dusk, so Caitlin couldn't gauge his reaction to these instructions from his secretary. "Instructions" was the correct word, too, Caitlin thought, shocked at this further evidence of Betty's dislike. The secretary had come close to forbidding Alec to drive Caitlin home.

A few moments passed, and when Alec finally spoke, he continued to stare out of the window. "You're quite right, Betty. Thanks for reminding me.

Caitlin and I will only be another few minutes and then I'll be ready for my next appointment.''

"Good," she said. "I have all the papers on my desk. And I'll call Ms. Howard a cab.''

Betty left the room and Alec turned away from the window, although he seemed to deliberately avoid meeting Caitlin's eye as he returned to his desk. Her hands started to shake, and she put down her cup to avoid spilling the dregs of her tea. It was an extraordinary feeling to look across the room at a man she had known for most of her life and realize that her knees wobbled and her heart pounded at the mere thought of his glancing up and meeting her gaze.

She wanted to run to his side, hurl herself into his arms and shout aloud how much she loved him, but a cruel voice deep inside her head whispered that if she did any such thing, she might well be humiliated. Twenty years of friendship linked their pasts, and yet she had no idea how Alec really felt about her. The cold truth was that she'd never allowed herself to consider his feelings. Her relationship with Alec had been dominated by *her* needs, *her* wishes, *her* desires. In a lifetime of friendship, she could remember few occasions when she'd inquired how Alec felt about a situation. She'd simply assumed—with blind arrogance—that he felt the same way she did. Their relationship was deeply rooted in the selfishness of her behavior, and she feared she would soon choke on the tangled weeds of her own creation.

Alec spoke at last. "Why did you come here this afternoon, Caity?"

She wanted to tell him. She searched for words that might begin to hint at the truths about herself she'd finally uncovered. Unfortunately she had no chance to speak. Betty displayed her unfailing knack for intruding at just the wrong moment and stuck her head around the door. "The cab will be here in ten minutes. The dispatcher wants you to wait downstairs, Ms. Howard."

Caitlin tried to sound properly grateful. "I'll be right down. Thanks for calling on my behalf."

"Anytime." Betty withdrew.

Alec leaned forward across his desk. The rays of the setting sun angled through the window behind him, burnishing the sheen of his dark hair and outlining his high cheekbones in a vivid contrast of light and shadow. Caitlin's stomach swooped in a visceral response to the power of his sheer male sexuality. Had she been willfully blind these past few years? How had she managed to spend so much time with Alec and yet still cut off all awareness of her own feelings and her own physical attraction to him?

"Caity." Alec sounded gentle again, and yet remote. "You really don't look well. Take care of yourself this weekend, okay?"

"Sure." His impersonal kindness irritated her lacerated nerves more than any brusqueness could possibly have done. Until it stopped, she hadn't realized how much she cherished the undercurrent of husky, intimate warmth that always flowed beneath their conversations. Overwhelmed by a sudden need for the privacy of her own apartment, she got up and prepared to leave. She couldn't smile, so she pretended to busy herself picking up her briefcase and smoothing her skirt.

"Do you have plans for tonight?" Alec asked politely.

She tried to sound casual and unconcerned. "Very important ones. I plan to sleep for twelve hours and vegetate for another twelve after that."

Alec's gaze narrowed as he escorted her to the door. "You know, you still haven't told me why you came."

She bit back a gasp of slightly hysterical laughter. *For protection from the big bad wolf,* she thought. *Except you turned out to be the wolf, not the protector.*

"It was business," she said, clutching at the first excuse that popped into her overtired, overworked brain.

"Business? Oh, you must mean my contract with Services Unlimited. My search for a wife."

She hadn't meant that at all, of course. She could hardly think of anything she wanted to discuss less than Alec's quest for marital bliss. She sighed and rubbed her eyes, which burned with fatigue.

"I came to straighten out a possible misunderstanding," she said at last. "I want you to know I don't consider Jodie Bergen a client of our agency. She isn't on our books, and she wasn't introduced to you as a serious candidate for the position of your wife. As far as I'm concerned, anything that's developed between the two of you is strictly personal and has nothing to do with our company.''

"Are you telling me I don't owe Services Unlimited any money?"

The question jarred and Caitlin gritted her teeth. "Naturally, since you and Jodie..." She cleared her throat and tried again. "In the circumstances, I'm willing to cancel your agreement with the company."

"You're jumping the gun a bit," Alec said. "I'm not sure I want you to do that."

They'd reached the door to his office and she stopped in surprise. "But you and Jodie—"

"Jodie is a great person, and we get on very well together, but marriage is a serious business. I'd certainly like to check out all my options before I take the final plunge."

Something wasn't right with this conversation, Caitlin thought, trying to prod her fuzzy brain cells into action. A few minutes ago, when she'd burst into his office, Alec had been calling Jodie "darling," and blowing kisses into the phone. Now he was talking about checking out the full range of his matrimonial options. The shift in his attitude made no sense, and Caitlin was about to say so. Second thoughts prompted her to keep silent. Heaven knew, after the way she'd behaved recently, she wasn't the right person to call other people's actions irrational.

"You were going to say something?" Alec prompted, ushering her out of his office.

Caitlin spoke in a low voice and hoped very much that Betty wasn't listening. "I just wondered...isn't it a little unfair to Jodie if you start dating other women?"

"Don't worry about Jodie—we understand each other much better than you'd expect," Alec said heartily. He gave a smooth smile and ushered her past Betty's desk toward the elevator. "Jodie's sweet, and I'm crazy about her already, but we both have a lot to consider before plunging into a lifetime commitment. So if you have a suitable bride on your books, I'd like to meet her. I trust your professional judgment, Caity, even if our old friendship is on rocky ground these days."

The wretched man was making absolutely no sense. Caitlin became aware of a complex new emotion, somewhere between excitement and anger, uncoiling in the pit of her stomach. "Let me get this straight," she said. "Despite the fact that you and Jodie are so attracted to each other that you spent every night this week together, you now want me to produce another candidate for the position of your wife?"

"That's right. And I'd appreciate a call from you every day or so tell me how your search is progressing. That way I can fill you in on my progress with Jodie, too." He made no effort to explain his motives or to defend his decision. She had the bizarre impression that, although they were discussing something that ought to have been of vital importance to him, his attention was elsewhere.

Caitlin abandoned her struggle to understand the incomprehensible. A thread of hope was added to her anger and her excitement. If Alec wasn't committed to Jodie, then Caitlin had been given another chance. Surely she could find some way to convince him that the perfect bride had been sitting under his nose for the past several years. She loved a challenge, and this was shaping up to be the most important one she'd ever tackled.

Caitlin found that she could smile again, and she flashed Alec one of her best professional smiles. "Okay, you've got a deal. As it happens, I have the perfect person in mind for you to date."

"You have?" He seemed startled, as well he might after her initial lack of enthusiasm for the assignment. "Well, er, great. What's her name?"

"Helen." Caitlin said the first name that popped into her head. "And that's all I'm telling you for now, Alec."

"When can I meet her?"

"Saturday evening."

"It's, um, rather short notice...."

"Take it or leave it, Alec. Helen's very much in demand. She has invitations for a party that the Mexican ambassador is hosting, and you could escort her. A genuine south-of-the-border fiesta, dancing, singing, good food and all the Washington bigwigs in attendance. Black tie. Eight o'clock. You can pick her up at my place. Interested?''

"I'll be there."

Caitlin's smile this time was entirely genuine. "Helen will be pleased," she said, and escaped into the elevator.

CHAPTER NINE

CAITLIN HAD ALWAYS considered herself smart, sensible and reasonably attractive. She could cope with most of life's intellectual challenges, although she wasn't an Einstein, or even a budding Ph.D like Jodie. She wasn't knockout gorgeous or gamin-cute like Michelle, but she had an acceptable face, perched on top of a decent body, with better-than-average legs and thick chestnut hair that was her secret pride and joy. Not bad qualities, all in all, even if she was so thickheaded about her own feelings that Alec had to be on the verge of marrying another woman before she noticed that she loved him.

By late Saturday afternoon, Caitlin was ready to revise her previous favorable opinion of herself. After hours of touring stores and trying on clothes, she reached the gloomy conclusion that she had seriously overestimated her physical attractions. On the evidence of the afternoon's shopping, she must be one of the ugliest, most misshapen women in the city of Washington. Nothing fit and she looked a fright in everything.

She'd given up hours ago on her dream of finding a dress so drop-dead stunning that Alec would take one look at her and realize what he'd been missing all his life. Now, she hoped for nothing fancier than a dress that would flatter her small waist and show off her legs, preferably in a color that didn't clash hopelessly with her hair. Hair that for some reason no longer appeared subtly chestnut, but seemed instead to glow more carroty orange with each outfit she tried on.

Smothering a sigh, Caitlin entered the small Georgetown boutique on Wisconsin Avenue that was her last stop before she gave up and went home. The Christmas merchandise was already in stock: rows of stiff dresses in heavy scarlet satin and black velvet; skirts and sweaters in winter white; and lots of blouses weighted down with sequins. None of it was even remotely like what she was looking for.

Without much hope, Caitlin turned from the new stock and poked through a rack of sale items, wondering why the capital of the United States of America was unable to provide such a simple commodity as one—just one—outfit capable of dazzling Alec Woodward.

When she first spotted the silk dress hidden among the bargains, she tried to damp down her flare of hope. But in the dressing room, staring at her reflection in the mirror, she couldn't restrain the quiver of pleasure that rippled down her spine.

The dress was everything she wanted. Of delicate green silk, shot through with a sheen of gold, the style was simple, with a close-fitting bodice, low neck and elbow-length sleeves. The skirt was gored and cut on the bias, so that its flare was subtle, starting below the hips and ending in soft swirls at the knee-length hem. Even without makeup and with her hair dragged back in a ponytail, the dress brought her closer to drop-dead stunning than she'd ever hoped to come. Surely Alec would take one look at her in this and forget all about Helen.

Which would be extremely fortunate, Caitlin reflected, owing to the fact that Helen didn't exist.

Her optimism lasted long enough to get her home, showered, zipped into the new dress and halfway through putting on her makeup. But somewhere between smoothing on lip gloss and stroking on mascara, doubt set in and she wondered if she was behaving like a total idiot.

Her plan had seemed quite straightforward yesterday, when it existed only inside her head: set up an interesting place to meet with Alec (the ambassador's Mexican fiesta); enjoy each other's company for a couple of hours (dance, eat tortillas, drink margaritas); then confess the truth about her feelings (Alec, I love you). The plan dissolved into vagueness at this point, but Caitlin had hoped it would include Alec sweeping her into his arms and setting a wedding date as they exchanged rapturous kisses.

Unfortunately, now that she was getting down to the nitty-gritty, her plan seemed to suffer from several gaping holes. Alec was too polite to refuse to go out with her when she failed to produce the nonexistent

Helen, but that was no guarantee the evening would be a success, or even a semi-success. If their encounter yesterday was anything to judge by, tonight could well be an unmitigated disaster.

Poking hairpins into a sophisticated, upswept hairstyle that refused to stay either upswept or sophisticated, Caitlin discovered the awkward truth that the more intense your feelings, the more difficult they were to put into words.

I love you. How could it possibly be difficult to say three such simple words to a man she had known most of her life?

She clipped on earrings that shimmered against her cheeks in a fragile burst of golden moons and crystal stars. The earrings had been a gift from Alec last Christmas, and Caitlin suddenly felt more cheerful. So what if she now realized she loved Alec Woodward? How could she possibly feel nervous about a date with him? Heck, the first time they met, he'd still been wearing braces and she was a third-grader with scabby knees.

Since leaving college, she'd slept on his sofa plenty of times and spent dozens of weekends in his company. She knew which part of the newspaper he read first on Sundays. He'd seen her looking hot and frazzled after mowing her parents' lawn, and she knew what he looked like before he drank that crucial first cup of coffee in the morning. Good grief, what was she worried about? They might as well be married already, they knew each other so intimately.

Her doorbell rang and her hand stopped in midair. Alec. It had to be Alec, otherwise the night watchman would have buzzed the intercom to alert her to visitors. Caitlin's stomach swooped as she stuck a final pin into her hair and left the bathroom. Her high heels sounded extraordinarily loud as she crossed the parquet floor of the tiny entrance hall. Tap, tap, tap. Her heartbeat echoed her heels, only twice as fast. Pitpat, pitpat, pitpat. She pushed at a wisp of hair that had already lost its moorings and drew a shaky breath. This was it! *Showtime.*

She threw open the door, smiling a cheery welcome. No point in making a mountain out of a molehill, she chided herself. Keep calm, think cool, and this won't be so bad.

It wasn't going to be bad, it was going to be terrible, far worse than her worst nightmare, she knew the moment she saw him. Immaculate in evening dress and starched white shirt, Alec stood on her doorstep, holding a small gift-wrapped box. He looked inches taller than she remembered him, a hundred times more suave and about a thousand times more sexy. His blue eyes swept her appraisingly, and for a split second, she saw the leap of some primitive emotion blaze in the depths of his gaze. Then the fire was banked, and he smiled at her with remote courtesy.

"Hello, Caity. You're all dressed up. Going somewhere exciting?"

She had to say something, invent some excuse, or

the evening would be over before it got started. "Come in, Alec, would you?" Her voice sounded high and squeaky, about as sophisticated as Minnie Mouse, and she coughed nervously.

"I'm afraid things, um…things aren't quite going to plan." Heaven knew, that was certainly true.

Alec strolled in and tossed his white silk scarf over the back of a chair. Men like Alec should be banned from wearing evening dress, Caitlin thought wildly. It wasn't fair to the female half of the population. How could she think when her entire body had transformed itself into a quivering collection of hormones?

"Where's Helen?" he asked, glancing around the empty living room. "I'm looking forward to meeting her and finding out how much we have in common."

Caitlin hoped she didn't look as guilty as she felt. "Um…there's a slight problem," she said. "I'm really sorry, but, um, Helen's been called away at the last minute. Urgent. A very urgent matter."

Alec looked startled. "Called away? That is a surprise. Nothing tragic has happened, I hope."

Caitlin sensed events slipping disastrously out of her control. By now she should have confessed to Alec that Helen didn't exist and they should both be laughing at the joke. But the simple words of explanation wouldn't come. Alec wasn't looking at her, he wasn't laughing with her, he scarcely seemed aware of her existence. At this precise moment, Caitlin would have preferred to enter the cage of a dozen starving leopards than confess the truth about Helen to Alec.

"It was a top-level meeting. International business. The people are only in town for one night," she said quickly. "Just one of those last-minute crises Helen is always coping with. She asked me to give you her sincere apologies. I'm afraid it may be a while before she's available again."

"I'm devastated. I was really looking forward to meeting her. What does she do precisely?"

"Do?"

"Yes, you know, what's her profession? Where does she work?"

"For the government," Caitlin said after a too-long pause. "Very hush-hush. Top-level security clearance. I really shouldn't say anything more."

"I'm flattered she wants to take time out from such an exciting job to meet me."

"Well, I've told her a lot about you."

He chuckled. "Then I'm even more surprised she wants to meet me. How did she come to be a client of yours?"

"She needed reliable cleaning help."

"And you managed to talk her into considering marriage to me? Wow! I always knew you were a good salesperson, but not that good. What color hair does she have?"

"Red." Caitlin said the first thing that came into her head.

"Like yours? What a coincidence."

"No, it's not a coincidence. She's nothing at all like me. She's more of a strawberry blonde."

"Mmm. Sounds delightful."

Caitlin tried to think of some witty comeback and failed totally. In fact, she couldn't think of anything to say at all. Alec broke the silence.

"Well, I can see you're ready to leave for somewhere fancy. I guess I'd better head for home."

"You could come with me," Caitlin blurted out. *Good Lord, what a mess she was making of this simple invitation!*

Alec picked up his scarf. "Oh, no, I wouldn't want to intrude on a special date."

"Don't worry, it's not a special date. I don't have a date. I got dressed up for you." She blushed hotly. "What I mean is Helen sent over her invitation cards for the Mexican fiesta and asked me to take you in her place."

He looked doubtful in the extreme. "But we don't want to go to a party together, do we? What's the point? We'd both be more usefully employed catching up on our paperwork."

"I'm not working this weekend, remember?"

"Then you certainly don't have to fill in for Helen, Caity. Relax and enjoy your mini-vacation. I quite understand why your client couldn't make it."

He was turning the doorknob, on the brink of leaving. Caitlin couldn't believe how badly she'd handled the situation. "I don't want to catch up on paperwork," she said flatly. "I really would like to go to this fiesta with you, Alec. If you feel you can spare the time, that is. I don't want to impose.''

Alec opened the door. ''I'm sorry, I really can't...'' He paused, then slowly swung around. She had the odd impression that he was annoyed with himself for staying. ''All right,'' he said curtly. ''Since we're both dressed up already, it seems a bit silly to end the evening before it's even started.''

''Oh, yes!'' she agreed fervently. ''We may as well go to the embassy and strut our stuff. It should be fun.''

''If you say so.'' Alec leaned against the doorjamb, finally looking at her with eyes that actually seemed to focus. ''I like your dress. Have I ever seen it before?''

''No, it's new.'' She tried not to feel crushed, but she'd hoped for so much more from this glamorous outfit than an offhand compliment. She was darn sure he would remember which dresses he'd seen Jodie wear and which ones were new. She forced a smile, drawing some comfort from the fact that her plans for the evening could still be salvaged. At least he hadn't refused outright to take her to the party. At least he was willing to spend a few hours in her company.

''You need a coat,'' he said. ''It's chilly out there tonight.''

''Right. If you'll wait a second, I'll get it.''

He smothered a yawn that appeared bored rather than tired. ''Take your time. No reason to rush.''

THE PARTY WAS in full swing by the time Caitlin and Alec arrived. Waiters circulated through the reception rooms carrying heavy silver trays laden with chilled champagne and foaming margaritas. Crowds of elegantly clothed men and women clustered around buffet tables that were almost invisible beneath bowls and platters of spicy seafood, fajitas, tacos, salsas, salads, salty breadsticks and colorful tropical fruits. Strolling musicians entertained the guests with folk songs, and in a vaulted room with two magnificently tiled alcoves, a larger band played traditional Mexican dance music for the few couples who seemed interested in dancing.

Caitlin was glad of the noise and the bustle of activity, since she and Alec seemed to have absolutely nothing to say to each other. Poised awkwardly near the end of one of the buffet tables, they nibbled food that Caitlin suspected neither of them wanted and exchanged polite platitudes about nothing in particular.

Alec finally suggested they should go to the room with the dancing, but the band had chosen that moment to take a break, and they were left with nothing to do except prop up one of the walls and sip margaritas. When Caitlin saw a diplomat who had been a client of Services Unlimited earlier in the year, she greeted him eagerly.

''Antonio, I'm so glad to see you. How are you?''

He bowed gracefully over her hand. Despite years at graduate school in the States and several more years in Washington, he hadn't lost any of his Latin charm. "All the better for seeing you, Caitlin. I keep meaning to fire my housekeeper so I have an excuse to call you and arrange a long, intimate lunch."

She laughed. "You don't need such a drastic excuse—just call. I'd love to have lunch with you. Although I'd be delighted to find you a new housekeeper if you really need one."

"Serafina keeps talking about retiring. Joking aside, I may have to contact you soon." His gaze roamed approvingly over her legs and lingered on the bare slope of her shoulders. "That's a terrific dress you have on, Caitlin, just the right color for you. And your hair looks more gorgeous than usual."

She smiled. "Thanks. I see you still manage to say all the things a woman wants to hear."

"With you, it's easy because they're all true." He held out his hand to Alec. "We haven't met, but I recognize you from the evening news on television. I am Antonio de las Canteras, information officer at the Mexican Embassy, and you are Alec Woodward, famous defense lawyer for the notorious Mr. Mancuso."

Alec grimaced as he shook hands. "Right now, I wish Mr. Mancuso were a little less well-known, and I wish the press hadn't decided to make his wife into their victim-of-the-month. The finer points of law tend to get lost when a trial is carried on in the full blaze of media attention."

"But you are well accustomed to such trials, no? You are famous for keeping cool under pressure."

Alec gave a tight smile. "If that's a compliment, I guess I'd better grab it and say thank-you."

"It was most certainly a compliment." Antonio broke off, cocking his head to one side. He smiled in delight. "Listen, the band is playing a tango—how fortunate for me. Caitlin, I'm going to beg and plead and make a pest of myself until you agree to dance with me. I have vivid memories of the last time we performed a tango together, and I'm going to claim the privilege of a host and insist on repeating the pleasure."

Caitlin was more than willing to accept. Not only was Antonio a superb dancer, but the tension between Alec and her seemed to be building by the minute, and she was frankly relieved at the prospect of spending some time away from him. She murmured a few conventional words to excuse herself and gladly followed Antonio onto the dance floor.

Handsome, slender and athletic, Antonio harbored no Anglo-Saxon hang-ups about modesty or not making a spectacle of himself. He knew from previous encounters that Caitlin loved to dance, and he quickly led her into a series of dramatic twirls, followed by a couple of even more dramatic lunges with her back arched over his supporting arm and her skirt swirling about his knees in a flash of golden-green silk. An appreciative audience gathered around the edge of the dance floor, and Caitlin allowed herself to strut, glide and swoop in response to Antonio's expert commands. The harder she threw herself into her performance, the easier it was to forget about Alec and the disaster this evening had become. Exerting every ounce of her technical skill, she did her best to lose herself in the pounding, exotic rhythm of the dance. When the music finally ended and the crowd applauded, she emerged blinking and disoriented into reality. A quick glance around revealed that Alec had left the room. Obviously he found her company so boring he hadn't bothered to stay and watch.

Antonio mopped his brow with a snow-white handkerchief, seized two champagne flutes from a passing waiter and handed her one. He raised his glass in a toast. "You get better every time, Caitlin."

"Thanks. So do you." She drank deeply, vaguely remembering that she'd already had two margaritas but too thirsty to care. She wondered where Alec had gone and wished he had been her partner for the tango. Dancing with Antonio was fun, but dancing with Alec was heaven.

"We seem to have lost your escort," Antonio murmured. "What a stroke of good fortune for me. I shall start my grand plan to seduce you immediately. Caitlin, you have the most adorable green eyes and a mouth that is so kissable I'm already driven insane with longing. Get rid of your uptight lawyer and come home with me tonight."

Caitlin laughed. "Don't say that with such a soulful sigh, Antonio, or some unsuspecting woman might believe you were serious."

He tucked her hand through his arm. "I am serious—why do you doubt me? I would like nothing better than to take you to my bed tonight.''

"On condition that I promise to leave before dawn tomorrow morning, right?''

He grinned. "For you, beautiful Caitlin, I would make an exception. You can stay until ten o'clock and help yourself to coffee and freshly squeezed orange juice before you leave.''

"What a deal! I'm truly flattered, but I guess I'll pass all the same.''

He sighed. "I knew I had no hope when I saw your glowering lawyer. He's tough competition even for a man like me.''

"He's not *my* lawyer,'' Caitlin said, then wished she hadn't spoken when Antonio looked at her with too much understanding.

"You sound frustrated, *pequeña.*''

"You're mistaken. Alec and I have known each other for years, but we're just good friends.''

"Ah!'' he said. "I see.''

"There's nothing to see.''

"But of course there is. You wish him to be something more than a friend, and he is not cooperating. Although why he refuses to cooperate I can't imagine. The mating behavior of you Americanos is often incomprehensible to the Latin soul.''

Caitlin swallowed the last mouthful of her champagne. The bubbles fizzed in her throat and she suddenly felt reckless enough to admit the truth. "You're right about one thing, Antonio. I want him to be a lot more than my friend.''

"Then tell him so. Better yet, show him.''

"I tried. He isn't getting the message.''

"You are too subtle in affairs of the heart. Don't beat around the bush. Don't drop delicate hints. Take him home to your apartment and make love to him until he's too tired to keep his feelings hidden behind those defensive shields he carries. I can't imagine any way for a woman to be more convincing than in her lover's bed.''

Caitlin wasn't sure whether to laugh or cry. "Antonio, you make it sound a snap. But somehow I don't think it's quite that easy to turn an old friend into a lover.''

"If you're willing to risk the friendship, it's easy. In your case, trust me. You have only to kiss your uptight, controlled lawyer with passion, to look at him with hunger in your eyes, to allow your body to show your needs, and I guarantee you will be in his bed as fast as he can get you there. Alec Woodward wants to make love to you, Caitlin, take my word for it. Desire is not something one man can hide from another, not even your oh-so-controlled lawyer.''

She traced the rim of her empty glass with her fingertip. "Maybe he does want to make love to me,'' she said. "But physical attraction isn't enough. What happens if our lovemaking doesn't work out? I'd hate to ruin a great friendship with Alec for the sake of an unsuccessful one-night stand.''

He shrugged. "Life is full of risks, Caitlin. You have merely to decide if winning the game is worth the stake you're investing."

She smiled ruefully. "I don't believe life's equations are as simple as you're making them sound, Antonio."

His answering smile didn't quite reach his eyes. "A cynic always finds other people's romantic problems easy to resolve. It is his own love affairs that he manages so badly." He gave her no chance to probe this brief glimpse beneath his facade.

"Look!" he said, all suave charm once again. "There is your heartthrob lawyer. He seems to have a harem of devoted admirers in tow."

"He usually does at parties like this."

"Then we must break him loose." Taking Caitlin's hand, Antonio drew her across the room and ended up in front of Alec, pushing her forward with a flourish.

"Mr. Woodward, I thank you from the bottom of my heart for allowing me to dance with Caitlin. She tangos with such fire and grace that it's always thrilling to be her partner."

"There's no reason to thank me," Alec said curtly. "Caitlin doesn't need my permission to choose a dance partner."

"How generous of you," Antonio murmured. "For myself, with such a beautiful woman as my date, I believe I would be a little more possessive." He took Caitlin's hand, dropped a kiss onto her fingertips and slipped away into the crowd without saying another word.

Alec disengaged himself from the cluster of women surrounding him. "This has been a terrific party and it's been great talking to you all. I appreciate your good wishes for Mr. Mancuso, and I'll be sure to pass them on to him. Caitlin, are you ready to leave now?"

She drew in a deep breath, wishing they weren't being overheard by so many people. "Are we in a hurry?" she asked. "I'd love to dance with you before we leave."

For a moment, she thought he was going to refuse. Then he shrugged and put his hand on the small of her back, guiding her to the dance floor without speaking. For once, luck seemed to be on her side. As Alec took her into his arms, the band finished an energetic mamba and segued into the compelling, melancholy rhythms of a folk song lamenting the heartache caused by a false lover.

As Alec drew her fractionally closer, Caitlin realized she was shaking. The longing to lean against him, to mold her softness against the hardness of his body, was intense enough to make her feel dizzy. Or perhaps the dizziness was caused by two margaritas and a tall glass of champagne. Or perhaps this was how people always felt when they were falling in love. She'd never understood before how accurate the word "falling" actually was. She felt disoriented, giddy, dazzled, by the intensity of her emotions.

Alec's hand rested lightly, noncommittally against

the small of her back as he guided her across the dance floor. The lightness of his touch drove her crazy. She wanted to feel his fingers clutch her with urgent need. She wanted him to drag her tight against him and drown her yearnings in a sea of endless, stormy passion.

Alec, however, might as well have been dancing with the Queen of England for all the passion he displayed. In fact, if he'd been dancing with the Queen, he'd have felt compelled to make polite conversation, which was a lot more than he was attempting right now. Frustration began to spice Caitlin's longing with a dash of desperation, and with a boldness that would have been unimaginable a couple of weeks earlier, she closed the six-inch gap between their bodies and allowed her hands to caress his back with erotic, feathery strokes. Emboldened by the shudder of his response, she clasped her fingers behind his neck and pulled his cheek down to rest against hers.

The smell of his after-shave filled her nostrils; the heat of his body warmed her soul. Desire and happiness bubbled through her veins. She wondered how she could have deprived herself of these incredible feelings for so many years. How could she have fooled herself into thinking she wanted Alec as a friend, when her entire being craved him as a lover? As a husband... The lights dimmed and she closed her eyes, rubbing her face softly against his.

His reaction was all she'd hoped for. He stumbled and for several seconds couldn't recapture the beat of the music. As soon as their steps were in sync again, he led her to the darkest corner of the dance floor, and she felt his clasp tighten around her, cradling her hips against his lower body, showing her how much he desired her. His hands no longer felt cool and remote, but hot and urgent, just as she'd longed for. Then he bent his head and for a few blissful moments she felt the brush of his hungry kisses in the hollow of her neck. Her skin tingled, her body pulsed with desire. Oblivious to their surroundings, she turned her head, lifting her face to receive the full-blown kiss she craved.

For an instant, his mouth hovered over hers. She saw his eyes darken with passion until they were almost indigo; she saw the tension in the tight line of his jaw and knew he wanted to kiss her as desperately as she wanted to receive his kiss. Then he snapped his head up, jerking away from her. And when he faced her again, his expression had completely changed.

"Tell me more about Helen," he said, as if two seconds earlier he hadn't been poised on the brink of kissing her senseless. "I'm really longing to hear all about her. Adventurous, dynamic, sure of herself— she sounds just my type."

Caitlin felt like Alice in Wonderland at the Mad Hatter's tea party. Why were they suddenly talking about Helen? Why was Alec guiding her with such determination toward the well-lit center of the room? She blinked, trying to slough the haze of desire that clung to her like a second skin. She couldn't think of anything she wanted to discuss less than the wretched, nonexistent Helen. She shook her head, frantically trying to collect her muzzy thoughts.

"Are you feeling all right?" Alec asked kindly. "We can sit out the rest of this dance if you prefer."

"Yes, that would be better. I think that last glass of champagne did me in."

Alec looked at his watch. "Actually, it's already eleven-thirty. Why don't we slip away before it gets really late? I'm sure you have as much to do tomorrow as I do, so we could both use an early night."

Caitlin stared at him in helpless silence, which he read as consent. As he ushered her briskly toward the exit, she had the bewildering sensation that somewhere between one blink of her eyes and the next, an alien had slipped into Alec's body and taken possession. It wasn't possible for the man who had trembled in her arms to sound this casual and cheery two minutes later.

"Alec...about Helen...about us..."

His smile never waivered. "Look, Caitlin, you don't have to explain. There is no *us*. I understand completely."

"What happened on the dance floor..."

"I apologize," he said with a disarming shrug. "What can I say? I'm a sucker for slow music. It has a crazy effect on my libido, but don't worry, Caity, I promise you it didn't mean a thing." He rushed on before she could say a word. "You know, I've been thinking about Helen. I'm not sure you should arrange a meeting between the two of us, after all. The more I think about it, the more I wonder how we'd make a marriage work. My schedule's impossible, and hers sounds as if it's even worse. Besides, Jodie is the ideal candidate. She hasn't established her career as yet, so her life-style is more flexible. We'll be able to accommodate each other's needs much more easily. It seems superfluous to bring another woman into the picture at this stage.''

"That's fine with me," Caitlin said. "Helen is history.'' She was so grateful to be let off the hook that she didn't risk pointing out that it had been entirely Alec's own idea to meet another candidate. If she hadn't felt so heartsick and bemused, she would have spared a few moments to inform Alec that he was behaving like a potential chauvinist, and that Jodie deserved more out of life than to be picked as a wife simply because she was young and not yet settled into a career.

Alec retrieved their coats from the cloakroom and helped Caitlin into hers with polite solicitude. "We'll consider the Helen situation settled, then.''

"Fine, terrific. Helen never existed.'' She blushed hotly. "As far as you're concerned, I mean.''

"Right, as far as I'm concerned, she was just a figment of your imagination.'' Alec whistled cheerfully, jingling the coins in his pocket as they waited for a parking attendant to bring them their car. "Well, I guess there's nothing left to say except here's to dear little Jodie, and congratulations to you, Caity, on your terrific matchmaking skills. Thanks to you, Jodie and I are making the perfect team!''

"Rah-rah," Caitlin said, horrified to discover she was choking back tears. The enormity of her loss almost overwhelmed her. Because of her emotional immaturity and her panicky refusal to see that marriage to Alec would bear no resemblance to her parents' constricting relationship, she'd thrown away her chance to marry the man she'd been in love with since her sixteenth birthday.

"I'm seeing Jodie tomorrow," Alec said, opening the car door for her and tipping the attendant at the same time. "I've decided we should start making serious plans for a wedding. We'll have to talk about setting the date." He smiled widely. "My mother's going to be so excited—she's been planning my wedding for years."

"She and Sam will both be pleased," Caitlin managed to say. "And your father, of course."

Alec chuckled. "Sam will be tickled pink. This is all his idea. With a little help from Dot and Betty."

"Betty! What's she got to do with it?"

"Betty's been on a campaign to get me married. She's a real sentimentalist at heart." He latched his seat belt, looking so darn pleased with himself that Caitlin had an almost irresistible urge to bop him on the nose. Beneath her hurt, beneath her aching sense of loss, she felt bewildered. Lord knew, her behavior tonight hadn't been very rational, but Alec's had been even less rational. She had the crazy impression he was laughing at some joke she didn't share.

"I'm going to go straight home and telephone Jodie," he announced, easing the car out into the flow of traffic.

"You're going to ask her to set a date for your wedding?"

"Not exactly." Alec's face split into another wide grin. "My mother's had the date of my wedding picked out for at least a month," he said. "I just need to make sure that Jodie and Sam can clear their calendars for the first Saturday in December."

"December fifth?"

"Right."

In less than six weeks, Alec would be married. To Jodie. "Congratulations," Caitlin said, and even to her own ears, her voice sounded hollow. "I hope you'll both be very happy."

CHAPTER TEN

"HE CAN'T DO IT!" Caitlin said, pacing the hearth rug in Dot's cozy apartment. "We have to get him declared temporarily insane, or something. Good grief, Dot, can you imagine how miserable they're going to make each other?"

"Jodie's a nice kid. She'll make a great wife some day."

"*Some day*—that's the whole point. Five years from now when she's got the tsetse flies out of her system. But right now, she's not ready to be married, especially to a dynamic, demanding man like Alec. He's such a powerful personality he'll chew her up into little pieces. And while Jodie's trying to work out how to put herself together again, he'll decide she's boring and demand a divorce."

"Sounds like typical male behavior," Dot agreed.

"Alec isn't callous, not in the least. But I know him better than anyone, his faults as well as his good points. He needs a strong partner to stand up to him, not a kitten still trying to decide what she'll be when she finally grows up and has a full set of claws."

Dot yawned. "You sound very passionate about all this, boss, and I can't imagine why. Maybe Jodie's smarter than you think. Maybe she'll refuse to set a date for their wedding.''

"Women never refuse Alec Woodward,'' Caitlin said gloomily. "Besides, she thinks she's in love with him. Everyone agrees on that.''

"Have you actually talked to Jodie herself about how she feels?''

"Well, no…''

"Then until you do, I suggest this conversation is premature. You know how I feel about marriage, it's not a subject I enjoy discussing, particularly on a Sunday morning before I've finished reading the newspaper. Have another blueberry muffin and let's talk about something else. Something more cheerful than marriage. How about income tax returns, or the Second World War?''

"I'm not hungry, thanks.'' Caitlin rubbed her forehead which had been throbbing with pain ever since she'd woken up that morning, a fitting punishment for too many margaritas and too little self-control. "Honestly, I think Alec has flipped. His behavior last night made absolutely no sense. One minute he was just about ready to make love to me right there on the dance floor—'' She stopped abruptly. "I need another cup of coffee. Can I get you something?''

"A dash of honesty would be nice,'' Dot said.

Caitlin straightened, full of righteous indignation. "What does that mean, for heaven's sake? I came here this morning because you're a friend and I need your help—''

"And so far, you've consumed three large mugs of coffee and spouted on about everything except what's really worrying you."

"Which is?" Caitlin asked, very much on her dignity.

"The fact that you're head over heels in love with Alec Woodward."

Caitlin opened her mouth to protest, then collapsed onto the sofa in a defeated heap. "Oh, boy, is it that obvious?"

"Well, I guess a deaf and blind visitor from another planet might not get the picture." Dot shot her a shrewd glance. "Alec Woodward might not get the picture, either, since he appears to be as thick-skulled as you, impossible as that might seem. All in all, I'd say the two of you make an ideal couple. There can't be many people around with sky-high IQs and such a total lack of common sense."

Caitlin stared at her hands. "Alec's known me for years. If he wants to marry me, why hasn't he ever suggested it?"

"Would you have said yes? Or would you have gone running a thousand miles in the opposite direction? Face it, lady, you've never made any secret of the fact that, until recently, you considered marriage barely one step up from a sentence of life imprisonment."

Caitlin wasn't prepared to concede the logic of Dot's argument. "If Alec had wanted to marry me, he'd have said something by now. He must have recognized how I feel about him.''

''I'd say that's highly debatable.''

''He's just trying to save my pride by refusing to give me any chance to discuss my feelings. He's doing his best to stop me from telling him I love him.''

''Honey, if you weren't so smart, I'd say you were terminally stupid.''

''What's that supposed to mean?''

''Hasn't it occurred to you that Alec may find it as difficult to be honest with you as you are with him?''

''No, it hasn't,'' Caitlin said slowly. ''The fact is, I have trouble seeing this situation from Alec's point of view. I keep trying to consider his emotions, his feelings, but my own needs get in the way. Right now, all I can think about is how much I want to be with him, how desperately I want him to hold me.'' She got up and renewed her pacing. ''This falling-in-love business is totally weird, you know, and I don't have any practice in coping. My sisters would have known years ago how they felt. Good grief, they'd probably have known from the day Alec moved in next door that they planned to marry him. Whereas dumb old me, I only noticed last week that I'm madly, passionately in love with the wretched man.''

''Madly?'' Dot queried with obvious interest. ''Passionately?'' She smiled. ''Well, boss, I guess that red hair of yours is coming into its own at last.''

''And a lot of good it's doing me,'' Caitlin said tartly. ''For heaven's sake, Dot, Alec and I are both adults. We're good friends. Why can't I just walk up to him and say, 'Alec, I love you. Would you be interested in spending the rest of your life with me?'"

Dot's laughter held a hint of pain. "Honey, I've been married three times, widowed once and divorced twice. If I knew the answer to that question I'd have written a how-to-manage-your-love-life book and made myself a fortune long before now. And I wouldn't have two divorces on my record. If you're looking for advice, you've come to the wrong woman."

"Maybe I should go over to his apartment tonight. Maybe I should go right now, before he meets with Jodie again." Caitlin squared her shoulders, mentally preparing herself for the task of confronting Alec. She looked at Dot and gave a gasp of embarrassed laughter. "You know, I really am going crazy. I've turned up on Alec's doorstep uninvited at least a hundred times. Suddenly, just because I've discovered I'm desperately in love with him, I can't do it."

"Love sure makes fools out of all of us," Dot agreed.

Something about Dot's tone penetrated the haze of Caitlin's self-absorption. "Dot, are you okay?" she asked. She looked more closely at her friend and saw that her eyes were suspiciously red-rimmed and her normally pink cheeks pale and sallow. Furious with herself for being so self-centered she had taken this long to notice that something was wrong, she knelt beside Dot's chair and took her hand. "Dot, what is it? Please tell me if I can help."

Dot stared at her empty coffee mug and the color came and went in her cheeks. Caitlin felt her heart constrict when Dot—the ever cheerful, ever cynical, ever self-possessed Dot—burst into noisy, wrenching tears.

Caitlin put her arm around Dot's shoulder and hugged her hard. "It'll be all right," she said soothingly. "Dot, tell me. Let me help. What is it?"

Dot's voice throbbed with tragedy. "I told Sam I'll marry him," she said. "Last night at nine o'clock. I promised him again this morning."

"You told Sam you'll marry him!" Caitlin repeated in a dazed voice. She rocked back on her heels, trying to absorb the stunning news. Keeping her arm around Dot, she probed the cause of her friend's tears as tactfully as she could. "You agreed because he's sick, is that what you mean? He wants to marry you, and you felt you couldn't refuse because he's suffered two minor heart attacks?"

Dot jerked out of Caitlin's comforting hug and stormed angrily across the room. "Of course not!" she said. "Sam's a wonderful, wonderful man and I've loved him for months. Oh, hell, where are the tissues?"

"Here."

Dot scrubbed her eyes and blew her nose. "I love Sam," she said harshly. "He's been asking me to marry him for weeks now, but I kept putting him off, telling him to find another woman.''

''Why would you do that?'' Caitlin asked cautiously. She was no expert in matters of the heart, but since Dot loved Sam and he loved her, she couldn't begin to understand why a proposal of marriage should have Dot hovering on the verge of hysterics.

Dot didn't answer directly. ''We've been dating each other on and off since our Fourth of July office party. Of course, I've tried to make it more off than on, but Sam won't take no for an answer.''

''That's good, isn't it? Doesn't that show how much he cares for you?''

Dot gave her a withering look. ''After everyone else left the office party, we went to the beach and dug for clams. Then we sat up all night on the porch of his beach cottage just talking.'' The memory of this sentimental occasion was apparently enough to send her off into a fresh noisy bout of tears.

Caitlin stared at her secretary and wondered if ''love'' was simply another word for insanity. So far, Dot's story had revealed absolutely no reason for sadness. Dot, clearly, was in love with Sam. Sam, presumably, was in love with Dot, since he'd asked her to marry him. Sam's health, provided he followed a sensible diet and exercise regimen, was unlikely to present further problems. Dot was healthy as a horse. They were both single and free to marry. Caitlin tried to think of any possible reason her secretary would announce the news of her engagement as if it were the greatest disaster since the sinking of the *Titanic*. Absolutely no rational explanation came to mind.

"Does Sam want a long engagement?" she asked with what she hoped was supreme tact.

She had, apparently, blundered straight to the heart of an emotional mine field. "He wants to get married next Saturday!" Dot wailed. "In his house, with all the children there, and his friend the judge to conduct the ceremony, and he's already booked the Grand Gourmet catering service to prepare the buffet for afterward."

"It sounds as if he has everything well planned," Caitlin said. "The Grand Gourmet people are very good." She waited nervously and saw with relief that she'd finally managed to say something that didn't send Dot off into paroxysms of tears. She plucked up her courage and tried again. "I could help you choose a dress," she suggested. "You'd look wonderful in deep rose, or even burgundy, which would be a great color for this time of year."

Dot huddled on the edge of an armchair, shredding tissues. "I can't marry him," she said tersely. "I'll ruin his life. Look at me, for heaven's sake! Forty-five years old, and three marriages already behind me. Face it, Caitlin, I'm a loser where marriage is concerned, a lousy three-time loser."

"You're scared," Caitlin said. "Too scared to carry through on the commitment you've made to Sam."

"Darn right I'm scared. I have reason to be. Sam's

a good man, a kind, generous man, who spent thirty years happily married to the same woman until he was widowed. He doesn't know what hell an unsuccessful marriage can be.''

"On the other hand, you don't know what heaven a successful marriage can be,'' Caitlin pointed out. "Your first husband died in Vietnam before you were nineteen, and your other two marriages ended in divorce.''

"Not entirely because my husbands were rats. Face it, Caitlin, I'm not easy to live with. I can be ornery as a hungry bear for no good reason and—''

"Whereas Sam is the model of sweet reason,'' Caitlin said, suddenly finding the situation almost amusing. "Five-thirty on Friday afternoons is just another example of his calm, cheerful approach to life. Come on, Dot, lighten up. In my opinion, the pair of you are two ornery bears who are going to make each other very happy.''

"Do you really think that?'' Dot sounded nothing at all like her usual confident, hard-edged self.

"Yes, I do,'' Caitlin said, and realized she was telling the absolute and complete truth.

"I get sick with nerves just thinking about telling his kids what we're planning,'' Dot said. "I'm supposed to go over to Sam's house for lunch today and face the music. Will you come with me?''

"Well, if you're sure it's not strictly a family occasion...''

"I need you.'' Dot managed a near-normal grin.

"Having you around is living proof that everyone behaves like a total fool when they fall in love."

Reminded of her own crazy situation, Caitlin hesitated. "Alec won't be there with Jodie, will he? He said something about having a date with her today."

"It must be for the afternoon," Dot said. "Sam set up this lunch with Jodie and Laura, his other daughter. His son's going to be there, too. He flies back to Chicago this evening. Please come, Caitlin. I need someone there who's on my side."

DOT COULDN'T HAVE BEEN more wrong in expecting to meet opposition from Sam's family. His children greeted the news of their father's impending marriage with crows of delight and fervent words of thanks to Dot for agreeing to take Sam in hand. They agreed with Caitlin that Dot would look wonderful in a wedding gown of deep rose and suggested that Caitlin would make a spectacular maid of honor in forest green. Laura confessed to being a whiz with a sewing maching, and Dot finally conceded that she *might* go out with Laura on Monday and choose the necessary dress patterns.

Sam, silver hairs spiking in a quiver of pleasure, sat on the sofa with his arm around Dot, looking as smug and self-satisfied as if he'd personally invented the concept of matrimony. His only complaint centered on Dot's insistence that he should toast their engagement with a glass of cranberry juice.

"Don't make a fuss," Dot said briskly. "I need you fighting fit for next Saturday."

"Ah, yes, the honeymoon," Sam said, looking extremely pleased with himself. "We're going to the Cayman Islands for a few days. Can you hold the fort at the office until I get back, Caitlin?"

"Covering for you will be a breeze, but I've no idea how I'll manage without Dot," she said, smiling. "But I'll try to keep everything together."

A ring of the doorbell interrupted a chorus of laughter from Sam's children. Jodie jumped up. "That must be Alec," she said. "I arranged to meet him here right around this time. I'll let him in."

Caitlin's laughter died abruptly. Conversation and jokes continued to ebb and flow around her, but she no longer heard them. She strained her ears and heard the sound of Jodie's voice raised in greeting and the low, husky murmur of Alec's response. They seemed to have an awful lot to say to each other out there in the privacy of the hallway, and at least ten minutes went by before Alec followed Jodie into the living room. He went straight to Sam and offered his hearty congratulations. Then he hugged Dot and told her she was a brave woman. Caitlin's presence he acknowledged with no more than a brief nod.

She watched him in the sort of rapt silence she'd always considered totally absurd in other people. The quirk of his mouth when he smiled, the restless energy of his body, the thickness of his hair all seemed new to her, and yet oddly familiar, as if they had always been part of her unconscious definition of masculinity. Last night, when he had worn evening dress, she had told herself it was the formal clothing that gave him such a compelling aura of magnetism. Today he was dressed in washed-out jeans and a loose-fitting, dark blue sweater, and he still dominated the room by his mere presence. Drinking in the reality of his nearness, it was all Caitlin could do to stay in her seat and not run to his side and beg for a few crumbs of his attention.

She wanted to laugh at the ridiculousness of what she felt. Unfortunately she had already learned that being in love left little room for lighthearted self-mockery. Intellectually, she recognized that she was overdramatizing her situation. Emotionally, she wondered how a person could feel anything as intense as what she felt for Alec and survive. Through the obscuring haze of her emotions, she felt someone touch her arm. She turned around and realized, belatedly, that Sam was talking to her.

"Well, are you surprised, Caitlin?"

She had absolutely no idea what he was talking about. "Should I be?" she asked.

"You were the one who told me Jodie would never be talked out of going to Africa."

Caitlin's heart seemed to explode in a flash of blinding, crippling pain. *This is how it felt to have all your hopes dashed in one swift, crushing blow,* she thought. She sensed everyone watching her, sensed an undercurrent of speculation, and pride forced her to gather her wits to try to respond normally. She cleared her throat several times before she could speak. "You must be very happy, Sam."

He snorted. "I suppose Mexico is a bit closer at least. Dot and I can visit her at Easter, I guess."

"Mexico?" she blurted out, staring first at Jodie and then at Alec. "You're going to move to Mexico?"

"Not me," Alec said shortly. "Jodie."

Damping down a leap of wild hope, Caitlin realized she had daydreamed through a very important piece of conversation. Unfortunately, she couldn't ask too many questions without revealing that she'd heard nothing anybody had said since Alec rang the doorbell.

"What made you decide on Mexico?" she asked Jodie, hoping the question was at least marginally appropriate.

"Alec persuaded me." Jodie hooked her arm through Alec's and looked up at him with an adoring gaze. "He put me in touch with a friend of his who runs a special research lab in Monterey, which is the second largest city in Mexico. The lab runs field projects all over the country, and they have connections to Stanford University, so I'll be able to get in some really important on-site research and work toward my doctorate at the same time."

"That's really great," Caitlin said. She tried not to show the relief that was washing over her in huge, ecstatic waves.

Alec isn't going to marry Jodie.

She forced her best imitation of a casual grin. "I guess that means I've blown my chance for making vice president of Services Unlimited before Christmas. You were my last hope as far as marrying off Alec was concerned."

"I should think we'd have women lined up on the sidewalk begging for a date," Sam said, casting her a sly sideways glance.

"Thanks for the vote of support," Alec said. "You know, Caity, there's always Helen. Somehow, in my heart of hearts, I'm convinced Helen is the right woman for me. Maybe it's the thought of her wonderful red hair. I've always been very partial to redheads. Do you think you could arrange a date for us?"

"Absolutely not," Caitlin said. "I'm sure you wouldn't suit each other at all."

"Why not? She sounds exactly like the woman I'm looking for."

"Two days ago, you were crazy about Jodie and convinced that Helen's career was too demanding! What in the world has gotten into you, Alec?"

Dot, Jodie, Sam and Alec all spoke at once. Alec finally cut through the babble of explanations. "I think Helen would agree to marry me if she'd only give me a chance to discuss our future prospects rationally."

"You'd never heard of her until two days ago!" Caitlin protested, thoroughly infuriated by Alec's cavalier attitude and even more infuriated by his resurrection of the nonexistent Helen.

"What's time got to do with romance?" he asked vaguely. "Helen meets all of my requirements."

"It's absolutely ridiculous to think you can choose a wife just by matching some woman to a prepackaged list of specifications, like selecting curtains for the bathroom. 'Must be blue, no ruffles, preferably machine washable.'"

Sam laughed, but Alec looked at her, his eyes suddenly dark and intense. "I'll cut you a deal, Caity. Bring Helen to my apartment tonight, and I guarantee you'll be astonished at the results. Don't you want to get your vice presidency by Christmas?"

Caitlin should have known better than to set her feet further on the slippery slope of deception, but her mouth gave the fateful agreement before her brain had the sense to veto it. "You're on," she said. "You want Helen, you've got her. Nine o'clock tonight at your apartment."

"Hey, wait a minute," Dot protested. "No woman is going to agree to a first meeting in a strange man's apartment."

"Don't worry about it," Alec said. "Caitlin will be there to reassure her that I don't bite, won't you?"

"I'll be there," Caitlin said. "You can count on it."

CHAPTER ELEVEN

CAITLIN SMOOTHED the palms of her hands over her jeans and waited for the butterflies in her stomach to stop swarming. They failed to oblige. Tonight, even her stomach refused to cooperate and make life a little easier.

The elevator was paneled with smoked glass, and she stared at her murky reflection in the vain hope that she would miraculously have become ten times more attractive during the short car ride from her apartment to Alec's. Unfortunately, no fairy god-mother had chosen to wave a magic wand. She looked pretty much the way she always looked. Probably, she thought despairingly, pretty much the way she'd looked when she was sixteen, and Alec, on the banks of the fishing pond, had tactfully rejected the offer of her overflowing teenage heart.

She scowled at her reflection, wondering why in the world she'd decided to wear jeans, which were calculated to create exactly the wrong sort of juvenile image. The elevator stopped, and she stepped out onto the fourteenth floor, Alec's floor, telling herself it was too late to worry about what she was wearing.

She had changed her outfit literally a dozen times

before settling on jeans and a shirt of turquoise silk, topped by a leather jacket. Not the sort of clothes to set a man's libido racing into overdrive, but since Alec was likely to throw her out the moment she admitted the truth about Helen, it had seemed a bit ridiculous to come obviously dressed for seduction.

Her breath caught in her throat, and her finger paused smack dab over Alec's doorbell. *Dressed for seduction.* At last she'd admitted the truth, at least to herself. Using Helen as an excuse, she had come here tonight to seduce Alec, to gamble everything on a final, high-stakes throw.

She didn't have much confidence in her powers as a seductress—her experience was far too limited—but she tried to reassure herself with the thought that Alec already liked her, so maybe it wouldn't take much to persuade him that he could make a happy marriage with her. Caitlin tried to keep her level of hope high, since right now hope was about all she had. Squaring her shoulders, she pressed the doorbell before her courage could desert her.

Alec opened the door. "Hi, Caity." He brushed her cheek in the sort of friendly greeting he had given her a thousand times before. She jumped as if he'd inserted red-hot needles under her thumbnails.

"Something wrong?" Alec inquired politely.

"Oh, n-no, nothing. I'm fine." *Great,* she told herself sarcastically. *You're going to make a wonderful seductress if you leap like a gazelle every time he comes within two feet of you.*

For a fleeting moment she thought she saw laughter in Alec's eyes, then the laughter vanished and he stepped out into the corridor, looking up and down and all around her. "Where's Helen?" he asked. "Did she get called away again, or was she just unwilling to meet me?"

"It's, um, a long story," Caitlin said. "Could I...could I come in, Alec?"

"Of course. My pleasure." He stepped back, the picture of a courteous host, and gestured for her to precede him into the living room.

"Let me take your jacket," he said, reaching up and helping her to slip it off without waiting for her agreement. His hands slid slowly down her arms, rubbing the silk of her blouse against her skin. He was standing so close behind her she could feel the whisper of his breath against her neck. Caitlin closed her eyes as her nerve endings went haywire.

"Is something the matter?" Alec murmured, his touch suddenly turning brisk. "You seem to be covered in goose bumps. Shall I turn up the heat?"

She catapulted out of his arms. "Oh, no, no thanks. I'm just fine. Perfectly fine."

He tossed her jacket over a chair. "Could I get you some coffee? A few Belgian chocolates for old times sake? I still have some of your private supply in the freezer."

"N-no. No, thank you." *Way to go, Caitlin. This is the sort of witty, sparkling dialogue that would seduce any man.* Angry with her gaucheness, she seized the dregs of her courage and swung around to face him. "We need to talk about Helen."

Alec smiled, the sort of predatory smile that had sent chills down the spines of innumerable witnesses for the prosecution. Caitlin's spine tingled, proving it was equally vulnerable. "Believe me, Caity, I'm looking forward to hearing everything you have to say." He tossed another log onto the fire. "Why don't you sit down and get comfortable before you start?"

Caitlin lowered herself onto the extreme edge of the sofa, feeling about as relaxed as a high-wire acrobat about to perform a triple-turn jump without a safety net. "Nice fire," she managed. "Is it your first of the season?"

"Yes, it is. And before you ask, the wood is cherry, and my supplier brings it in from Maryland."

"The wood smells wonderful. You must...you must give me his name."

"I'll do that. Later, if you still want it. Now, tell me about Helen." Alec sat down on the sofa next to her, so close she could feel the heat of his body, so close she smelled the subtle tang of his cologne with every breath she drew. Alec leaned back against the sofa cushions, and the shifting of his weight inevitably caused her to tumble back with him. Her head ended up resting on the crook of his shoulder, and she squirmed hastily away.

Alec waited until she had repositioned herself in her former awkward position at the edge of the sofa. "Feeling better now?"

"M-much better, thanks."

"Personally, I'm feeling frustrated. I've spent most of the afternoon fantasizing about the way this evening might end. And it certainly wasn't with you perched on the edge of your seat looking as if someone had shoved a steel rod down your back."

Caitlin's precarious hold on her self-control snapped, and she jumped up. "Then you've fantasized in vain," she said crossly. "Not just for tonight, but forever. There *is* no Helen, there *was* no Helen, and there never *will* be a Helen. I invented her—she doesn't exist!"

Alec jumped up, too. "I can't believe it!" he said, sounding astonished, which Caitlin supposed wasn't unreasonable. And yet, his astonishment didn't ring true. She had the peculiar impression that in reality he wasn't even marginally surprised. He reached out and put his hands on her shoulders, his gaze suddenly very intent. "Why did you invent her, Caity? It seems like a curious thing to do, especially for you."

She told him half the truth. "At the time, you seemed set to marry Jodie Bergen, and I didn't think you were at all suited to each other."

Alec grinned. "Mama Maria doesn't agree. She said we were a perfect couple, and you know she claims to have second sight."

"She obviously needs an eye examination. She said we were a perfect couple, too. Remember?"

He crooked his finger under her chin and tilted her

face upward. "You're right. I guess that ought to warn me not to trust Mama Maria's judgments."

"Her pizza's more reliable than her folk wisdom," Caitlin said, hoping Alec wouldn't notice that she was perilously close to tears. "I can't believe you took Jodie to Mama Maria's," she wailed. "That's our special place."

He brushed his thumb over her lips, his touch gentle. "Is it?" he said huskily. "I didn't realize you felt so possessive about where I take my dates to eat pizza."

She swayed toward him. His head inched fractionally lower. "Choosing pizza toppings is a very intimate process," she whispered. "It tells you a lot about a person."

"Like kissing," he said, and closed the tiny gap between their mouths. "Like making love."

She knew from previous experience exactly what would happen the moment their lips touched. Sure enough, the fireworks exploded, the brass band began to play, her heart melted, her soul caught on fire. But none of the clichés really expressed the way she felt. She'd come home, Caitlin realized. With Alec's arms holding her, she felt as close to perfect happiness as she was likely to find here on earth.

When their kiss finally ended, he cupped her face in his hands and looked down at her, his eyes dark with tenderness. "It's time for us to stop playing games," he said softly. "No more lies, no more half-truths, no more mythical Helens, no more pretending

I'm interested in little girls like Jodie Bergen. Are you ready to stop running, Caity?''

She laughed shakily. "I can't run. My legs have turned to jelly."

"Great. But maybe I'd better kiss you one more time just to make sure." He captured her mouth again, covering her lips in a passionate, seeking kiss, miraculously tempered by sweetness. Caitlin closed her eyes and let the desire build slowly, fiercely, inside her.

"Caity." This time his voice was huskier. "Caity, I want to make love to you. Come to bed with me."

"Yes," she said, the last of her doubts vanishing in a blaze of fierce longing. "Alec, I love you so much."

His laughter held more than a hint of pain. "I've been waiting for years to hear you say that."

"You have? Does that mean you love me, too?"

He held her tight against his body. "Let me show you how much," he murmured, and took her hand to lead her into the bedroom.

LATER, SNUGLY WRAPPED in one of Alec's robes, Caitlin curled up in his lap in front of the fire. Resting her head on his shoulder, she sipped contentedly at a cup of fresh-brewed coffee.

Alec twined his hands around hers. The warmth from the cup seeped through their fingers. "Marry me?" he asked.

She smiled radiantly. "Yes, please."

"Does December the fifth sound like a good day? In Hapsburg, Ohio, with both our families present in full force?"

"I'd like that a lot." She gazed at him, replete with love, drowsy with happiness. "Do you think our families will be pleased?"

He laughed. "Only you could ask that question, Caity, my love. Our families have been trying to arrange this wedding for the past ten years at least. My mother finally got desperate and told me she was going to book the church and the Veterans' Hall for the reception, so I'd darn well better produce you as the bride!"

"She did?" Caitlin went pink with pleasure. "You mean you're not just marrying me because you've decided it's time to settle down? You really do love me?"

"Caity, my beloved idiot, I've loved you passionately, insanely and totally for years. Probably ever since you were sixteen and came to me by the fishing pond. Even then, you had the most kissable mouth I'd ever seen."

"Then what did you mean with all that nonsense about hiring Services Unlimited to find you a suitable bride?"

"I wouldn't call it nonsense, since it seems to have succeeded in capturing your attention at last. I can't claim credit for the idea, though. My mother suggested it to me, and I decided I had nothing to lose."

"You certainly grabbed my attention. I was furious

when you casually announced that you'd decided to get married. It took me about a week to realize why I was so angry. I wanted you for myself.''

''I kept trying to tell you how I felt, but you wouldn't listen. You just weren't ready to make a commitment, and I was terrified of scaring you off for good. Every time I tried to change the basis of our relationship, you ran a hundred miles in the opposite direction.''

''It's taken me a while to realize that marriage to you doesn't mean total loss of my identity.'' She sighed. ''You know, we'll have to do some hard thinking about juggling our careers. However much I love you, I'm not ready to give up my job. I'm just not the domestic type, Alec.''

''I wouldn't want you to change.'' He took her hand and brought it to his cheek. ''We'll make it work, Caity, don't worry.''

She knew there would be problems ahead, particularly when they had children, but she also knew that the rewards of marriage to Alec were going to make those problems seem trivial by comparison. She leaned forward and kissed him. ''Yes,'' she said. ''We'll make it work.''

The answering kiss he gave her was so intense it was a long time before either of them had breath or energy for any more conversation. Several minutes passed before she stirred in his arms. ''What about that woman your mother told me you wanted to marry? I think I'm jealous. You never told me her name."

He kissed her tenderly on the nose. "Idiot," he said lovingly. "That woman was you. My mother was trying to find out how you felt about me."

"You could have asked me yourself."

"And sent you fleeing? You weren't ready to get married, Caity. It's taken you a long time to realize that marriage isn't a trap, but a gateway."

"I got engaged to David," she protested.

"Because he was safe," Alec said. "I was terrified you might drift into marriage with him, but in my heart of hearts, I knew the two of you were never going to follow through on your commitment. David was kind, he was decent, and you didn't care two cents for him. That's why it felt safe for you to get engaged."

"Are you going to insist on psychoanalyzing me once we're married?"

He kissed her tenderly. "Only when I can't think of anything better to do." He straightened and poured her more coffee from the pot heating by the hearth. She smiled at him over the rim of the cup. "Mmm...what a fabulous man you are. You do realize I'm only marrying you for your coffee, don't you?"

"Don't forget my chocolates. Although I can't help thinking my superb skills in the bedroom must have something to do with your change of heart."

She pretended to consider. "No," she said at last. "It's definitely the coffee."

"Liar." He leaned over and expertly removed the cup from her fingers. Then he trailed tantalizing kisses over her cheeks and the hollows of her throat, while his hands wrought magic over the rest of her body. She arched toward him, immediately responsive, but he simply smiled, tormenting her with his refusal to give her the deeper, more satisfying kisses she craved. His lips hovered a breath away from hers.

"You can't win this game, Caity," he murmured. "Now, let's try again. Why did you agree to marry me?"

"For—your—coffee."

His hands brushed over the swell of her breast. His eyes danced with laughter—and desire. "Why are you marrying me?"

"Because I love you, you arrogant beast!"

"Amazing! That's the very same reason I'm marrying you."

"Prove it to me," she whispered.

He did.

EVEN THE OLD-TIMERS agreed that Hapsburg, Ohio, had never seen a more splendid wedding than that of Caitlin Elizabeth Howard and Alec Harrison Woodward. The locals were delighted that two of their own had shown the good sense to fall in love with each other, and they were forgiven for having taken so long to make up their minds.

The bride, looking ethereal in ivory satin, was declared the prettiest of the decade, and the groom—whose successful defense of Leon Mancuso had made news headlines across the country—looked both handsome and passionately in love. The maid of honor, Mrs. Sam Bergen, was pronounced too old for the role, but most guests conceded she looked more than okay in a gown of deep rose silk, which someone declared had been her own wedding dress.

If Hapsburg found the maid-of-honor situation rather odd and "big city," the flower girls met with unstinted approval, and the ring bearers, Matt and Zach, were considered amazingly well behaved. Both little boys refrained from throwing up until more than halfway through the reception, which everyone agreed was a minor miracle given the quantity of wedding cake they consumed.

Hapsburg wasn't impressed by the parade of Washington bigwigs who ventured into the Midwest hinterland for the wedding—it took more than a tuxedo and a fancy accent to impress a Hapsburgian—but the Grand Gourmet caterers were acknowledged to have done a terrific job with the buffet dinner, and the band from Cleveland was rated hot stuff. All in all, the Howards and the Woodwards had put on a darn good show, worthy of third-generation natives. The townfolk were content.

IN THEIR HOTEL SUITE in the Bahamas, Alec took Caitlin into his arms with a sigh of profound relief.

"Alone at last. Would you care for some champagne, Mrs. Woodward?"

"Mmm. Yes, please." She took the flute of champagne and followed him out onto the balcony overlooking the ocean. She felt a familiar thrill of pleasure as his arms closed around her waist, drawing her back against his body. Looking out across the endless vista of dark ocean, it seemed that her life shimmered ahead of her, dazzling with new possibilities and fresh horizons. A tropical breeze blew off the sea, warm, perfumed and gently caressing, the perfect benediction at the end of a perfect day. Caitlin wished she could capture her feelings at this moment and store them forever.

Alec's voice rippled over her, low, husky and full of promise. "I love you, Caity."

She turned in his arms. "I love you, too." She thought back over the day just ended. "I think everything went off well, don't you? Our families were ecstatic and our friends had a good time."

"Everything went wonderfully. Maybe even too well. From the gleam in my mother's eyes, I think we've just whetted her appetite."

"How so?"

"A few minutes before we left, I heard her discussing baby showers with you mother. And she wasn't talking about Merry."

Caitlin laughed, but her body flushed with the heat of sudden longing. "How much time to you think we

MONDAY MAN

Kristin Gabriel

For my sister, Linda,
who can always make me laugh.

CHAPTER ONE

MONDAYS WERE BAD DAYS for Nick Chamberlin. He'd come down with the chicken pox on a Monday. He'd wrecked his '79 Thunderbird on a Monday. He'd kissed his first girl on a Monday. Okay, technically that was a good thing. Only, the girl of his seven-year-old dreams didn't appreciate his advances and promptly knocked out his front tooth, which was eventually repaired by a sadistic dentist. On a Monday.

But that was all a very long time ago. Surely, today would be different. He was older now. Wiser. Immune to chicken pox and fast cars and dangerous women.

Nick studied the guy seated across the booth from him. A small ink stain bled though the pocket of his crisp white shirt, and a spot of ketchup smeared the front of his green clip-on tie. His plastic name tag read Captain Robby and his freckles and peach fuzz told Nick the kid couldn't be a day over seventeen.

A Monday-killer if he ever saw one.

"Interesting résumé, Mr. Chamberlin," Robby said, flipping the pages in the blue-bound folder.

"We've never had a cop apply at Farley's Fish Hut before."

"*Ex*-cop," Nick clipped.

Robby nodded. "Right." Then he folded his freckled hands together and cleared his throat. "One of my duties here is to hire responsible, dedicated people to serve on our crew. You'll have to start out as a cabin boy even though you're—" Robby flipped over the employment application "—thirty-three years old. That means you're not allowed to run the cash register or operate the French fry machine. But with some self-motivation and hard work you can advance to deckhand, then first mate, and maybe after that..." his reedy voice grew cocky "...even a captain."

Nick closed his eyes and reminded himself he didn't have any other viable options. "When can I start?"

When Robby didn't answer, he opened his eyes and found the teenager still staring at the employment application.

"Is there a problem?" Nick asked, steeling himself for the inevitable.

Robby cleared his throat. "This says...um...under felony convictions..."

"That I spent the last fifteen months in the Pickaway Correctional Center."

"You're an ex-con?" Robby shifted in his molded plastic chair.

Nick nodded, not bothering to explain how he had voluntarily taken the rap for someone else, and in the process ruined his career and his reputation. He'd also apparently even ruined his job prospects at Farley's Fish Hut, one of the few places in town that had granted him a job interview since his release from prison a week ago.

"Cool," Robby exclaimed. "I thought you looked kinda tough."

A minimum-security prison was hardly Alcatraz, but Nick didn't have time to explain the subtle nuances of the penal system. "Listen, Captain Robby," he said, checking his watch, "I'm due to pick up my grandmother at the library in ten minutes...."

"No problem." Robby held out his hand. "You start training tomorrow at two o'clock. Welcome aboard, Mr. Chamberlin."

Nick looked down at the flattened sheet of colorful cardboard in Robby's hand. "What's this?"

"Your hat. All the crew wear one when they're on deck. It's required."

Nick slowly reached for it. "It doesn't look like a hat."

Robby grinned. "You have to put it together. It's shaped like a cod. That's our specialty. Oh, that reminds me, you'll need to memorize the menu list and our slogan. Oceans Of Fish, Fries, And Fun For Everyone."

But Nick was still staring at the hat. So it had come to this. A thirty-three-year-old man with a college degree wearing a cod on his head and working his way up to the French fry machine. For five dollars and fifteen cents an hour.

Another Monday bites the dust.

THIS WAS Lucy Moore's lucky day.

She'd lost three pounds and found ninety-seven cents buried in her sofa. And she'd arrived at the Heritage Library employee parking lot just in time to save Gigi, Letitia Beaumont's pedigreed poodle, from a fate worse than death—the amorous attentions of a junkyard mutt cruising the nice side of town, where respectable dogs wore rhinestone collars and bows on their ears.

Not that Gigi couldn't use a little of the mutt's scrappy tenacity in her gene pool. So could her owner, the horrified and nearly hysterical chairwoman of the Heritage Library Foundation, Lucy thought as she gently shooed the mutt back toward his neighborhood—and hers. But she wisely kept that opinion to herself. Letitia expressed her eternal gratitude by promising to remember Lucy when the position of assistant senior librarian opened up.

Assistant senior librarian. It had a nice ring to it. Of course, not quite as nice as senior librarian, or even director of the Heritage Library. But not bad for a twenty-eight-year-old bookworm who grew up dirt-poor on the wrong side of Westview. And certainly better than her current position as staff librarian.

Lucy ran one hand over the smooth, green marble counter, warmed by the late-afternoon October sun slanting through the library windows. She couldn't wait to write to her brother Melvin and tell him all about it. Not that he would ever read it. He still returned all her letters unopened. Refused to take her phone calls. And generally irritated her with that masculine mix of bravado and martyrdom that always set her teeth on edge.

He'd been just as stubborn when they were growing up together. Of course, she'd been stubborn, too. She'd needed that mental toughness to survive the peer pressure on Bale Street. Avoiding the street gangs so she could earn a high-school diploma instead of a juvenile record. Spending all of her Saturday nights studying so she could win a full college scholarship to Ohio State University.

Through it all she'd always had her brother's support. Which was why she simply couldn't believe that now he expected her to sit back and do nothing while his life fell apart. He'd told her more than once to forget about him. To pretend she didn't even have a brother. To stay out of it, for her own good.

If she waited around for Melvin's consent, she'd never get anything accomplished. He simply worried too much. Recalled too many of her past mishaps. Like that annoying incident with the bleach. Pink underwear never hurt anybody. And weren't men of the nineties supposed to explore their feminine side?

It was time for Lucy to take matters into her own hands. Maybe once she proved herself to him, he'd learn to loosen up a little. Melvin needed help. Her help. And she needed a street-smart sidekick to do the grunt work. Someone tough and tenacious. Dependable and desperate. Someone like the man Sadie Chamberlin boasted about every week at the library's Monday-afternoon meeting of the Merry Widows Book Club.

Now the only question was, how lucky could Lucy get?

"I can't wait to meet your grandson," she said to the silver-haired woman approaching the circulation desk. "I hope he's the right man for the job. I need someone who's not afraid to get his hands dirty. A man who's not afraid, period."

"He's perfect," Sadie Chamberlin replied, shifting the bulging library tote bag from one blue-veined hand to the other. "Very well-rounded."

"I can't pay much," Lucy warned for the third time that afternoon. "That's why every P.I. in Westview has turned me down."

Sadie smiled and reached over to pat Lucy's hand. "The money won't be a problem, dear. Nicky just finished doing a little work for the state, so he's in between jobs at the moment. I'm sure he'll be thrilled with anything you have to offer."

A little of Lucy's enthusiasm wavered. Nicky sounded almost too good to be true. She'd heard Sadie's glowing accounts of his youth, the summers spent in Westview, Ohio, with his adoring grandparents. Maybe Sadie saw him through rose-colored bifocals. Maybe Nicky Chamberlin was a no-account nerd. Just like Lester Bonn, the director of the Heritage Library. He snorted when he laughed, wore his pants a good two inches above the top of his shoes and whined about *everything*. A man—and she used that term loosely—only a mother could love. Or a doting grandmother.

"I want to see him before I make up my mind for sure," Lucy announced. "I always go by first impressions."

"Fine, dear. Now stand up straight. My grandson should be here any minute."

Lucy tucked a stray wisp of hair behind her ear. "Shouldn't we have some sort of signal."

"Signal?"

"A code word to let you know if I want to hire him. I mean, if he's not the right man for the job I wouldn't want to hurt his feelings." *Or make him cry.*

Sadie's faded blue eyes lit up. "A secret code! That's a wonderful idea. How about…'Mary, Mary, quite contrary, how does your garden grow?'"

Lucy wrinkled her nose. "That might be a little hard to work into the conversation. How about 'nice hat.'"

"Nicky doesn't wear a hat. Now his grandfather never went out of the house without one. Always a distinguished gentleman, my Nicholas. Did I tell you Nicky's named after him?"

Only about eight hundred times. Lucy smiled, warmed by Sadie's affection for her late husband. "You've mentioned it."

"Do you like spaghetti with meatballs?"

Lucy shrugged. "Once in a while. Why?"

"No, dear, I mean for our secret code."

Lucy nodded. "That's perfect. If I want him, I'll ask for your recipe for spaghetti with meatballs."

Sadie clucked her tongue. "No, that won't work. I never cook Italian."

"Well, we've got to come up with something—" Lucy said, before Sadie interrupted her with an excited whisper.

"Here he comes!"

Lucy looked toward the door and her mouth went dry. Nicky Chamberlin looked nothing like a nerd. No horn-rimmed glasses. No short, rail-thin body. No high-water pants. He looked big and bad, with short, jet-black hair slicked back, piercing gray eyes and a square, don't-mess-with-me jaw.

He looked like a man who could take apart a building brick by brick with his bare hands. And judging by the stubborn set of his chin, he'd do just that if he thought it was necessary.

A street-smart soldier for hire. Cheap.

Lucy told herself to remain calm as a bolt of excitement surged through her blood. She didn't want to act hastily. Or do anything impulsive. She needed to give this some serious thought. Weigh the pros and the cons. Check into his background, at the very least.

She took a deep breath, gazed directly into Nicky Chamberlin's gunmetal eyes and said, "Spaghetti with meatballs."

NICK DIDN'T THINK his Monday could possibly get any worse. Until a bee stung him on his way into the library. So now on top of a throbbing headache from his interview with Captain Robby, he had a throbbing pain in his right shoulder from the sting. And a wide-eyed librarian talking nonsense to him.

He turned to his grandmother, taking the heavy tote bag out of her grasp. "Ready to go?"

Sadie frowned up at him. "Nicky Chamberlin, I expect you to mind your manners and speak to Lucy."

"Who's Lucy?"

The librarian raised her hand.

He turned toward her, the embedded stinger in his shoulder grating against his shirt. Nick noticed her eyes first—probably because they were big and round and staring openly at him—brown eyes flecked with gold and fringed with lush, dark lashes. He dropped his gaze from those eyes and found full, pink lips below a small, pert nose. Deliciously supple lips. Lips just made for kissing.

He mentally shook that image from his head, stunned to find himself fantasizing about Marian the Librarian. At least her hair looked the part, drawn back into an efficient knot at the nape of her neck. Except for those wisps of honey blond curls spilling over her smooth cheeks, teasing him with the promise of silky softness, tempting him to reach out and brush them off her face. Nick curled his hand into a fist to prevent him from doing just that.

He'd obviously been in prison too long.

"It's a pleasure to meet you, Mr. Chamberlin," she said at last, extending a slender hand for him to shake.

Nick reached out to grasp it, wincing as the stinger shifted painfully under his shirt at the movement. "Ow."

Lucy dropped his hand and frowned. "I'm sorry...I didn't mean to hurt you. My brother always believed a woman should be able to handle a firm handshake. I must have squeezed too hard." Her words sounded apologetic but her tone implied he was a wimp, and her big, brown eyes softened with disappointment.

Nick clenched his jaw, wondering why he cared about her opinion of him, especially when he'd stopped caring about anyone else's opinion a long time ago. Fifteen months to be exact. "No problem."

"What's the matter with you?" Sadie asked. "You look a little pale."

"Maybe he should lie down," Lucy suggested.

"It's nothing serious," he said. "It's just this damned—" he skittered a glance toward his grandmother "—darned stinger in my shoulder. A bee got me on the way in."

"You got stung?" Sadie asked, her pale blue eyes clouding with concern. She looked at Lucy. "Oh, dear. Now what?"

"Why don't I take him into the office and have a look at it?" Lucy suggested.

Sadie smiled. "That's a wonderful idea."

"No," Nick insisted. "I'll be fine."

"Unless you're allergic," Lucy said. "Then you could be dead in ten minutes. We've got a book called *How To Survive Venomous Bites and Stings.*" She began pecking at the keys on the computer in front of her. "I can see if it's on the shelf and look up the symptoms. We don't want to take any chances."

"That's not necessary," he said.

"Now you look flushed," Sadie observed, laying her palm on his forehead. "Maybe you should go rest for a while."

"I think that's an excellent idea," Lucy exclaimed, and then turned toward the back office with a frantic wave.

"Look, this is ridiculous," Nick interjected as a short, balding man in a tweed jacket and bow tie joined Lucy behind the circulation desk.

"Is there a problem, Lucy?"

"As a matter of fact, Lester, there's a very serious problem." She pointed at Nick. "This man just got stung by a bee and seems to be suffering some sort of reaction."

"I never..." Nick sputtered, but his grandmother placed a quieting hand on his shoulder, right on top of the stinger, turning his protest into a muted gasp of pain.

"You can see how much he's suffering," Lucy continued with a pitying glance at Nick. "We can only hope he doesn't sue the city for damages."

"A lawsuit?" Lester squeaked.

Nick rolled his eyes toward the tile ceiling and wondered if this Monday would ever end.

"Imagine the publicity, Lester," Lucy continued. "Vicious killer bees preventing entrance to the Heritage Library. Our patronage dwindles down to nothing. The staff protests the dangerous working conditions with a walkout. And the city council looks for a scapegoat."

"And I suppose everyone will assume this is my fault," Lester whined.

"Well, you are the library director," Lucy replied.

Lester nervously licked his thin lips. "What do you suggest we do?"

Lucy circled around to the front of the desk and hooked her arm through Nick's. "I'll take Mr. Chamberlin into the office so he can recover and rethink this pesky lawsuit idea of his. Can you handle the checkout line?" She motioned toward the long line of impatient patrons behind Nick and Sadie. "Mindy is still on break."

Lester nodded, his scanty mustache twitching nervously under his nose.

Sadie patted Nick's sore shoulder, and he had to steel himself to keep from flinching at the pain. "I'll just go visit with the members of my Merry Widows Book Club until you're through, dear," she said, nodding toward a small circle of white-haired women at a corner table. "Edith is telling her gall bladder story again, and I don't want to miss out on the good part."

Nick didn't say a word as Lucy led him into the

cramped library office and closed the door behind them, flipping the lock. Then she pushed him gently down into a worn office chair, swiveling it away from the sight of Lester's half-eaten peanut butter and jelly sandwich lying on top of the desk. "Alone at last."

The hair on the back of Nick's neck prickled at her words. It had been a long time since he'd been alone with a woman, but he still recognized the subtle signs of physical attraction. The assessing glances. The flush of anticipation. The locked door. Then he reminded himself that this was a sweet, innocent librarian. And that he'd always had an overactive imagination.

She moved around to face him and he couldn't help but notice how well she filled out her caramel silk pantsuit. "Will you take your shirt off for me?"

Nick blinked at her. "What did you say?"

"Your shirt." She reached into the desk drawer, pulling out a pair of tweezers. "I'll remove that stinger for you."

Nick shook his head. "Forget it. I'm not going to sue."

"Oh, that," she said with a beguiling smile. "That was just a ploy to get you alone."

He swallowed. *Alone.* Had he been that obvious in his attraction to her? He took note of the way she was looking at him with that hopeful gleam in her brown eyes.

"Look, Marian…" he began.

"The name's Lucy. Lucy Moore. And don't be

scared," she said, leaning over him as she briskly unbuttoned the front of his shirt. A stray wisp of her hair tickled his cheek. "It won't hurt too much."

His breath caught in his throat as her fingertips grazed against his bare chest. He stared up at her in disbelief as she peeled his shirt back over his shoulders.

"Now that I think about it," she mused, frowning down at him, "squeezing it might make it worse."

He shifted uncomfortably in the chair. "Squeezing *what?*"

"The stinger. I think you're supposed to scrape it off. Squeezing it injects more venom into the skin."

"Just get it out," he said, trying to ignore the fact that she'd just half undressed him.

She moved around to his back and tenderly traced one finger around the stinger. He closed his eyes at the bittersweet sensation.

"I'll have to use something else. Hold still."

He held still, every muscle relaxing under her touch. "Ouch!" he suddenly yelped, inching away from her. "What was that?"

"My fingernail. I used it to scrape off the stinger. There," she said cheerfully, lightly patting his shoulder, "all better."

"It doesn't feel better," he grumbled as he heard her fumbling through the desk drawers.

"You really do have a low tolerance for pain, don't you? Now sit still, while I find some ointment to rub on it."

"Don't bother."

"It's no bother, and I promise it won't hurt." Her fingers gently smoothed a thick salve over his shoulder blade. "You might even like it."

His animosity faded. It wasn't her fault this was a Monday. Or that a bee had stung him. Or that he still couldn't figure out how to put together that stupid cod hat. She just wanted to help him. Besides, she was cute and quirky and harmless, if he overlooked how she'd scraped her fingernail across his back. And her touch did feel good as she slowly rubbed the ointment into his sore shoulder. Too good.

"Listen, Lucy, I need to go…"

"Your grandmother said I could have you."

"What?" He shot halfway out of the chair.

She pushed him back down. "Don't move. I still need to put on a bandage."

He unclenched his jaw as she briskly pressed a bandage across the sting. "I don't know what you and my grandmother have cooked up, but I'm just not interested." *Nice, Chamberlin, crush her poor little librarian's heart.*

Lucy walked around to the front of the chair, wiping her fingers with a tissue. "But you haven't even heard my proposition yet."

"I don't want to hear it." He leaned forward, his tone softening. "It's nothing personal. I just don't have room for any complications in my life right now."

"I'll pay you."

Nick shook his head. She couldn't be that desperate. "Sorry, I'm still not interested."

She rolled her eyes. "Your grandmother said you were stubborn, but this is ridiculous."

"I'm not stubborn," he said. "I'm a total stranger. You don't know anything about me."

She tilted up her chin. "Yes I do. Sadie's told me everything about you. I know your favorite color is blue. Your favorite meal is fried chicken with mashed potatoes and cream gravy and apple pie for dessert. And I know that you've got a scar on your left knee from a skateboard accident when you were eight years old."

"Did you know I'm married?" he lied, ready to put an end to her fantasies once and for all.

Lucy blinked. "No…but that doesn't matter to me."

"It might matter to my wife," he said indignantly.

She shrugged her slender shoulders, her brow furrowed. "I don't see why it should. Unless your wife objects to us spending time together."

"I think it's *how* we'll be spending that time together that she'll object to," he said, feeling more ridiculous by the moment for having this hypothetical argument. He didn't have a wife. Didn't want a wife. Not even as a figment of his imagination.

"This is pointless." Nick rolled his sore shoulder, trying to assuage the odd tingling sensation near the sting. "The bottom line is I can't give you what you want."

She frowned. "Why not?"

For a librarian, she was incredibly dense.

"Because I'm not attracted to you."

Something flickered in her brown eyes until she blinked it away. "Does that really make a difference?"

"To me it does." He knew she already suspected he was a wimp. Why not seal the impression? He clenched his jaw, forcing the words out. "I'm a... sensitive guy."

"I've noticed." She narrowed her brown eyes. "I realize it might get a little rough, but I really thought you could handle it."

He swallowed. "What kind of librarian are you?"

"A very desperate one at the moment."

"I've noticed." He plowed one hand through his short hair, almost wishing he was back in prison. Anywhere but with this luscious, love-starved librarian who wouldn't take no for an answer. "But don't you think it's just a little dangerous to ask perfect strangers to have sex with you?"

Her mouth fell open. And stayed open. Until Nick shifted uncomfortably in his chair and wondered if he might have possibly misunderstood her. Possibly made an asinine fool of himself. And just possibly turned this into the worst Monday on record.

"So let me get this straight," she said at last, her cheeks a rosy pink. "You think I want you to..." she moistened her lips with her tongue "to *pay* you to..."

Nick cleared his throat. Twice. "Isn't that what you meant?"

"No. Absolutely not. It never even crossed my mind." Her gaze fell to his bare chest and her blush deepened. "Will you *please* put your shirt back on?"

He pulled the shirt back over his shoulders, ignoring the prickly sensation around the sting, while his fingers fumbled over each other in his haste to button it. "I'm sorry, I must have misunderstood...."

"Obviously," she said. Then a small smile tipped up her lips. "I suppose your wife would object to *that,* wouldn't she?"

Nick looked at her. "Well, actually...I'm not married."

Her smile faded. "You're not?"

He shook his head, his discomfort with the situation increasing at the same rate as the maddening itch on his shoulder. "I just wanted to make it clear that I'm not..."

"Interested," she finished for him. "I know. You've mentioned it at least five times now. I got the message loud and clear. You don't need to worry anymore, your virtue is safe with me."

"I—I don't want you to get the wrong impression," he stammered. "It's not that you're not appealing. I think you're absolutely gorgeous."

She narrowed her eyes in disbelief.

"All right, maybe not gorgeous. I mean...it's been a long time for me, so any woman looks pretty good...."

She raised one golden brow, daring him to bury himself even deeper.

Unfortunately, Nick could never refuse a dare. "You're very appealing for a librarian. I'm sure if the circumstances were different I might even be tempted myself...."

"Don't worry, Mr. Chamberlin," she assured him briskly. "The circumstances will *never* be different. I promise. Now can we get down to business?"

"Call me Nick," he said, absently rubbing his shoulder against the back of the chair. "And what business? Does my grandmother owe a small fortune in overdue fines?"

"No. This business is strictly personal." She held up both hands. "And before you get the wrong idea again, let me explain. I want to hire you to help my brother."

"Do I have to wear a hat?"

"What?"

"Never mind. Sadie obviously told you I'm looking for work, but I've already found a job."

"Oh." Her face fell. "Then you really aren't interested?"

Maybe it was a sense of misplaced guilt for turning down what she'd never offered in the first place. Or the distracting itch in his shoulder. Or just a case of temporary insanity. Whatever the reason, he thought the least he could do was hear her proposition. "What kind of job is it?"

She hesitated, her teeth grazing her lower lip. "Well...I'd call it a research project, of sorts."

"Could you be more specific?"

She squared her shoulders and looked him straight in the eye. "My brother is in jail on arson charges. His trial starts in six weeks. Sadie told me you used to be some kind of crack investigator. I want you to help me find evidence that proves he didn't do it."

Nick opened his mouth and then closed it again. At last he said, "And just how am I supposed to do that?"

"By helping me find the person who did start that fire. And enough evidence to set Melvin free."

"Melvin. Melvin Moore," he said, rolling the name over his tongue. It sounded vaguely familiar.

"I'll pay you three hundred dollars a week," she added. "That pencils out to eighteen hundred dollars for six weeks' work. That's all I've got left in my savings account."

Three hundred dollars a week was considerably more than Farley's Fish Hut. Plus the fringe benefits: no hat and no Captain Robby breathing down his neck. He could do some respectable detective work instead of spending his days dishing up fish nuggets and tuna dogs. *Dogs.* Then it clicked.

"Your brother is *Mad Dog Moore?*"

She tipped up her chin. "His real name is Melvin."

"He torched the old Hanover Building downtown. Wasn't it some kind of historic landmark?"

"It still is," Lucy said. "Most of the damage was

due to smoke and water. That building can still be restored. Melvin knew it needed work when he bought it eight months ago. He planned to turn the ground floor into a sports bar and renovate the upper floors into apartment units. So why would he burn it down?''

"For the insurance money,'' Nick replied, remembering the articles he'd read in the newspaper. One of the few pleasures of prison life. "He took out a hefty policy on that old building only a few weeks before the fire. It's a simple open-and-shut case.''

Lucy tipped up her chin. "Somebody obviously framed him.''

"Is this the same man who drove his motorcycle into traffic court and asked the judge if he'd like to go for a spin?''

"That was a long time ago. He's changed.''

"And didn't I read that he hot-wired the mayor's car as part of a gang initiation?''

"He was only fifteen at the time,'' Lucy explained. "Besides, everybody makes mistakes.''

Nick knew that only too well.

She folded her arms across her chest. "If you don't want to take the job, I'll find someone who will.''

"Maybe you should do that. Just how much did my grandmother tell you about me?''

Her expression softened. "A lot. She's very proud of you.''

"Did she tell you where I've been for the last fifteen months?''

"She said you had a job with the state."

He shook his head. Leave it to Gram to make his prison stay sound like a career opportunity. "I suppose you could say that. I was at the Pickaway Correctional Center."

"Oh, were you a guard?"

"Actually I worked in the laundry."

"But I thought prisoners usually worked in the laundry."

"That's right."

It took a moment for his words to sink in. "You mean you're an ex-convict?"

He nodded, waiting for the usual reaction. It would be interesting to see how she wiggled her way out of her job offer now.

"But that's wonderful! You'll be perfect."

He blinked. "I will?"

"Of course. Whoever framed Melvin isn't going to surrender easily. It could get rough out there. I need someone tough and cagey on my side. Someone who thinks like a criminal."

"Don't you even want to know my crime?"

She shook her head. "It doesn't matter. If you were only there for fifteen months, it couldn't be that bad, right? Besides, we need to concentrate on Melvin. That is, if you'll take the job."

He sighed. "You really think he's innocent?"

"No," she replied. "I *know* he's innocent. Despite all his brushes with the law, Melvin has never lied to me. My brother swears he didn't start that fire. And now I intend to prove it, with or without you.''

Nick closed his eyes. He admired her loyalty, but the word of a miscreant like Mad Dog Moore didn't hold much weight with him. Which left him with two choices. He could take this woman's money when he *knew* her brother was guilty. Or he could let someone else take her money, while he mopped the deck at Farley's Fish Hut. With a paper cod on his head.

He reached back to scratch the persistent itch on his shoulder blade. Maybe he should just take the job and prove to her that nobody but Mad Dog could be guilty. Prove it to her before she spent every cent she had on a worthless cause. Or before she let some greedy, incompetent private eye bleed her dry.

''All right, I'll do it,'' he said, trying to ignore that guilty twinge in the pit of his stomach. Knowing he'd never take the case if Farley's Fish Hut weren't his only other alternative. ''But I can't make you any promises.''

''I don't need any promises,'' she said cheerfully. ''Just results.''

''Speaking of results, I don't think this stuff is working.'' The ferocious itch spread in an ever-widening circle around the sting. ''Just what kind of ointment did you put on my shoulder?''

Her brown eyes widened with concern. ''Why? Isn't it any better?''

''No. And the itching is making me crazy.'' He

rubbed the back of his shoulder against the cracked vinyl padding on the chair.

She sighed. "That's too bad. I thought it might work."

"You thought what might work?"

"The peanut butter. It was all I could find." She smiled innocently at him. "You know that old saying Put Butter On A Burn. I thought maybe peanut butter might work for a sting."

Nick closed his eyes and took two deep breaths. "You put peanut butter on my shoulder?"

"From Lester's sandwich. I rubbed it in really well."

He didn't know whether to laugh or rip his shirt off and beg her to rake her fingernails across his back again. "I'm not allergic to bee stings, Lucy," he said with a preternatural calmness. Even now he could feel the huge, itchy, red welts rise up over his back and shoulder. "But I am allergic to peanuts."

"Oh, Nick, I'm so sorry. I shouldn't have experimented on you." Lucy nibbled her lower lip. "I hope this won't make you change your mind about working for me."

"It's not your fault," he said with a sigh of resignation. "It's a Monday."

Despite his discomfort and his lingering doubts, he'd given his word. He couldn't walk away now. Or run, as some small part of his brain was urging him to do at the moment. Warning him that Lucy Moore just might be the most dangerous woman he'd ever met.

He shoved that ludicrous thought back where it belonged, into his overactive imagination. Marian the Librarian didn't have a dangerous bone in her delectable body. Her most risky escapades probably involved eating raw cookie dough and not rewinding rented videotapes before she returned them.

He didn't have anything to worry about. *She was a librarian, after all.*

How dangerous could she get?

CHAPTER TWO

"THIS IS ILLEGAL. I can't believe I'm letting you talk me into this," Nick muttered as his gaze quickly scanned up and down the darkened street.

"We're not *technically* breaking in," Lucy said, wishing he'd stop worrying so much and just jimmy the lock already. Or let her do it. Her fingers itched to give it a try. For the first time in her life, she'd be participating in an adventure instead of just reading about it. "I really do have a key to this place somewhere. I just can't seem to find it."

She peered over his shoulder, watching him wiggle the nail file she'd given him into the keyhole. "I'm guessing you didn't serve time for breaking and entering. Why is this taking so long?"

"Because I'm giving myself a manicure!"

"You don't have to yell at me."

"I am not yelling at you," he said, slowly enunciating each word. "I'm all yelled out from your slamming that car door on my foot."

"I already told you that was an accident. And for somebody who said he didn't want to attract any attention, you certainly made enough noise."

Lucy heard him swear softly under his breath, but

she wasn't sure if the oath was directed at her or at the stubborn lock. That antihistamine he'd taken earlier was obviously making him cranky.

"I never should have agreed to come here tonight," he muttered, more to himself than to her. "We should have waited until tomorrow to search this place. On a nice, safe Tuesday."

"I have to work tomorrow," she said. "Besides, somebody might see us roaming around in here during the day." Somebody who might not like her snooping around the Hanover Building again. Maybe the same person who kept making crank phone calls to her apartment in the middle of the night and leaving footprints in the flower bed outside her bay window.

She watched Nick's back muscles shift under his chambray shirt as he picked the lock. She felt safer now, with him by her side. And more than a little guilty for not telling him about the possible danger. But she didn't know for certain if the phone calls and the footprints and the eerie sensation of someone watching her were connected to the fire and Melvin. And he hardly seemed like a man who would trust a woman's intuition. Especially hers.

"So what if somebody does see us?" he asked, twisting the file in the lock. "Your brother still owns this place, right?"

Lucy considered the question. "Well, actually..."

But a sharp, metallic click interrupted her. Nick turned to her and smiled. "We're in."

She followed him into the building, inhaling the faint, residual odor of acrid smoke in the cool, musty interior. Old places like this had always held a fascination for her. Full of untold stories of the people who had come and gone. She loved to imagine the events played out here over the last hundred years.

She sighed inwardly, thinking of Melvin's unfinished story. Hopefully she and Nick could steer it in the right direction. Because Lucy always hoped for happy endings.

"Stay here," Nick ordered. "I'll check out the upper floors."

He left her side before she could tell him she had no intention of becoming a bystander in this investigation, although she admired his take-charge attitude, his professional demeanor. And she really liked his smile, realizing it was the first time she'd seen it today. She especially liked that tiny cleft in his chin that made him seem almost friendly.

Unfortunately, his command hadn't sounded very friendly. It had sounded brusque. Impatient. And downright bossy. It reminded her of similar commands she'd reluctantly obeyed as a girl. Melvin's commands, delivered in an equally aggravating manner. *You stay put, Lucy. And stay out of trouble.* He hadn't trusted her to evade the bad crowd that was always so easy to find on Bale Street.

He'd never let his baby sister tag along with him and his rough-and-tumble gang of misfits, either.

Boys like Snake and Buzz and Weasel. Melvin didn't want her tangled up in his wild adventures.

Her brother had always worried about her. When she was six, she'd developed severe asthma, and suffered from chronic bouts for several years. Her wheezing terrified him. Especially since he was responsible for her while their mother worked double shifts at the potato chip factory. Their father spent most of his time at the corner tavern, in between visits to his parole officer.

Melvin and Lucy had soon learned to depend on each other. She'd help him with his homework, while he'd administered her medication and kept her supplied with library books. She spent most of her childhood curled up with a book, keeping company with a fascinating array of fictional characters.

Even in high school, she preferred the heroes in her books to the aimless boys hanging out on the street corner. Too many of her friends had gotten sidetracked by a handsome face. Bale Street was filled with women who had loved the wrong man. They'd traded their dreams for broken marriages and dead-end jobs and children to support.

But not Lucy. She'd woven her own fantasies, inspired by the feisty, indomitable characters that filled the pages of her books. She knew that a better life than Bale Street was possible for herself and her family. A life of respectability and opportunity and promise. So she played by all the rules.

After her parents died in a car crash when she was

twenty, Lucy only had Melvin left. And her dreams. It was a long, hard climb, but she was almost there. Only it wouldn't mean anything without her brother.

It just wasn't fair.

He'd made a break from his troubled past, but now faced twenty years in the state penitentiary for a crime he didn't commit. She was determined to face any obstacle, take any risk to set him free. Especially since she'd always wanted to do more than read about daring escapades and spine-tingling adventures.

Lucy wasn't going to play by the rules anymore.

She walked toward the south end of the Hanover Building, to the makeshift apartment Melvin had lived in during the renovations. Stopping in front of the door, she was surprised to find it slightly ajar. The fire hadn't come close to this part of the building and the last time she'd been here, shortly after his arrest, this door had been locked.

She pushed it open, assuming the police had come back at some point for more so-called evidence. And done a very sloppy job of it, she observed, as she moved into the middle of the disarray Melvin used to call his living room. The love seat and both armchairs lay overturned on the scuffed linoleum floor, foam stuffing spilling out of the jagged tears in the fabric. Glossy posters hung haphazardly on the wall, and dry cereal was piled in sugary pyramids on the kitchen counter next to the empty boxes.

All courtesy of the Westview police, who obviously didn't bother to clean up after themselves. No doubt they assumed a former resident of Bale Street wouldn't notice the difference.

Lucy tried to swallow the lump in her throat, but it wouldn't budge. As she turned into the tiny, utility kitchen for a glass of water, she heard footsteps outside the apartment door.

"Nick?" she called out, hearing something scrape against the closed door and then more footsteps.

"Nick?" Lucy called again, only louder this time.

No answer. No sound at all now outside that door. Lucy's breath caught in her throat as she heard the distinct shuffle of feet overhead. Nick checking out the upper floor. Which meant...

Which meant somebody else was down here with her. Somebody who didn't want her to know it.

Lucy plastered her back against the wall next to the door and frantically dug through the purse slung over her shoulder for some kind of weapon. She found a barrette, a pack of gum, a bookmark and an old throat lozenge. But nothing really useful like a gun or a baseball bat. Unfortunately, Nick still had her nail file.

She heard a low grunt on the other side of the wall and then more footsteps. Her fingers suddenly curled around another object inside her purse. It might not stop whoever was out there, but it could possibly slow him down long enough for her to escape.

She took a deep, shaky breath as more sounds emerged from beyond the door. She had two choices. Stay trapped in here while the intruder planned his next move, or confront him, using the element of surprise.

I can do this...I can do this...I can do this. Lucy pulled the impromptu weapon out of her purse and took a step toward the door. Then two. Then three.

The sounds had stopped again, but the hair prickling on her arms told her someone was still out there. She pulled the door open, wincing at the creak of the hinges, and peered out into the murky expanse. The silence seemed ominous now, the shadows malevolent, the air really dusty.

She sneezed—twice. Her gut twisted and her heart slammed against her ribs as she moved quickly away from the door, edging along the hallway wall. Even through her fear she sensed a frisson of excitement zipping through her body. The realization that her first adventure was just about to begin.

She could only hope it wouldn't be her last.

She froze as the soft patter of footsteps echoed just around the corner. They were steady now; determined. Her arms trembled slightly as she held them out straight in front of her, her weapon at the ready. She resisted the urge to turn and bolt, to flee instead of fight, and then a strange detachment settled over her. When the intruder suddenly rounded the corner, bearing down on her, she didn't scream or throw up or faint like she'd always imagined she might when confronted with danger. She just screwed her eyes tightly shut and squeezed the nozzle under her fingertip.

A yelp of pain ripped through the silence, followed by a thud. Lucy cracked open one eye to see the intruder hunched down on his knees, his face bent to the floor.

"Gotcha!" she exclaimed, ready to strike again if he so much as moved one of those bulging muscles. She tightened her hold on the travel-size can of hair spray and aimed the nozzle toward his dark head.

The man took a deep, shuddering breath. "Are you some kind of deranged lunatic?"

She opened both eyes and stared down at him in horror. "Nick?"

"Of course, it's me," he roared. "Who were you expecting...Jack the Ripper? I think you've blinded me. What is that stuff? Pepper spray?"

"No, it's hair spray. Super Hold. Unscented. I'm pretty sure it's nontoxic."

He slowly straightened up, then reached for his shirt pocket. He fumbled inside it for a moment before pulling out a handkerchief. "*Pretty sure.* Well, that's a big relief."

He wiped the sticky hair spray out of his eyes. Then he swabbed at his wet forehead, the dark strands of his hair stiff and glistening in the slivers of moonlight streaming through the grimy windows. "Don't you think you've already done enough damage to me for one day?"

"You don't understand. I heard footsteps." She dropped her voice down to barely a whisper. "Someone's in here with us."

"Yeah, well, if it's the hair police, I'm safe."

"Just listen," she implored.

He cocked his head to the side and listened for all of two seconds.

"I still don't hear anything."

"That's because you're yelling at me again. You've probably scared him off by now."

He stuffed the handkerchief back into his shirt pocket. "See how much easier that is than assaulting people with hair care products."

Lucy resisted the childish urge to stamp her foot on the floor. *Why wouldn't he take her seriously?* "But it might be the arsonist, returning to the scene of the crime."

He shook his head. "You've been reading too many mystery novels. That hardly ever happens. If you did hear something, it was probably just a mouse."

Then the distinct sound of loose bricks cascading to the floor echoed from one dark corner of the building.

"Loud mouse," she said dryly. "Do you want me to check it out?"

He got slowly to his feet. "No, you and your hair spray have done enough harm for one night. I'll handle it. You stay here."

Stay here. Again. Lucy pressed her lips together. Hadn't she just shown him that she could take care of herself?

But Nick didn't stick around long enough to see if

she obeyed his order. He turned and moved silently along the wall that led to the far corner.

Adrenaline still pumped through her veins and her can of hair spray still had at least one or two good shots left in it. Nick needed backup and she needed to redeem herself for spraying the wrong guy. And prove to him that she could hold her own in this investigation.

So she crept after him, unable now to even see his silhouette in the deepening shadows, but priding herself that her footsteps were just as soundless as his. Only one day in the cloak-and-dagger business and she'd already disabled a man who outweighed her by at least sixty pounds and was now tracking down a bad guy as if she'd been doing it for years. Lucy Moore—master spy.

Her fantasy came to an abrupt—and bruising—halt when she bumped up against something big and hard and immovable. Something that made her heart leap to her throat. Something that grabbed her tight and wouldn't let go.

Nick.

''Sorry,'' she gasped as he whipped her around so fast, her head snapped against the wall. He pressed her back hard against it, the full length of his powerful body pinning her in one easy motion. Her breath caught in her throat at the sheer strength of him. The painful grip of his hands on her shoulders loosened, but he didn't let go. She wriggled against him, her hands trapped against his hard chest.

"Don't move," he whispered, his lips brushing against her ear.

"Did you see something?"

He nodded, listening intently, his hands still grasping her shoulders and his rough cheek grazing her soft one. He stood there for several long, silent minutes. Then he lifted his head just far enough to look into her eyes, his mouth just a hairbreadth from her own. His heart beat a rapid tattoo beneath her fingertips as his steely gaze flicked to her mouth.

Lucy swallowed, mesmerized by the expression on his face. He leaned toward her, the motion so slight she couldn't even be certain he'd moved at all. Then he pulled his head back abruptly and his flinty gray eyes narrowed. "What are you trying to do to me?"

"I'm not doing anything to you," she whispered. "I'm just trying to help."

A muscle flickered in his jaw. "Lady, I don't need your kind of help." Then he pulled away from her, robbing her of the warmth of his body and any wild notions she might have entertained about Nick treating her like an equal partner in this investigation.

"Maybe you don't," she whispered, trying not to sound disappointed. "But Melvin does. Do you think I'm going to just stand around, just *stay put,* when I could help find the proof we need to set him free?"

He closed his eyes. "Lucy…we're not going to find any…"

A strangled cry echoed through the building as a wiry figure shot up from the corner and barreled through a pile of cardboard boxes as though pursued by demons. Nick spun around, one long arm extended to clothesline the man around the waist as he sped by, knocking the air out of him. The intruder went down like a rock, his eyes wide open and panicked as he gasped for air.

Nick towered over him, one foot pressed against the side of his neck, almost daring him to move.

"We caught him!" Lucy exclaimed.

The man on the floor swallowed convulsively, his prominent Adam's apple bobbing in his throat, then pointed one shaky finger in the direction of the corner. "R-r-rat," he breathed. "A big one."

Lucy squinted down at him. "Weasel?"

Nick looked at her. "He said *rat*." Then a hopeful gleam lit his eyes. "Lucy, if you're afraid of rats, why don't you wait for me in the car? I can handle this."

"I'm not afraid of rats," she informed him evenly. "I'm not afraid of Weasel, either." She smiled down at him. "Hey, Weasel, how's it going?"

"Hey…Lucy," Weasel said, his panicked expression fading as he blinked up at her. His admiring gaze traveled slowly up the length her body. "Wow, you look great. Really hot."

"Thanks," she replied, a blush warming her cheeks as she self-consciously smoothed down her blue mohair sweater.

Nick shifted his weight, until Weasel's eyes bulged out and odd gurgling noises bubbled out of his throat.

Lucy frowned up at him. "You're choking him. Get your foot off his neck and let him get up."

Nick eased off the pressure. "First, he answers a few of my questions." He glared down at him, looking as if he'd rather squash him than interrogate him. "How do you know Lucy?"

Weasel took a deep, unhampered breath and then his mouth twisted into a smirk. "She's my woman."

BY THE TIME Nick abandoned the temptation to grind his heel down Weasel's windpipe, Lucy had the guy up off the floor and resting comfortably in one of the wounded armchairs in Mad Dog's apartment.

Nick watched while she crooned over him, dabbing at the microscopic scrape on his forehead and reassuring him that the rat wouldn't make any sudden appearances. And if it did, she vowed to annihilate it with her hair spray.

Lucy the Terminator. Or in this case, *Exterminator*.

Nick rubbed one hand over the thick stubble on his jaw and wondered how he'd let his life get so out of control. He thought he could handle starting over. Playing it safe while he rebuilt his life. Structuring some sort of future, however bleak.

He thought he could handle Lucy.

Until those brief, tantalizing moments he'd had her backed against the wall. Her body soft and curvy in all the right places. Her silky hair smelling like vanilla. Her full, pink lips slightly parted and so tempting that his body tightened at the memory.

Then he shook the image from his head. At least she didn't seem to notice his short departure from reality. Probably because she couldn't keep her eyes or her hands off that…Weasel. Nick's gaze narrowed as he studied the man sprawled in the chair. He wore a black mesh muscle shirt and faded blue jeans with a trendy rip in each knee. His brown hair was neatly pulled back into a short ponytail. A colorful tattoo adorned each brawny arm.

He certainly hoped the guy wasn't serious about that "She's my woman" crack. Not that Nick wanted any claim to Lucy himself. His life was screwed up enough without involving himself with a kooky librarian—or any woman, for that matter. He didn't want that kind of responsibility, that kind of distraction. Not until he resolved his own problems, his own disappointments.

But Lucy could certainly do better than this lowlife.

"That feels so good," the lowlife said, his head lolling against the back of the chair. His eyelids fluttered shut as Lucy massaged his temples. "You've got magic fingers, Luce."

Nick stalked over to them. "It's time for Lucy and her magic fingers to take a rest. You've got some explaining to do."

Weasel cracked one eye open. "Are you still here?"

Nick leaned down, his voice low and menacing. "Here and in your face until you tell me what I want to know."

Lucy scowled at him. "Nick, have a little compassion. Weasel hit his head on the floor when you tackled him. He's got an awful headache now, possibly a concussion, as well as a nasty cut on his forehead."

"Maybe you should rub some peanut butter on it."

She tipped up her chin. "Maybe *you* should apologize."

She couldn't be serious. "Me? Apologize? I'm the good guy, remember?" He pointed to Weasel. "He's the bad guy."

Weasel held both hands up in front of him in mock surrender. "Hey, I'm innocent until proven guilty. I know that much."

Nick snorted. "I'll just bet you do. So let's lay out the incriminating evidence we've got against you so far." He counted off the offenses with a flick of his fingers. "Number one—breaking and entering into private property. Number two—stalking. Number three—"

"That's not fair," Lucy interjected, laying one hand on Weasel's burly shoulder. "Give him a chance to explain. And quit treating him like a common criminal."

Nick shrugged. "Hey, if the handcuffs fit…"

"It's all right, Luce," Weasel said, patting her hand. "I'm used to it." Then he arched his neck to look up at her. "But does Mad Dog know you're hanging around with a cop? I visited him at the jailhouse yesterday and he didn't say a word about it."

"Nick's not a cop," she assured him. "He's my private investigator."

Weasel turned to scowl at him. "He *smells* like a cop."

"You're way off base," Lucy said with a smile. "Tell him, Nick."

"I'm a cop," Nick replied, thoroughly enjoying the brief flare of panic in Weasel's eyes. Then he saw the puzzled look on Lucy's face. "All right, I'm not a cop," he admitted. "Not anymore."

"What's that supposed to mean?" she asked. "I thought you were an ex-con."

"I am."

"But that doesn't make any sense...."

Nick's jaw clenched. "Do we have to talk about this right now?"

Weasel clasped his hands behind his head. "No time like the present. So tell us, how did you land the big house? I'm guessing you're a dirty cop who got caught. Am I right? Was it a little money under the table? Some racketeering?"

"Actually, I killed a guy for asking too many dumb questions."

Lucy's brown eyes widened with apprehension. "You...killed a guy?"

"No," Nick replied, wishing he'd kept his mouth shut. Now she'd want to know all about him. He resisted the ridiculous urge to confide in her. To make her understand what he didn't fully understand himself. To assuage his sense of loss and betrayal. But this wasn't the time and certainly not the place. Besides, it would be a totally selfish act, and stupid. He couldn't tell her, or anyone. No matter what she thought of him now.

"I got released from duty for an ethics violation and served fifteen months in prison for possession of stolen property," Nick snapped. "Can we get on with the investigation now?"

Weasel shook his head. "The only thing worse than a cop is a *dirty* cop. Get rid of him, Luce. You don't need his kind of help."

"Yes I do," she said firmly. "This means he can think like a criminal *and* like a cop. He's just the man for me."

Her words thawed some frozen place deep in his soul, warming him from the inside out. Where others saw failure and disgrace, Lucy saw possibilities. She believed in him despite his past, believed he could prove her brother innocent.

Too bad he'd have to let her down. Because despite Lucy's optimism, Mad Dog was still the most obvious suspect. The *only* suspect. And the sooner she accepted that fact, the better.

Which was why he didn't tell her about the matchbook. The dirty, dilapidated, charcoal-smudged matchbook he'd found stuck under the floorboard after she'd nailed him with the hair spray. It had once been white, etched with now barely legible gold lettering. The police must have missed it while sorting through all the debris. And Nick was almost certain any prints they'd find on it would belong to Mad Dog Moore.

So he kept it hidden away in his shirt pocket. The last thing he wanted to do was get her hopes up. She was already the most dangerously optimistic person he'd ever met.

"Look, we've wasted enough time here already," Nick said gruffly. His gaze fixed on Weasel. "Ready to tell us your story?"

Weasel smirked up at him. "Once upon a time…"

"Weasel, please," Lucy murmured, gently squeezing his shoulder.

"All right," he said reluctantly. He looked up at Nick, his gaze serious now, but still belligerent. "What do you want to know?"

He wanted to know everything. Why Weasel chose tonight to break into the Hanover Building. What he was looking for. Why Lucy obviously liked him so much. Why it bothered Nick that she did.

"What's your connection to Lucy?" he asked, his curiosity getting the better of him.

"We go way back."

Nick propped one foot on a corner of the chair, his forearm resting on his knee. "Care to elaborate?"

Weasel leaned back in the chair. "I already told you, she's my woman."

"In your dreams, pal," Nick said, certain she wouldn't associate with a two-bit hood like Weasel. Nick had seen enough of his kind during his years on the force. Crass. Disrespectful. Lazy. He probably knew Lucy from the library. Sometimes bums hang out there.

"Hey, she wanted to marry me, *pal*," Weasel retorted. "But I'm a confirmed bachelor, so I had to turn her down."

Lucy planted her hands on her hips. "You might want to mention that I was only ten years old at the time."

Weasel feigned disappointment. "You mean the offer isn't good anymore?"

She smiled. "You're a confirmed bachelor, remember?"

Then she turned to Nick. "Actually, Weasel and I do go way back. We both grew up in the same neighborhood, on Bale Street. He lived two doors down and used to hang out with Melvin."

Bale Street? Somehow he couldn't imagine Lucy living in that decrepit, lawless part of town, although Weasel would fit right in.

"So what are you doing here now?" Nick asked him, casting a purposeful glance toward the scorched north wall. "Reliving the good old days? A little looting? Some breaking and entering?"

"*I've* got a key," Weasel said with a sneer. "How about you, Officer? Trying to impress the lady with some breaking and entering of your own?"

"It was my idea," Lucy interjected. "I couldn't find my key, but my nail file worked just as well."

Weasel shook his head. "Your key wouldn't have

worked at all, Luce. All the locks have been changed.''

"Who changed them?'' Nick asked, looking from Weasel to Lucy and back again. A faint, reminiscent gnawing in the pit of his stomach told him he didn't want to hear the answer. The same gnawing he used to get on the police force when something unexpected, and really bad, was just about to happen. And the guilty look on Lucy's face didn't make him feel any better.

"It must have been Vanessa,'' she mused.

He was almost certain he didn't want to know, but the cop in him made him ask the question. "Who's Vanessa?''

"Vanessa Beaumont,'' Weasel supplied. "She's Mad Dog's woman. Or at least she used to be until he became eligible for twenty years in the state pen. Princess Vanessa likes the bad boys, but only if they're available.''

"So who gave her permission to change the locks? Mad Dog?''

Weasel looked at Lucy. "You didn't tell him?''

Nick closed his eyes as his stomach clenched and twisted. After a Monday like this, he'd probably get an ulcer. And he'd name it Lucy. "Tell me what?''

She cleared her throat. "I must've forgotten to mention it in all the excitement.'' The wail of police sirens nearby almost drowned out her next words. But not quite. "Neither Melvin nor I actually own this building.''

"YOU HAVE THE RIGHT to remain silent," the police officer droned. The harsh red glare of the flashing lights illuminated the stark, implacable expression on Nick's face. "Any statement you make can be used against you in a court of law. You have the right to consult with an attorney...."

Lucy couldn't let another minute go by without at least trying to rectify this mess. *Her* mess. If only he'd given her a chance to explain! But Nick had simply stared at her when she'd admitted the truth. Shocked into silence, he'd allowed Weasel to slink away and the police to arrive, ignoring her suggestion that they make a run for it, as well. By the time the officer assessed the situation and easily apprehended Nick and Lucy, the shock on his granite face had faded to grim resignation.

"This is all a big misunderstanding," she interjected, cutting off the uniformed officer's recitation of the Miranda warnings.

"Shut up, Lucy," Nick said evenly.

The officer, a young man with a boyish face dusted with freckles, scowled at Nick before swinging his gaze to her. "Would you like to make a statement, ma'am?"

"Yes I would," she replied.

"No she wouldn't," Nick countered.

She stifled a sigh of exasperation. Didn't he realize that they could end up spending the night in jail over a simple misunderstanding? That might not bother him, but she still had a reputation to maintain.

"Yes, I'd like to make a statement, Officer," she insisted. "Several, in fact."

A pale blue sedan pulled up behind the police cruiser. The driver cut the lights and then lumbered out of the car.

"What have we got, Madison?" the new arrival asked, hitching up the baggy slacks of his wrinkled brown suit. His craggy face and thinning gray hair marked him in his late fifties. His world-weary attitude and the shoulder holster Lucy glimpsed beneath his jacket marked him as a plainclothes police officer.

Officer Madison nervously flipped through the notepad in his hands. "Looks like we interrupted a burglary in progress, Lieutenant," He held up Lucy's nail file. "They picked the lock with this."

She reached for it. "That's mine. I'd like it back, please." She knew they probably needed it as evidence, but it was one of a kind and had a lot of sentimental value. The fingernail file had belonged to her grandmother, also named Lucy, and had the letter *L* artfully etched in the genuine mother-of-pearl handle.

"All in good time," the man said, slipping her nail file back into the evidence bag. Then his gaze slid to Nick, and he stiffened with recognition. "Been a long time, Chamberlin."

"Lieutenant Delaney," Nick acknowledged with a slight nod of his head. "You're working late tonight."

"I'm pulling a double shift. We're a little short-handed down at the station. How long have you been—'' Lieutenant Delaney cleared his throat ''—back in town?''

''About a week.''

The lieutenant eyed the Hanover Building. ''You're keeping busy, I see.''

Lucy took a step forward. ''It's not what it looks like, Lieutenant. Nick didn't want to break into the building, but I forced him.''

''Lucy...'' Nick's voice sounded low and dangerous, but she ignored it, as well as the incredulous expression on Officer Madison's freckled face.

''He thought I owned this building. I told him I had a key.'' She caught her lower lip between her teeth. ''Well, actually, I do have a key. It just doesn't fit the lock anymore.'' She could feel Nick's piercing glare fixed on her. ''Did I mention that I want to file a complaint against the Westview police department?''

There was a pregnant silence.

Then Lieutenant Delaney looked at Nick. ''Is she for real?''

''Unfortunately for me, yes.''

Lucy bristled at the exchange. ''Yes, Lieutenant, I'm for real. So is my brother, the man your police department wants to send to prison for a crime he didn't commit. And then—'' she pointed toward the building ''—you add insult to injury by destroying his apartment. Melvin's personal belongings are my responsibility now. And I intend to see that...''

"Melvin?" Lieutenant Delaney interjected, his bushy gray brows furrowed with confusion.

"Mad Dog Moore," Nick supplied. "Meet his sister, Lucy."

The lieutenant's wrinkled forehead cleared, and to Lucy's astonishment—and chagrin—the man looked like he was trying to hide a smile.

"I think I'm beginning to understand the situation." He turned to Officer Madison. "I can handle it from here, Johnny. You go back to the beat. Oh, by the way—" he hitched up a thumb "—good job."

He waited until the police cruiser edged away from the curb and into the deserted street before turning back to Nick and Lucy.

"He's a good kid, but fresh from the academy. I try to keep an eye out for him." He looked at Nick and his face sobered. "Like your grandfather did for me. I…uh…never got a chance to offer you my condolences. Nicholas Chamberlin was a great cop. I'll never forget everything he did for me."

"Thanks," Nick said stiffly.

"That's why I'm gonna let you two off the hook," Lieutenant Delaney said, handing Lucy the bag containing her nail file, "this time. The building's secure and no harm's done. So stay out of trouble from now on, and don't make me sorry I cut you a break."

Lucy's knees went weak with relief. A night in jail might be a whole new adventure but it certainly wouldn't look good on her résumé, or help her secure the promotion she wanted so badly. "Thank you,

Lieutenant. You won't be sorry. I'm still new at this, but I'm a fast learner. And I can almost guarantee you that we won't break any more laws during our investigation.''

Nick groaned, covering his eyes with one hand.

''Good luck to you, Chamberlin,'' Lieutenant Delaney said, clapping Nick on the shoulder. ''Looks like you're gonna need it.''

CHAPTER THREE

HE'D TELL HER TONIGHT.

Nick tugged at one end of the black bow tie around his neck, unfurling the crooked knot for another attempt at tying it on straight. He never should have accepted Lucy's invitation for dinner. But she'd been so apologetic about the incident with the police and so determined to make it up to him. In the end, she'd simply worn him down. To the point that he'd agreed to wear a tuxedo, because she wanted to take him somewhere special.

Nick evened out the ends of the tie, then carefully began to knot it. He doubted this monkey suit would soften the blow when he told Lucy that he couldn't pursue the case because there simply was no case. He'd spent the last three days researching the Hanover Building fire and Mad Dog Moore and the insurance angle. He still needed to talk to his friend and former partner, Cole Rafferty, who had led the fire investigation, about any possible leads, new or old. But that was just a formality. Cole had obviously come to the same conclusion. Mad Dog Moore set that fire and now he had to face the consequences.

At the moment, those consequences almost seemed

preferable to facing Lucy when he told her to accept her brother's guilt and get on with her own life. Maybe he'd take away all her cutlery beforehand, just to be on the safe side.

With an impatient yank, Nick loosened the mangled bow tie once more, leaning closer to the small mirror in the attic bedroom. He'd used this room on visits to his grandparents' house ever since he was eight years old. His own parents, busy with careers and active in state politics, had shipped him off to Ohio every summer. As he grew older, it seemed only natural that Nick would follow in the footsteps of the grandfather he loved and admired so much. He attended the police academy in Cleveland, then joined the Westview force, a rookie the same year his grandfather was promoted to police chief.

It all seemed like a lifetime ago. His parents still lived in Oregon, exchanging cards with him at Christmas and birthdays. But they'd never invited him back home since his conviction.

Nick sighed. He knew he couldn't stay with Gram forever. This visit had already extended beyond his original intentions. Maybe he needed to take his own advice and get on with his life. Look for an apartment. Another job. A remote control with a mute button.

Because if he had to listen to one more song from *Oklahoma,* Gram's favorite musical, he was going to take his Glock 9 mm out of retirement and shoot the television set. She watched the videotape at least three times a day and listened to the soundtrack CD in between.

Not that living with Gram didn't have its advantages. He loved her cooking and her company. Enjoyed running errands for her and tinkering with her car. But when he caught himself humming "Surrey with the Fringe on Top," he knew it was time to start looking for a place of his own. A very *cheap* place.

He had to admit he'd miss his grandmother. Even if she did periodically drive him crazy. Because she also loved him unconditionally. She had been too torn apart by her husband's death a year and a half ago to even comprehend the events surrounding Nick's arrest and conviction. She'd always just accepted his vague explanation of making a few mistakes.

She'd never criticized or censored him, just offered her unending support and a promise that she'd be waiting for him when he got out. She'd also sent two dozen home-baked cookies every week, making him the most popular guy in his cell block.

Her unquestioning acceptance of his confession of the crime sometimes made him wonder if he suspected the real truth, but didn't want to face it. Prison had given him ample time to go over the event that changed his life forever. To wonder what would possess his grandfather, a highly respected former chief of police, to steal that marijuana from the evidence room at the police station. He'd come up with dozens of scenarios, but none of them made sense. And now, almost two years later, he still had more questions than answers.

Finally satisfied with the bow tie, he stared at his reflection in the mirror. The tux still fit after all this time, the black lapels neatly pressed and in stark contrast to the crisp, white, pleated dress shirt. He looked like the maître d' at Château Pierre. Maybe that's where Lucy planned to take him for dinner. Maybe they'd have a job opening.

The last time he'd dined at the Château Pierre had been two years ago at his grandfather's retirement party. The Westview Police Department had spared no expense to celebrate the exemplary thirty-five-year career of Police Chief Nicholas Chamberlin. He died a short four months later with his reputation and his secrets still intact.

Nick intended to keep it that way.

"Don't you look handsome," Sadie exclaimed as he descended the staircase that led into the living room. "And wait until you see Lucy." His grandmother swept one arm toward the stone fireplace, where Lucy stood studying the framed photographs on the mantel.

"Isn't she a dream, Nicky?"

More like his worst nightmare. Then she turned and smiled at him, and his heart stopped beating for one paralyzing moment.

What happened to his librarian?

Her honey blond hair swept down in gentle waves around her shoulders, framing her face and deceptively innocent smile. A shimmering ice blue cocktail dress clung to her slender figure, revealing surprisingly seductive curves in all the right places, curves that caught and held his attention longer than good manners or political correctness allowed. But Nick couldn't help himself. She looked delicious and wanton and more dangerous than she ever had before.

"Isn't she, Nicky?" Sadie asked.

He swallowed. "Isn't she…what?"

"A dream," Sadie insisted.

He nodded. A dream. He was dreaming. That had to be it. Or delusional. That hair spray she gassed him with probably wasn't hair spray at all, but some toxic, slow-acting nerve gas. He closed his eyes. Remember the hair spray, he told himself. The peanut butter. The other disasters Lucy Moore could lead him to with just one crook of her little finger.

He opened his eyes and breathed again. After tonight, he'd never see her again. After he told her about the overwhelming amount of evidence confirming Mad Dog's guilt, she'd never *want* to see him again.

"Hold still, dear," Sadie said, reaching up to straighten his tie. "There. Perfect. Now go stand next to Lucy. I've got to have a picture of the two of you."

"This isn't the prom, Gram," he protested. "And I'm sure Lucy made reservations. We don't want to be late."

"Don't worry," Lucy said. "We have plenty of time."

"Lucy, scoot over closer to Nicky," Sadie ordered, pulling the camera out of the case. "Nicky, relax. You look like you're facing a firing squad. Lucy, hook your arm through his. That's right. Now stand a little closer together. Closer..." Sadie held the viewfinder up to her eye. "All right everybody, smile! Say...spaghetti with meatballs."

"Take off the lens cap first," Nick advised.

She removed the lens cap and then frowned down at the 35 mm camera in her hands. "It seems like I'm forgetting something else."

"Film?" Lucy guessed.

"Batteries?" Nick asked.

Sadie snapped her fingers. "Oh, I remember now. Goodness, how could we forget? Nicky, go into the kitchen and get Lucy's corsage."

"Corsage?" he echoed.

"Yes, dear," Sadie said with a sly wink in his direction. "The corsage you ordered from the florist this afternoon. It arrived while you were dressing and I put it in the refrigerator for safekeeping."

"A corsage!" Lucy clasped her hands together. "Oh, Nick, you shouldn't have."

She was right. He shouldn't have. In fact, he hadn't. But he couldn't very well admit that now. Not with Lucy looking at him like that, flushed with pleasure. His grandmother, however, would have some explaining to do when he got home tonight.

But first he needed to figure out how to pin the delicate champagne rose corsage on Lucy's dress without actually touching her. He stood close to her, his head bent as he tried to pin on the flower, resisting the urge to look down her dress. Her silky hair brushed against his cheek and his fingers kept grazing the soft, warm skin beneath her collarbone as he fumbled with the pin, jabbing himself three times.

"Got it," he said at last, stepping away from her so fast, he tripped over the andiron next to the fireplace.

"Smile," Sadie chimed, snapping the picture just as he fell at Lucy's feet.

And it wasn't even a Monday.

LUCY'S GRIP TIGHTENED on the steering wheel as she drove through downtown Westview and fumed silently.

Three days. Three whole days without a word from him about the investigation. Nick sat in the passenger seat beside her, quiet, aloof. Already she could read him as well as any book. He was shutting her out of the case. Making her *stay put* while he continued to search for clues without her.

The aromatic scent of the corsage weakened her outrage. It almost made her feel guilty about pretending to take him out for dinner. How did he know champagne roses were her favorite? She'd never expected it, especially from Nick. He didn't seem like the romantic type.

He did, however, seem like the irritating type. The strong, silent, let-me-handle-everything type. The type who didn't bother to tell her he used to be a cop. *A dirty cop.* She still couldn't believe it. He seemed so noble. So forthright. So annoyingly honest.

Nick might not be a cop anymore, but he acted like a cop, thought like a cop. And if he thought he could exclude her from this investigation, then she was more determined than ever to prove him wrong.

"We're here," she announced, pulling into the crowded parking lot and cutting the engine.

Nick peered through the windshield at Westview's new civic auditorium, a gleaming brick-and-steel structure bathed in the numerous spotlights scattered over the manicured grounds. "I see that. The only question is why? I thought you were taking me out for dinner."

"Just stay close behind me and follow my lead," she said, hopping out of the car before he could question her further.

"Lucy!"

But she just kept walking, hearing Nick's muttered curses and hurried footsteps echoing behind her. Her heart raced in her chest as she approached the front entrance. She'd never done anything like this before in her life. It was calculated. Conniving. Simply wonderful.

She took a deep, calming breath and assessed the situation. A grim Jeeves at twelve o'clock, checking the invitations of the guests as they filed through the door. Security guard at two o'clock. He was well armed, but pudgy, and had to be at least sixty years old. Lucy was almost certain she and Nick could outrun him if it became necessary.

She ascended the first two steps, ready to put her plan into action, when Nick grasped her by the elbow.

"Do you mind telling me what's going on?"

Lucy shook her head. "Not now. They'll get suspicious. Just play along." She wiggled out of his grasp and moved up to the top step.

"Your invitation, madam?" the doorman requested, holding out one white-gloved hand.

"Of course," Lucy said, reaching into her beaded purse. She pulled out a card of ivory parchment and handed it to the doorman. Her pulses pounded as he looked at it.

"Mr. and Mrs. Reginald Van Whipple," he read aloud, then began checking his invitation list.

"That's right. And what is your name?"

"Alfred, ma'am," he murmured, his gray brow furrowed as his gaze moved up and down the list.

"Alfred." Lucy turned to Nick with a bright, phony smile. "Remember that name, Reggie. We'll want to tell Letitia how fortunate she is to have such a competent man on staff." She leaned forward, resting her hand on Alfred's forearm. "Reggie and I just flew in from Palm Springs. It was an exhausting trip, but we just couldn't let Letitia down. And it *is* all for charity."

"Yes, of course..." Alfred muttered. "I'm sorry, Mrs. Van Whipple, but I can't seem to find your name on Mrs. Beaumont's list."

"Oh, dear, we simply *must* be there. We're always invited to all the best parties. Dear Letitia and I go way back. Did she ever tell you the story of how we first met eleven years ago? It was March third, a rainy Friday..." she began, eliciting impatient groans from the gathering crowd behind them.

"Perhaps the omission was just an oversight," Alfred said. "After all, you do have an invitation."

"Indeed, we do," Lucy said, her knees weak with relief. "Reginald, tip this darling man."

Nick looked at her. "What?"

"A tip, darling." Would it kill him to help her out a little here? "Just a little something to show Alfred our appreciation."

Nick reached for his wallet. "Anything for you, my darling Cruella. But all I've got is a twenty."

"Very good, sir," the doorman said, neatly plucking the bill out of Nick's hand. "Please enjoy your evening."

Lucy sailed into the ballroom foyer. She pulled a stem from a large vase of white carnations while she waited for Nick, snapping off the blossom with her fingernail.

"That was quite a performance, Mrs. Van Whipple," Nick said, joining her. "What do you do for an encore?"

She stuck the carnation in the buttonhole on his lapel. "I dance," she replied, pulling him onto the ballroom floor before he could protest.

"So who are the Van Whipples?" he asked as he

circled his arm around her waist, clasping her hand in his.

Lucy smiled up at him. "We are, for tonight anyway. Mr. and Mrs. Van Whipple are the lead characters in one of my favorite mystery novels, *High Society Sleuths.*" Then she scowled. "And her name is Penelope, not Cruella."

"My mistake." He skillfully maneuvered them around an elderly couple performing an impromptu tango.

"So how exactly did Reginald and Penelope get an invitation to this shindig?"

"We're crashing. The Beaumonts do a lot of charity work, and tonight they're hosting a fund-raiser for the Friends of Westview Association. Letitia Beaumont also heads the Heritage Library Foundation. She often uses the library staff for personal business, so I wasn't surprised when she asked me to address the invitations."

"Enter the Van Whipples."

"Only because I couldn't afford the one-thousand-per-plate donation needed to finagle an invitation."

He whistled low. "A thousand dollars per plate? Must be some great food." Then he looked at her. "Don't you feel the least bit guilty, Mrs. Van Whipple, for enjoying a dinner you don't intend to pay for?"

"Don't worry," she told him, nestling her head against his sturdy shoulder as they swayed to the slow, languorous music. "I intend to contribute something."

She closed her eyes, aware of the pressure of his broad hand on the small of her back. *No harm in enjoying a brief respite from their mission while waiting for phase two to begin,* she thought to herself as they floated across the dance floor. No harm in pretending to enjoy Nick's arms around her, either. Or the bulge of muscles beneath her fingertips. Reminding her of his strength. His power. His endurance.

"Ouch," he exclaimed as she missed a step, grinding the spiked heel of her shoe into his foot.

"Oops, sorry," Lucy apologized, embarrassed at her lack of coordination. Reginald Van Whipple never complained about a little discomfort. Even when his wife accidentally shot him in the leg, mistaking him for the villain. "Are you all right?"

"I'm fine," he replied. "Just promise me that Reginald doesn't suffer some horrible, torturous death before the story ends."

"Of course not. You worry too much," Lucy murmured next to his ear. "Relax. Trust me."

"Said the spider to the fly."

She didn't understand his cynicism. They'd made it through the door. Now they could enjoy the party until it was time to put her plan into action. "Maybe I just want to show you a good time. Maybe I thought you could make some connections here that might benefit the case."

"Listen, Lucy. We need to talk about the case."

"I agree," she said. "You've been shutting me out of the investigation, Nick. I'm intelligent, resourceful. All I want is a little respect."

"I do respect you," he said softly against her ear. "As a librarian. You are not, however, Penelope Van Whipple, high society sleuth. And you don't seem to realize that all these silly games of yours could lead to serious trouble."

"I know this isn't a game," she replied. "My brother's future is at stake. I may be all that stands between his freedom and twenty years in the state pen."

"So do you mind telling me how crashing this party to sip champagne and dance the night away accomplishes that?"

"Not at all," she said. "My instincts tell me Vanessa knows something about the fire. But we need to get close to her to find out."

"Vanessa Beaumont? The current owner?"

Lucy nodded. "She financed Melvin's purchase and renovation of the building. According to the contract, if he missed more than two payments, an option clause allowed the ownership to revert to her."

"So while Mad Dog sits in jail awaiting his trial, Vanessa exercised the option clause," Nick deduced. "Not a very understanding girlfriend, is she?"

"Ex-girlfriend," Lucy clarified. "She broke up with him after his arrest. Vanessa isn't exactly the loyal type."

"How did they ever get together in the first place?"

She sighed. "They met at a literacy reception at the Heritage Library. Letitia brought Vanessa and I invited Melvin. Unfortunately, he's attracted to thin, gorgeous and shallow."

"And Vanessa's here tonight?" he asked, looking eagerly around the room. A little too eagerly in Lucy's opinion.

"Yes."

"So why not just give Vanessa a call and ask to talk about the case?"

"I tried that already."

"And?"

"And she said no. We're not exactly in the same social circle."

"So you're hoping that rubbing sequined elbows together tonight might convince her to open up?"

"Of course not. I'm hoping my donation will convince her."

Nick raised a brow. "I was under the impression you don't have much money."

"I don't. But I'm not donating money."

"What then?"

She grabbed his hand, pulling him off the dance floor. He still didn't seem ready to join in the spirit of the occasion. Maybe he was hungry. "Shall we go help ourselves to the appetizers?"

"Not until you finish answering my questions."

"They have shrimp cocktail. And I think I saw some buffalo wings."

"Lucy…"

"Or a vegetable tray if you're trying to stay in shape. Did I mention how nice you look in your tux?"

"Thank you. Did I mention how good you are at evasion?"

She smiled. "Thank you."

He shook his head. "I didn't mean it as a compliment."

She looked wistfully over at the crowded buffet table. "Why don't we finish this discussion after we eat?"

The squeal of a microphone forestalled his reply as a portly gentleman in a white tie and tails stepped onto the raised platform in the center of the room.

Just in time.

Nick moved a step closer to her, his tone softening. "Why are you afraid to tell me about your donation, Lucy? Is it…I mean, there's nothing…illegal about it, is there?"

She blinked up at him in surprise. "Of course not. Whatever gave you that idea?"

"Maybe because you're acting so guilty about it."

The man on stage tapped the microphone several times. "Testing one, two, three…"

"That's silly. I don't feel the least bit guilty."

"So then tell me," he insisted.

"Tell you what?"

A muscle flickered in his jaw. "What you're donating to lure Vanessa into discussing the case."

"You."

He gaped at her. "What?"

Lucy reached up to straighten the white carnation on his lapel. "Didn't you understand my answer?"

"Didn't you understand my question?"

"Ladies and gentlemen, may I have your attention…"

"You're my donation, Nick. Now I don't have a lot of time to explain, so just go with the flow. I already signed you up. You can't back out now."

He frowned at her. "Signed me up? For what?"

"…it's now time for that exciting event you've all been waiting for…."

She gave his hand an encouraging squeeze. "Don't look so apprehensive. It's painless, I promise you."

"I don't like the sound of this," he announced. "What exactly did you get me into?"

"…if the usherettes will please escort all the gentlemen wearing white carnations to center stage."

Lucy smiled up at him. "The bachelor auction."

A perky usherette hauled Nick off before he could say another word—which was fortunate for Lucy, judging by the look on his face. That wait-until-I-get-my-hands-on-you look. And she knew without a doubt that the only place his hands wanted to be were wrapped around her neck.

His look only confirmed her earlier decision not to tell him about the bachelor auction in advance. Sadie had warned her that Nick didn't like to call attention to himself. Tended to be touchy about public exhibitions. Hated surprises.

But Sadie hadn't said anything about an aversion to charitable donations. As Lucy watched him reluctantly ascend the stage, she knew she'd made the right decision. He probably just avoided events like this out of a sense of self-preservation.

Because what woman wouldn't want a man like him?

Not her, she told herself firmly. She needed to concentrate on the investigation, not her love life. Besides, he was an ex-con, which made him definitely off-limits. She hadn't clawed her way up from Bale Street to a respectable life and career to throw it all away for a pretty face.

She wanted to fall in love—someday. With a man who met all her requirements. He needed a good career, a steady income, a spotless background. No Bale Street bums for her. Unfortunately, Nick didn't fit into any of her required categories. He was unemployed, broke and had a criminal record as well as a reputation as a dirty cop. She'd seen enough women on Bale Street dragged down by the men in their lives.

Not that she ever had to worry about choosing between him and her dreams of success. Nick had made it crystal clear in the library office last Monday that she couldn't interest him if she danced buck naked on top of his bed. Those weren't his exact words, but she didn't need to be hit over the head with a book of rejection lines to get the hint.

However, from a perfectly objective viewpoint, she couldn't help but notice how easily he surpassed the other bachelors gathered on the stage. He wasn't movie-star handsome. His nose crooked just a little in the middle, as if a break never quite healed properly. That, combined with the small scar on his square chin and his flinty gray eyes, gave him a subtle edge of roughness that appealed rather than frightened.

His impressive height made him stand literally head and broad shoulders above the rest. She swallowed, remembering the sight of those bare, brawny shoulders, and that wide expanse of hairy chest that gradually narrowed to a lean waist and taut, rippling stomach. The feel of those hard muscles flexing beneath her fingertips…

Lucy swallowed again, her throat uncomfortably parched. Then she glanced over to the other side of the stage, hoping she wasn't the only woman to notice how easily Nick Chamberlin stood out in this crowd of pampered blue bloods.

She wasn't disappointed.

Vanessa Beaumont sat at a cordoned table adjacent to the stage, sharing a shrimp cocktail with her adoring father while her eyes feasted on Nick.

She'd taken the bait.

Lucy let out her pent-up breath, relieved that her assessment of Melvin's old girlfriend had proven right on target. Vanessa had grown up rich and pampered, cutting her capped teeth on premed preppies and boys from Snob Hill. Now she preferred men with more raw edges. Tough and gritty, with a hint of danger about them. Men like Nick.

She experienced a momentary twinge of uneasiness watching Vanessa drool into her napkin. Nick certainly wouldn't be duped by Vanessa's blatant sexuality and millions of dollars in the bank. He had more sense and integrity than that.

Didn't he?

"Good evening," the emcee bellowed into the microphone. "I'm Ralph Rooney, president of the Friends of Westview Association, and I'll be your emcee. Welcome to our third annual fund-raiser and bachelor auction."

The crowd erupted into applause.

"I'd like to thank Harold and Letitia Beaumont for hosting the event this year. According to the association's police liaison, Lieutenant Ed Delaney, last year's donation has made it possible for the police department to continue the Protégé Project. This is a project that gives at-risk juveniles and inner-city residents temporary employment. It provides them with a paycheck, plenty of job experience and networking opportunities for those individuals with the drive and the gumption to succeed."

Ralph waited for the applause to fade before he continued. "We have several participants in the Protégé Project working here tonight. They're employed as valets, coat-check clerks and bartenders. So tonight you can actually see your donations at work.''

Lucy politely applauded with the rest of the crowd until she saw Letitia Beaumont squinting in her direction. She surreptitiously moved behind a potted palm.

''Now the moment you've all been waiting for,'' Ralph announced. ''Ladies, have we got a fine selection of bachelors here for you to choose from this evening.''

Piercing wolf whistles and shouts from the female audience members filled the air.

''Over here, big boy!''

''Pump it up, fellas!''

''Let's see some skin!''

The Friends of Westview Annual Fund-Raiser and Bachelor Auction generated a lot of money and drew women from all over the state, most of them successful, aggressive career women who weren't afraid to go after what they wanted—or whom.

Several of the bachelors on stage grew fidgety. Some pranced and preened to the appreciative cheers of the crowd of ravenous women. Nick just stood there and glared at Lucy.

She tugged up the corners of her mouth with her fingers, motioning for him to smile.

''The rules are simple,'' Ralph continued. ''The highest bidder gets her man for a date on the town. For simplicity and convenience, the bachelors will be notified of the arrangements through the Friends of Westview office secretary.''

A muted drum roll sounded from the orchestra pit. ''So without further ado,'' Ralph bellowed, ''it's time for our bachelor auction. And to kick off tonight's affair we've received a special request from the audience—'' he winked in Vanessa's direction ''—to begin with this bachelor right here.'' Ralph clapped his hand on Nick's shoulder.

The cheers and applause grew even more raucous.

Ralph conferred for a moment with Lucy's reluctant donation and then checked the information card she'd sent in yesterday. ''We've got a fine specimen here, ladies. Mr. Nick Chamberlin. A real man's man. Nick enjoys moonlit walks, candlelight dinners and cuddling.''

Nick visibly cringed.

''Do I hear a bid of two hundred dollars?''

Several women screamed their bid at once. So many of them wanted Nick, it was hard for Lucy to keep track as the bidding quickly escalated.

''Five hundred!''

''Seven fifty!''

''One thousand dollars!''

Lucy couldn't even see Vanessa anymore as a throng of potential buyers, young and old, milled around the edge of the stage. She rose on her tiptoes, scanning the crowd through the palm fronds as the emcee whetted their appetites even more.

"Turn around, Nick, and let the ladies see the whole package," Ralph Rooney insisted.

A soprano chorus of appreciative oohs and aahs mingled with wolf whistles from the crowd of women.

The emcee egged them on. "Any woman who wins a date with this bachelor will certainly have her hands full. Take a good look, ladies, before you pass up this hunk of USDA prime beefcake."

"Fifteen hundred dollars," screeched a frantic matron next to Lucy.

"Fifteen seventy-five," a hoarse debutante called out.

Lucy stumbled over the potted plant and almost got trampled in the process.

"Sixteen fifty."

"Seventeen hundred."

Gradually the frenzied pace of the bidding slowed until only a few, determined voices remained in the fray.

"Going once," the emcee called at last.

Lucy caught her breath and held it.

"Going twice."

Nick mouthed a few words at her from the stage that at first she interpreted as "I'm going to kill you." But he couldn't be *that* upset about an innocent bachelor auction. He probably meant he was going to *bill* her. And, of course, she intended to pay him for a good night's work.

"Sold! For two thousand dollars," Ralph Rooney announced, "to Miss Vanessa Beaumont."

"THE MONEY GOES to a good cause," Lucy stated, driving through the lighted streets of Westview. She wondered how much longer Nick could last without saying a word.

Maybe he was a little bit upset after all.

"It's not like I sold you into bondage. It's only one date."

Nick shifted in the passenger seat, piercing her with his merciless gaze.

"Look on the bright side. Most men would give a year's salary to go out with Vanessa," she continued. "Although personally, I don't see the attraction. In my opinion, she's a total flake. I can't figure out what guys find so appealing about her. I mean, unless you're into big breasts, long legs and flawless skin, what is there to like? She's shallow, greedy and possessive."

He just kept staring at her.

"Don't you think this silent treatment is just a bit childish?" she exclaimed, unnerved by his unblinking perusal. "If you're upset about what happened tonight, just say so."

"I'm upset about what happened tonight."

Lucy smiled. "That's better. It's not healthy to keep your feelings all bottled up inside, Nick. Now that we've got that out into the open, we can concentrate on our next step. I think we need to expand our list of suspects. Vanessa is my choice as pyromaniac of the year, but I overheard talk tonight that Ralph Rooney made an offer to buy the Hanover Building. Maybe we should keep an eye on him, too.''

He met her suggestion with more tight-lipped silence. His attitude bewildered her. Tonight had been a major success. Vanessa had fallen right into their trap. But Nick certainly didn't act very happy about it. Maybe he resented Lucy springing the bachelor auction on him without warning. Or maybe he simply didn't like taking orders from a librarian. As a former police detective, he was probably used to running the show.

She looked over at him, anxious to make amends with her new partner. ''So, Nick, do you have any ideas?''

He drew himself up in the seat, one hand gripping the dashboard so tightly, his knuckles turned white. ''Just one.'' The softly spoken words belied the menace in his tone. ''I'm resigning from this job. Effective immediately.''

Her mouth dropped open. ''You can't do that.''

He settled back against the seat. ''Just watch me.''

She turned off the street into a restaurant parking lot, certain he couldn't be serious. Quitting meant giving up, and Lucy simply didn't believe in giving up. Giving up meant spending your life on Bale Street. Giving up meant watching your brother serve twenty years in state prison. Giving up meant forfeiting your dreams. It simply wasn't an option.

She cruised up the drive to the fast-food menu box. "You're not thinking clearly. Where could you find a job more exciting than this one?" she asked as she rolled down her window. "You're probably just hungry. You'll feel better after we eat."

"Ahoy, mate!" crackled a voice from the speaker. "What's your pleasure?"

Lucy leaned her head out the window. "I'll have an order of fish nuggets, large fries and a Farley's Hurricane shake. Chocolate."

"Would you like candy sprinkles or minimarshmallows with that Hurricane, ma'am?"

"Sprinkles." She turned to Nick. "What do you want?"

He stared disconsolately at the bright neon Farley's Fish Hut menu box, topped by a large, plastic cod. "I just want to wake up from this nightmare."

"Don't you want something to eat?" she asked, feeling a twinge of guilt. "I promised you supper tonight and you haven't eaten a thing. They've got great fish nuggets here. Or you might want to try the cod fingers. Cod's their specialty."

Nick paled. "So I've heard. Thanks anyway, but I think I'll pass."

Lucy pulled up to the drive-thru window and gave her money to a pimply-faced teenager with a cod hat on his head.

"Hey, Nick," the teenager called, leaning down to peer through the driver's side window. "Good to see ya, buddy."

Lucy turned to her stony companion. "Do you know him?"

"That's...Captain Robby," he replied, acknowledging the teenager with a short nod.

Lucy took the bulging, greasy sack Captain Robby handed her and then rolled up the window. The aroma of fish and fries filled the car. Maybe the food would work its magic on Nick. There was nothing like a sack full of salty, saturated fats to bring her out of a bad mood.

"Mmm," she breathed. "Doesn't it smell heavenly? Are you sure you're not hungry?" She held up a fried fish nugget. "I'm willing to share."

He turned his gaze away from her food and stared out the window. "No, thanks. I've lost my appetite."

"That's too bad," she said, munching on a French fry. "So where did you meet Captain Robby?"

"Listen, Lucy," he began, raking a hand through his hair. "About my resignation... I might have been a little hasty."

She looked up from her Farley's Hurricane shake. "Really?"

He hesitated a moment, his gaze fixed on the colorful dancing cod decorating the take-out sack, then he nodded. "Really. I'm not quite ready to resign yet."

"I knew you'd see it my way," she said, cheerfully munching on a crispy fish nugget. "And you'll see the wisdom of this date with Vanessa, too. You just need a little time to adjust to the idea."

"Time," he echoed, leaning back against the headrest as he closed his eyes. "Yeah, that's what I need…a little time."

THIRTY MINUTES LATER, Lucy was humming under her breath as she unlocked the door to her apartment, proud of her part in tonight's success. *Mission accomplished.* With a well-paired investigative team like her and Nick, the real arsonist didn't stand a chance.

"I'm home," she called out, closing the door behind her and hanging her purse on the coat tree.

A plaintive meow sounded from under the sofa.

Lucy bent down to coax the black cat out of its hiding place. "Hello, Sherlock. Sorry I took so long, but I brought you a treat."

She pulled a lukewarm fish nugget out of the crumpled take-out bag, peeling the crispy layer off the top. Then she crumbled the flaky white meat into a small plastic bowl. "From Farley's Fish Hut. Your favorite."

The cat just looked up at her and meowed again.

"What's the matter, Sherlock?" Lucy asked, scooping him up into her arms. "Did we get another one of those phone calls?"

She looked over at the answering machine and saw it blinking at her.

Not again.

With a sigh of resignation, she punched the message retrieval button. The first call sounded uncomfortably familiar: a man breathing heavily while he called her name in an eerie singsong voice. Like Tiny Tim with a head cold. Creepy, but probably harmless.

It was the second call that made her heart jump into her throat.

"Hey, Luce. It's me, Melvin. We've got trouble."

CHAPTER FOUR

MELVIN "MAD DOG" MOORE sat in the visitors' room of the county lockup the next morning and glared at his sister. Usually his baleful expression and brawny build sent both men and women scurrying across the street to avoid crossing his path. But Lucy just smiled at him, knowing full well his bark was worse than his bite.

"You look wonderful," she said, sitting across a wide wooden table from him, a twelve-inch-thick pane of Plexiglas between them. She took in his wavy blond hair, dark brown eyes and smooth-shaven cheeks. "I'm glad you got rid of the beard. I've always loved that dimple on your chin."

"It's not a dimple," Melvin growled. "It's a scar. I got it in a fight at Harrigan's Bar."

"Who was your opponent? A plastic surgeon?"

His hard mouth tipped up in a smile. "All right. So I can't keep any secrets from my baby sister. Just don't let that dimple story get spread around. Remember, I know the truth behind those rolled-up socks you used to wear. And I don't mean on your feet."

"I was a sophomore in high school and underde-veloped for my age." Lucy crossed her arms in mock outrage. "I can't believe you'd resort to blackmailing your own sister."

"Prison has been a bad influence on me."

Her smile faded. "What's wrong, Melvin? You said there was trouble."

"My lawyer quit yesterday." He sighed. "Looks like you spent all that money on him for nothing."

She sat up straighter on the hard wooden chair. "He can't just quit! Your trial is in less than a month. I'll sue him. I'll report him to the state bar association. I'll picket in front of his office until he agrees to represent you again."

Melvin shook his head. "Hey, if he's not on my side, then I don't want him. The last thing I need is for my own *lawyer* to believe I'm guilty."

"Is that what he said?" she asked, knowing that her brother valued loyalty above all else. So did she. When you grew up on Bale Street, rife with crime and double-dealing, trust and loyalty were priceless commodities.

He shrugged. "Close enough."

She hit the scratched tabletop with her fist. "This is so unfair! You are not guilty. And I intend to prove it to that slimy lawyer and everybody else in this town."

He folded his beefy arms across his chest. "That's the other thing I wanted to talk to you about."

The hairs on Lucy's neck prickled at his tone. It wasn't that she was afraid, just a natural reaction to twenty-eight years of being bossed around by a big brother. A six-foot-three, two-hundred-and-twenty-pound big brother.

"Well, we both know you're innocent," she began.

"And?" he prompted.

"And I won't rest until I prove it. I'll find another lawyer...delay the trial...hire a psychic. I know we can find the evidence to clear you."

He arched a thick, blond brow. "We?"

She swallowed. "I've hired someone to help me with the investigation."

"A man?"

"Nobody you know," she said quickly. Melvin had never quite accepted that she was old enough to date. "He's retired from the police department and lives with his grandmother. He's perfectly harmless."

Melvin snorted. "Weasel's already told me all about this *harmless* friend of yours. Nick Chamberlin. Thirty-three-years old. Ex-con. Sex maniac."

Her mouth dropped open. "He's no sex maniac. I can guarantee you that."

"And what's that supposed to mean?"

"Well, he got stung by a bee," she began.

"Sounds painful, but hardly a permanent disability. Are you telling me this bee sting has affected his love life?"

"Not exactly."

"Then what, exactly?"

She decided to skip the rest of the story. "It means Nick Chamberlin isn't interested in my body. Only a paycheck. My relationship with him is strictly business.''

"Not according to Weasel. He told me the guy practically drools every time he looks at you. Weasel's worried about you, Luce, and so am I. Especially since I can't keep an eye on you from in here.''

"I can take care of myself,'' she said softly.

He rolled his eyes. "Right. As long as you've got your nose buried in a book. But this isn't fiction, Lucy, it's real life. You don't know what, or who, you're up against.''

"Nick is on our side. He's one of the good guys.''

"I have a feeling *good old Nick* is on the side that can pad his bank account. He's after your money,'' he said, his face darkening, "and anything else he can get. Forget him, Lucy. Forget me. You've got your own life to live. You don't need me to drag it down.''

"You're my brother,'' she whispered, her throat tight. "The only family I've got left. And I'm not about to let you spend the next twenty years in prison for a crime you didn't commit.''

"You don't need to worry about that. I've got a plan.''

She didn't like the sound of that. "A plan?''

He nodded. "If it all works out, I won't need another lawyer.''

"So are you going to fill me in?''

"No way. The only reason I contacted you at all is so you don't send any more money to that lousy lawyer. The less you know, the better.''

She rolled her eyes. If he was going to start that nonsense again, she'd never get anything accomplished. So she resorted to a tactic that had worked on him since she was eight years old. "Actually, I already know all about it. Weasel told me."

Melvin scowled at her.

"You do not."

"Do, too."

"Do not."

"Do, too."

"Do not!"

She shrugged, feigning unconcern. "Fine. You don't have to admit it. But I'm really hurt that you would try to keep something like this from me." She sniffed for good effect. "I'm your sister. At least Weasel understands that I have a right to know."

"Man, he did tell you!" He shook his head in disbelief. "How could Weasel let you get mixed up in something like this? I never should have told him my plan to bust out of here."

She blinked. "You're *what?*"

Melvin narrowed his eyes. "So you really didn't know," he accused. "Damn! I hate it when you do that to me, Lucy."

She leaned closer to him. "Melvin, are you crazy?"

"Yeah. Crazy to stick around this place for so long. To even think I stood a chance of an acquittal. You don't know what it's like in here, Luce. My cellmate, José, talks to his invisible friend. The bedsheets are giving me a rash. And I've named the spiders living in my toothbrush holder Harvey and Doris.'' He raked his fingers through his hair. ''I'm cracking up, Luce. I've got to get out of here.''

She wanted him out of there, too, but planning a jailbreak definitely wasn't the answer. It was all so unfair. He'd been ready to make something of his life. Instead of leaving the old neighborhood, he had a plan to make it better. Provide jobs for a decent wage and better housing for reasonable rent. And just like Lucy, he wasn't a quitter.

Lucy couldn't let him give up now.

''Melvin,'' she whispered, ''if you try to escape, they'll lock you up and throw away the key.''

''They'll have to catch me first.''

''But you shouldn't have to run away. You haven't done anything wrong.''

He leaned forward and said softly, ''I know you believe life should be fair, Lucy. Maybe it's that way in books, but I realized a long time ago that sometimes we have to make our own happily-ever-after.''

''Just wait a little while before you do anything rash. I know Nick and I can find the real arsonist.''

''The only thing Nick Chamberlin is going to find is trouble if he lays one finger on my little sister. I know his type. At the moment, I'm surrounded by them. He's not going to solve this case. He's just going to clean out your bank account.''

''You've got it all wrong,'' she said, her mind racing for a way to convince him to delay his escape attempt.

"I'm right about this, Lucy," he countered. "I want you to dump this guy."

"All right."

He blinked. "What did you say?"

She swallowed. "I said all right. I'll dump him."

He smiled.

"In two weeks."

His smile twisted into a scowl. "What's wrong with today? Or better yet, yesterday."

"Because I need him. I may be the brains in our investigation, but he's the brawn. Like you said, we don't know who—or what—we're up against. Give us two weeks to find enough evidence to clear your name before you do anything drastic."

"No way."

"Would you rather have me do this on my own?"

"I'd rather lock you in a closet until I'm safely in Mexico City."

"I've recently learned how to pick locks, so that won't do you any good. But I will make you a deal."

He narrowed his eyes. "What kind of deal?"

"I'll dump Nick Chamberlin in two weeks if you'll promise to stay put for that long."

"Stay put?" he asked innocently.

"You know what I mean. No midnight taco runs."

"All right," he agreed grudgingly. "It will take me that long to work all the details out anyway. But I don't like the idea of you spending even one more

day with this guy, much less two weeks. I'm going
to make sure Weasel keeps an eye on you."

Just what she needed. Another man peeking
through her windows. "That really isn't necessary."

"I think it is. No offense, Lucy, but you don't
know guys like I do. They're not like those romantic
heroes in your favorite novels." He cleared his throat.
"Men and women are made differently."

She bit back a smile. "I think we covered this
about fifteen years ago. I distinctly remember the di-
agrams."

A blush stained Melvin's stubbly cheeks. "I'm not
talking about physical differences. Men and women
think differently. Now take Vanessa…"

"You take her," Lucy quipped. "Or better yet,
let's give her to your ex-lawyer and show him the
real meaning of cruel and unusual punishment."

"I know Vanessa is spoiled and vain and selfish,
but she has her good points, too."

"Thanks to liposuction."

"Face it, Luce. Men are attracted to beautiful
women. It's been that way forever. We're also attracted to not-so-beautiful women. And tall women.
And short women. And skinny women. And—"

"I think I get your point," Lucy interjected. "If
it's in a skirt, it's fair game."

"Exactly. And I don't like the idea of Chamberlin
using you for target practice."

"I told you Nick isn't like that."

"*All* guys are like that. If they can't have a fantasy

woman like Vanessa, then they'll take the next best thing.''

''Gee, thanks.''

''You know what I mean.''

Unfortunately she did. Nick might be immune to her charms, but according to Melvin he would fall right into Vanessa's web—with his arms wide open.

''Men are such idiots,'' she murmured aloud.

''Now that's what I like to hear,'' he said. ''Keep that thought whenever you're around Chamberlin during the next two weeks.''

Lucy blinked. ''Oh, right. Two weeks.'' For the first time she noticed the shadows under Melvin's eyes and the loose fit of his bright orange prison uniform. He'd lost weight. For a brief moment she felt a pang of guilt for making him stay incarcerated even one more day. ''Just two more weeks. Can you wait that long, Melvin?''

''Sure,'' he said with his familiar, cocky grin. ''I'll put the time to good use. José and his invisible friend are giving me Spanish lessons.''

NICK WALKED into the Westview police station on Monday afternoon. Surprisingly, it looked the same as it had that day eighteen months ago when he'd been escorted from the premises. Same pea-green walls. Same blinking telephones. Same leaky coffeepot. He sidestepped the coffee-soaked paper towels on the tile floor as he strode past a silent, staring trio of uniformed officers.

His face wasn't on any of the Ten Most Wanted posters, but he was greeted with the same looks of suspicion and disdain as public enemy number one. He really couldn't blame them. Nobody liked a dirty cop.

Nick walked past the reception desk to the tiny office he used to share with his partner. Cole looked the same, too, sitting in front of his computer monitor with a pencil clamped between his teeth. His tie hung loose around his neck, his dark hair was ruffled. He pecked at the keyboard with one finger, intent on his work.

"Still trying to learn the alphabet, I see," Nick said, stepping through the doorway.

"Nick!" Cole jumped out of his chair, slapping his old friend on the back. "Man, it's great to see you."

Despite Cole's laid-back attitude, his athleticism and quick instincts had made him invaluable on the streets. Even after Nick's arrest, Cole had never let him down. His long, humorous letters had gotten Nick through more than one sleepless night in prison.

"So what brings you here?" Cole asked, clearing a chair of haphazardly stacked file folders so Nick could sit down.

"I'm doing some investigative work."

Cole's dark brows shot up. "Really? That sounds right up your alley. You always were the smart one."

"If I was the smart one, what does that make you?"

Cole grinned. "The good-looking one."

Nick shook his head. "You haven't changed a bit, Rafferty."

"I'm betting neither have you. You're still the same decent, upstanding cop you were eighteen months ago. The one who pleaded guilty to a crime I know he didn't commit."

"Let's not get into that."

Cole perched on the corner of his desk. "Why not? I've been over it a hundred times. Your grandfather suffers a massive heart attack, you're driving his car to the hospital when you're pulled over for...what?"

"A routine traffic check."

"Right. And that's when they found all that marijuana stashed in the trunk of the car. The same marijuana missing from the evidence room at the station. But what really doesn't make sense is your confession. I *know* you'd never do something like that."

"I confessed, didn't I? I wasn't about to put my grandparents through a lengthy, messy investigation and trial. Not with everything else they were going through. Look, I paid the price. It's over and done with now. Let's just forget it."

"Can you do that, Nick? You lost everything."

"I'll do whatever I have to do."

Cole knew when to stop pushing. "So tell me about your case."

"Does the name Mad Dog Moore sound familiar?"

"Are you kidding? The guy's practically a legend around here. But he really blew it when he torched the Hanover Building. I thought he was smarter than that.''

''So you're convinced he did it?''

''Positive. I was the lead investigator. It's an open-and-shut case.''

''What about his alibi?''

Cole shook his head. ''Weak. Very weak. You'd think a guy with Mad Dog's colorful past would be more creative.''

''He claims he was driving around Westview when the fire started?''

Cole nodded. ''Some passerby called in a report of smoke coming out of the windows. Mad Dog finally showed up after the fire department put out the blaze.''

''I suppose nobody saw him between the time of the fire and when he arrived on the scene?''

''Not a soul.'' Cole picked up a paper clip off his desk, twirling it with his fingers. ''So why all the questions? Don't tell me Mad Dog hired you?''

''Nope. His sister, Lucy. She thinks he's innocent.''

Cole whistled. ''Mad Dog has a sister? I'll bet she's something to see. Let me guess, she's got spiked purple hair, missing teeth and twice as many tattoos as her brother.''

Nick bit back a smile. ''Not exactly.''

''Well, she must be nuts if she thinks Mad Dog is innocent. In his apartment we found traces of the gunpowder he used as an accelerant. And the place was full of combustibles—all kinds of paint and varnish cans from the remodeling.'' Cole threw the mangled paper clip into the trash can. "As far as a motive, it's the usual.''

"Money?'' Nick guessed.

Cole nodded. "He insured the place a few weeks earlier with a replacement policy for almost twice the building's original purchase price. Mad Dog claimed it would be worth that much after the renovations, but they'd barely begun when the place got torched.''

"Didn't he realize the insurance company would never pay the full amount of the policy?''

Cole shrugged. "Guess he wasn't thinking straight. He sure wasn't thinking when he torched that place. It's a textbook arson case, Nick. And the trail literally leads right to Mad Dog's front door.''

Nick sighed. "That's what I keep trying to tell Lucy.''

"And she's not buying it?''

"Nope. She's convinced someone else is to blame. She's determined to find the *real* arsonist.''

Cole grinned. "So what's your plan?''

Nick stretched his long legs out in front of him. It felt good to be back here like this, discussing a case with his old partner. Almost like old times.

"First I'm going to check out Ralph Rooney. Then—''

"Wait a minute,'' Cole interjected, holding up one hand. "Ralph Rooney? *The* Ralph Rooney? The president of the Friends of Westview Association? The man who's planning to run for mayor in the next election?"

"I know," Nick replied. "It's a long shot. But the least I can do is check him out. I mean, she *is* paying me to investigate the case."

"And Rooney's your only lead?"

Nick cleared his throat. "Not exactly. After I check out Rooney, Lucy has *arranged* for me to...um... interview Vanessa Beaumont."

"You've interviewed suspects before. Why do I get the feeling there's more to this story?"

"Because the way she arranged it was by having Vanessa buy me at a bachelor auction. We have a date next Friday night."

Cole laughed. "I've *got* to meet this Lucy. Sounds like you have your hands full, Chamberlin."

"You have no idea." Nick reached into his pocket, pulling out a plastic bag. "By the way, I'd like to have this checked out."

"What is it?"

"A matchbook."

Cole looked at the smudged, tattered matchbook through the plastic. "Where did you get it?"

"At the crime scene."

"You're kidding. We turned that place upside down."

"It was wedged under a floorboard. Lucy helped me find it." He decided not to go into details. "Can you get the lab to check it for fingerprints?"

"Sure thing." Cole frowned. "But it looks pretty

fragile. I'm not sure how well it will hold up under testing.'' He squinted at the gold lettering barely visible through the charcoal smudges. ''Is there writing on it?''

Nick nodded. ''I checked it out with a magnifying glass. The only words I could make out were *old, Fort* and *Ann*.

''Old Fort Ann? What is that? The name of a bar?''

Nick shrugged. ''Who knows? This is probably a long shot anyway. I didn't even tell Lucy about it. I don't want to get her hopes up.''

Cole nodded. ''I'll let you know the report as soon as I get the lab results.'' He tossed the bag onto his desk. ''Hey, why don't you meet me at Bailey's Bar and Grill tonight after my shift is over? We'll grab a burger, a pitcher of beer, and watch the game on the big screen. It'll be like old times.''

''Sorry, I've got to work tonight. A stakeout at Rooney's place.''

''With your new boss?'' Cole grinned. ''Some things never change. The only thing that ever kept you from 'Monday Night Football' was a woman.''

''I'll be on my own this time. And it's a good thing, too.''

''Because Lucy Moore is scarier than her brother?''

''Nope,'' Nick countered. ''Because it's a Monday.''

LATER THAT EVENING, Nick hunkered down in the driver's seat of Sadie's '89 Buick and told himself it could be worse. He could be sweeping up fish nuggets off the floor at Farley's Fish Hut.

The car sat like a big yellow U-boat along a curb on Aspen Drive, in the ritziest neighborhood in Westview. If the homeowners' association had a rule against ex-cons scoping out the condos and gated estates, he was in big trouble. He could just imagine trying to explain all this to his parole officer. Somehow the excuse, "A librarian made me do it," sounded lame even to his ears.

But this particular librarian seemed able to make him do just about anything. It worried him, because he'd never been a pushover with women before. He'd always been the one calling the shots, whether it was with an investigation or a relationship. He wasn't domineering, just in control of his own life.

Except with Lucy.

So far, he'd broken into a building for her, put himself on the auction block for her, and now he was spying on rich people for her. He needed to figure out this power she had over him, before she got any more brilliant ideas.

Maybe it was her eyes. Soft, big brown eyes that could sparkle with mischief one moment and melt his defenses the next. Or her blond hair, as unmanageable as Lucy herself. Or that crooked smile of hers that niggled something way down deep in his gut. Then there was her body.

Even after fifteen months without a woman, he still had a discerning eye. Most men wouldn't look beyond those conservative clothes she wore at the library. But he had a great imagination. And he'd seen her in that blue dress. Seen her soft, enticing curves. The gentle sway of her hips. Those long, long legs.

He closed his eyes as he leaned back against the headrest. Thanks to his great imagination he could now see her *out* of that blue dress. Her skin warm and silky smooth. Her lips pink and slightly parted as she walked toward him. His gaze falling on those legs and that tempting mouth and everywhere in between.

His eyes snapped open and his head jerked up. He definitely didn't want to start having fantasies about Lucy, especially a *naked* Lucy. He looked around the front seat, desperate for something to distract him from his too-vivid imagination.

Picking up the flattened cardboard hat off the dashboard, he scowled at the colorful dancing cod. In the dim glow provided by the streetlight, he studied the directions on the inner panel. *Insert flap A into flap F. Tuck flap B under flap H. Fold flap D along the dotted line.* His fingers fumbled over each other as he tried to manipulate the small paper tabs. *Bend flap C over flap E.* Flap C? Nick turned the cardboard over in his hands. Where the hell was Flap C?

Maybe he wasn't ready for the French fry machine. He couldn't even put together a simple cardboard hat. But that meant staying with Lucy. How long could he continue taking money for a case that was already solved? He tossed the mangled hat into the back seat, wishing he could toss his conscience aside just as easily. Most people already thought he was without morals or ethics. So why not fulfill their expectations? He certainly didn't have anything more to lose.

Except possibly his sanity.

"Nick."

The eerie whisper startled him out of his reverie. He peered out the car windows but saw only the silhouette of looming willow trees and the soft glow of lights in the gated estate windows. As the wind rustled the tree leaves, he thought he heard the sound again.

"Nick."

The hairs prickled on the back of his neck. He'd never questioned his sanity before, but hearing voices wasn't a good sign. He knew if he started talking back he would really be in trouble. He began humming to drown out the disconcerting sound.

But he could still hear that husky voice calling to him.

"Nick," it rasped. "Ni…i…ck."

At that moment he chose to start singing the chorus to "Surrey with the Fringe on Top" while tapping his fingers in rhythm against the steering wheel.

A head suddenly appeared in the passenger window. Startled, his body jerked in reaction, his knee slamming against the steering column. "Ow!"

"Did you hurt yourself again?"

Lucy. He should have known. He reached over to unlock the passenger door, then popped it open. She was crouched in the grass, dressed entirely in black—

from the knit cap concealing her blond hair to the black leotard that stretched over her slender body to the black leather boots on her feet.

"Who are you supposed to be?" he asked, as she climbed into the seat. "Catwoman?" Then another thought occurred to him as he warily eyed the bulging black knapsack slung over her shoulder. "Don't tell me we're crashing a masquerade party, because I'm putting my foot down, Lucy...."

She closed the car door, then looked at him, her brow crinkled above her brown eyes. "What are you talking about? We're on a stakeout. I just didn't want anyone to see me."

"Where did you come from? I didn't see any headlights."

"I parked around the corner and sort of moved from tree to tree until I reached the car."

"You're soaking wet," he observed, uncomfortably aware of the way the leotard clung to her body.

She pulled off the knit cap, her damp hair falling haphazardly out of its bun. "That's because you left me sitting out on the lawn until the automatic sprinklers came on!"

"I was singing," he muttered, as she slid the knapsack off her shoulder.

"I heard. You do have a great voice," she said. "And I love show tunes, especially from *Oklahoma*. Do you know the words to 'I Cain't Say No'?"

He knew it down to the dance steps, but he wasn't about to admit it. "What are you doing here?"

"I brought you something." She unzipped the knapsack.

"Valium?"

"Even better," she said, reaching inside. "I've got some great stuff here. Pretzels, peanuts, caramel corn, potato chips, chocolate bars, diet soda…"

"Diet soda?"

"I'm trying to watch my weight."

"Lucy," he began as she tossed him a beef jerky stick, "what's with all the junk food?"

She pulled a pretzel out of the bag. "To keep up our energy. It could be a long night."

"For me, maybe. But I work alone."

She shook her head. "Unwise. According to Leo Bronski, stakeouts require at least two people so the investigation isn't compromised. It's too easy to fall asleep or start daydreaming and miss something important when you're all by yourself."

He didn't mention the type of daydreams he'd been having before she showed up. Daydreams he couldn't quite forget while she was sitting next to him in that revealing leotard.

"Who is Leo Bronski?" he asked, popping open a can of diet soda.

"I can't believe you don't know," she said, munching on her pretzel. "His books, *Under the Gun* and *The Felony Files,* are national bestsellers."

Nick rolled his eyes. "Not more of those supercop books."

"He's a great writer," she said, rolling up the pretzel bag, "and a retired police detective. So all his stories are based on real-life experiences. They're fascinating. And he's been on hundreds of stakeouts."

"Lucy, this isn't some storybook fantasy," he said, finishing off his beef jerky. "In fact, it's actually a complete waste of time. We're not going to find out anything about Melvin's case here. Ralph Rooney is a prominent, respected businessman. He's even on the governor's crime-prevention panel."

"Which is why no one would ever suspect him. Did you know he made several offers to buy the Hanover Building before the fire, but Melvin refused to sell it to him?"

"So Rooney decides to torch the place? That just doesn't make sense."

"Well, somebody torched it."

"Lucy..."

"Duck!" She suddenly grabbed him by the shirt-front and pushed him down lower in the seat. The back of his head bumped hard against the armrest on the door as his legs tangled with hers.

Nick reached up to rub his head. "What do you think you're doing?"

"Don't move," Lucy whispered, her lithe body stretched out on top of him, her hands gripping his shoulders. "I think someone is looking over here."

"Well, if he saw us, he's really going to be suspicious now."

She looked down at him. "Not if..." Her voice trailed off and he saw her swallow.

"Not if…what?"

Her fingers flexed on his shoulders. "Not if who-ever is out there thinks we're just…parking."

"I've been parked here for the last thirty minutes."

She wrapped her arms around his neck. "That's not exactly what I mean."

He opened his mouth but Lucy's lips met his before he could say a word. His vivid imagination never even came close to the reality of Lucy in his arms. Her tentative, feather-light kiss. Her mouth moving over his, gentle and delving, luscious and lingering.

Nick's arms wrapped around her, his hands caress-ing the length of her back, warming her cool, moist leotard. Her body relaxed into his. Her mouth tasted salty and sweet. So sweet that he almost groaned aloud when she finally broke the kiss.

"Nick," she breathed heavily, her brown eyes wide and slightly dazed, her mouth still only scant inches from his.

The beam of a flashlight swept slowly past the windshield, now partially steamed over.

"He's still out there," Nick whispered raggedly.

She hovered above him, lightly brushing his hair with her fingertips. "Good."

She kissed him again, her tongue tentatively ex-ploring his mouth. He moaned low in his throat, his hands moving to her hair. He pulled the bobby pins out and let his fingers luxuriate in the thick, damp curls that spilled over her shoulders. Every nerve ending in his body reacted as Lucy shifted atop him, deepening the kiss.

He wondered briefly what book taught her to kiss like this; then he stopped thinking at all. He only wanted to feel—feel her soft, pliant body molded against his own, her hands everywhere. He anchored one arm around her narrow waist and slowly turned them both on the wide seat until their positions were reversed. He'd never loved this big, roomy boat of a car more than he did at this moment.

She broke the kiss with a gasp of surprise as she now found him on top of her. "I don't think..." she began.

He silenced her with another kiss. A raw, sensual kiss filled with all the pent-up frustration and desire he'd felt ever since he first laid eyes on her. A kiss he never wanted to end.

The soft whimpers emanating from her throat thrilled him—at first. Then they made him hesitate. Were they whimpers of passion? Or protest? Maybe he'd been without a woman so long, he'd lost control. Maybe she was as terrified by his response as he was.

He lifted his head, his breathing as fast and shallow as hers, and stared into her wide brown eyes.

"Oh, Nick." He swallowed at the tremor in her voice. Darkness blanketed the fogged car windows. "He's gone. I think we fooled him."

"What?"

"The guy with the flashlight," she said, rising up on her elbows. "He must have believed we were really lovers." She blinked up at him, the heat fading from her eyes. "You can get up now."

He didn't want to get up. He wanted to sink into her soft body and kiss her breathless. He wanted to explore every inch of her under that leotard. He wanted to hold on to Lucy and never let her go.

"I can't breathe," she said.

With a deep sigh, he reluctantly shifted his weight off her, his foot catching on the door handle and his elbow connecting solidly with the steering wheel. The sharp blare of the car horn covered his grunt of pain.

"So much for keeping a low profile," Lucy cried, struggling to get out from underneath him.

He emitted a stifled groan. "Watch your knee."

"Sorry," she murmured, pulling herself up to a sitting position. Then she frowned at the front windshield. "It's all steamed up in here. I can't see a thing."

The windows weren't the only thing steamed up. Nick tugged at his shirt collar. If only the automatic sprinklers would come on again so he could have the best alternative to a cold shower. He took several slow, deep breaths and tried not to think about Lucy. Or that hot, passionate kiss. Or that he really wanted to kiss her again. That he really wanted her.

He was starting to hyperventilate. If he didn't calm down, he'd get dizzy. Maybe he'd pass out. Maybe Lucy would have to give him mouth-to-mouth resuscitation.

This was really getting pathetic.

"I can't stand it anymore," she said, rolling down her fogged window.

That made two of them, Nick thought.

He turned to reach for her as a swift gust of brisk night air blew across the front seat. But it was the sound of a familiar masculine voice that chilled his hot blood.

"Hey, Luce. How come you never kissed me like that?"

CHAPTER FIVE

"WEASEL," LUCY EXCLAIMED, brushing her tousled hair out of her eyes. "What are you doing here?"

"Wishing I'd taken you up on that marriage proposal." Weasel leaned in the open window, his arms resting on the door frame. "Or at least asked you out on a date. I take it you've changed your policy."

"Policy?" she echoed, still shaken by the impact of Nick's kiss. It scored at least a 9.5 on her own personal Richter scale.

"About not dating anybody with jail time—which pretty much excluded every guy on Bale Street," Weasel said with a good-natured shrug. "Mad Dog explained it to all of us one night after you'd turned down Snake. He said it was nothing personal, you just didn't want to get involved with a loser."

"I don't think I ever put it quite like that," she said, unable to deny it completely.

Nick sat silent and unmoving beside her. He could have been two hundred miles away from her instead of only two feet. He obviously didn't understand that she'd established that policy for a very good reason. She couldn't let anything, or more specifically, anyone interfere with her goals.

Her avid reading had taught her a lot, including how the main character in a novel always set a goal, then stopped at nothing to achieve it. Lucy had followed the same example in her life. In high school, her goal was to win a college scholarship. In college, her goal was to get her degree in library science. After accomplishing each goal, she set a new one, always determined to reach higher. And she'd never let love or lust get in her way. Until now.

Instead of pursuing her newest goal, which was fighting for her brother's freedom, she'd been making out in a parked car with an ex-con. Time to get her priorities straight.

"I made that policy for a reason," she explained.

Weasel nodded. "Hey, I understand. Why drag yourself down with a no-account bum when you're on the way up, when you've got such big dreams? Like a house in the Eagle Estates. The top job at the Heritage Library. A seat on the city council."

Her mouth fell open. "How do you know about that?"

"Me and Snake broke into your locker in high school and read your diary. Not too juicy, but you've got great penmanship."

She turned to Nick. "You can shoot him now."

"What exactly are you doing here," Nick growled, "besides spying on us?"

"I'm working as a valet. It's all part of the Protégé Project. Rooney hires me to park cars whenever he throws one of his ritzy dinner parties. He likes to

bestow temporary employment on the underprivileged. It makes him feel special.'' Weasel's green
eyes narrowed. ''What exactly are *you* doing here,
Chamberlin? Besides feeling up my best friend's sister.''

His jaw clenched as Weasel's smirk widened.
''Don't you have some cars to park?''

''I'd offer to park yours, but somehow I don't think
you're here for the party.''

''We're spying on Ralph Rooney,'' Lucy said.
''Trying to find out if he has any connection to the
fire.''

''Oh.'' Weasel's smirk faded. ''Gee, Luce, is there
anything I can do?''

''Confess to the crime?'' Nick suggested.

''No, thanks,'' Weasel said. ''But I do have some
information—'' he paused, flicking an invisible piece
of lint from his jacket ''—if you're willing to deal.''

''What kind of deal?'' Nick asked.

''One hundred dollars or…''

''Or what?''

Weasel's gaze fastened on Lucy. ''One kiss.''

''You're not my type,'' Nick clipped.

''Good, because Lucy is definitely my type,'' Weasel said. ''What do you say, Luce? Do we have a
deal?''

Before she could even open her mouth, Nick tossed
a wad of bills at Weasel. ''Enough fooling around,
Malone. What have you got?''

Weasel stuffed the bills in his shirt pocket with a

disappointed sigh. "You don't know what you're missing, Lucy."

"Just tell us what you know," Nick growled.

"Okay. The night of the fire…"

"Yes," Lucy prompted, her heart beating faster.

"There was an eyewitness."

Nick snorted. "No kidding. Half the neighborhood turned out when the fire trucks showed up."

"No, I mean a real eyewitness. A person who saw somebody leave the Hanover Building around midnight. And *that* somebody wasn't Mad Dog."

Lucy's fingers clutched the armrest. "Then who was it?"

Weasel shrugged. "She didn't say."

"She?" Nick asked.

"One of the girls who works a corner downtown. I heard about her from a friend of a friend."

"A prostitute?" Lucy guessed.

"That's right. I think her name is Daisy. Or maybe Rose. Some flower name."

"You *think?*" Nick said. "I just paid you a hundred bucks. I expect some quality information for that price. How do we even know it's true? And why didn't she report this to the police?"

Weasel laughed. "The police? Yeah, right." He stepped back from the car, looking toward the house. "Looks like the party is starting to break up. I've got to get back to work."

"Thanks, Weasel," Lucy called as he strolled away. He'd just given them the biggest lead in the case. She could barely contain her excitement as she turned to Nick. "This is it! I can go undercover. She'll probably talk to me if she thinks I'm another hooker. And I've got the perfect dress...."

"No way."

"But Nick..."

"Forget it, Lucy. It's out of the question. In the first place, you could never pass as a hooker."

She wasn't sure if he meant that as an insult or a compliment. Either way, she hoped it wasn't true. She had to pass for a prostitute if she ever wanted to find Daisy, or Rose, or Magnolia.

"And in the second place," Nick continued, "it's much too dangerous down there at night. Believe me. I used to work that beat when I was a rookie. It's no place for a librarian."

Now *that* was an insult—and a challenge. One she fully intended to meet. She could pull it off, too. All she needed was a little time, some tenacity...and a Miracle Bra.

"I'M READY for a good, juicy murder."

Lucy hid a yawn behind one hand as she scribbled Sadie Chamberlin's comment on her notepad. Ever since the stakeout three nights ago, she'd been up late researching every book available on the world's oldest profession. Now she could barely stay awake for the Merry Widows Book Club meeting. As discussion leader, it was her responsibility to provide good reading recommendations.

She looked around at the time-weathered faces of the club's five regular members: Sadie Chamberlin, Edith Cummings, Veda Tavlik, Lenora Eberly and Goldie Schwartz. They all had two things in common: dead husbands and a love of books.

"Any other suggestions?" Lucy asked, trying to focus her mind on fiction. Lately, real life had demanded all of her attention. She only had eight more days until Melvin attempted his prison break, and twenty-four more hours until she transformed herself from a librarian into a lady of the evening.

A tingle of anticipation shot through her. While Nick was on his date with Vanessa tomorrow evening in search of information, she'd be walking the streets in search of the eyewitness. Her costume was almost ready and she'd stocked up on hair spray just in case she encountered trouble.

"I want something challenging, like a complicated murder mystery," Edith said. Shortly after her retirement, Edith had qualified for the semifinals of the senior citizens' tournament on the "Jeopardy!" TV game show. She loved to read mysteries, solving most of them before the group got halfway through the book.

"Nick and Lucy are trying to solve a real mystery," Sadie announced. "Her brother is accused of arson and they're trying to find the real culprit."

"How fascinating!" Goldie exclaimed. At forty-eight, Goldie was the youngest member of the Merry Widows Book Club. She qualified for membership after the death of her fourth husband, newspaper magnate Wilson Schwartz. Though now financially independent, she still wrote her popular gossip column for the *Westview Herald*.

"Frustrating is more like it," Lucy said with a sigh. "If we could just find the real arsonist, Melvin could be free. But we're running out of time, and the police are convinced he's guilty."

Veda, a sixty-eight-year-old grandmother who jogged three miles a day, leaned forward in her chair. "Are you saying your brother didn't start that fire, but someone else is letting him take the blame?"

Lucy nodded. "The real arsonist is feeling smug and safe while an innocent man goes to jail."

Edith brushed a speck of lint off her neatly pressed "Jeopardy!" T-shirt. "Just like Horace Dexter in that book, *Murder for Sale*. Remember, girls? We read it last summer."

Sadie nodded. "Horace killed the doctor, then framed that nice young lady. Nobody would have discovered the truth if the detective hadn't tricked him by planting that article in the newspaper."

Veda snapped her fingers. "That's right. The one that said he'd found the murder weapon and planned to have it tested for fingerprints."

For a moment no one said a word. Lucy tried to tell herself it could never work, but the more she thought about it, the more possible it seemed. "Do you think I should do it? Try to flush out the real arsonist by claiming there's new evidence that will break the case wide open?''

"Well, it certainly couldn't hurt," Sadie mused.

"I could put an item in my column," Goldie offered, her blue eyes gleaming with excitement. "Give a review of the case and then put in the plug about the new evidence. All with my trademark flair, of course."

Sadie clapped her hands together. "Then when the real arsonist reads it, he'll panic and possibly reveal himself."

"*If* he reads it," Veda said.

Goldie sniffed. "*Everybody* in Westview reads my column." Then she smiled at Lucy. "I'll make sure it gets in tomorrow's paper."

"Goldie, that would be wonderful," Lucy exclaimed, almost afraid to get her hopes up. "Thank you all so much. Now I've taken up enough time with my personal problems. We're here to talk about books."

Lenora, the group's oldest member at eighty-two, held up a thick volume in her hand. "I just finished *Out of the Blue*. It's got some nice gory parts in it, but it's a little light on the sex."

"I'm in the mood for another good love story," Veda Tavlik said, pulling knitting needles and a skein of baby blue yarn out of her tote bag, "like that one we read last month. It was really hot."

Sadie nodded. "Wasn't that Stone character a hunk?"

"He reminded me of your grandson," Goldie chimed.

"Nicky is quite good-looking," Veda added, clicking her knitting needles together, "with those big broad shoulders. He's certainly handsome enough to take a young girl's breath away. Don't you think so, Lucy?"

Lucy blinked, her mind still on the image of Nicky Chamberlin's broad, bare shoulders. "What?"

"Lucy and my grandson went on a date last week," Sadie confided to the group. "He got her the loveliest corsage."

Lenora's thin, blue-veined hand fluttered up to her chest. "Isn't that romantic? I think flowers are such a poetic way for a man to express his true feelings. My Henry always gave me bouquets of lavender."

"What kind of flowers did Nicky give you?" Edith asked.

"Roses," Lucy replied. "Champagne roses."

The women oohed and aahed until Lenora had to take a whiff from her oxygen tank.

"Roses can mean love," Goldie informed them.

"It was only our first date," Lucy said. "And *I* asked *him* out."

"But you do like him?" Sadie asked.

Edith snorted. "What's not to like? That grandson of yours is one handsome hunk of man, Sadie. If I were a few years younger, I'd set my cap on him myself."

"I think you mean a few decades younger, Edith,"

Veda said with a smile. "Besides, we don't want Lucy to have any competition. You are almost thirty, aren't you, dear?"

"In two years," Lucy admitted, wondering how the discussion had turned from hot books to her not-so-hot love life.

Lenora reached over and patted her hand. "Don't worry, Lucy, you still have a little time left. Nicky is a fine man, and there comes a time when a woman can't be so choosy."

"Why don't you come over to the house tomorrow evening?" Sadie suggested. "I'll fix a nice, romantic dinner for two, and then disappear."

"Make oyster stew," Edith said. "Oysters are an aphrodisiac."

"The man's been in prison for over a year," Goldie reminded them. "I hardly think he'll need any additional stimulation. One kiss and he'll be a goner."

Lucy swallowed. The memory of Nick's kiss last Monday night still made her woozy. Or maybe it was lack of sleep. She didn't have enough experience with men to know if kisses usually caused such a strong physical reaction.

"You're right, Goldie," Veda said, counting the stitches on her knitting needle. "It will be almost too easy."

"Like shooting fish in a barrel," Lenora piped up.

Sadie clapped her hands together. "Then it's all

set. Dinner for two at my house tomorrow night. Eight o'clock. Nicky will be thrilled."

Lucy couldn't keep silent any longer. "We'll have to do it another time. Nick will be at the Château Pierre tomorrow night…with Vanessa Beaumont." Five pairs of bifocals turned in her direction.

"On a date?" Edith asked.

"With whom?" Sadie asked in a weak voice.

"Vanessa Beaumont." Lucy twisted the ballpoint pen in her fingers. "She and Nick are having dinner together. It was…sort of my idea."

"Lucy, dear," Goldie said gently. "Men have such short attention spans. It's not a good idea to distract them by throwing other women in their paths."

Edith arched one silver brow. "Especially a woman like Vanessa."

Lucy wondered if she could possibly steer the conversation toward bunions again, an earlier topic of the evening. "It's not like that. Nick isn't romantically interested in her." She saw Veda and Goldie exchange glances. "Really. Vanessa may have information about the fire. That's the reason for the date. The only reason."

"So Nicky is sacrificing himself for you," Veda said. "Isn't that sweet?"

Lucy didn't know any man who would consider dating Vanessa a sacrifice. And what if the women were right? What if Nick was vulnerable? Lonely? An easy victim to Vanessa's obvious charms?

She closed her eyes, telling herself it didn't matter.

Telling herself as long as Nick kept his focus on the case, his private life was his own affair. Telling herself she didn't care what tactics Nick used to make Vanessa talk.

As long as he didn't touch her. Or order anything with oysters.

"I CAN'T BELIEVE you're here." Nick stood alone in the foyer of Château Pierre the next evening, glaring at the potted palm in the dimly lit corner. The palm fronds rustled suspiciously as he took a step closer.

He'd been on edge all week, wondering how Lucy would infiltrate herself into this phase of the investigation. He could hardly bring her along on his date, but hiding in the foliage seemed a little desperate, even for Lucy.

"I can't do my job if I have to keep looking over my shoulder, waiting for you to interfere. I am a former police detective. I can handle this investigation all by myself."

No response from the potted palm. He wondered briefly if Lucy knew how she affected him, how she drove him to do things a normal, thirty-three-year-old man shouldn't do. Like make out in a car. Or fantasize about a librarian. Or argue with a plant.

She also made it impossible for him to remain distant and cynical and hopeless. Because when she'd thrown herself on top of him in that car, he'd started hoping all kinds of things—things he'd soon learned could never come true. Because Lucy had a policy against men like him. And as soon as she accepted her brother's guilt and gave up on this case, she'd be out of his life. Forever.

"Don't you feel just a little bit ridiculous?" he asked, glimpsing a flash of blue between the leaves.

The maître d' approached, clearing his throat. "Excuse me, sir," he said, his gaze moving warily between Nick and the plant. "My name is Jacques. Is there a problem here?"

"Nothing I can't handle."

"Perhaps I can be of some assistance?"

Nick shook his head. "This is a private conversation."

Jacques moved back a step. "I see. Well, then perhaps it would be best to seat you now. We have a very attractive fern next to a private table in the back."

"My party hasn't arrived yet."

The maître d' glanced at the plant. "Do you have a reservation?"

He had plenty of reservations. This so-called date with Vanessa Beaumont was not only a dead end, but a potential disaster—especially with Lucy around. She was too unpredictable, too impulsive, too dangerous.

Hadn't he been punished enough in the last fifteen months?

He scowled at the potted palm as he reached into his jacket, pulling out the appointment card he'd received from the Friends of Westview Association.

"Reservations for two at Château Pierre," he said, handing the card to Jacques.

"Ah. The Beaumont party. One moment, please." Jacques moved back to his station.

Nick's gaze fell on a newspaper lying open on a mahogany pedestal table. He picked it up, a name highlighted in the Goldie's Nuggets gossip column catching his eye. His jaw dropped as he scanned the column.

Goldie foresees sparks between a certain Westview librarian named *Lucy* and a former police detective who can still heat up an investigation. They're working together to solve the case of the Hanover Building fire. While the courts want to lock up a certain *Mad Dog* in a cage for the crime, this hot twosome is on the trail of the real smoking bandit. And they've got sizzling new evidence that could blow the case wide open just in the *Nick* of time. Stay tuned for *Moore* details of this smoldering story....

Nick couldn't believe it. He blinked and read the column again. Not only did the item link him and Lucy romantically, it claimed new evidence that just didn't exist. Where would Goldie Schwartz come up with such a ridiculous story? There could only be one answer.

He turned back to the potted palm. "This time you've gone too far."

Jacques approached, clearing his throat. "Pardon me again, sir. Miss Beaumont has already arrived. If you'll just follow me...."

With one last warning glance at the quivering palm fronds, Nick stepped after the maître d'.

Lucy's description of Vanessa hadn't prepared him for the woman seated at the small, secluded table. He'd been too stunned by the bachelor auction to notice the top bidder. Although looking at her now, he wondered how he ever could have missed her.

Vanessa Beaumont was blatantly beautiful.

Sleek, dark hair framed a heart-shaped face. Deep green eyes gleamed beneath thick, lush lashes. A small, upturned nose and pouty, pink lips completed the picture of a breathtaking woman.

She smiled up at him, her face ethereal in the glow of the candlelight. "Hello there."

"Miss Beaumont," he said, seating himself across from her.

"I simply won't be satisfied unless you call me Vanessa," she said, running one finger around the rim of her wineglass. "And for two thousand dollars, I certainly expect plenty of satisfaction."

Great. His status had fallen all the way from respected cop to paid gigolo. Just how far did Lucy expect him to go to obtain information? He picked up his wineglass, swallowing the Burgundy in one long gulp.

"I took the liberty of ordering for us," Vanessa

said. ''The cuisine here is excellent. We'll start off with Champagne Oysters followed by Turtle Soup.''

''Fine,'' he said,

Vanessa leaned forward. ''Then, for the main course, Roast Capon in Peanut Sauce. How does that sound?''

''Itchy,'' he muttered.

''What?''

He reached for the wine bottle to refill his glass. Maybe he should just relax and enjoy the inevitable. Vanessa Beaumont seemed designed to make a man forget about his troubles. ''I was just wondering what's for dessert?''

''Anything you'd like, Nick,'' Vanessa murmured, ''anything at all.'' Then he felt her foot crawling up his pant leg.

The wine toppled over the top of the glass, spilling onto the white linen tablecloth and dripping down onto his suit.

He bolted out of his chair, wiping his pants with his napkin. ''Excuse me for a moment.'' With a polite nod, he headed toward the sanctity of the men's room. He needed some solitude, some time to regroup—an escape plan.

Once inside, he took off his jacket, tossing it onto a chair. Then he bent over the sink, splashing cold water on his face. He straightened and mopped his face dry with a paper towel.

The reflection he saw in the mirror made him gasp out loud. A woman with big red hair winked at him with her thick, false eyelashes. For a moment he panicked, thinking he'd entered the ladies' room by mistake.

"You missed a spot," said a familiar voice.

Lucy. Slowly turning around, it took a moment to register the fact that this woman with the big hair and the even bigger chest was his librarian. But it was definitely Lucy. He glimpsed a skimpy red dress beneath the long, brown trench coat. He took a deep breath. "This is the men's room."

"I figured that out already," she said. "The urinals gave it away." She took the paper towel out of his hand and reached up to dab at his damp temple.

"I can't believe you followed me in here, especially after what I told you in the foyer."

She blinked. "Foyer? I wasn't in the foyer."

He folded his arms across his chest. "Don't give me that innocent act. You were hiding behind the potted palm. I saw the leaves moving."

"It must have been a draft, because I've been waiting in here for the last twenty minutes." She shook her head. "It was a real eye-opening experience. You wouldn't *believe* how many men don't wash their hands."

He swallowed. "You mean, I was talking to a plant the entire time?"

"I guess so," she said. "But don't feel bad. You're supposed to talk to plants. It helps them grow."

"Except I kept expecting the plant to talk back to

me.'' He shook his head. ''No wonder the maître d'
was looking at me like I was nuts.''

''Why would you think I'd be hiding behind a
plant? I'd never do anything that dumb.''

''Gee, I don't know, Lucy. Why would you put
peanut butter on a bee sting? Why would you attack
me with hair spray? Why would you show up in the
men's room?''

''Because we need to map out our strategy. Now,
I don't have much time....''

''Our strategy?''

She nodded. ''This is the perfect opportunity to
catch Vanessa off guard. Wine and dine her. Then go
in for the kill.''

''Excuse me?'' Nick was still trying to find the real
Lucy under that atrocious wig and all that makeup.
Did she really think she could fool anyone with this
ridiculous disguise?

''I want you to leave,'' he said. ''Leave the men's
room. Leave the restaurant. Leave me alone.''

''I will,'' she said, then noticed the skeptical expression on his face. ''I promise. I have plans tonight,
too. But first I want to give you something.''

He backed up a step as she reached into the pocket
of the trench coat. She pulled out a small sheet of
paper.

''I made up a series of questions. Try to work them
into the conversation.''

He looked down at the list. ''You've got to be kidding.''

"You can do it," she said. "Just use your imagination."

"I can just hear it now." He cleared his throat. "Vanessa, I'm on fire for you. And speaking of fires, did you happen to burn down Mad Dog's building?"

Lucy frowned at him.

"Or how about this," he continued. "Vanessa, you are the most beautiful woman on earth. Please say you'll be mine. Confess your love and your participation in the crime that took place on April nineteenth."

He shook his head. "Not only would it never work, it's a complete waste of time. We shouldn't be focusing the investigation on Vanessa."

"Why not?"

"Because she isn't the most logical suspect."

"If you're going to tell me she's too beautiful to be guilty..." Lucy began.

"No," he replied, dabbing at the wine spots on his jacket. "I mean, obviously she's a beautiful woman. Exquisite, really, if you like..."

"Please get to the point," Lucy interjected. "If Vanessa isn't guilty, then who is?"

"Weasel."

Her mouth dropped open. "Weasel? My Weasel?"

"How many other Weasels do you know?"

"That's ridiculous," she sputtered. "I've known him since he was eight years old. He used to practically live at our house. He might be a little rough around the edges, but he's actually very sensitive. Besides, he's Melvin's best friend. He'd never do anything to hurt him.''

''Then why was he in the warehouse the night we broke in?''

''He told us…'' Lucy sputtered to a stop.

Nick shrugged into his jacket. ''You see. He never gave us a reason. And the police showed up before I could get any answers out of him.''

''He had a key.''

''He *said* he had a key. We never saw it.''

''But that doesn't mean anything. If he didn't have a key, he could have been in there for a good reason.''

''Like returning to the scene of the crime?''

She scowled at him. ''You told me that never happens.''

''It *rarely* happens. But Weasel doesn't exactly strike me as the most brilliant criminal mind. Maybe he was in the warehouse that night to recover evidence that might prove him guilty.''

''And this is what you're basing your suspicions on?''

''No. I'm basing them on the fact that in 1982, Walter 'Weasel' Malone was arrested and charged with two counts of second-degree arson. His lawyer later got him off on a technicality.''

''1982?'' Lucy said. ''But that would only make him…fourteen years old at the time.''

''Maybe he was in training.''

Lucy folded her arms around her inflated chest. ''Look, Weasel's had a rough life growing up with a single mother in a houseful of kids. He's made a few mistakes along the way, but anybody who leaves dog food out in the alley for all the stray mutts can't be that bad. You're just saying all this because you don't like him."

"Maybe you're just intent on accusing Vanessa because you don't like her," Nick countered. "She could be an innocent victim in all of this."

Lucy rolled her eyes. "*Innocent* is not the word to describe Vanessa."

"Oh, that reminds me..." Nick said, thoroughly enjoying himself. It was nice to see someone else confused and frustrated for a change. "How far do you want me to go?"

"Go where?"

He straightened his tie. "With Vanessa. I mean, it's fairly obvious she's attracted to me. I suppose I'd be willing to sacrifice myself in the line of duty...."

"You are totally disgusting."

A toilet flushed. Lucy ducked behind the heavy fabric draped over the long French windows, the toes of her spiked red heels peeking out underneath.

Jacques emerged from one of the stalls. He eyed Nick, then looked furtively around the posh rest room, his gaze finally falling on the potted philodendron suspended from the ceiling. "I thought I heard a woman talking."

Nick pressed his lips together. The last thing he needed was to try and explain Lucy's antics to the management of the Château Pierre. ''There's nobody in here but me.''

''So I see.'' The maître d' glanced at the philodendron again. ''Pardon me for interrupting, sir,'' he whispered, quickly washing his hands before ducking out the door.

''That was a close one,'' Lucy said, emerging from below the drapery.

''Forget about him. And forget about Vanessa. I can handle her.''

She arched one heavily penciled brow. ''That's what I'm afraid of. You'll be drooling over her before they even serve the second course, and you'll blow a great opportunity.''

''Give me a little credit,'' Nick said. ''I've got great willpower. I probably won't start drooling until the fourth course.''

''I didn't know you had a sense of humor,'' she said, looking completely unamused.

''No extra charge,'' he quipped, saluting her as he walked out the door.

CHAPTER SIX

NICK GLANCED at his watch as Vanessa droned on about her favorite subject: herself. He wasn't in any danger of drooling by the fourth course, but falling asleep was a definite possibility.

"And then I wrote a poem about my traumatic experience in the Miss Ohio Beauty Pageant," she said, retrieving a package of cigarettes from her beaded handbag.

"Bad hair day?" Nick ventured.

"Actually my hair looked absolutely fabulous." She fluffed her thick mane over her shoulders. "My hairdresser Raoul used a special avocado herbal shampoo blend with just a hint of real organic lemon juice. The lemon is supposed to bring out my hair's natural highlights."

"You were telling me about your traumatic experience," he prodded before she could begin another dissertation on blow-drying.

"Oh, right. The interview question."

She shuddered slightly, drawing a long, slim cigarette out of the pack. "It still haunts me."

"A tough one?"

"It was a trick question. The emcee asked me how

the United States could solve the problem of illegal aliens.''

''And what did you say?''

''That the United States is the greatest country on the planet and we shouldn't let any UFO's land here without permission.''

Nick opened his mouth, then closed it again.

''Who knew he was talking about invading *foreigners?*'' She sighed. ''I lost a crown, the judges voted nay, when the emcee stumped me that day…. That's how my poem starts. My writer friend, Niles, just thought it was so powerful. He said reading it was physically painful for him.''

''I can imagine.''

She held up her cigarette. ''Do you have a light?''

''Sorry, I don't smoke.''

She fumbled around in her purse. ''I should have a lighter in here somewhere… Ah, this will do.'' She pulled out a white matchbook with shiny gold lettering on the front. It looked disturbingly familiar.

''Allow me,'' he said, taking the matchbook out of her hand. The first line on the cover read Harold & Letitia, followed by Happy Fortieth Anniversary. It was a lot cleaner, but otherwise identical to the one he'd found in the warehouse. All the letters fit, too. Old in Harold, Fort in Fortieth, and Ann in Anniversary.

''Who are Harold and Letitia?'' he asked, as he struck a match, then held the flame up to the tip of her cigarette.

"Mommy and Daddy." She took a deep drag, moaning softly with appreciation. "They had a big bash last April for their anniversary."

Nick slowly flipped the matchbook back and forth between his fingers. "When in April?"

She blew a stream of smoke into the air. "The nineteenth."

Nick felt a suspicious gnawing in the pit of his stomach. *April nineteenth.* The same night as the fire. "Personalized matchbooks. Must have been quite a party."

She shrugged. "It was a total bore for me. I'd just had a big fight with my boyfriend. But, of course, as hostess, I had to stay until the party ended. There's nothing quite like watching a group of tipsy senior citizens dancing the conga at two o'clock in the morning."

"And they gave away these at the party?" he asked, holding up the matchbook.

She rolled her eyes. "Dozens of them."

"Can I have this one?"

She shrugged her bony shoulders. "Sure. We've got a ton left over at home."

"Thanks," he said, pocketing the matchbook. "So, what kind of man would let his girlfriend dance the night away without him?"

Vanessa sighed. "Mad Dog threw an absolute fit when I forbade him to go to the party with me. But what could I do? He was a real cool guy, but naturally he just wouldn't fit in with Mommy and Daddy's crowd.''

"Naturally," Nick agreed with a sardonic twist of his lips. *What did Mad Dog Moore ever see in this woman?*

"Who knew he'd go berserk and try to burn down his own building?''

"Maybe he didn't do it.''

Vanessa took another drag on her cigarette. "That's what he claimed afterward. But he was obviously throwing a temper tantrum that night. He wouldn't even answer his phone when I called.''

"What?''

"I called him around eleven-thirty," Vanessa said, "to see if he was through pouting. But he didn't pick up.''

According to the police reports the fire had started shortly before midnight. Was it possible Mad Dog's alibi really was true? "Did you tell the police this?''

She shrugged. "I don't remember. They asked me all sorts of questions. But then they found all that gunpowder that started the fire, so we all knew Mad Dog did it.''

Nick had barely digested this new twist in the case when Jacques approached the table carrying a cordless telephone receiver. "Excuse me. You have a phone call, Mr. Chamberlin.''

Surprised, Nick took the phone. With a polite nod, Jacques returned to his post.

"Hello?" Nick said, cradling the phone on his shoulder.

"Hi, Nick. It's me, Lucy. Pretend you don't know me."

"Believe me, I've tried." He glanced at Vanessa, who was dipping her spoon into the turtle soup.

"Is Vanessa still there?"

"Yes."

"Has she spilled anything yet."

"Just a little cleavage." Static crackled over the line. Then Nick thought he heard the sound of screeching tires. "Where are you?"

"I'm doing a little undercover work."

He didn't like the sound of that, or the ferocious gnawing in the pit of his stomach.

More static. "Oops. Someone's coming," Lucy said, her voice sounding far way. "Gotta go."

"Hey, wait a minute...." he began, but all he heard was the sound of a dial tone in his ear. Nick frowned at the phone in his hand before placing it on the table. Lucy obviously wasn't in the men's room anymore. But where the hell was she?

Vanessa looked up from her soup, her perfect brow wrinkled with annoyance. "Important call?"

Nick shook his head. "My librarian. She has something she wants me to check out."

The phone chirped. Once. Twice.

Nick reached for it, but Vanessa got to it first. She pushed the power button off. "You're all mine tonight, Nick, and I'm not a woman who likes to share. Now where were we?''

"About to move on to the next course," he said, more than ready to end this date. Especially since he had a new lead and a librarian to pursue. He picked up the dessert menu, pretending to study the choices while he tried to figure how to make a graceful exit. Vanessa might be visually stunning and every man's fantasy on the outside, but she certainly wasn't his fantasy woman. She wasn't warm. She wasn't kind. She wasn't…Lucy.

Of course Lucy wasn't exactly Lucy tonight either, dressed up like a three-dollar hooker. If he didn't know better…

A three-dollar hooker. Nick set the menu on the table as the realization washed over him. That costume she had on earlier obviously meant she intended to go undercover as a prostitute to catch this supposed eyewitness. He was torn between outrage and resignation. Maybe he should just let her play out this ridiculous charade. Let her stand on that street corner…in that skimpy red dress…in one of the worst sections of Westview…alone.

He stood up, tossing his napkin beside his plate. "It's been great, but I've got to go."

Vanessa looked at him in surprise. "Go? You can't just go. You're bought and paid for. You're all mine tonight, Nick."

"Maybe the Friends of Westview will give you a

refund,'' he said as he placed a generous tip on the table.

Vanessa was still sputtering as he strode out the door of Château Pierre. Part of him felt like a heel for deserting her in the middle of their date, but he didn't have any choice.

Lucy was in big trouble. Again.

LUCY CLUTCHED her big handbag against her chest as she huddled against the cold brick wall of the Hanover Building. Somehow, going undercover as a prostitute wasn't quite as adventurous as she'd imagined. Teetering on her spiked heels, she looked up and down the shadowed street. So far, she'd gotten three leg cramps, two blisters and a run in her nylons—but no inside information from the regulars that walked the streets of downtown Westview.

She'd expected the women to either ignore her or laugh at her, but not to compete with her. Every time a prospective customer approached, one of the regular girls would sidle over so he could do some comparison shopping. Not that Lucy wanted to sell her body—for any price. Which was a good thing, because no one was buying.

And she was really trying not to take it personally.

At least her efforts weren't completely wasted. She'd handed out several bookmarks with the library's address and hours to the women on her corner, recommended books on everything from beauty tips to auto repair, even invited those who were interested to a library seminar on job training.

Lester wouldn't be happy, but then Lester was a bit of a snob. Every time she suggested implementing a literacy program for the underprivileged or inviting inner-city kids to the weekly story hour, he'd look at her as if she'd proposed an orgy. Of course, he'd led a sheltered life. At forty-seven, he still lived with his mother and spent most of his spare time with his collection of cheeses from around the world. Still, she got tired of his constant toadying to the wishes of Mrs. Beaumont and the other members of the Heritage Library Foundation. As library director, Lester needed to remember that the public library belonged to *all* the citizens of Westview.

Lucy stifled a yawn as she glanced at her watch. Fifteen more minutes, then she'd head for home. Maybe she'd try it again tomorrow night.

A pair of headlights shone in the distance. Lucy's fingers curled around her handbag. A light blue Ford Escort had tailed her all the way to the Château Pierre restaurant earlier this evening, the same Ford Escort she'd been seeing in her rearview mirror for the past several weeks. But it had never been quite close enough for her to identify the driver.

The car passed under a streetlight, illuminating the shiny silver exterior. She let out her pent-up breath. It wasn't the same one. Probably just another over-sexed seventeen-year-old with twenty dollars to burn. She'd given the last one a lecture on the dangers of sexually transmitted diseases and sent him on his way.

The car slowed as it approached her, the driver anonymous behind the shaded windows. Then it stopped, the whir of the electric window blending with the sounds of the street.

"Get in the car."

Lucy peered through the passenger window. "Nick, is that you? Where did you get the car?"

"Just get in, Lucy."

"You didn't steal it, did you?"

He closed his eyes. "Sadie's car is in the shop. This is a loaner. Now get in the car."

"How did you find me?" Lucy edged closer. "And what happened to Vanessa?"

"We aren't going to discuss this now," he said, his voice strained. "Get in the car."

"I'm fine. Really. There was a little mishap between some rival gang members earlier, but it's pretty quiet now." Lucy waved him on. "You're going to blow my cover. I'll call you in the morning. We'll compare notes."

He dropped his head forward, banging it lightly against the steering wheel.

She walked to the curb, leaning into the open window. "Are you all right?"

He sighed as he lifted his head. "I think I'm having a nervous breakdown."

"Well, don't have it here! I'm trying to flush out

a witness—the woman who might be able to identify the real arsonist.''

''In that outfit, you'll flush out every pervert in Westview! Now, are you going to get in this car, or do I have to come after you?''

She tugged up the low neckline of her costume, a red sequin cocktail dress she'd bought for a New Year's Eve party ten years ago, but which was now two sizes too small. ''I'm trying to blend in.''

He shook his head in disbelief. ''Don't you realize how dangerous it is out here?''

''Don't worry about me,'' she said. ''I've got plenty of hair spray and great instincts. Besides, I grew up in the meanest neighborhood in Westview. I can take care of myself.''

Nick got out of the car, circling the front bumper to stand beside her on the sidewalk. ''We are not going to argue about this anymore.'' He grabbed her elbow. ''Now let's go.''

A voluptuous bleached blonde appeared out of the darkness. Her neon pink hot pants clashed with the orange halter top that stretched across her ample chest.

''What's your hurry, darlin'?'' she asked, snapping her bubble gum. ''How 'bout letting Babette join the party?''

Lucy whirled out of Nick's grasp and extended her hand to the prostitute. ''Good evening, Babette. I'm Lucy. Have you been working this neighborhood long?''

Babette's gaze moved from Nick to the shiny Buick Century. "Long enough to know a big spender when I see one."

Nick folded his arms across his chest. "We're looking for a woman named Daisy, or Chrysanthemum, or…some flower name. Do you know her?"

Babette ran one long fingernail down the length of his coat sleeve. "Honey, you don't need to look any farther. I'm your woman. You want something from Babette, you just have to ask."

"And pay," Nick said dryly.

Babette shrugged. "Business is business, darlin'."

"That's what I thought." He grasped Lucy's elbow. "Let's go."

Lucy didn't budge. Her instincts told her Babette knew something. She looked up at Nick. "No, not yet. She might really be able to help us."

"Lucy…"

She squeezed his arm. "Please."

With a reluctant sigh, Nick took out his wallet and withdrew a twenty-dollar bill. He handed it to Babette. "Now what do you have to say that's so important?"

Babette tucked the bill inside her generous cleavage, then drew out a shiny silver badge. "You're under arrest, darlin'."

"YOU'RE OFF THE HOOK, Chamberlin," Cole Rafferty said as he strode into his tiny office at the Westview police station, "thanks to your friend Lucy."

"Lucy is the one who got me into this mess in the first place," Nick muttered, raking his fingers through his hair. "She's impossible."

Cole grinned. "At last, a woman who can put a few dents in the Chamberlin armor. Sounds like a keeper."

Nick scowled at his old friend. "Very funny. Keep it up, Rafferty, and I'll have her demonstrate some of her self-defense techniques. You'll never be the same again."

"Actually, I might take you up on the offer. I've always been partial to big brown eyes."

"Stay away from her," Nick barked. Then his tone softened. "She's a dangerous woman."

Cole laughed out loud. "Dangerous? That sweet librarian, who must be all of five foot three? Give me a break, Nick. Just tell me she's off-limits and I'll keep my distance."

"She's off-limits."

Cole tipped back in his chair, clasping his hands behind his head. "So my old partner has finally taken the fall. Was it love at first sight?"

Nick frowned. "More like hives at first sight. Love has nothing to do with me and Lucy. She hired me to do some investigative work. That's it."

Cole smiled. "Right."

"If you don't believe me, just ask her."

"I did. She told me your relationship is strictly professional," Cole said. "And that Babette misunderstood your little transaction."

"Babette." Nick shook his head. "Is that really her name?"

"Yep. The department's newest recruit. A good cop, but a little overzealous in her work."

"Overzealous?" Nick echoed, rolling one stiff shoulder. "That woman put me in an headlock so fast, I could hear bones cracking. Where did you find her? 'American Gladiators'?"

"Hey, we had to fill the void somehow after we lost you."

A terse silence filled the room.

"Ready to tell me what really happened eighteen months ago?" Cole asked.

"That case is closed," Nick said evenly. "I'd rather talk about the case against Mad Dog. Did you find any fingerprints on that matchbook I gave you?"

Cole shook his head. "Nope. And it pretty much disintegrated during the testing. So I guess you're at a dead end."

"Maybe not."

That got Cole's attention. He leaned forward, resting his elbows on top of the scratched desktop. "You've got a new lead?"

"I'm working on it." Nick fingered the new matchbook in his pocket. "Could you do me a favor?"

"Name it."

"Harold and Letitia Beaumont held an anniversary party the same night as the fire. I'd like to see a guest list."

"I'll see what I can do." Then Cole's brow furrowed. "Are these Beaumonts related to Mad Dog's old girlfriend?"

Nick nodded. "Her parents. But Mad Dog wasn't invited to the party. He and Vanessa had a big blowup about it."

"That's right." Cole rubbed his chin. "Actually, that plays into his motive. He wanted to impress his rich girlfriend, so he set fire to the warehouse for the insurance money."

"Lucy thinks he's innocent."

Cole grinned. "So she's pretty, sexy *and* loyal. A lethal combination. No wonder you're a lost cause. Does she have a sister?"

"As I said before, you haven't changed a bit, Rafferty."

"Hey, somebody has to ask the tough questions. Why don't you and Lucy join me for a beer after my shift is over? I can tell her about the time you commandeered a hang glider to pursue a suspect."

"No way. Those days are over for me. I'm playing it safe now. And I certainly don't need Lucy to get any more crazy ideas. After this last stunt, I'm tempted to lock her inside her apartment and throw away the key."

"You don't approve of her undercover work?"

Nick stood up and began pacing back and forth across the office. "Approve of her masquerading as a prostitute in one of the most crime-ridden sections of Westview? No I don't approve. She could have been assaulted…nabbed…killed.'' He swallowed hard. ''I don't even want to think about it.''

''You want to tell me again how she doesn't mean anything to you?''

''It's not like that,'' he explained, trying to understand these odd feelings himself. ''I just feel responsible for her. She's alone, vulnerable and…''

''Dangerous?''

Nick stopped and let out a deep breath. ''Extremely.''

Cole nodded. ''I think you may be right, Nick. Lucy Moore may just be the most dangerous woman you've ever met.''

LUCY COULD SENSE a lecture coming on, and she just wasn't in the mood. A full moon glowed in the night sky. A lilting ballad played softly on the car radio as Nick pulled up along the curb in front of her apartment building. The roomy front seat of the loaner car reminded her of another car…another front seat… another night alone in the moonlight with Nick. And a kiss she couldn't seem to forget.

She swallowed a sigh, fingering the bright red curls of the wig on her lap. She'd scrubbed off all her makeup at the police station and pinned her gaping bodice shut with the safety pin Nick had thrust at her. He'd barely said two words to her since the arrest, but she could see his jaw working and knew he couldn't contain himself much longer. She settled back against the seat, waiting for the lecture to begin.

"Let's go," he snapped, switching off the ignition.

She blinked. "Where?"

Nick turned to look at her. "Up to your apartment. We have some things to discuss."

She didn't like the sound of that. And she definitely didn't want him to see her apartment in its current condition.

"Come on, Lucy," he prodded. "I've wasted enough time tonight already."

"My place is a mess."

"I won't even notice." He popped the door open and stepped out of the car before she could say another word.

For an employee, he wasn't very good at taking orders.

Lucy dragged herself behind him, all too aware of his loose-hipped stride and the wide breadth of his shoulders. She forced herself to look away. Melvin was running out of time, she was running out of money and Nick was running out of patience. The last thing she needed to do was fantasize about the hired help.

She had to keep her head, because no matter how good he looked in his clothes—or how much better he might look out of them—she still had to face facts. Nick Chamberlin was an ex-con. A dirty cop. A thirty-three-year-old man who lived with his grandmother.

But he was also a great kisser.

Unfortunately, that probably wasn't enough to base

a relationship on. Not that he seemed interested in pursuing a relationship with her, or even seducing her. Maybe she simply wasn't his type. Maybe he liked them big and busty, like Babette. Or shallow and slinky, like Vanessa.

"I hope you're giving some thought to all the trouble you caused tonight," he said as he held open the door to the apartment building.

She stopped in the doorway, turning to face him. "Actually, I was wondering what type of woman you find attractive."

Nick looked baffled. "What does that have to do with the case?"

"Nothing. I was just curious."

His eyes narrowed. "I think you're trying to change the subject. We're talking about the stunt you pulled tonight. The one that almost put me back behind bars, thanks to Babette."

"Did you find Babette attractive?"

"It's hard to fantasize about a woman when she's got you upside down in a bone-crunching headlock. I'll probably have nightmares about her."

"What about Vanessa?"

"Vanessa won't give me nightmares," he said, leaning against the open door.

She swallowed. "She is pretty."

"Stunning."

"And rich and sexy and skinny," Lucy muttered.

"And boring as hell."

She blinked. "What? You mean you didn't fall under the spell of the Wicked Witch of Westview?"

Nick shook his head as he followed her inside the building. "She might not be guilty of arson but she could certainly bore a man to death. I could barely stay awake through the meal." He scowled down at her when they reached her apartment door. "But then I realized you were off masquerading as a hooker, and perked right up again."

"Vanessa *bored* you?" she asked, stopping in front of her door and inserting the key into the dead bolt.

"Right up until the time she dropped the biggest clue of this case into my lap, figuratively speaking."

Lucy spun around. "A clue? Really?"

"Possibly," he amended. "But I don't want you to get your hopes up."

That was like telling her not to breathe. She threw her arms around his neck. "Oh, Nick. A clue. A real clue. A chance to save Melvin."

His arms went around her. Lucy was suddenly very aware of his earthy scent, the long, hard length of his body and the nearness of his mouth to her own. Her breath quickened. She wanted him to kiss her, to lose control. To make her forget all about her policy against ex-cons.

They backed away from each other at the same time.

Lucy's heart skipped a beat as she struggled for something to say.

"I have to go," Nick announced, his eyes half-lidded and unreadable.

"Wait a minute." She reached out to grab his forearm before he could escape. His muscles tensed under her fingertips. "What about the clue? Tell me everything."

"I don't think that's a good idea."

She dropped her hand, staring up at him in disbelief. "You're not going to tell me?"

"No."

"That's ridiculous. I have to know."

"Why? So you can hatch some new harebrained scheme?" He folded his arms across his chest. "Forget it."

She resisted the urge to stamp her foot. "But I've got a right to know. I'm paying you for information."

"You're paying me to find evidence to clear your brother of arson charges. That's what I'm doing. And the last thing I need is a lunatic librarian interfering with the case."

"Don't you think 'lunatic' is a little extreme?"

"I was being nice. You're actually the most dangerous woman I've ever met. I'm lucky to still be alive."

"You're exaggerating. And you're shutting me out of the case because of a few little mishaps."

"Mishaps? Lucy, I almost got arrested tonight—for the second time in less than two weeks. You've tried to blind me with hair spray. And don't forget about the peanut butter."

She rolled her eyes. "Well, if you're going to bring up every little incident, I could lodge a few complaints myself."

"Such as?"

"Such as…kissing me the night of the stakeout." She tipped up her chin. "I'd hardly call that professional behavior."

"As I remember it, you kissed me."

"But you kissed me back."

He rifled a hand through his short dark hair. "I've been in prison for the last fifteen months. What did you expect?"

Her cheeks grew warm. "Flattery will get you nowhere."

He opened his mouth, but she held up her hand to ward off his apology. At least she hoped it was an apology. "Let's just forget about that kiss."

"Believe me, I've tried," he muttered. "Just like I've tried to figure out how I ever got into this mess. Because when we were in the library, you looked harmless. Did you hypnotize me? Use mind control? Voodoo?"

"Quit trying to change the subject. I want to know about the new lead in the case. At least give me a hint."

"No."

"Does it involve Vanessa?" she asked, then waved her hand in the air. "What am I saying? Of course it does. She was at dinner with you tonight. She must have made some kind of slip-up. Did she say something incriminating? Reveal a motive? Use the wrong fork?''

''I'm not going to stand out in the hallway playing Twenty Questions.''

''Then let's go inside,'' she said, placing her hand on the doorknob.

''That's not a good idea.''

''I'll make coffee. We can talk about the case and plan our strategy.''

''I don't drink coffee.''

''Then I'll give you tea, beer, milk of magnesia—anything you want.''

''How about the silent treatment?''

''You're impossible!'' she exclaimed, wanting to shake him. Didn't he realize how important this was to her? How much she was willing to sacrifice for her brother? ''Not to mention irritating, stubborn and evasive. Didn't they teach you any communication skills in prison?''

''I guess we were all too busy with those ballroom dance lessons.''

''Well, you've got tap dancing down pat,'' Lucy said in a fit of exasperation. ''You've avoided answering all of my questions. You won't tell me about the new clue. And I think you're trying your hardest to start an argument.''

He just stood there watching her, his jaw clamped tightly shut.

''You are, aren't you?'' she accused. ''In fact,

you've been like this ever since we met. It's like you purposely try to pick fights with me.''

''You're right,'' he admitted, taking a step closer to her. ''I do.''

Suddenly Lucy became very aware of all six feet two inches of solid, potent male. She swallowed. ''Why?''

''Because it keeps me from doing something stupid.''

She stared up at him, confused. ''Like what?''

''Like this.'' He lowered his head and captured her mouth with his own.

Her breath caught in her throat at the unexpected onslaught of his lips. His mouth melded against hers with raw desire and molten heat. Desire flared inside her as his arms wrapped around her waist, pulling her tightly against him.

Lucy leaned into him, her hands pressed against his chest. Her fingers flexed against hard, unyielding muscle until he moaned low into her mouth, deepening the kiss. She slid her hands up to his shoulders, wrapping them around his neck to pull him even closer. Then she held on tight as he kissed her again. She kissed him back, shutting out everything but the fierce intensity of their embrace.

When he finally ended the kiss, she could barely breathe, much less think clearly. So he did find her attractive. The very idea made her light-headed. Or maybe it was lack of oxygen. Nick was certainly taking up his fair share, breathing hard and fast, his mouth only scant inches from her own.

"Now do you understand?" he rasped, his hands gripping her shoulders. "I want you, Lucy. I want you all the time. Right now I'd like nothing better than to take you into that apartment and lock the door. To shut out the rest of the world. To keep you there, in my arms, for a week…a month…a year. I want to make love to you until we both pass out from exhaustion. And then I want to love you all over again."

His communication skills were definitely improving.

"Why…" she began, the word sticking in her parched throat. She licked her lips, unnerved by the way his gaze followed her tongue. "Why didn't you say something before?"

"Because it's impossible. You have a policy against guys like me. And even if you didn't, I can't afford to take that kind of risk." He stepped away from her. "You're trouble, Lucy Moore. You've been trouble since the first day we met."

The loss of his body heat didn't explain the sudden chill deep inside her. He meant it. Stubborn determination steeled his gray eyes. How could he kiss her like that one moment, then want nothing to do with her the next? Was it possible that he hadn't experienced the same emotional upheaval during that kiss? Was it possible that she was falling in love with Nick Chamberlin?

Lucy sucked in her breath. "I don't know what you mean. I've just been trying to help with the case."

"That's the problem. From now on, I'm working solo."

She blinked back her shock at his unexpected announcement. "You can't be serious."

"No more contact between us. Except by telephone. It's the only way I'll agree to keep working for you."

She couldn't believe it. He was actually afraid of her. What next? A clove of garlic around his neck to keep her at bay? "This is ridiculous. I'll admit I'm attracted to you, too." A serious understatement, considering her knees were so weak, she needed to lean against the wall to remain upright. "If we both exercise some self-control, I'm sure we can resist temptation."

"I can't," he said baldly. "Not anymore."

"Just until after the case," she promised.

A muscle flickered in his jaw. "Nothing is going to change once the case is over. I don't want any complications in my life, and you can't risk your dreams by becoming involved with an ex-con—a dirty cop who will never be accepted in this city."

"So you're doing this for me?" she asked, helpless and frustrated as she saw her newest, most precious dream slipping away. The dream conceived in Nick's arms. Tears stung her eyes. "For a dirty cop, you're annoyingly noble. Besides, I'm old enough to make my own decisions."

''The decision's already made. I won't let you sacrifice your life, too.''

''What does that mean?''

''Nothing. End of discussion.'' He reached around her to open the door. As it swung open, he turned her around and gave her a gentle shove.

She took one look inside her apartment and screamed.

CHAPTER SEVEN

"Wow," NICK SAID, stepping over the threshold. "This place really is a mess. Have you ever thought about hiring a cleaning service?"

"I didn't do this," she exclaimed, looking around her living room in disbelief. "I may not be Martha Stewart, but I'm not a total slob. Someone must have broken in."

She wrapped her arms around herself, attempting to ward off the cold emptiness growing inside of her. Her apartment was in total disarray. Clothes from the laundry basket she'd left by the door were strewn all over the floor. All the books from her bookshelf lay open in haphazard piles. Every drawer of the antique buffet stood open and empty, the contents of each dumped onto the carpet below.

"Don't touch anything," Nick warned just as she reached down to pick up a shattered photograph of Melvin on his motorcycle. "The police will want to check for fingerprints."

"Police." She mouthed the word under her breath, still not ready to believe this could really be happening to her.

Nick pushed her gently onto an easy chair. "You sit here while I check out the rest of the apartment."

His words had barely registered before he was back by her side. "The kitchen, bathroom and your bedroom all look like this one. The intruder was certainly thorough."

"But not very neat."

"Can you tell if anything is missing?"

She looked around the disheveled room again as the reality slowly began to sink in. "Actually, it looks like he added stuff. I can't believe all this mess belongs to me."

Then her eyes widened in horror. "Someone was inside my apartment. Do you know what that means?"

Nick nodded. "You probably feel violated."

"What I feel is embarrassed! Some total stranger saw my apartment." She closed her eyes. "All those dirty dishes on the counter. I didn't even have time to wipe off the kitchen table after breakfast this morning. And the bathroom..." She groaned and leaned her head back against the chair. "I was going to mop the floor tomorrow. Really."

"Don't be ridiculous," he snapped. "Who cares what the scum who did this thinks?"

She stood up. "I've got to clean up before the police get here."

"I told you not to touch anything."

"Just a little dusting," she said, eyeing the thick

layer on top of the buffet. "Maybe give the bathtub a quick wipe."

"Lucy," he said, pulling her back down into the chair. "You can scour the place from top to bottom *after* the police check everything out. I called them from the bedroom. They should be here any minute."

"Great. First they think I'm a lousy hooker, and now they'll think I'm a lousy housekeeper." A lump lodged in her throat as she swallowed a sob.

Nick kneeled down next to her chair, gently brushing her hair off her cheek. "Everything will be all right. We'll catch the jerk who did this to you. I promise."

If only he'd hold her in his arms…make her feel safe…make her feel comforted. Make her feel like he was paying attention. "Nick?" she said, as he stared at something over her shoulder.

He stood. "Your answering machine is blinking." He walked over to the telephone stand. Picking up a pencil, he pushed the play button with the tip of the eraser.

She was experiencing one of the most traumatic moments of her life, and he was worried about retrieving phone messages. "Were you expecting a call?"

"No. But the burglar might have called earlier to make certain the apartment was empty. It's a typical M.O."

The first message was an insurance salesman who, ironically, offered a special one-month rate against theft and burglary. The second was from Letitia Beaumont, wondering if Lucy could serve tea at the meeting of the Heritage Library Foundation.

The third caller didn't identify himself. "Hello, Lucy," he said, the voice sounding muffled and far away. "Will you pick up if you're there? Lucy? I have an important message for you. Pick up, Lucy."

"Do you know who that was?" Nick asked, as the answering machine beeped twice to indicate the end of the messages.

She shook her head. "I don't think so. He doesn't sound the same."

Nick slowly turned around to face her. "The same as what?"

"As the other guy." She wrinkled her nose. "This one sounds rougher, meaner. Floyd's voice is higher, and he has kind of an asthmatic wheeze when he talks."

"Who is Floyd?"

"My stalker," she said, then shrugged her shoulders. "Well, that's not really his name. I just call him that."

Nick sat down on the sofa next to her chair. "Slow down a minute. Someone is *stalking* you?"

She shrugged again. "Well, maybe not technically stalking me. He leaves bizarre messages on my answering machine. Once in a while it seems like a light blue Ford Escort is tailing me. But there have to be hundreds of those around, right?"

"Anything else?"

"I've found footprints outside my window. But that could be the gardener or the meter man."

"It's October, Lucy. All the plants and flowers are dead. And I saw the gas meter on the way in. It's next to the laundry room."

"Well, there has to be a reasonable explanation for the footprints. I can't believe someone would actually spy on me."

"How long have you been getting the phone calls?"

She thought a moment. "Just for the past few weeks."

"And you call this guy Floyd?" Nick asked in a strangled voice.

"It made it all seem less scary. I didn't want to overreact to a few crank phone calls. Besides, why would anyone be stalking me?"

"Why would anyone break into your apartment?" he asked, pacing back and forth across the living room. "Or frame your brother? I can't believe you didn't tell me about this sooner."

"Oh, Nick," she exclaimed, smiling amidst the chaos. "This is wonderful. You finally believe someone framed Melvin."

He stopped pacing. "I think it's a possibility. But I don't want to talk about your brother at the moment. I want to know about Floyd—every little detail."

"GUESS THAT ABOUT WRAPS it up," Lieutenant Delaney said as the evidence crew left the apartment with all their samples in tiny plastic bags. "Are you certain nothing is missing, Miss Moore?"

"I don't know," Lucy said, hugging Sherlock to her chest. She'd finally found him underneath her bed, guarding the dust bunnies. "He didn't take my mother's pearl ring or the gold bracelet Melvin gave me for my college graduation."

"Her television set and all the appliances are still here, too," Nick added. "Seems like the perp was on a search-and-destroy mission."

"Searching for what?" she asked.

Lieutenant Delaney seated himself on the vinyl ottoman, flipping open his notebook. "That's what we need to figure out. Now Nick told me you've been receiving some unusual phone calls."

"He told you about Floyd?"

Nick rubbed his temple. Leave it to Lucy to give her stalker a name. Next, she'd be leaving him milk and cookies on the doorstep.

Lieutenant Delaney jotted the name down in his notebook. "Do you know Floyd's last name?"

"I don't even know his first name. I just call him Floyd."

Delaney looked at Nick.

"Don't ask," Nick said. "The important thing is Lucy doesn't think Floyd left the latest message on the answering machine."

Delaney nodded. "I listened to it several times. Sounds like his voice is disguised."

"Which means it could still be Floyd," Nick said.

"Or someone else she knows," Delaney added.

Lucy's mouth fell open. "You think I might know the person who did all this?" she asked, indicating the disaster area that used to be her living room.

Nick sat forward in his chair, his elbows on his knees. "Check out a guy named Walter 'Weasel' Malone," he told Delaney. "See if he can explain his whereabouts for the past eight hours."

"Weasel would never do this to me," Lucy said. "Besides, he's allergic to cat hair. He wouldn't last five minutes in here with Sherlock. It's probably just some random burglary that could have happened to anyone."

Nick turned to her. "How many burglars do you know leave the house empty-handed?"

"Number one, I don't know any burglars...anymore. And number two, my stuff isn't that nice. Maybe Jamie thought it wasn't worth the effort."

"Jamie?" Nick and Delaney said at the same time.

"I think that's what we should call him to avoid confusion," Lucy said. "Or her. After all, this is the nineties. I'm sure there are as many women in the burglary business now as there are men."

"Perhaps you should see a crisis counselor," Delaney suggested gently. "I'm sure this has been an upsetting experience for you."

Lucy blinked at him. "There's nothing wrong with me. I'm perfectly fine."

Delaney looked skeptically at Nick.

Nick gave a brief nod. "Don't worry about Lucy. She's always like this."

The lieutenant cleared his throat. "Fine. Then let's proceed. Did you leave any doors or windows unlocked today?"

"I always leave the north bedroom window open about four inches for Sherlock."

"Now wait a minute," Delaney said. "You've got a stalker named Floyd, a burglar named Jamie and now Sherlock. Who is he and what's his crime?"

"Sherlock's my cat," she explained. "And he's not guilty of anything except drooling over my neighbor's pet parakeet. He likes to lie on the windowsill and enjoy the breeze. Maybe Jamie got in that way."

Delaney jotted the information in his notepad. "Does anyone else have a key to your apartment?"

Lucy nibbled her lip. "Melvin did have one, but he gave it back to me after his arrest. Oh, and I used to have a roommate."

"Male or female."

Lucy could feel Nick tense beside her. "Female," she said. "Barbara moved to England last year."

"I think you should make a list of all your friends and acquaintances," Nick suggested. "And anyone who might hold a grudge against you."

"Jamie probably doesn't even know me," Lucy said, not wanting to believe any of her friends could do this to her. "What if he lost his job and has three small, hungry children and a pregnant wife? Desperation drove him to break into my apartment, but then he came to his senses and—"

"Lucy," Nick interjected, his voice hard-edged and impatient, "this isn't some fairy tale. This is real life. Someone broke into your apartment. A criminal. A thief. A murderer, for all we know. When I think you could have been alone here with him…"

"Miss Moore's wild imagination seems to be contagious," Delaney said. "I deal in facts. Someone broke into your apartment, went through everything with a fine-tooth comb but took nothing. Which means he didn't find what he was looking for."

"But what was he looking for?" Lucy asked. "I don't have anything valuable."

Nick turned to her. "The evidence."

Her mouth fell open. "From Goldie's gossip column?"

"Is this the column that claimed you found new evidence in the case against Melvin Moore?"

"You saw it, too?" Nick asked the detective.

Delaney snorted. "It was big news down at the station. You know cops don't like to be accused of shoddy investigating—especially Cole Rafferty."

"I wanted to flush out the real arsonist," Lucy explained. "Goldie offered to help me."

"And that's when you told her about this new evidence?" Delaney asked. "The proof that can set your brother free?"

"It does exist," Lucy insisted. "I just haven't

found it yet. But I was hoping the real arsonist would panic and do something stupid—reveal himself.''

''Looks like he panicked all right,'' Nick said.

Delaney tapped his pen against the notepad. ''So let me get this straight. You made it all up? There is no new evidence in the case?''

''That's why the burglar left empty-handed,'' Nick concluded. ''But that doesn't mean he won't be back.''He turned to Delaney. ''I think Lucy should be under police protection.''

Delaney shook his head. ''We just don't have that kind of manpower, Chamberlin. Unless you want me to put her in the lockup—for her own protection.''

Lucy shot to her feet. She knew Nick wanted to be rid of her, but locking her away seemed a little extreme. ''One Moore in your jail is already one too many. You can't put me there against my will.''

''She's right about that,'' Delaney agreed, ''although I think it may be for the best.''

Lucy shook her head. ''No way.''

Nick stood up and folded his arms across his chest, stubbornness practically oozing from every pore. ''Then I've got an even better idea.''

''THIS IS NICKY'S ROOM,'' Sadie said, leading Lucy into a large attic bedroom with a double bed and a dresser tucked in one corner. A round stained-glass window spilled a rainbow of colors on the polished hardwood floor. ''You can unpack while I make us a nice pot of chicken gumbo for dinner.''

"I don't know how to thank you," Lucy said, setting down her suitcase, her legs still shaky from the shock of seeing her home torn apart. "I still think Nick's overreacting, but he wouldn't take no for an answer. He insisted I stay with you while he camps out at my apartment."

"He does have a stubborn streak."

"Tell me about it." Lucy sat down on the bed, then plopped backward, sinking into the downy comforter. "He never listens to a word I say. He's bossy and opinionated and bullheaded."

"All the things I love about him," Sadie chimed. "But he has his faults, too."

"What if the burglar does come back to my apartment?" Lucy asked, voicing the fear that had been niggling at her for the last hour. "Nick could be in danger."

"Don't worry. My grandson knows how to take care of himself." Sadie stepped back and eyed Lucy from head to toe. "I think it will just about fit."

"What?" she asked, distracted by the scent of Nick on the bedcovers. It made her stomach flip-flop to think of him sleeping here, cozy and rumpled and practically naked. Unless he slept in pajamas. But for some reason, pajamas and Nick Chamberlin just didn't seem to go together.

"My wedding dress. We might have to take up the hem a bit, but otherwise I think it will be perfect."

Lucy sat up. "Your wedding dress?"

"It's a long satin gown. Very simple. Nothing elaborate or fussy.'' Sadie tapped her chin with one finger. ''And I think a circlet of delicate silk flowers for your hair. Or would you prefer a veil?''

''Sadie, I'm not planning a wedding.''

''Oh, I know that, dear. Not yet. First we have to settle this little mix-up with your brother. But once he's out of jail, there's no reason for you and Nicky to wait any longer.''

''Me and Nicky?'' Lucy squeaked. She'd imagined herself married someday. When the right man came along. But that man couldn't be Nick, with his unsavory background and dead-end future. *Could it?* Just the thought of spending the rest of her days and nights with him made her feel dizzy. Probably not a good sign.

''You two are made for each other. I've never seen Nicky as animated as he is around you. He can't take his eyes off you.''

''I think it's a form of self-defense. He still hasn't forgotten about that peanut butter incident.'' Lucy stared up at the thin, jagged crack in the plaster ceiling, wondering how many times Nick had stared up at the same crack, wondering how many dreams he'd made for himself while lying awake in this bed.

Had any of his dreams ever come true?

''You'll both laugh about it someday.'' Sadie moved over to the closet, making room on the rod for Lucy's clothes. ''Nicky has a wonderful sense of humor.''

She'd rarely even seen him smile. But the few

times he had, her knees had gone weak. Nick revealed himself to her in bits and pieces, like a jigsaw puzzle that promises a great picture, but drives you crazy as you try to put it together.

Now he didn't even want to see her again, much less marry her. He'd made that perfectly clear after kissing her senseless outside her front door.

"Nicky doesn't want you to tell anyone you're staying here," Sadie reminded her. "He'll forward your mail and relay any important phone calls. And you're not to go anywhere except work without his permission."

"This is ridiculous," Lucy cried, frustrated with Nick and the way her life was spinning out of control. She didn't know what she wanted anymore. "I'm twenty-eight years old. I'm a college graduate. I'm an honorary member of the Book-of-the-Month Club. He can't tell me what to do!"

"Take it from me, Lucy," Sadie said, patting her shoulder sympathetically. "Never argue with a Chamberlin man. It's a waste of breath."

"YOU'RE WASTING your breath, Chamberlin," Cole Rafferty said the next morning. He sat with his feet propped on the desk while he munched on a doughnut. "A matchbook isn't exactly a written confession. You never would have released a suspect on such flimsy evidence. Bring me something more solid and we can reopen the investigation."

"We've got a tip," Nick announced. "There may

be an eyewitness. A woman who saw the man that started that fire.''

Cole's eyes widened. ''Now this is what I mean by solid. Give me something I can go on. Have you got a name?''

Nick shook his head. ''Not yet. But I've got this.'' He flipped the matchbook Vanessa had given him onto the desk. ''Harold and Letitia Beaumont, Happy Fortieth Wedding Anniversary. April nineteenth. The same night as the fire. Now tell me how an identical matchbook ended up in the Hanover Building?''

Cole stared at the matchbook on his desk, then shrugged. ''It could have belonged to Mad Dog himself. You know the guys in the lab couldn't find any prints.''

''Mad Dog wasn't at the party.''

Cole pulled his feet off the desk, sitting straight up in his chair. ''He wasn't *invited*. But we both know someone with Mad Dog's background isn't adverse to crashing a party.''

''Then let's interview the guests to see if anyone spotted him there. Did you get the list?''

Cole shook his head as he licked powdered sugar off his fingertips. ''Nope. The Beaumonts disposed of the invitation list shortly after the party. According to Mrs. Beaumont, over two hundred people were invited.'' Cole sighed. ''My invitation must have gotten lost in the mail.''

''The Beaumonts were probably afraid you'd

charm the designer stockings off their daughter. Of course, they don't know you like I do.''

"Hey," Cole said, holding up both hands, "I'd know better than to abscond with Mad Dog Moore's woman. I value my life."

"Maybe that's it," Nick ventured. "One of those smooth, preppy boys fell for Vanessa but couldn't compete with Mad Dog, so he decided to get him out of the way."

"I think you've been spending too much time with that lovely librarian. That scenario sounds straight out of a mystery novel."

Nick had to agree. He was getting desperate for an explanation, any explanation other than the one Lucy didn't want to hear—that her brother was guilty of arson. If only they had something more concrete to go on. So far, all their investigation had turned up was a couple matchbooks and a possible unknown eyewitness with a flower name. Hardly enough to justify reopening the investigation.

He rubbed his jaw, frustrated with his lack of progress in the case. "Can you come up with a better scenario?"

Cole grinned. "Maybe Floyd and Jamie teamed up to do it."

Nick folded his arms across his chest. "Very funny. I take it Delaney can't keep his big mouth shut?"

Cole shook his head. "That Lucy is priceless. Not

to mention creative, sweet and incredibly sexy in a red wig. Are you *sure* she doesn't have a sister?''

"Believe me," Nick said, pocketing the matchbook, "Lucy is one of a kind."

"GOOD AFTERNOON, LADIES," Lucy said, hurrying into the Monday-afternoon meeting of the Merry Widows Book Club. "I'm so sorry I'm late. We've got several new patrons, so we're busier than usual around here today."

"How nice," Veda said. "Mr. Bonn must be pleased."

Lucy just smiled as she took her seat. Lester wasn't pleased. In fact, he was mortified. Most of the new patrons were people Lucy recruited the night she went undercover as a prostitute. They'd brought in their children for the reading hour and signed up for library cards and had the library director scurrying to the telephone to call his mother. He didn't like change, believing the library to be an almost sacred institution.

He reminded her of the starchy librarian she'd been terrified of as a small child. The one who had always made Lucy and the other kids from Bale Street wash their hands before they touched any of the books.

Lester had looked like he wanted to scour the library from floor to ceiling with disinfectant. Fortunately for him, the library closed at six o'clock on Monday evenings so they could find room in the tight city budget to be open on Sunday afternoons. He only had to handle three more hours of these unconventional library patrons. Though Lucy sincerely hoped they returned to take advantage of all the Heritage Library had to offer.

An empty chair caught her attention. "Where's Sadie?"

"That's what we were wondering," Edith said. "We can't start the meeting without her. She has to read the minutes."

Lucy blinked. "Minutes? But we're a book club. We don't have minutes."

"We do now, dear," Veda said, pulling out her knitting needles. "We voted Sadie in as secretary after our last meeting."

"Oh," Lucy said, still confused. "Why?"

"Some of us suffer from short-term memory loss," Goldie explained in a whisper.

Lenora Eberly bristled. "I may be forgetful, but I'm not deaf. Besides, I think it's a good idea to keep a record of our meetings."

"Especially since they've gotten so exciting lately," Edith piped up.

Goldie turned to Lucy. "You can bring us up-to-date while we wait for Sadie. Tell us everything." The small circle of women fluttered with anticipation.

Lucy didn't know where to begin. "Well…we still haven't found the real arsonist, but he did break into my apartment because of that item you planted in your column."

Goldie clapped her hands. "That's wonderful!"

Lucy nodded. "Actually, it is. Because now Nick

really believes Mad Dog is innocent. Of course, he also thinks I might be in danger, so he forced me to move out of my own home. And he won't tell me about the new lead in the case."

"Isn't that romantic?" Veda cried. "He's trying to protect you."

Or avoid her. She hadn't even seen him since the night of their arrest two whole days ago. Ignoring her might work for Nick, but it only made Lucy very aware of how much she missed him. It probably didn't help matters that she'd been sleeping in his bed, wrapping her arms around his pillow every night just to breathe in his scent. Pathetic, but true.

"The problem is that I want to help solve this case," Lucy said. "But Nick just won't listen to reason."

"He is a man, dear," Lenora reminded her.

Edith nodded. "Just give him some time. He'll come around to your way of thinking."

"They always do," Veda added. "Love makes people act pretty crazy sometimes."

"But we're not in love," Lucy protested, feeling a telltale blush creep into her cheeks.

They all smiled and Goldie winked at her. She was outnumbered. A dozen reasons why she couldn't love Nick Chamberlin battled on the tip of her tongue: his prison record, his sullied reputation, his uncertain future. But they didn't seem to matter much anymore. Not when she thought about the Nick she'd come to know. How he took care of his grandmother, sang show tunes…kissed with a consuming intensity that made her cheeks burn just to think about it.

She fanned a sheet of paper in front of her face, ready to introduce a safer topic, like fictional serial killers, when she saw Lester in the doorway, waving frantically at her.

Excusing herself, she walked over to him. "What is it, Lester?"

"Another one of *those women* has arrived," he hissed, motioning behind him. A petite young woman with straight, blond hair that reached almost to her waist stood next to the huge globe in the corner.

"Mother said I'm not to associate with anyone wearing leather or a nose ring," he said, his thin lips pinched with disapproval. "Since you're responsible for bringing this rabble to the library, you can deal with it. I'll send Mindy up to handle your book club duties."

Lucy bit back an angry retort. "Fine. I'll be more than happy to assist her."

Lester sniffed. "Wait until Mrs. Beaumont hears about all this," he mumbled as he strode away.

Lucy sighed inwardly, used to Lester's dissatisfaction with her unorthodox ideas. Over the years, he'd submitted a series of complaints about her. The last typed report critiquing her conduct had been four single-spaced pages long.

Telling herself to forget about her problems with Lester, she turned to the waiflike woman in the baggy blue sweater and skin-tight black leather pants. The flush in the girl's cheeks told Lucy she'd overheard Lester's tantrum.

"I'm Lucy," she said with a welcoming smile. "How can I help you, Miss…?"

"Vyne," the girl said softly. "But you can call me Lily."

CHAPTER EIGHT

Lucy's heart skipped a beat. "Lily?"

She nodded. "I heard you were looking for me. One of the girls gave me a bookmark with the name and address of this place. I thought the library might be a safe place to…" Her voice trailed off and her blue eyes grew wide with apprehension as voices sounded in the stairwell.

Lucy pulled her into the audiovisual room, closing the door behind them. "We can have some privacy in here," she said, flipping on the lights. Then she turned around. "You're the one, aren't you? The eye-witness."

Lily sank into a chair. "I know Melvin didn't start that fire."

"You call him Melvin?" Lucy hadn't heard anyone call him by his real name for years. When he was twelve he'd earned the moniker Mad Dog by facing down a vicious street mongrel and coming out on top. During his teen years, he spent most of his time in trouble, just trying to live up to his reputation. Only Lucy had known there was really a sweet puppy dog beneath all that bluster.

A rosy blush suffused Lily's pale cheeks. "He

asked me to call him Melvin. I'd see him sometimes on the street. Not that he ever wanted to do any… business. Melvin was always very kind to me.''

Lucy's heart melted. ''I'm glad. My brother may act tough, but he's really just a big pushover—especially for a pretty girl.''

Lily's blush deepened. ''He always treated me like a lady. I couldn't believe it when they arrested him.''

Lucy slid into the chair next to her. ''Why didn't you come forward? Try to help Melvin? Go to the police and tell them what you saw?''

''No one would have believed me.''

''I'm sure that's not true.''

''I am.'' Lily chewed on her lower lip. ''The guy wore a tuxedo that night, but I still recognized him. He didn't see me standing there in the shadows. Shortly after he left Melvin's place, I saw smoke rolling out of the windows.'' She twisted her fingers in her lap. ''I called 911 from the phone booth on the corner to report the fire. Then I ran.''

''Oh, Lily, you recognized him!'' Her mind raced to absorb this new information. *A tuxedo?* Fancy dress for such dirty work. ''Now we can nail the real arsonist. You can identify him….''

Lily shot to her feet. ''No. I can't.''

''I'll go down to the police station with you,'' Lucy promised. ''You can tell them who you saw. Then all you'll probably have to do is pick him out of a lineup.''

Lily emphatically shook her head and started backing toward the door. "I've probably said too much already. If he finds out…"

Lucy rose. "But Lily, you may be the only one who can help Melvin."

"I'm sorry," Lily cried. "I can't. I just…can't." Then she turned and bolted out the door.

Lucy raced after her, knowing she might never see her again if Lily didn't want to be found. Her heels skidded on the polished tile floor as she rounded the corner. She slammed straight into a hard, broad chest that emitted a resounding "Ooomph!"

"Sorry," she gasped, her gaze still on Lily's retreating back. She tried to step away, but two strong arms held her firmly in place. She looked up to find Nick gazing down at her with molten gray eyes.

"We've got to stop meeting like this," he said.

She pointed toward the swinging library door. "That was her. That was the eyewitness!"

"Marigold?"

"Her name is Lily," she said, very aware of the heat of his body and the way his long fingers spanned her waist. She took a step away from him so she could think more clearly.

Nick was still staring at the door. "I can't believe it. Weasel actually gave us a legitimate tip. Do you want me to go after her?"

"No," Lucy said, really wanting him to hold her again. But she had to think of her brother first. Even if just the sight of Nick Chamberlin made her heart thump in her chest.

She took another step back from him, still not quite trusting herself. "What are you doing here?"

He held up a canvas tote bag. "Gram forgot her books. I thought she might want them for the meeting."

"I'm sure she will, but she isn't here yet."

He frowned. "That's impossible. She said she had a ride to the library. And I found the tote bag sitting out on the front stoop."

Lucy motioned toward the open door of the meeting room. "See for yourself. Everybody's here but Sadie."

Nick looked in the room, then looked at Lucy. "If she's not here, then where the hell is she?"

She shrugged. "I don't know. She never misses a book club meeting. Maybe we should ask the other members. They might have talked to her."

Lester rounded the corner. "Excuse me, Miss Moore. You have a telephone call."

Lucy looked up at Nick. "I'd better take it."

He nodded. "Go ahead. I'll ask the ladies if any of them have talked to Gram today. If they don't know anything, I'm contacting the police." He rubbed one hand over his midsection. "I have a bad feeling about this."

So did Lucy. She hurried to the telephone, telling herself not to worry—only she knew Sadie never missed a meeting of the Merry Widows. Anxiety trickled through her as she stepped over two toddlers to reach for the phone. "Hello?"

"Lucy, thank God. I thought I'd never find you." The masculine voice on the other end sounded strained, yet familiar.

"Weasel?" she guessed.

"Yeah, it's me. I've been trying to reach you all afternoon."

"Weasel, turn your television down," she said. "I can hardly hear you."

"I said I've been looking for you everywhere," he yelled. "That twit who answers the phone kept saying you can't receive personal calls. I finally told him it was an emergency."

Lucy's heart froze in her chest. "An emergency? Oh my God! Is it Melvin?" Her two weeks weren't up yet. Had he gotten impatient? Made his prison break early? She sucked in her breath. "Has something happened to him?"

"No, no, nothing like that." He paused a moment, and she could hear strains of music playing in the background. "But you've got to get over here."

"Where are you?"

"My place. The apartment on Bale Street. Number 503."

She twisted the phone cord in her fingers. "This really isn't a good time...."

"Please come, Luce," he said as the music blared louder. "Please. I...don't know what else to do."

The hairs prickled on the back of her neck. But it wasn't Weasel's frantic, harassed tone that unnerved her. It was the music she heard on the other end of the line, the music she finally recognized. The theme song to *Oklahoma*.

"I'll be there in ten minutes."

ONE HOUR and one flat tire later, Lucy arrived on Bale Street. It looked the same as it had when she was ten years old. There was still litter in the streets, gang members on the corners, and a sign in Rigetto's Bakery window offering free weight-loss classes.

Apartment buildings lined the rest of the block—tall, stark brick structures with broken windows and graffiti sprayed on the front stoops. Her old house had been torn down long ago, replaced by a Jiffy Lube. Even with all the changes in her life, part of her would always think of this street as home. Growing up here had made her both strong and stubborn. More importantly, it had taught her to dream.

Only now, her dreams went beyond a successful career and a house in a nice neighborhood. She wanted family around her. Not only Melvin, free and happy, but a family of her own—a husband and children, a house that was really a home and a kind of love she'd never dared dream of before. The kind of love that survived whether you lived on Bale Street or the Eagle Estates. The kind of love she had for Nick.

Reconciled with her past and optimistic about her future, she strode into Weasel's apartment building, smiling at the ragtag little girl of about nine standing just inside the front door.

"Hey, lady," the girl said, her chin jutting out, her wispy blond braids falling over her shoulders. "Wanna buy a genuine gold bracelet? Only twenty bucks."

Lucy looked at the tin bracelet in the girl's grubby hand. She'd bet a lot more than twenty bucks that the *genuine gold* bracelet would turn her wrist green in less than a day. She knew a con when she saw one. And she also knew no one on Bale Street respected a sucker.

"Twenty bucks for that Cracker Jack toy?" Lucy replied skeptically. "I won't pay a dime over ten."

"Deal," the girl said instantly, trying to hide a toothy grin.

"You didn't let me finish," Lucy said, trying to hide a grin of her own. "I'll pay you five dollars now and the another five when you show up at the Heritage Library and check out a certain book that I know a smart girl like you will just love. I'm a librarian there and read the same book when I was about your age."

The little girl shrewdly eyed Lucy's tailored silk suit. "Make it ten bucks when I check out that book, and you've got a deal."

"Deal," Lucy said, exchanging the cheap bracelet for a crisp five-dollar bill and knowing the little girl would be getting something so much more out of the bargain. This is what Lucy wanted to do with her life: help people find their dreams.

As she rode the elevator up five floors, she added

to the graffiti on the walls. With a red flair pen she wrote: For A Good Time, Call This Number. Then she printed the Heritage library's telephone number below.

She just hoped Lester didn't find out about her newest promotional idea.

When she reached the fifth floor, Lucy walked down the long, narrow hallway, looking for her destination. To her surprise, the door to apartment 503 stood wide open. Most residents of Bale Street knew not only to lock their door, but to invest in a deadbolt, chain lock, motion alarm, and if they were smart, a hungry pit bull.

Nobody left their door wide open.

Lucy stepped gingerly over the threshold, impressed by the spotless appearance of the living room and tiny kitchen nook. The roar of a vacuum cleaner sounded from a back bedroom. "Weasel?" she called.

When no one answered, she seated herself on the threadbare sofa to wait until he finished. She'd never known him to be meticulously neat, but perhaps he had changed over the years…or developed an obsessive-compulsive disorder.

She picked up a magazine off the polished coffee table, flipping through the pages of *The Mercenary Gazette*. It was filled with articles on all the latest assault weapons as well as letters from mercenary enthusiasts. Correct grammar and spelling obviously weren't high on their list of requirements.

"Lucy."

She looked up to see Weasel standing at the front door, a bag of groceries in each arm.

"Thank God you're here," he said, setting the bags on the coffee table. "What took you so long?"

"I had a flat tire," she explained. "The door was open so I just walked in. I thought you were vacuuming." They both turned toward the noise emanating from the back room.

He groaned. "So she's still here."

"Who? Your mother?"

He shook his head. "Worse."

"Who could possibly be worse than your mother?" Lucy asked, remembering the acerbic Mrs. Malone.

Weasel sat down on the sofa, burying his head in his hands. "I don't know how I ever got into this mess. A few easy bucks isn't worth what I've been through."

Lucy sat down next to him, almost afraid to voice her worst fears. "It's Sadie Chamberlin, isn't it? You've got her here."

He nodded, his face still hidden.

"You kidnapped her," she breathed. "*You really kidnapped her.* I can't believe it. Weasel, how could you ever do such a thing?"

Raising his head, he took a deep breath. "I didn't kidnap her. I'm just...detaining her for a while. She was delivered this morning. My instructions were to keep her here until further notice."

"Instructions? From whom?"

He shrugged. "I don't know his name. Some guy who calls me whenever he wants a job done."

She shot to her feet. "Like kidnapping? I thought you went straight, Weasel."

"I did. *I am.* I usually turn him down when he calls. I've certainly never done anything like this before." He wrung his hands together. "But this job came up and the money was too good to turn down. I want to get out of this neighborhood, Lucy, just like you did. And I might have a chance if my book is a hit. But I need some fast cash to cover printing and promotional expenses."

She blinked back her surprise. "Book? What book?"

A blush stained the skin under his whiskers. "I write…poems. My publisher says they're good, but he's just got a small press. If I want good distribution, I have to kick in some bucks."

"Oh, Weasel," she said, sinking back down onto the sofa. "There are other ways to get money. Grants, loans, a second job. I've heard they have an opening at Farley's Fish Hut."

"For minimum wage? That would take forever. I'm already thirty years old. Sometimes I think I'll never get out of this neighborhood." He rubbed his temple with his fingertips. "This was my ticket out, Luce."

Her pity for him turned to anger when she remembered exactly what he'd done. "By manhandling a defenseless old woman? Poor Sadie! Not only have you kept her locked away here against her will, you're forcing her to clean your apartment.''

"You don't understand...."

"Oh, I understand." She leapt to her feet. "I understand that Nick was right. You're still a two-bit hood. And I've been defending you!"

He rose with his hands up, backing away from her as she stalked toward him. "Now wait a minute...."

"If you've harmed one hair on her head..." she warned.

"I'd never do that."

"But you'd make her grandson go crazy with worry," she accused, grappling in her purse for her hair spray. "And you'd make Sadie feel alone and afraid."

Weasel tripped over a footstool, falling to the floor. "I'm the one who's afraid," he clarified, holding one arm up in self-defense. "I'm afraid she'll never leave. In the last few hours, Sadie Chamberlin has made my life a living hell."

Lucy lowered the hair spray. "What are you talking about?"

He swallowed. "She's driving me crazy. Why do you think the door is wide open? For fresh air? I've tried everything to get her out of here. I even called her a taxi."

"You expect me to believe that?"

"It's true! She took control as soon as she stepped over the threshold. She made me watch *Oklahoma.*"

He ran a shaky hand over his forehead. "And now I can't get those songs out of my head!"

She took a step back. "You let her watch *Oklahoma?*"

He snorted. "*Let her?* I haven't *let* her do anything. She just does exactly what she wants to do. If you don't believe me, just ask her." He hitched his thumb toward the hallway.

Lucy looked up to see Sadie pushing the upright vacuum cleaner toward a corner closet.

"Lucy," Sadie exclaimed with a wide smile. "What a nice surprise. Walter, get up off that floor. I just vacuumed in here. And take those shoes off. I told you I want to give them a good polish."

"But they're tennis shoes," he squeaked, rising to his feet. "*Canvas* tennis shoes."

"And just think how nice and bright they'll look after I whiten them up." She set the vacuum cleaner in the closet, then shut the door. "Oh, by the way, I told your next-door neighbor, Vinnie, to keep the noise down or you'd be over to teach him a lesson. And I strongly suggested he take a bath."

He gulped. "Vinnie the Viper?"

"Is that what was tattooed on his chest? I thought it was a caterpillar. It was hard to tell with all those chains."

An oven timer chimed from the kitchen. "There are my sticky buns," Sadie said, moving toward the kitchen. Then she turned to Weasel. "I put that prune sauce in the refrigerator for you. That should help take care of that little problem we talked about earlier.''

When she was out of the room, Weasel turned to Lucy. ''You've got to help me. Please take her with you. I'll never do anything like this again. I've learned my lesson.''

''Then prove it,'' Lucy replied, still upset with him. ''Tell me who hired you to do his dirty work.''

Weasel sank down onto the sofa. ''I already told you I don't know his name. But I think he's connected to the Protégé Project.''

Lucy sat down next to him. ''The Protégé Project? But that doesn't make any sense. They hire people to mow lawns and paint houses, not commit felonies.''

Weasel shrugged. ''All I know is that every once in a while, me or one of the other guys in the program gets a call to do a job that pays a heck of a lot more than parking cars.''

What could be going on? Whatever it was, Weasel did seem genuinely remorseful. She almost couldn't blame him for succumbing to temptation. She knew that burning desire to get off Bale Street, to make a better life for yourself. But just how far would Weasel go? She leveled her gaze on him. ''So did this mystery man send you to the Hanover Building the same night Nick and I were there?''

''No. Mad Dog sent me there to get the keys and title to his car. He wanted to sell it so you wouldn't have to pay his legal fees.'' He sighed. ''And I know what you're thinking, Luce. But I didn't start that fire, either.''

Lucy stood up. "I don't know what to think. And what am I going to tell Nick?"

"I don't know…I don't care at this point." Weasel wrung his hands together. "Just take that woman with you."

They both looked up as Sadie walked back into the living room, wiping her hands on a dish towel. "Sticky buns, anyone?"

"Why don't we go home now, Sadie?" Lucy suggested. "You've done enough work for one day."

"I've barely scratched the surface," Sadie replied. "Poor Walter needs a woman's touch around here. I could probably stay a month and find plenty to keep me busy."

Weasel visibly paled.

"But Nick's worried sick about you," Lucy said. "He thinks…you've been kidnapped."

Sadie frowned. "Now that's just plain silly. A taxi-cab arrived at the house this morning, and the driver told me I'd won a free ride. Does that sound like kidnapping?"

"No," Lucy admitted. "But it does sound a little odd."

Sadie nodded. "The cab dropped me off in front of the building and Walter met me at the front door. I thought it was all part of that community mentor program I signed up for at the library."

"And I can't thank you enough," Weasel said,

pulling Sadie toward the door. "Really. This is a day I'll never forget."

Sadie patted his cheek. "You are such a sweet boy. And I think with a proper haircut, you'd be a real charmer."

Weasel reached for his ponytail. "Haircut?"

"I'll bring my scissors next time," Sadie promised.

"Next time?" he squeaked.

"And you can keep that copy of *Oklahoma* until then."

"Oh, no," he protested. "I absolutely couldn't do that."

"Of course you can. I've got two more copies at home. Work on those dance steps, too. You almost had it this afternoon."

"Maybe you can teach me a few, Sadie," Lucy said as they walked out the door. She had a feeling she'd need them when she tried to explain all this to Nick.

"LET'S GO OVER our story one more time," Lucy said as she and Sadie hovered in the darkness outside the back door of Sadie's house.

"You really think Nicky will be upset?"

Lucy rolled her eyes. "Upset? I think he'll be homicidal, especially when he finds out Weasel is the reason you've been missing for the last several hours. I just hope he hasn't called the police yet."

"Oh, dear," Sadie murmured. "And Walter is such a sweet boy. I think he just needs a little attention."

"Well, he'll get plenty of attention if Nick has him arrested for kidnapping," Lucy replied. She knew Weasel had screwed up, but didn't he deserve a second chance? Just like Melvin? *Just like Nick?*

"Kidnapping?" Sadie echoed. "Now that's just plain silly. Perhaps the circumstances of my meeting Walter were a little unusual, but I like to think it was fate. It felt nice to be needed. And I was never held there against my will. Walter made it perfectly clear to me that I was free to leave. In fact, he mentioned it several times."

"Nick might not see it that way. In fact, I can almost guarantee it."

"Then we simply won't tell him."

"So we're agreed? No matter what happens, we won't mention Weasel's name?"

"Agreed." Sadie reached out to pat Lucy's cheek. "Don't look so worried, dear. I can be very creative. Now let's go in and put Nicky out of his misery."

Nick did look miserable when Lucy walked into the living room with Sadie close behind her. He sat on the sofa, his face buried in his hands. Obviously lost in his thoughts, he didn't even look up as they entered the room.

"Hi, honey, we're home," Lucy announced, hoping to lighten the tense atmosphere blanketing the room.

He slowly lifted his head, his gray eyes bleak and haggard. He looked from Lucy to his grandmother, and back again. "Where the hell have you two been?"

"Now, Nicky," Sadie said, hanging her purse on the coatrack, "you know how I feel about cursing. We're back now, that's all that matters." She took off her blue cardigan sweater and hung it next to her purse. "You must be hungry. Shall I warm up that leftover Stroganoff?"

"That's sounds wonderful," Lucy exclaimed. "Beef Stroganoff is one of my favorites."

He scowled at Lucy. "Stroganoff? *Stroganoff?* Gram disappears without a trace. Then you disappear from the library, leaving me some vague note about running an errand. I don't hear a word from either of you for hours, and now all you two can talk about is Stroganoff?"

"Well, if you don't want Stroganoff, I've got Swedish meatballs in the freezer," Sadie replied.

He closed his eyes. Lucy could see the muscle working in his tightly clenched jaw. "I don't want Swedish meatballs and I don't want Stroganoff. All I want is an explanation."

"We can do that." Sadie looked over at Lucy. "Right?"

"Right," Lucy agreed, scrambling for a plausible explanation that would keep Weasel from writing his poetry behind bars. "Sadie was…auditioning roles for a possible community theater production of *Oklahoma.*"

"I need to find someone to play Judd," Sadie explained, taking it from there. "Nicky, you'll play the hero Curly. You already know all the songs and are certainly handsome enough for the part. And Lucy, you'll be perfect in the role of Laurie."

"And you can play Aunt Eller," Lucy suggested.

Sadie shook her head. "No, dear. I'll be too busy directing. Veda will make a good Aunt Eller and Edith can do the costuming. She's an excellent seamstress."

"Hold it." Nick stood up. He didn't look convinced by their story. Harassed, impatient and incredibly sexy, but not convinced. "Look, you two," he said, his voice low and urgent, "no more games. I need to know everything. And I mean *right now.*"

Lucy bit her lip. She'd never been a good liar. Obviously Nick had seen right through her. And maybe he did need to know. No harm had come to Sadie today, but what if someone other than Weasel had been hired to *detain* her? Sadie might truly be in danger.

"You're not going to like it…" Lucy began.

"That's a given," he said, his voice tight.

"I really think it's better if you just let it go, Nicky," Sadie said. "Lucy and I agreed to keep this little episode between ourselves."

"Episode?" he echoed, his voice strained. "Is that what you call it? An…episode?"

"Nick, it's not as bad as you think," Lucy interjected. "I think Sadie even enjoyed herself."

"I really did…" Sadie began, before the chime of

the doorbell interrupted her. She turned toward the door. "Well, it looks like we've got company."

"It's not company," Nick said grimly. "It's the police."

NICK WATCHED Lucy's face turn pale at his announcement. It confirmed his worst suspicions, making his gut clench and twist into a hard knot. A harried Lester Bonn had called the house fifteen minutes ago to announce that the police were on their way over. They'd come to the library looking for Lucy and he'd given him this address. One question had played over and over in his mind since that phone call.

What had she done now?

But before he could ask her, Sadie escorted two uniformed police officers into the room. He recognized the freckle-faced Officer Madison from their encounter outside the Hanover Building. And he'd never forget Babette.

"Good evening, folks. I'm Officer Madison," the young cop said, then motioned to his partner. "And this is…"

"Babette," Lucy said in surprise.

"I prefer Officer Gryzynski," Babette said as she pulled a notepad and pencil out of her pocket. "We'd like to ask you a few questions, Miss Moore."

"What k-kind of questions?" Lucy stammered, seating herself next to Nick on the sofa.

Office Madison exchanged glances with Babette.

"We'd like to ask you about your activities earlier today."

"Look, this really isn't necessary," Lucy replied. "Sadie's here now. She's fine. We appreciate all your efforts, but I'm afraid you've been called out on a false alarm. I'm sure you've got more important things to do."

"Unless you'd like to stay for Stroganoff," Sadie offered. "I've got plenty to go around."

"No, thank you, ma'am," Officer Madison replied. "Officer Gryzynski and I are still on duty. We've got a job to do. And we won't rest until this case is closed."

Nick rolled his eyes. Great. Two rookie cops who had weaned themselves on reruns of "Dragnet." He knew the department was shorthanded, but this was ridiculous.

Babette tapped her pencil on the notepad. "Earlier today, Vanessa Beaumont's residence was broken into and burglarized."

Lucy blinked. "What does that have to do with me?"

"We'd like to know your whereabouts from 4:00 p.m. until now," Officer Madison replied.

Nick stifled a groan. *Burglary?* How was she ever going to talk herself out of that one?

"Lucy was with me," Sadie announced. "I was rehearsing the song-and-dance numbers from the musical *Oklahoma* with a very nice young man. He has a strong voice, although he had a little trouble with some of the steps.''

Nick closed his eyes. Their story sounded lame even to his ears. But maybe the inexperienced cops wouldn't notice. Or see the guilt written all over Lucy's face.

Babette's gaze narrowed on Lucy. "Are you sure you want to stick with that story, Miss Moore? We all know you've been pursuing an investigation to clear your brother's name."

"In fact, the first time I met you," Officer Madison said, "you'd just broken into the Hanover Building looking for evidence."

"I told you that was a misunderstanding."

Babette snorted. "Right. Just like your jaunt as a hooker was a misunderstanding. What other illegal activities have you indulged in to help your brother?"

"Now wait a minute," Lucy said, rising to her feet. "You've got it all wrong."

"We don't think so, Miss Moore," Babette countered, flipping through her notepad. "We think you spent the afternoon attempting to frame Miss Beaumont. We even have a quote from your superior at the Heritage Library, Lester Bonn. He overheard you refer to Vanessa Beaumont as the Wicked Witch of Westview. He also said you believed she was responsible for the fire."

"I never told him that," Lucy said, indignant. "You're accusing me of a crime just on Lester's word?"

"No," Officer Madison said, deadly serious behind all his freckles. "We've got more solid evidence. The perpetrator left something behind at Miss Beaumont's town house."

"Two things, actually," Babette said.

"The first is a tin of gunpowder, the same brand used in the Hanover Building fire. Obviously meant to implicate Miss Beaumont in the incident."

"And the second?" Nick demanded, suddenly hopeful that the evidence against Lucy was all circumstantial, that these two rookies had nothing more to go on than a theory and a quote from a wimpy library gossip.

"We found a fingernail file with a mother-of-pearl handle still stuck in the keyhole," Office Madison said. "I knew it looked familiar."

"But my fingernail file is one of a kind," Lucy protested.

Office Madison arched a sandy eyebrow as he held up a plastic evidence bag. "With the initial *L* etched in it?"

Lucy's mouth dropped open. She looked at Nick, her expression one of horrified disbelief.

Nick's heart lurched. If it was true, his librarian had gotten in way over her head this time. Now she was possibly facing a felony. And the police already had more than enough evidence to lock her away for a long time.

All they needed to cinch the case was a confession.

"Lucy didn't do it," he heard himself say, his mind

clouded with images of Lucy undergoing arrest and a trial. Sitting in a cold, empty jail cell until all her optimism and exuberance and dreams faded away.

Babette rolled her eyes. "Come on, Chamberlin. You used to be a cop. A real hotshot, from the stories down at the station. We've got previous criminal activity, a statement that points to motive and even the fingernail file she used to pick the lock. If she's not guilty, then who is?"

"Me."

CHAPTER NINE

EVERYONE IN THE ROOM turned to gape at him. Nick met Lucy's gaze; her big brown eyes reflected a raw emotion that made him swallow hard and look away. His unplanned outburst surprised him almost as much as the rest of them. But he did it for Lucy. And he'd do it again in a heartbeat.

"That doesn't any make sense," Babette said at last.

Nick folded his arms across his chest, hoping his bluff worked well enough to delay an arrest—at least long enough for Lucy to get an alibi, or a good lawyer. "It does if you actually follow through all the leads in the case. You should have learned that your first week at the police academy. Have you even interviewed the *alleged* victim?"

Officer Madison and Babette looked guiltily at each other. "Well...not yet. The victim's mother, Letitia Beaumont, reported the burglary. She was quite upset about it and wanted immediate action. We haven't been able to locate Miss Beaumont."

Nick shook his head. "So you two go off half-cocked and accuse an innocent woman of the crime? That's not exactly proper police conduct."

Babette bristled. "*You* should talk, Chamberlin! You just got out of prison for *improper* conduct."

"That's right," Nick said, keeping his voice relaxed and even, hoping some of Lucy's vivid imagination and storytelling techniques had rubbed off on him. "My prison record is what Vanessa found so appealing about me. We had a date last Friday evening. You can verify it with Jacques at Château Pierre. I'm sure he'll remember me."

Babette scribbled the name in her notebook.

"That's when Vanessa asked me to play out her little fantasy," Nick continued. "I think she called it The Criminal and the Debutante."

"I knew that girl was trouble," Sadie muttered under her breath.

Nick cleared his throat, more than a little uncomfortable describing a sexual fantasy with his grandmother in the room. Lucy didn't look too happy, either. In fact, his sweet librarian looked downright lethal.

"I was supposed to break into her town house and ransack it until I found her in the bedroom," he said, hurrying through the story. "And then…well, I'm sure you can figure out the rest."

Officer Madison tugged at his shirt collar. "Gee whiz."

"But Vanessa wasn't in the bedroom, or anywhere else in the place," Nick said, before Lucy could grab the nearest aerosol can. "She must have forgotten to mark our date down on her social calendar."

"So how do you explain the fingernail file we found? The one belonging to Miss Moore?" Babette asked.

"Easy," Nick replied. "I've been staying at Lucy's place for the last few days, so I've had access to all her things."

"Then we'll find your fingerprints on it?" Officer Madison asked.

"I wore gloves and a ski mask," Nick explained. "It was all part of the fantasy." He cleared his throat. "Now you can find Vanessa and verify the story or you can arrest me...or Lucy, and give the cops down at the station a good laugh."

Officer Madison's freckled cheeks flushed with embarrassment. He turned to Babette. "Maybe I'll go out to the squad car and radio Lieutenant Delaney about the situation."

Babette nodded. "And I'll try phoning Miss Beaumont at her town house again. If she's still not there, I'll call around to see if I can track her down."

"You can use the telephone in the den," Sadie said, leading her from the living room as Officer Madison ducked out the front door.

"The Criminal and the Debutante?" Lucy asked once they were alone.

"I know what you're thinking." He moved closer to her, dropping his voice to a whisper.

"I don't think you do. I could strangle you."

He held up both hands. "Wait a minute. I made up that story about Vanessa and her fantasy."

"I know you made it up," she said. "It was a great story. Very creative. There's no way you could have had a rendezvous with Vanessa this afternoon. I saw you in the library, remember? You were too worried about your grandmother to indulge in any fantasies."

His fingers brushed a honey blond curl off her cheek. "I don't know about that," he said huskily.

"Pay attention, Nick," she warned. "I'm not through with you yet."

He dropped his hand, frowning at the fierce expression on her face. "If you don't believe my story, why do you look like you want to annihilate me?"

She rolled her eyes. "Because, you big, dumb, noble *jerk,* we wouldn't be in this mess if you weren't always trying to protect me! *I* didn't break into Vanessa's town house, either."

As soon as she said the words, Nick knew she was telling him the truth. He also realized he might have overreacted just a little to the police interrogation. Like confessing to a crime he didn't commit. Again.

He closed his eyes. "I don't believe it."

"Believe it," she said, misunderstanding him. "Somebody set me up while I was busy rescuing your grandmother from her kidnapper. Or rather, the kidnapper from your grandmother."

His eyes flew open. "Gram was *kidnapped?*"

"More like 'voluntarily detained.' Look, Nick, I think it's time we compare notes. Someone is trying very hard to distract us from this case, which can only mean one thing. We're getting too close for comfort."

He couldn't agree more. He'd been fighting the urge to wrap her in his arms since she walked through that front door with his grandmother in tow. He'd wanted to kiss Lucy silly when she'd spouted that convoluted story. And now he wanted to haul her over his shoulder and go on the lam before one of them ended up behind bars.

Nick knew at that moment he loved her.

This revelation was unexpected, overwhelming and inconvenient as hell, considering the circumstances. But his heart overflowed with love for Lucy Moore.

She planted her hands on her hips, looking angry and exasperated and simply adorable. "We're in this together. So no more shutting me out of the case, Chamberlin. Let me be an equal partner in this investigation...or else."

He bit back a smile at the fierce gleam in her eye. "Or else what?"

She tipped up her chin. "Or else I'll be forced to do something drastic. I've got peanut butter and I'm not afraid to use it."

He held up both hands. "All right, I surrender. From now on we're together all the way. But before we can figure out who set you up, we need to get rid of Freckles and Babette."

Sadie hurried into the living room. "Nicky Chamberlin, I could wring your neck!"

"Get in line," Lucy muttered. "Can you believe he'd confess to something he didn't do?"

Sadie took a deep breath. "Yes, I can. He did it a

year and a half ago. It seems to be turning into a bad habit."

"He what?" Lucy exclaimed.

Nick looked in disbelief at his grandmother. "You knew?"

She shook her head, her lower lip trembling. "No, not at the time. I was still in shock. Your grandfather was my entire life. I knew something had been troubling him for weeks. Then he suffered those heart attacks and the next few months passed like a nightmare for me. When I woke up, you'd already been convicted and sentenced."

Lucy stared up at him as if she'd never seen him before. "You sacrificed your career and your reputation and your freedom for someone else?"

He shrugged. "It was just something I had to do."

"I should have known," she said huskily. "You've always been too honest and noble for your own good."

Nick turned to his grandmother, unnerved by the raw emotion shining in Lucy's eyes.

"Why do you think Grandpa did it?"

She took a deep breath, then set her mouth in a determined line. "I think neither my husband nor my grandson was guilty of committing the crime. Or any crime, for that matter. And I refuse to sit idly by and watch it happen all over again. So what can I do to help?"

Lucy snapped her fingers. "I've got it! A way to get rid of the cops." She turned to Sadie. "Do you remember that book the Merry Widows Club read last July? The title was *High Society Sleuths Go to Vegas.*"

Nick groaned. "I don't think I want to hear this."

A slow smile dawned on Sadie's lips. "Yes, I do remember, and I think I know exactly the scene you mean. But will it work?"

Lucy grinned. "If it worked for Reginald and Penelope Van Whipple, it will work for us."

THE CLOSET DOOR CLOSED, blanketing Nick and Lucy in total darkness. Nick heard the scrape of a key in the keyhole, then the sound of Sadie's footsteps fading away.

"This is your great idea?" he asked, disoriented by the blackness surrounding him and the odor of mothballs in the air. "Locking us in a closet?"

"It worked in the book." Lucy's voice floated toward him. "The mobsters thought they'd gone out the back door and ran after them. That gave the Van Whipples a chance to escape. When Sadie tells the cops we went out the back door to search for Vanessa ourselves, they'll take after us. That should buy us a little time."

"I just hope it's enough."

Silence as thick as the darkness descended between them. Clothes hangers jabbed Nick in the back as he moved to find room in the stuffed closet. His foot collided with a bowling ball, and he swallowed his grunt of pain.

"Are you all right?" she asked.

"I'm fine," he said through clenched teeth, trying to ignore the throb in his big toe. "We need to put the pieces of this case together and come up with a plan."

"Good idea. You go first."

"I found a matchbook at the Hanover Building the night we broke in. Vanessa had an identical matchbook. It was from the Beaumonts' anniversary party on April nineteenth."

"The same night as the fire. It makes sense now."

"What makes sense?" he asked.

"Lily Vyne, the eyewitness. With everything going on, I haven't had a chance to tell you. She saw a man leaving the Hanover Building only moments before the fire. He was in a tuxedo."

"Now all we need is a list of all the guests that attended the party. Cole tried to get it from the Beaumonts but came up empty."

He heard her quick intake of breath. "What's wrong?"

"I've got it."

"What?"

"The list. The invitation list. It's on a computer disk at the library. Mrs. Beaumont always uses the library staff as if we're her social secretaries. I guess she thinks it's one of the fringe benefits for serving on the Heritage Library Foundation. I remember typing the list into the computer and fuming because Melvin wasn't invited."

"Lucy, do you know what this means?" he asked, his blood surging with adrenaline. As a cop, he'd always felt this way right before he'd cracked a case. "Between that list and the eyewitness and the matchbook, we should have enough evidence to convince Cole to reopen the investigation. And it would help if we could prove that you weren't anywhere near Vanessa's place this afternoon. Did anyone else see you besides Gram?"

"A little girl on Bale Street," Lucy replied. "And Weasel."

"Weasel? Why the hell were you with Weasel?"

"Not so loud," Lucy whispered. "I'll tell you later. We don't want Babette and Officer Madison to hear us."

"*I* can hardly hear you," he replied. "You sound all muffled."

"All these coats are smothering me," she complained. "And I can't see a thing."

He reached out for Lucy, grabbing a fistful of faux fur instead. "Just move toward the sound of my voice."

He moved his hands around, searching for her among the old coats and dresses and suits. Then he found her. "I've got your shoulder," he said, squeezing it gently to reassure her. Only, the flesh beneath his hand was round and warm and incredibly soft.

"I know it's been a long time for you, but...that's not my shoulder."

"Lucy," he breathed, his hand lingering there for

a long moment before skimming down over her ribs to her slender waist. He pulled her close, inhaling the familiar, sweet scent of her skin. Her hair tickled his nose. All his senses came alive in the darkness. Sound…smell…touch… Now he wanted more than anything to taste her.

He drew his hand slowly back up along her body, allowing it to guide him to her mouth. He heard her intake of breath, felt the delicate skin on her throat pebble beneath his fingertips. Then he found her chin, tipping it up, while his fingers caressed her lips.

"Kiss me, Nick," she said in a sultry whisper. "Kiss me like you never want to stop."

He knew he wouldn't want to stop, knew this was the worst possible time to indulge in the fantasies he'd been having ever since the first moment he met her. But he'd delayed living his life long enough. From now on, Nick Chamberlin planned to enjoy every moment and take advantage of every opportunity.

He gently cupped her face between his palms, then lowered his head until his mouth touched her face. He brushed his lips over hers, so lightly that she moaned for more. His tongue traced the seam of her lips until they parted. He deepened the kiss, moving his mouth against hers in a slow, evocative rhythm. His lips made a leisurely journey across her neck, tasting and caressing, awakening every nerve cell in his body.

"Oh…Nick," she murmured, her lips seeking his once more, teasing and tantalizing. He moaned into her mouth as her hands joined in the fray. She touched him with an enthusiastic curiosity that kindled the fire inside him. The darkness heightened all his senses, making each touch, each sound, each taste, an intimate caress.

Nick forgot about everything except the beautiful, sensuous woman in his arms—until the closet door swung open. They reluctantly pulled apart, squinting at the sudden infusion of bright light.

Sadie stood before them. "I got rid of the heat."

Nick looked at Lucy's flushed cheeks, her red lips and the passion glowing in her big brown eyes, wishing he could just carry her upstairs instead of carrying on with this investigation. But the sooner they solved this case, the sooner they could finish what they started in the closet.

"Ready?" he asked.

She nodded. "I'll go to the library and get the list."

"And I'll track down Cole and we'll meet you there. If he's not home, I've got his pager number back at your apartment. I have a feeling when we tell him about Lily Vyne, this case will break wide open."

"What if she still refuses to talk to the police?"

Nick brushed a stray curl off her cheek. "She'll talk to Rafferty. He's always had a way with women."

Lucy arched a blond brow. "What about you, Nick?"

He grinned. "There's only one woman I'm hoping will want to have her way with me."

Sadie cleared her throat. "Time to get moving, you two." She reached up to kiss Nick's cheek. "Good luck. I'll keep the Stroganoff warm until you come back."

LUCY DIDN'T NEED her nail file to break into the Heritage Library. Her key worked perfectly. But she still felt like an intruder as she moved among the rows of bookshelves, her footsteps echoing in the deserted building.

She'd been in the library after closing time several times before, but the silence seemed ominous now, almost eerie. The streetlights outside illuminated the interior of the library just enough for Lucy to make her way around inside without bumping into anything.

The hairs on the back of her neck prickled as she made her way across the main floor. Her instincts told her that she wasn't safe, but her instincts weren't all that reliable. They hadn't told her that Nick wasn't really a criminal, or that Babette wasn't really a prostitute. Or that peanut butter could be dangerous.

So maybe her uneasiness was due to her overactive imagination. Nick trusted her to handle this part of the investigation alone while he tracked down his old partner. They just had to convince Cole Rafferty to reopen the investigation—and soon, if she wanted to keep Melvin from going through with his escape plans.

Tapping sounds drew her attention to the large windowpanes overhead. She stood immobilized as she peered into the darkness, reminding herself of the tall oak trees lining the walk outside the library. Branches hitting the windowpane. No reason to panic. Neither was that loud creaking noise above her. She looked up at the tiled ceiling. Probably just the building settling. All old buildings made unusual noises. Didn't they?

Lucy told herself she didn't have time to figure out the source of every mysterious creak and clank. It was only a matter of time before the police tracked her down to question her some more about the break-in at Vanessa's town house. Time that she was wasting by jumping at shadows.

She took a deep, fortifying breath before heading into the tiny audiovisual room. The tables inside were crowded with the library's computers, audiotape recorders, overhead projectors, a VCR and two microfilm readers.

She sat down at a computer terminal and booted up. The library network allowed all the computers to access information from one another. The computer screen glowed a bright phosphorescent green, lighting up the area around her. She typed in her password, then accessed Letitia Beaumont's social file, scrolling down the length of text until she finally found it: the invitation list for Harold and Letitia Beaumont's fortieth anniversary party.

Lucy highlighted the list of over two hundred

names, flipped on the laser printer, then clicked on the print icon.

The whir of the printer sounded unusually loud in the empty room. But not quite loud enough to cover the sound of the door to the room creaking open.

A shiver tingled down her spine. She held her breath as her instincts screamed at her to run. Maybe they were wrong again. Maybe Nick had arrived early. Or a ghost roamed the library at night. Or her stalker finally wanted to meet her in person.

"Hello, Lucy."

She turned around, breathing a sigh of relief at the sight of a familiar face in the doorway. "Hello, Lieutenant Delaney. You startled me."

"Sorry about that," he said, sauntering inside the room. "Seems you're wanted downtown for questioning. According to Officers Madison and Gryzynski, you're involved in a burglary."

Her heart sank. She just needed a little more time. Her gaze fell to the printer, slowly spitting out the second sheet of paper full of names and addresses. "I know, Lieutenant. Somebody set me up. Nick and Detective Rafferty should be here in about twenty minutes. Then we can get this all straightened out."

"Let me guess," he said, stepping out of the shadows. "This has to do with the case against your brother."

"I think we've got enough evidence to reopen the investigation," Lucy said, her voice quivering with excitement. "An eyewitness came forward."

His eyes widened at that announcement. "No kidding? An eyewitness?"

Lucy nodded. "She came to the library this afternoon and told me she saw a man in a tuxedo leaving the Hanover Building shortly before the fire started."

The lieutenant shook his head in disbelief. "That's incredible."

"We're close to finding the real arsonist, Lieutenant," she said as the last sheet of paper fell onto the printer tray. "Very close."

He took a step toward her. "A little too close, Lucy," he said, pulling his gun out of his shoulder holster and aiming it straight at her.

NICK CREPT THROUGH the bushes beside Lucy's apartment building, intently watching his prey. He almost hadn't seen the stalker in his race toward Lucy's place to retrieve Cole's pager number. But now there was no mistaking the sound of leaves crunching underfoot and the flash of green polyester between the bare twigs.

"Bird-watching, Lester?"

The man crouching under the window of Lucy's apartment emitted a high-pitched scream. He bolted up to make a run for it, but Nick had already hooked his arm around Lester's throat. "Or maybe you're peeping through windows again?"

Lester whimpered. "Please let me go. I didn't do anything wrong."

"Now that's a matter of opinion, Les." Nick released his hold, but stood blocking the only path to the street. Lester was trapped by hydrangea bushes on one side and the three-story brick apartment building on the other.

"I need to go home now," Lester said, his gaze darting frantically around him, searching for an escape route. "Mother's expecting me. She'll…she'll have my milk ready. She makes me warm milk every night. It helps calm my nerves."

Nick stood with his feet planted wide apart, twirling a stray twig in his hands. "Why would you be nervous, Lester? I'm a perfectly nice guy. Of course, the fact that I'm an ex-con sometimes makes people nervous. You know, we tend to be violent. Explode easily. Sometimes lose control." Nick snapped the twig in half.

Lester emitted a tiny squeak. "What do you want from me?"

"I want to know why you've been stalking Lucy."

"I was not stalking her," Lester said, his indignation momentarily overcoming his fear. "I was spying on her. There's a big difference."

"I'd say about three to five years in the state penitentiary."

Lester blanched. "No! It wasn't my fault. He told me to keep on eye on her. That she might be involved in criminal activity." He swallowed, his Adam's apple bobbing in his throat. "He said it was my civic duty. And I also have a responsibility as library di-

rector." Lester sniffed. "We can't have riffraff working at the Heritage Library."

"Riffraff?" Nick echoed, taking a step closer.

Lester backed up against the brick wall, his eyes
wide. "Not that I think Miss Moore is riffraff, even
if her brother is in jail. She's very pleasant, even
though she's always trying to change things around
the library. In fact, I wasn't even planning on watching her tonight, but I…I…" His voice trailed off.

"You what?"

"Well, she's very pretty, and Mother doesn't let
me date much, so watching Lucy has become sort of
my new hobby." Lester tugged at his shirt collar. "I
just couldn't stay away…even after you told me that
you were handling the investigation."

Nick's eyes narrowed. "I've never even talked to
you before tonight."

Lester's head bobbed up and down. "Yes, you did.
I was there that night at the Château Pierre, hiding
behind the potted palm."

"You?" His jaw clenched. "You followed Lucy
to the restaurant?"

"I was supposed to keep an eye on her. Report any
suspicious activity. But when you warned me to stay
away, I figured he'd told you to spy on Lucy, too."

"Who is *he?*"

"That policeman. Lieutenant Delaney," Lester explained. "He gave me the assignment a few weeks
ago. Sometimes I'd call her just to see if she was

home, and other times I'd come over here and check on her.''

Nick sucked in his breath. *Delaney?* Delaney ordered Lester to keep on eye on Lucy? Why? It just didn't make sense. But the gnawing in Nick's gut told him he didn't like it one bit.

He grabbed Lester by the shirt collar, pulling him toward the street. ''I'm going after Lucy. I want you to go down to the police station and tell them everything you told me. Got it?''

''I'll have to call Mother first....'' Lester shouted, but Nick didn't hear him as he raced for his car.

CHAPTER TEN

LUCY SWALLOWED as she stared into the barrel of a really big gun. Trying not to panic, she asked herself what Penelope Van Whipple would do in this situation. Cause a distraction. Come up with a delay tactic. Wait for the author to write her out of this mess.

The books in the library were filled with heroes. She'd read of their chivalrous escapades countless times. If only one of them would jump off the pages and come to her rescue.

Reginald Van Whipple, where are you when I need you?

Lucy had never wished for a happily-ever-after more than she did at this moment. Only, this wasn't fiction. And that gun gleaming in Delaney's hand wasn't make-believe. She'd have to depend on herself.

"I don't understand," she said, her mind racing in a hundred different directions. She didn't want to die. She needed to keep him talking. Ignore the gun. Buy cat food. Tell Nick she loved him.

That would be the first item on her list when she saw him again—*if* she saw him again. She took a deep breath. "Is this some kind of joke?"

Delaney snorted. "I thought you were a joke the first time we met. A harebrained librarian out to catch a criminal. Even with Chamberlin I didn't think you stood a chance of success. I covered my tracks too well." He motioned to the computer with his gun hand. "You can delete that file now and then turn all those machines off."

Lucy turned back to the computer screen, glimpsing the name of Lieutenant Ed Delaney on the invitation list before she reluctantly hit the delete button. Then, with her hands shaking, she methodically flipped buttons on the machines in front of her.

Delaney moved to the printer, sweeping up the papers she'd just printed off. He folded them and tucked them into his suit coat. "I don't suppose you have any books here on how to silence nosy librarians?"

"I'll have to check the card catalog," she said, edging away from him.

He took another step toward her. "Don't bother. I was never much of a reader anyway. I prefer action."

"Is that why you torched the Hanover Building?" Lucy asked, moving so a table full of audiovisual equipment stood between her and Delaney. "And then framed my brother for the crime?"

He shrugged. "I was just doing my job. As the police liaison for the Friends of Westview Association, that is. They pay me extremely well. Sure beats that measly pension I'll get from the police department. All I have to do is take care of any little problems that crop up—like disposing of traffic tickets or unsuitable men dating their precious daughters.''

''The Beaumonts paid you to get rid of Melvin?''

Delaney nodded. ''Good old Letitia didn't want to know any of the details. She just wanted Mad Dog Moore out of her daughter's life.''

Lucy wished she had a can of hair spray handy right now. Industrial strength.

Delaney sighed. ''It all went perfectly until you started digging around in the case. I thought I could keep an eye on you.''

''It was you who broke into my apartment.''

He shrugged. ''That's what you get for planting phony tips in the newspaper. But now it's getting too messy. Madison and Gryzynski have botched up the investigation of the Beaumont break-in so much that I'll never see you convicted and out of the way. So I guess it's up to me to tie up loose ends.''

He pulled a length of clothesline cord out of the back pocket of his slacks. ''Good thing I brought some rope.''

Just what she needed. A killer with a sense of humor. ''You won't get away with this.''

''Sure I will. Everybody will think *Floyd* did it.'' Delaney snorted. ''Besides, the only man who ever came close to catching me was old Captain Chamberlin. He suspected the Protégé Project was a front from the very start. I even went to the trouble of planting contraband in his car to discredit him. But then he conveniently had a heart attack. Of course, I never could have predicted his grandson would confess to the crime.'' He laughed, slapping the rope against his knee. "Isn't that a hoot? The old man never let me out of his sight when I was a rookie. Always hounding me. Passing me up for the big promotions. He didn't think I deserved to be a cop. Just because I cut a few corners along the way and roughed up a couple of hookers. Big deal.''

Lucy swallowed. Poor Lily. No wonder she didn't want to come forward.

"Next thing I know, he reports that I've got a gambling problem and Internal Affairs is breathing down my neck. So I decided it was time to get even.'' Delaney chuckled. "Now the old man's dead and his grandson's brought shame on the great Chamberlin name. Talk about poetic justice.''

"You framed Nick,'' she said, adrenaline fueling her anger. "Then you framed my big brother.'' She threw back her shoulders. "And now I'm going to make you pay.''

"Oooh, I'm scared,'' he mocked, laughter shaking the big belly hanging over his belt. "The big bad librarian is going to get me.''

"You should be scared,'' she warned. "Librarians are very resourceful.'' Then she flipped on the power switch of the overhead projector in front of her, the intense beam aimed directly at his face.

The bright light blinded him. His gun hand faltered as he brought up his other hand to shield his eyes from the glare.

Lucy ran for the door, making a wide arc around Delaney. She heard his muttered curses as she pulled it open, then his footsteps behind her as she headed for the locked front entrance. Grabbing a book off the shelf of new releases, she hurled it through the electronic sensor near the front doors, then ran for the rows of towering bookshelves.

A piercing alarm sounded throughout the building. Lucy leaned against the biography section, gasping for breath. She knew the security alarm rang at the police station after library hours. She also knew it would take them at least fifteen minutes to get here.

"Don't make me shoot you," Delaney said, his voice carrying over the stacks. "I was going to go easy on you. Tie you up. Set fire to the building. You'd die of smoke inhalation before the flames ever got to you."

Lucy edged around the nonfiction section, listening intently. By the sound of his footsteps, he was checking each row. *Cautiously* checking each row. Score one for the librarian; she'd obviously taught him not to underestimate her.

Unfortunately, the only weapons left in her arsenal were a hairpin and a number two pencil.

"Letitia Beaumont has been itching to build a new library," Delaney said, his voice uncomfortably close. "Maybe they'll even call it the Lucy Moore Memorial Library."

She swallowed the bubble of hysteria in her throat. Was this supposed to tempt her out of hiding?

"This is your last chance, Lucy."

She could see him now through a small gap in the books on the shelf. Only one row away. He crept nearer, the rope in his hands, his gun still tucked inside his holster—which meant he still didn't consider her much of a threat.

Librarians just don't get enough respect.

She braced her hands on the heavy frame of the ten-foot oak bookshelf. He stood directly opposite her now, only the bookshelf between them. His gaze fell on her through the same small gap. Then he smiled.

Lucy pushed with all her might, tipping the shelf far enough for a cascade of books to rain on Delaney. His shouts filled the air as she rounded the bookshelf to make her escape, Delaney right on her heels.

Then she saw Nick standing by the front desk. Her handsome, brave, *unarmed* hero.

"Nick! I love you!" Lucy shouted, barely avoiding the large rolling book cart in front of him. "Run for it!"

Delaney saw Nick, too, skidding to a stop just before he got within swinging distance. He dropped the rope, reaching for his gun.

"There will be no shooting in the library," Nick said, ramming the solid wooden book cart into Delaney's gut. The lieutenant flipped headfirst into the waist-high cart, his gun skidding away harmlessly, and his head hitting the bottom of the cart with a resounding thud. His flailing legs stuck straight up as he struggled to right himself.

Lucy picked up an oversize edition of *Webster's Unabridged Dictionary* off the front desk and flung it on top of his head. The ten-pound version. Delaney stopped moving.

Nick looked down at her handiwork. "Remind me to look up the word *concussion* whenever I start underestimating librarians." He took a closer look at the unconscious man. "Or maybe the words *fractured skull.*"

"I didn't mean to hurt him that badly," Lucy said, frowning down at the still body.

"Forget about him." Nick slowly drew her to him, wrapping her in his strong, protective arms. "Did you mean it, Lucy? Do you really love me?"

She gazed up into his gray eyes, her throat tight with emotion. She'd never seen him look so vulnerable, so full of hope. "Yes, Nick. I meant it. I love you. Now and forever."

He hugged her, burying his face in her hair, squeezing her so tightly she couldn't breathe. And she didn't care.

A weak groan emanated from the book cart. Nick turned her away from it, still holding her close to him. She could feel his heartbeat melding with her own.

"Don't worry about Delaney," he murmured against her ear. "He'll live. Let's just hope he doesn't plead amnesia when it's time to take the witness stand."

"It doesn't matter," she said, pulling away just far

enough to smile up at him. "I've already got his confession."

His brow furrowed. "What do you mean?"

"When Delaney showed up in the audiovisual room, I punched the record button on a tape recorder. He thought I was just shutting down the computer." She took a deep breath as Nick's strength and warmth flowed into her, slowly thawing the icy fear inside her. "So I kept him talking. I thought if he killed me, at least I could save Melvin. Someone would hear that tape and know the truth."

"You amaze me," he whispered, pressing his lips to her hair. Then his mouth sojourned along her jaw, lingering at every point along the way.

"And that's not all," she murmured, distracted by his kisses. "Your grandfather didn't do it."

His lips stilled on her neck. He pulled away just far enough to gaze into her eyes. "What did you say?"

"I said your grandfather was innocent. Delaney knew your grandfather was on to him, so he planted the marijuana in his car. Only, you took the blame instead. I've got it all on tape."

"You've got it all on tape?" he repeated, looking completely stunned. "*You got it all on tape?*"

She nodded. "I keep telling everyone librarians are very resourceful. Why won't anyone believe me?"

"I believe you," he declared, lifting her up in his arms and whooping with joy. He twirled her around until she was dizzy, before setting her back on her feet.

"And I love you, Lucy," he said, proving his point by kissing her senseless. "I want to spend the rest of my life with you." He grinned. "And then some."

Lucy melted against him. Dizzy, breathless and happier than she'd ever been in her life. Only a tiny twinge of doubt remained. "I love you, too, Nick," she said. "I think I've loved you since the night of the stakeout. But are you sure? Absolutely sure? I know I've been nothing but trouble for you since the first day we met."

"You are trouble," he agreed, his gray eyes shining with passion and promise. "Just the kind of trouble I want in my life."

THE WESTVIEW POLICE station buzzed with the news of the veteran officer gone bad. Cole ushered Nick and Lucy into his office to escape the pandemonium.

Cole perched on the corner of his desk. "We're bringing Letitia Beaumont in for questioning, as well as Ralph Rooney and several other members of the Friends of Westview Association. Looks like they had quite a setup."

"What about my brother?" Lucy asked.

"Mad Dog Moore's been notified about the new developments in the case. He'll go before a judge tomorrow morning to have the charges dropped, but that should just be a formality. Then he'll be a free man."

"You did it," Nick said, wrapping his arms around Lucy, and pulling her close. "You saved your brother."

"*We* did it," she replied, snuggling against him. "Proved Melvin innocent. *And* you. Neither one of you is guilty of anything."

"Except loving you." Nick kissed the top of her head. "This is the luckiest day of my life. And believe it or not, it's a Monday." He shook his head in disbelief. "Or maybe the luckiest day of my life is the day we met."

"That was a Monday, too," Lucy reminded him. "And I knew you were the perfect man for the job. The police department was crazy to let you go."

"It just so happens the police captain agrees with you," Cole replied.

"What are you saying?" Nick asked, his arm circling Lucy's waist.

Cole grinned. "Due to the severe shortage of police personnel and the fact that Delaney confessed to framing you a year and a half ago, the captain wants you reinstated on the force. Effective immediately."

Lucy turned into his arms. "Oh, Nick! How exciting!"

Cole chuckled. "Nick may not agree with you."

Nick forced his attention from a warm and loving Lucy to his old partner. "Are you kidding? I can't wait to get back to police work."

"That's great," Cole replied. "Because you've already been given an assignment—a suspected embezzlement scheme. And it's one of those good news, bad news cases.''

"Save the good news for last," Lucy said, a rosy blush in her cheeks. "I like happy endings."

Cole nodded. "Okay, the bad news first, then." He turned to Nick. "You're going undercover as one of the employees at Farley's Fish Hut."

Nick groaned. "And the good news?"

"You get to wear this really cool cod hat."

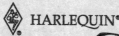

HARLEQUIN® Duets™

Receive 75¢ off your next Harlequin Duets® book purchase.

75¢ OFF!

Your next Harlequin Duets® book purchase.

RETAILER: Harlequin Enterprises Ltd. will pay the face value of this coupon plus 8¢ if submitted by customer for this product only. Any other use constitutes fraud. Coupon is nonassignable. Void if taxed, prohibited or restricted by law. Void if copied. Consumer must pay any government taxes. For reimbursement submit coupons and proof of sales to: Harlequin Enterprises Ltd., P.O. Box 880478, El Paso, TX 88588-0478, U.S.A. Cash value 1/100¢. Valid in the U.S. only.

Coupon expires July 31, 2003.
Redeemable at participating retail outlets in the U.S. only.
Limit one coupon per purchase.

110439

5 65373 00075 5   (8100)0 11043

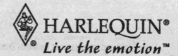

HARLEQUIN®
Live the emotion™

HARLEQUIN®

Duets™

Receive 75¢ off your next Harlequin Duets® book purchase.

75¢ OFF!

Your next Harlequin Duets® book purchase.

RETAILER: Harlequin Enterprises Ltd. will pay the face value of this coupon plus 10.25¢ if submitted by customer for this product only. Any other use constitutes fraud. Coupon is nonassignable. Void if taxed, prohibited or restricted by law. Void if copied. Consumer must pay any government taxes. Nielson Clearing House customers submit coupons and proof of sales to: Harlequin Enterprises Ltd., 661 Millidge Avenue, P.O. Box 639, Saint John, N.B. E2L 4A5. Non NCH retailer—for reimbursement submit coupons and proof of sales directly to: Harlequin Enterprises Ltd., Retail Marketing Department, 225 Duncan Mill Rd., Don Mills, Ontario M3B 3K9, Canada. Valid in Canada only.

Coupon expires July 31, 2003.
Redeemable at participating retail outlets in Canada only.
Limit one coupon per purchase.

52604674

Visit us at www.eHarlequin.com
NCP03HD-CANCPN
© 2003 Harlequin Enterprises Ltd.

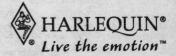

HARLEQUIN®
Live the emotion™

FTD.COM®

SHOP ONLINE OR DIAL 1-800-SEND-FTD

$10.00 OFF

COUPON

Expiration Date: April 30, 2003

To redeem your coupon:

Log on to www.ftd.com/harlequin and give promo code 2198 at checkout.

Or

Call 1-800-SEND-FTD and give promo code 2194.

Terms and conditions:

Coupon is redeemable at face value only for merchandise available for purchase at www.ftd.com/harlequin at the time of redemption and any applicable service fees and taxes. Limit 1 coupon per order. Cash value 1/100 of 1¢. Void if taxed, prohibited or restricted by law. Coupon cannot be used in conjunction with any other programs. If the order total exceeds the face value of this coupon, the remaining balance must be paid with a valid credit card. Coupon will not be replaced if lost or stolen. FTD.COM reserves the right to change these terms and conditions from time to time at its discretion. Valid in the U.S. and Canada only.

This offer is not available in retail stores.

NCP2198